SWEET VALLEY UNIVERSITY

COLLECTION

INCLUDING

College Girls

and

Love, Lies, and Jessica Wakefield

BANTAM BOOKS
NEW YORK · TORONTO · LONDON · SYDNEY · AUCKLAND

SWEET VALLEY UNIVERSITY COLLECTION
A BANTAM BOOK 0553 507214

This collection first published in UK in 1999

Cover photograph by Oliver Hunter

including:

COLLEGE GIRLS

First published in USA by Bantam Books, 1993
Bantam UK edition published 1995

LOVE, LIES AND JESSICA WAKEFIELD

First published in USA by Bantam Books, 1993
Bantam UK edition published 1995

Conceived by Francine Pascal

Produced by Daniel Weiss Associates, Inc., 33 West 17th Street, New York, NY 10011

Bantam Books are published by Transworld Publishers Ltd, 61-63 Uxbridge Road, Ealing, London W5 5SA, in Australia by Transworld Publishers, c/o Random House Australia Pty Ltd, 20 Alfred Street, Milsons Point, NSW 2061 and in New Zealand by Transworld Publishers, c/o Random House New Zealand, 18 Poland Road, Glenfield, Auckland.

Made and printed in Great Britain by Cox & Wyman, Reading, Berkshire.

SWEET VALLEY UNIVERSITY

College Girls

Written by
Laurie John

Created by
FRANCINE PASCAL

BANTAM BOOKS
NEW YORK · TORONTO · LONDON · SYDNEY · AUCKLAND

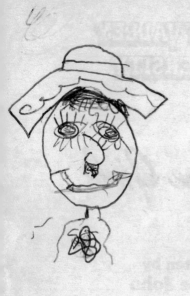

For Molly Jessica W. Wenk

Chapter One

"Look at that!" Elizabeth Wakefield had been dreamily staring up at the sky, her head on Todd Wilkins's shoulder, her long, golden-blond hair falling onto his chest. She sat up and pointed through the windshield of the BMW at the brilliant light streaking through the night sky. "It's a shooting star!"

Todd squeezed her hand. "The perfect ending to a perfect night."

Elizabeth smiled. "It is perfect." There was no doubt in her mind that this was one of the most important nights of her life. Tonight she and Todd were celebrating their "last date." They'd gone to all their favorite places, beginning with a romantic dinner at the Box Tree Café and ending with a milk shake with the old crowd at the Dairi Burger.

Old crowd. Elizabeth repeated the phrase in her head. It was hard to believe. After four happy and

1

successful years, she had really graduated from Sweet Valley High. She was no longer just a high school kid; she was eighteen and about to start her freshman year of college. About to leave home and all the things that were familiar to her.

That's why she and Todd had planned this night. It might not be the last time they ever went to the movies in Sweet Valley, or drove through the hills outside of town, or tossed a coin to see if they were going to go to Guido's for a pizza or to the Dairi Burger for fries. They'd be back home for vacations and summers. But it was the last night of their old life. Soon there would be new places, new friends, and new experiences.

"Who knows where we'll be a month from now," Todd said, as though reading her thoughts.

A slightly troubled look came into Elizabeth's eyes. She hadn't wanted to admit it to herself, but she was feeling the unfamiliar tingle of fear. Starting a new life meant leaving behind the things she loved.

"Are you scared?" she asked quietly.

"Scared?" Todd put his arm around her waist and held her close. "What is there to be scared of?"

"I don't know," she whispered. "It's just that when I try to picture my life somewhere else— without my mom and dad and our house and everything . . ." Her voice trailed off. *All I can see is a dark, empty space,* she finished silently.

Todd took her hand in his. "Don't think about

2

what's ending. Think about what's beginning. Besides, it's not like you're going to college in Alaska, Liz. Not everything's going to change. After all, you'll still have Jessica to drive you crazy."

At the mention of her twin sister, Elizabeth started to laugh with relief. Todd was right. There were some things that would never change. Flighty, frivolous, scheming Jessica would be at Sweet Valley University too. Where would Elizabeth be without her?

They were the famous Wakefield twins. Identical on the outside, opposite on the inside. Of course, they'd changed some over the years. Their hair was longer, they'd grown a little taller, and according to most people, even more beautiful.

But Elizabeth was still responsible and hard-working. She'd graduated with honors and a special award for her work on the school newspaper. She still preferred hanging out with Todd or her best friend, Enid Rollins, to partying.

And Jessica was still . . . Jessica. If there was a party in Sweet Valley, Jessica was at it; if there was a cute guy around, Jessica was after him. Jessica was still charming and stubborn and always got exactly what she wanted.

"Of course you're right," Elizabeth said. "After a week of sharing a room with Jess, I'll probably wish I *had* gone to school in Alaska."

Todd's laughter was warm and reassuring. "And let's not forget the most important thing." He pushed a long strand of yellow hair away from her face. "You'll still have me, you know."

Elizabeth snuggled against him. Todd was one of the most important things in her life. They were going to have an incredible year together. And, Elizabeth reminded herself, she'd still have dependable, wonderful Enid, too. What could she possibly be worried about?

"Just wait," Todd said. "No more rules. Nobody telling us what to do. We're about to have the time of our lives." He bent his head close to hers. "We're about to start really living."

"I don't know when we're supposed to go to classes," Elizabeth said to Enid, looking up from the Sweet Valley University bulletin. "It looks like every minute of the day is crammed with other things to do. Sorority events, clubs, parties, tryouts, dances . . . I'm exhausted just reading about it all."

"That's fine with me," said Jessica from behind the fashion magazine she was reading. "Personally, I don't see how they can expect us to fit in boring junk like science and English when there are so many more important things to do."

"I just hope I still find time to keep up my journalism," Elizabeth continued, ignoring her sister. "SVU has a great TV station. Only, I don't want my grades to suffer."

"You don't have to worry, Liz," Enid said

earnestly. "I'm sure you'll be able to do both, just like you always have."

Jessica groaned inwardly. Here she was, about to begin one of the most important and exciting times of her life, and she was surrounded by the Deadly Duo, Elizabeth and Enid, two of the dullest people in Southern California.

She stared hopelessly at the smiling model in the magazine. She really wished that her best friend, Lila Fowler, were there with her now! Lila worried about stuff that really counted, like having the right clothes and meeting gorgeous men.

But unfortunately Lila had gone to Europe for the summer and hadn't come back. She was supposed to have returned last week, but all Jessica had heard so far was from a postcard of some old church in Venice that said simply and mysteriously, "Slight delay. I'll call soon."

"Oh, give me a break, will you?" Jessica demanded, her face appearing over the top of the magazine. "We haven't even gotten there yet, and already you're moaning about your grade-point average."

Elizabeth rolled her eyes. "Not all of us are going to college just so we can buy a new wardrobe," she teased. "Some of us are hoping to get an education."

"Who cares about books when there's a whole campus full of boys to learn about?" Jessica replied.

"It's a good thing I know you're joking, Jessica Wakefield," Mrs. Wakefield said pointedly, coming over to the kitchen table and setting the coffeepot in the center. She sat down beside Enid. "There's Butler Hall," she said, pointing to a photograph in the bulletin of a pretty brick building surrounded by trees. "I used to have a lot of classes there." She turned the page. "And look, there's La Palma Drive. Look how it's changed! There used to be only a few old houses there and now it's all built up."

"Now they have electricity and running water, too," Jessica joked.

Mrs. Wakefield ignored her. "You know, I really envy you girls. Some of the best years of my life were spent on that campus. I hope you enjoy your college days half as much as I did."

Enid turned to her. "You belonged to a sorority, didn't you, Mrs. Wakefield?"

"Belonged to a sorority!" Elizabeth gave her mother a mischievous smile. "My mother was only president of Theta Alpha Theta—the most elite sorority on the entire campus."

Mrs. Wakefield nodded. "The Thetas were wonderful," she said, her eyes sparkling. "We had the best time. It was like having a ready-made family. Girls who shared your values and goals, and who were always ready to help you out . . ." Her voice trailed off as she stared out the window, lost in her memories.

Enid smiled. "I'm convinced," she said emphatically. "I'm definitely going to pledge a sorority. I'm sure it's the best way to find the right crowd."

Jessica peered over her magazine at Enid, one perfect eyebrow raised in surprise. If Lila were there and not stuck in a gondola somewhere in Venice, she and Jessica would have been laughing hysterically by now. The idea of Enid Rollins, the biggest drip since the invention of water, wanting to belong to the "in" group was too funny for words.

"The right crowd?" Elizabeth said with a smile. Jessica could tell Elizabeth found the idea as bizarre as she did. "I don't think I've ever heard you talk about the 'right crowd' before. Getting in with the right crowd is a Jessica Wakefield concept."

"But we're going to be in college now, Liz," Enid argued. "I don't want to do what I've always done. I want to change. I want things to be different." Her green eyes flashed. "I've made a big decision this summer. In high school I just let things happen to me. In college *I'm* going to decide what happens." She looked from Elizabeth to Mrs. Wakefield and back again, a smile lighting up her face. "To begin with, I'm changing my image."

Jessica couldn't contain her laughter for another second.

"Changing your image?" Elizabeth demanded. "But why? There's nothing wrong with your image, Enid. You're great as you are."

Mrs. Wakefield started pouring the coffee. "Enid does have a point," she said. "One of the most wonderful things about the next four years is having the opportunity to explore and grow."

"I couldn't agree with you more, Mom!" Jessica cut in enthusiastically. "I'm already thinking of myself as the Christopher Columbus of Sweet Valley University, exploring the new, uncharted world of sophisticated college men."

Her mother turned to her. "You, young lady, could do with a little less exploring and a little more growing."

Elizabeth put a hand on Enid's arm. "How are you going to change your image? You're not going to pierce your nose or anything, are you?"

Enid looked at her and laughed.

"There's nothing outrageous about experimenting a little," Mrs. Wakefield said. "You're allowed to do things like that when you're eighteen." She smiled to herself. "My first semester in college, I grew my hair long and dyed it black."

Jessica dropped her magazine and gazed at her mother in surprise. "That's great!" she cried. "Were you a hippie, Mom?"

"A real radical," her mother murmured.

"So, Enid, what are you planning to do?" Elizabeth persisted.

Enid sat up a little straighter, her eyes darting around the table. "Do you really want to know?"

Jessica ducked behind her magazine again. "Oh, yeah," she muttered. "Make my day."

"I'm changing my name!"

"Changing your name?" Elizabeth cried. "To *what*?"

Enid scowled at her. "To Genghis Khan," she said sourly. She put down her mug heavily. "What do you think, Liz? That I was just going to make something up? I'm going to use my middle name, Alexandra. I think it's a lot cooler than Enid."

"Even Genghis Khan is cooler than Enid," Jessica commented.

"Alexandra is a lovely name," Alice Wakefield said, lifting her own mug to her lips. "It's very sophisticated."

Enid smiled. "Thanks. I think so too."

Elizabeth was still staring at Enid in disbelief. "Since when are you so worried about being sophisticated?"

"Since I really started thinking about what I wanted out of college," Enid said.

"But—"

Jessica cut her off. "Face it, Liz," she advised. "The times they are a-changin'."

"But do they have to change so fast?" Elizabeth said, more to herself than anyone else.

Elizabeth looked at her watch. In less than an hour, Todd, Winston Egbert, and Enid, alias Alexandra, would all be pulling up in front of the house for the two-hour drive across sprawling Sweet Valley County to Sweet Valley University. Although they were each bringing a car, they'd decided it would be more fun to convoy. "Sort of like a wagon train," Winston had joked.

"Except nobody will be shooting at us."

Elizabeth picked up two small framed photographs, taken at a beach party when they were all high school juniors. In the first, she and Todd had their arms around each other and were laughing hysterically. In the second, she was between Todd and Jessica, and the three of them were grinning happily.

Elizabeth could remember the exact moment they had been taken as though it were yesterday. They'd been playing volleyball when suddenly the boys, who were ten points behind, decided it would be more fun to drag the girls into the water than continue losing. Todd had come charging under the net, scooped her up, and raced to the ocean with her in his arms. Jessica had raced after them with the camera. "I can't believe it!" she'd been screaming. "Liz and Todd are having a spontaneous moment!"

Elizabeth had planned to leave the snapshots behind, waiting on her dresser for her return at Thanksgiving, but remembering how the three of them had laughed that day, she changed her mind and laid them carefully on top of the box on the bed.

Elizabeth looked around the room once more. There were so many memories here that part of her wished she could just fold the whole thing up and put it in her trunk.

"You're being ridiculous," she scolded herself. "You'll be back in a few months."

But her eyes filled with tears at the sight of the worn koala bear and blue lop-eared rabbit sitting abandoned on her half-empty bookshelf. Jessica had laughed at her when she'd tried to pack them. "We're going to college, not nursery school!" Jessica had said. "You can bring a basic black dress and a linen suit with you, but you cannot bring a blue bunny."

Elizabeth gave herself a shake. Thinking of her sister reminded her that they'd better finish loading the Jeep.

She turned toward the bathroom connecting her room with her sister's. "Jessica!" she called. "Are you almost ready?"

Elizabeth came to a sudden stop in the doorway. Her sister's room didn't look heartbreakingly empty as hers did. It looked messier and more cluttered than it had when she started packing.

"Jessica, what are you doing?"

Jessica looked up from the floor, the picture of innocence. "I'm packing. What does it look like?"

Elizabeth put her hands on her hips. "It looks like you're digging for the ruins of an ancient temple." Her eyes scanned the room, from the small mountains of clothes on the floor to the boxes spilling over with papers and books. She gave an exaggerated sigh. "You have got to be the only person in the world who can pack for two weeks and still end up with more junk than you started with."

Jessica's sea-green eyes flashed indignantly. She

11

scooped up another armload of shoes and dumped them into her purple canvas bag.

"Maybe all *you* need are some notebooks and a few pens." She went back to her closet and removed a few more laden hangers. "But *I'm* going to have an adventure." She held up a long dress patterned in red and gold. "Isn't this great? These are *the* colors of the season." She smiled mischievously. "After all, a girl does have to dress for adventure. You can't leave these things to chance."

Elizabeth eyed the stunning red-and-gold dress, with its tight bodice and low-cut back. Like most of the clothes that were heaped around the room, it was new in more ways than one. Jessica had never owned clothes so obviously sophisticated before. Apparently Alexandra Rollins wasn't the only person changing her image this autumn.

"Well, I'm planning to have an adventure too," Elizabeth said, a little defensively. "I'm not going to just stay in our room and study, you know."

Jessica threw the season's colors on top of her suitcase, turning back to her twin with a serious expression. "Can we get one thing straight right now, Liz?"

"Sure," Elizabeth said, a little surprised by her sister's tone. "What is it?"

Jessica frowned. "I don't want you pulling your 'I'm the big sister' routine on me anymore. I've agreed to share a room with you, but not if you're going to act like you're my mother. I don't want you nagging me about cleaning up. I don't want you asking me where I've been or when I'm coming back. And I definitely don't want you telling me who I can date."

Elizabeth opened her mouth to answer, but nothing came out. Jessica made it sound as though she were doing Elizabeth a favor by sharing a room with her.

"I have no intention of telling you *whom* you can date," Elizabeth finally managed to squeak. "But if you think you can keep *our* room the way you keep this dump—"

"You see? I knew it!" Jessica tossed back her head, her eyes blazing. "I knew you were going to get on my case the first chance you had."

"Me? I didn't get on your case. You're the one who—"

"I'm not going to take it, Liz, I mean it." Jessica folded her arms, her cheeks flushed. "For eighteen years all I've ever heard is how you're four minutes older than I am, like it's some big deal or something. Like it gives you the right to boss me around. Well, I don't care if you're forty years older than I am! Now that we're in college, I'm going to do exactly what I want!"

Elizabeth had to laugh. "Since when have you ever done anything else?"

"Me?" Jessica's voice was shrill with indignation. "Are you accusing me of being self-centered, Elizabeth Wakefield? *You?*"

13

Elizabeth stared at her sister in disbelief. Where had Jessica been for the past eighteen years? There wasn't a person who knew her who hadn't accused her of being self-centered at one time or another. Aristotle believed that the earth was the center of the universe, Aristarchus believed that the sun was the center of the universe, and Jessica Wakefield believed that the center of the universe was Jessica Wakefield.

"What do you mean, *you*?" Elizabeth raged. "Are you suggesting that *I'm* the one who's self-centered?"

Jessica marched over to the closet and yanked out another clump of skirts and blouses. "Oh, no, not *you*," she sneered. "Not Princess Perfect, the Girl Who Can Do No Wrong." She started pulling the clothes from their hangers and stuffing them into her bag. "You've been bossing me around since we were little. But we're adults now, Liz, and I'm really not going to take it anymore!"

"Well, don't!" Elizabeth yelled back. "See if I care!"

It's a good thing we know we're adults now, Elizabeth thought as she stormed back to her own room, *because we sure sound like kids.*

"Well, that's that," Mr. Wakefield said as the last suitcase was finally wedged into the back of the Jeep. He slammed the rear door and turned to his daughters with a smile.

Jessica groaned inwardly. The smile on Ned Wakefield's face was one of his embarrassed I-Am-Your-Father smiles. This meant that he had a little farewell speech he'd been preparing. Much as she loved her father, Jessica had never been a fan of his serious talks.

Jessica looked down Calico Drive, hoping to be rescued by the sight of Winston's beat-up old Beetle or even Todd's BMW turning the corner. There was nothing coming.

Mr. Wakefield cleared his throat. "Well . . ." he said again. "This is a day your mother and I have been planning for since you two were born."

Jessica turned back to him with a grin. "You mean finally getting us out of the house?"

Mr. Wakefield laughed. "No, of course not," he said, moving forward and putting an arm around each of his daughters. "You know how much we're going to miss you. The house is going to seem very empty . . ."

"We're going to miss you and Mom, too, Dad," Elizabeth said.

Ned Wakefield coughed, giving them each a squeeze. "I just want you to know if there's anything you need, anytime . . . If you need to talk to me or your mother, if you need some advice about school . . . or boys . . . or anything like that—"

"Sure, Dad." Jessica hadn't meant it to sound sarcastic, but she wasn't exactly in a hurry to get her dad's opinion on guys.

Mr. Wakefield turned his gaze on her, a new

concern on his face. "I understand that you're very excited about all your new freedom, Jessica," he said slowly, "but with freedom comes responsibility. And being away from home doesn't mean you can run wild. Before you agree to go out with someone—whether it's a boy or even a girlfriend— I want you to ask yourself, 'What would my mother and father think of this person?'"

Jessica stared back at him with a glazed expression in her eyes. *What would my mother and father think of this person?* Some cute guy was going to ask her out and she was supposed to stop and ask herself if her father would want her to date him? As sweet as her father was, he was so completely out of touch with reality sometimes that it was a wonder he functioned at all.

Mr. Wakefield released his hold on them and folded his arms. He looked up at the few clouds lazily drifting through the sky. "Let me tell you a story," he said, smiling to himself. "I was your age once myself, believe it or not. I know how you feel. I remember when I first went away to college. I thought I was a big man. I had everything worked out. . . ."

Jessica tried to catch Elizabeth's eye, but Elizabeth was looking up at their father earnestly. Maybe Elizabeth was taking the move to college harder than Jessica had thought. Worrying about classes was one thing, but seriously listening to one of Mr. Wakefield's When I Was Your Age reminiscences was something else.

Just when Jessica feared that nothing was going to save them, the back door opened and a golden streak ran out, hurling itself at them with a happy bark.

"Prince Albert was afraid you were going to forget to say good-bye to him," Alice Wakefield said with a laugh, following him out to the driveway.

Jessica had never been so happy to see him before. She leaned down and gave him a hug. "I'm going to miss you, boy," she told him as he nuzzled against her ear. "I bet there's nobody at Sweet Valley University who can fetch a stick like you can."

Elizabeth bent down beside them, resting her head on Prince Albert's silky neck.

Jessica glanced over. Amazingly enough, there seemed to be a tear in her sister's eye. "Oh, come on, Liz," she whispered. "You're not going to start crying over the dog, are you?"

Elizabeth shook her head. "I'm not crying. I was just thinking about the first day we got him. Don't you remember how little and cute he was? Remember how he couldn't get up on our beds without help?"

"Oh, look!" Mrs. Wakefield said. "There's Todd and Alexandra."

"And Winston," Mr. Wakefield added as the putt-putt-putt of the bright orange Beetle suddenly sounded on Calico Drive.

Jessica waved as the cars drew up to the curb.

17

"We'll be right there!" she called, practically tripping over herself in her desire to get going. "Well, we'd better go," she said, giving her parents each a quick hug and slapping Prince Albert on the head. "Come on, Liz. We don't want to miss one minute of our new lives, do we?"

"Not one," Elizabeth mumbled.

Jessica marched past her. She was already at the Jeep when she realized that her twin wasn't behind her. Turning around, she saw Elizabeth hurling herself into Mrs. Wakefield's arms.

Talk about long good-byes, Jessica thought as her sister and her mother both brushed tears from their cheeks. "Come on, Liz!"

"I'm coming!" Elizabeth shouted back.

Jessica started the engine. However bizarre Elizabeth was acting, she was sure that once they were at Sweet Valley University, Elizabeth would forget all about how cute Prince Albert was when he was a puppy and she'd be fine. "The College Express is about to depart!"

Elizabeth didn't move.

Of course, it was going to be very hard for Elizabeth to settle into college life if she refused to leave the driveway.

Chapter Two

In the clear afternoon, the campus of Sweet Valley University looked even prettier and more perfect than it did in the colorful brochures. From the sun-dappled tree-lined streets, to the beautiful red-tiled buildings, to the groups of students laughing and talking as they strolled across the lawns, everything about the campus seemed to say, "Welcome to college. Welcome to freedom."

"We made it!" Jessica shouted as she followed Todd's BMW through the gates of Sweet Valley University. She sounded the horn. "Hello, freedom, here I come!"

Elizabeth felt an unexpected ripple of excitement herself. Her sister was right—they had made it! They really had! They weren't little kids anymore. They weren't just visiting their brother, Steven. This was where they lived now. They were college freshmen, adults in the real world.

19

"I love it, I love it, I love it!" Jessica screamed. "I really do." She gestured out the window. "Look at it, Liz! Isn't it beautiful?"

Elizabeth looked. Although it was the beginning of freshman orientation and classes wouldn't start for another week, it looked as though the entire student body had already arrived for a week of fun. And Jessica was right, it was beautiful. Suddenly her anxieties of the past few days seemed foolish. She felt as though she'd been in one of those troubled nights when you lie awake worrying about everything. Elizabeth sighed with relief. Arriving at Sweet Valley U was like waking up to find the sun streaming through the window and her problems no more than phantoms of the night.

She smiled happily as she gazed out the window. She could see herself walking down the steps of the library. She could see herself sitting on one of the wooden benches along the pathways, reading a book. She could imagine throwing a Frisbee on the lawn with Todd. Elizabeth's confidence began to return. She'd been worried about nothing. College was going to be great.

"This is definitely the place to be," Jessica said, heading toward Dickenson Hall, their new home. "I mean, will you look at that, Liz? Just look over there."

Elizabeth turned. "Oh, wow! That's the new art and drama complex. They must have finished it over the summer. Doesn't it look great?"

Jessica groaned. "My sister, the android. I point out one of the cutest boys I've ever seen, and all you see is a dumb building." She shook her head. "Maybe you're not ready for college after all."

Dickenson Hall was a modern, multistoried dorm with a lush, green expanse of grass in front and a parking lot behind. Its halls were filled with talk and laughter, and scores of girls and their friends and families carrying everything from leather suitcases to life-size cardboard cutouts of James Dean.

Elizabeth took a bag from the Jeep and followed Jessica and their brother, Steven, into the large white building that was now her home. All the noise and activity were reassuring. Everyone they passed said hello.

Jessica looked over her shoulder at her. "Isn't this cool?" she asked, her blue-green eyes almost glowing with excitement. "It looks just like one of those singles apartment complexes you see in movies. All it needs is a pool."

"And all you need is a mule," Steven Wakefield groaned as he staggered up the stairs ahead of them with Jessica's trunk. Like the good brother he was, Steven had agreed to meet the twins outside their dorm to help them unload the Jeep. "I don't understand why you have so much stuff." He banged against a wall. "When I first came here, I had two suitcases and a box of books."

"That's because you're a boy," Jessica said,

21

coming up behind him. "Boys are simpler creatures. Their needs are fewer."

"My needs are going to include a new back after this," Steven said. He dropped the trunk on the landing and collapsed on top of it. "What have you got in here, your bathtub?"

"Clothes," Jessica said, sailing past him with a box of tapes in her arms.

"Clothes?" Steven stared after her. "What kind of clothes? Armor?"

"Clothes for every conceivable occasion from afternoon tea to a midnight scuba-diving party," Elizabeth said. She put a comforting hand on his shoulder. "She wanted to hire a moving truck, you know, but Dad put his foot down."

Steven watched Jessica make her way down the corridor, searching for room 28. "When is she going to have any time for classes?" he asked. "She's going to be changing her clothes from morning to night."

Elizabeth laughed. "I'm not sure Jess realizes she has to go to any classes."

"Hey, you two!" Jessica called from the other end of the hall. "Here's our room!"

"You better hope it's bigger than my first college room," Steven said as he got back to his feet. "Or with all the stuff Jess has, you'll be sleeping in the hall."

And I thought Dickenson Hall was noisy, Elizabeth thought as her eyes scanned the campus snack room for her best friend. The place was packed with people, most of them shouting to be heard above the jukebox blaring music from the corner.

"Where are you, Enid?" she mumbled, her eyes darting from table to table. Even though everyone she'd met so far seemed very friendly, the newness of the place was a little overwhelming. Suddenly she felt as though a dozen people were looking at her, and she forced herself to smile as though she knew what she was doing.

She was just about to give up and wait for Enid outside when she saw someone waving from across the room. Elizabeth's heart jumped with relief. Enid had already changed into an outfit Elizabeth had never seen before, but it was definitely her, grinning happily from the entrance to the food line.

"I can't tell you how happy I was when you called," Elizabeth said as she reached her friend. "I really needed to be rescued from that room. I can't believe Jessica abandoned me like that. Five minutes, Enid. That's exactly how long she stayed. I timed it." She took a chocolate doughnut from the snack-bar shelf. "Five minutes and she was out the door, leaving me to set up the room all by myself. I wanted to kill her."

"Alexandra, Liz, not Enid." Enid filled a cup from the coffee machine. "Or maybe Alex. Alex sounds pretty cool, doesn't it?"

The irritation Elizabeth was feeling with her sister transferred itself to her friend. "Enid, Alexandra, Alex, Lucretia Borgia, who cares?" she snapped. "I'm trying to tell you something."

In her heart, Elizabeth knew that she was overreacting, but she wanted some sympathy. She'd assumed that Steven was going to spend some time with them since it was their first day, but after they unloaded the Jeep he'd made some excuse and went back to his off-campus apartment. *Well, at least I've got Jess,* Elizabeth had told herself.

But Jessica stayed just long enough to grab the bed by the window and half of Elizabeth's closet, and then raced off in search of fun.

Enid dropped a container of yogurt on her tray. "I care, Elizabeth," she said shortly, moving toward the cashier. "But you're not telling me anything that I haven't heard a million times before, and the truth is, I'm getting pretty tired of hearing it." She reached into her bag for her wallet. "So Jessica's acting like a spoiled brat and leaving you to do all the work. So what else is new?"

Feeling slightly stunned, Elizabeth watched Alexandra Rollins pay for her coffee and yogurt and then scan the snack bar for a table. How could somebody change so quickly? Elizabeth and Enid had been best friends for years, and in all that time Enid had always been sympathetic and supportive. She had never hidden the fact that she thought Jessica was a spoiled brat, but she'd also never

24

come out and said so in so many words. Not in that tone of voice.

"Let's sit over there." Enid gestured toward a table in the center of the room and then, not waiting for Elizabeth's answer, strode over to it.

Elizabeth fumbled in her pocket for change. And Enid had never sounded quite so snotty with her before. It wasn't as if Elizabeth was the annoying member of the Wakefield family. She was the Wakefield twin everybody loved.

Her eyes followed Enid as she crossed the snack bar. Not only was her personality changing, but she seemed to be walking differently too: slower, more deliberately. Frown lines appeared on Elizabeth's forehead. Alexandra was wearing an outfit that Enid wouldn't have been caught dead in—tight jeans and a form-fitting bodysuit.

"Are you planning to pay for that or are you just going to stand there staring into space?"

Elizabeth turned around. The woman at the register was glaring at her unpleasantly.

"You're holding up the line," she said.

Elizabeth glanced behind her. Several unsmiling students were standing there, waiting impatiently. One of them had actually started eating his sandwich.

Elizabeth felt her cheeks turn red. "Oh, of course . . . I—I'm sorry . . ." She pulled out a handful of coins. In her haste to hand them over, several spilled from her grasp. They sounded to Elizabeth like fire-

25

crackers going off as they landed on the linoleum floor. No one made a move to help her pick them up. She bent down, scrabbling around people's feet to retrieve the dimes and pennies.

"Your change is on the tray," the cashier snarled.

The line moved forward. The guy behind her, under whose heel Elizabeth had spotted a nickel, stepped over her.

Forget the money, Elizabeth told herself. *Just get your stuff and get out of here.* She stood up so quickly that the next girl in the line slammed into her. Elizabeth picked up her tray. Coffee had sloshed all over, making a small pool on which her doughnut sat like an inner tube on a lake.

"Freshmen," said the cashier as Elizabeth fled. "It's the same thing every year."

"At last," Winston Egbert said as he pulled the VW into the parking lot outside Oakley Hall. "I was beginning to think this place didn't exist."

Once the Sweet Valley convoy had entered the college grounds, the girls had gone off to find their rooms and Todd had headed to the special high rise that housed the varsity athletes, leaving Winston to find his dorm by himself. Only, he hadn't been able to find it. Most of the male dorms were grouped near one another, but though he'd driven around in circles for half an hour, from building to building, he hadn't been able to find Oakley Hall. Finally, seeing a very pretty young woman who looked as though she knew her way around, Winston stopped and asked.

"Oakley?" she said, giving him an almost conspiratorial smile. "Sure, it's right over there. Third on the left."

And there it was, third on the left, set down in the middle of the female dorms like a rooster in a flock of chickens. *This must be my lucky day,* Winston thought as two attractive girls in shorts and tank tops sauntered past the Beetle.

One of them slapped the bumper. "Cute car," she said in a loud, clear voice.

"Isn't it great?" the other one said.

Winston beamed. And he'd been worried that the Beetle might interfere with the sophisticated, worldly, man-about-campus image he was hoping to create for himself. He checked himself in the rearview mirror. The new hairstyle was still in place. The Ray Bans he'd squandered a large chunk of his graduation money on still looked cool. He gave himself a wicked, worldly grin. Yes, this was clearly his lucky day.

Whistling to himself, he climbed out of the car, hauling a leather carryall—another large chunk of his graduation money—and a box of books out of the back. Several more girls walked by, all of them giving the Volkswagen and its owner warm looks. *I have the feeling I'm really going to enjoy college life,* he thought happily.

By the time he'd located his wing and his hallway, Winston's mood had begun to dim slightly. He had the uneasy feeling that something was wrong. The corridor was crowded with people who were looking for their rooms. Already, music blared from several doorways and there was a lot of loud talk and laughter. The funny thing was, though, that every voice he heard, and every person he saw, was female.

I must have made a mistake, Winston thought. *I must be in the wrong wing or something.*

He lifted his sunglasses and looked up at the sign on the wall. *Wing B—Rooms 11–20.* He looked at the letter in his hand. He'd been given room 18, in wing B, which was supposed to be made up of small, single rooms. He checked the letter again. Yes, that was what it said: wing B, room 18. And it was definitely in Oakley Hall.

Winston smiled self-consciously as another group of girls struggled past him, their arms filled with boxes. They all smiled back. He saw hair dryers and makeup mirrors, curling irons and coffee machines. These girls were not visiting; they were moving in.

It must be a coed dorm, he decided. Relief engulfed him. That would explain it. It was a coed dorm, the guys were already in their rooms, and he had somehow gotten himself on the wrong floor.

Winston took a deep breath and sidled down the hallway, trying to appear as inconspicuous as possible. He glanced into each room out of the corner of his eye. There was a redheaded girl in number 12 who waved as he passed. There were three girls sitting on the single bed in number 16, drinking sodas and talking. They all looked up as he passed. "Are you lost?" one of them called to him.

Winston froze. "Me?" *Please don't let them know I was a clown in high school,* he silently prayed. *Please don't let me blush, please don't let me stammer, and please don't let me smile like Daffy Duck.*

The girl in the middle, who had the longest legs he had ever seen on anyone who wasn't a professional basketball player, laughed. Her laugh was nothing like a professional basketball player's. Her laugh was pure crystal. Winston felt his solar plexus beginning to dissolve.

"No," she said, "that guy behind you." She laughed again. "Who are you looking for? I'm the resident assistant for this floor, Maia Stillwater. Maybe I can help you."

An RA, that was just what he needed. By not breathing he managed to keep his voice steady. "My name's Winston Egbert,. And maybe you can help me." He took a step forward, but because the dark glasses made indoor visibility poor, he misjudged the doorway, and instead of striding forward in a commanding, masculine way he crashed into the frame and catapulted himself into the room.

There was a creaking of springs as the three attractive young women collapsed on the bed in hysterical laughter.

29

"Are you okay?" Maia gasped.

Winston could feel the new, cool Winston Egbert wobbling and Winston the clown trying to take over. "Yes, yes," he said quickly. "I'm fine. I must have tripped over something." He gave himself a shake, and hanging on to as much dignity as he could, completed his journey into the room.

"This is Candy Fierro," Maia said, nodding to the girl on her right. "And this is Anoushka Koll." The two of them were still laughing.

"Hi," said Winston, deciding that he could forgive them because of Candy's almost-purple eyes and Anoushka's heart-melting smile.

"So what's the problem?" Maia prompted. "You can't find your girlfriend?"

Winston tore his attention away from those eyes and that smile. "Well, no. Actually the problem is that I can't find my room."

The three girls exchanged a glance.

"Here?" Maia sounded incredulous.

"Well, I thought it was here." Winston handed her the letter. "I guess I must've made some kind of mistake or something."

Candy and Anoushka leaned over Maia's shoulder while she read. "This is Oakley Hall," Candy said.

"And this is wing B," Anoushka said.

Maia looked up. "And room eighteen is right next door." She grinned. Her smile was not quite up to Anoushka's, but close. "There aren't any men living here, though. It's strictly women." She read the letter again. "I don't get it. How could they have made a mistake like this?"

Suddenly Candy started laughing again. "Look!" she cried, stabbing at the paper with a daggerlike metallic-pink nail. "Look, there's what happened. The computer got your name wrong."

Maia and Anoushka started laughing too.

Winston sat down beside Candy, looking at the top of the letter where her finger was pointing.

"Oh, I don't believe this," he groaned. He must have read the letter at least ten times, and somehow he'd never noticed its first, basic mistake. *Dear Winnie Egbert,* the letter began.

Candy put an arm around him. "Cheer up, Winnie," she said. "I'll let you borrow my electric curlers anytime you want."

"You coming with us, Todd?"

Todd shut the dresser drawer he'd been filling with clothes and turned around. He'd spent so much time getting introduced to the other guys on his floor that he'd just started to unpack.

Bryan Mars, captain of the basketball team, was standing in the doorway of Todd's room. Behind him, several of the other team members were talking and fooling around.

"Where are you going?" Todd asked.

Mark Gathers, the team's undisputed star, poked his head over Bryan's shoulder. "We're going to

31

this great Cajun diner a couple of miles up the road. You've got to come, Todd. You haven't lived till you've tried their red beans and cornbread."

Todd stared back, suddenly confused. They couldn't be going for dinner yet? He felt as if he'd just gotten here. "What time is it?"

Bryan looked at his watch. "It's seven, amigo. Chow time."

Seven! Todd couldn't believe it. Only a little while ago it was four o'clock and he was going to ride over to Dickenson Hall and look for Elizabeth. But another bunch of guys had arrived, and they'd all started talking, and then a couple of the other guys had gone off to unpack and that had seemed like a good idea . . .

"We don't want to stay out too late tonight," one of the other freshmen said. "We have to get up early to take advantage of priority registration."

Todd hesitated, looking at the grins on the faces of Bryan and Mark. They were great guys. He really wanted to hang out with them some more. And red beans and cornbread sounded pretty good, too. But what about Elizabeth? She was probably expecting to eat with him tonight.

"Come on, Todd!" someone else shouted. "We haven't told you the end of the story about the game with U of O yet. You're going to lose it when you hear what Murgatroyd did."

On the other hand, Elizabeth had Jessica—*and* Steven. Steven was helping them move in; he'd

32

probably planned to take the twins back to his place for dinner. Todd didn't have to feel guilty about Elizabeth. She was fine. She was the one who should feel guilty about him. It hadn't even occurred to her to invite him to dinner with Steven. And besides, Todd really wanted to hear what Murgatroyd had done.

"Okay," Todd said, reaching for his jacket. "Sounds great."

As they all piled into the elevator, it crossed Todd's mind that he could give Elizabeth a ring from downstairs. Just to make sure she was at Steven's and that everything had gone all right. But as they came into the lobby, Mark Gathers caught up with him.

"There's no reason for all of us to take cars," he said. "Why don't you come with me and I can fill you in on all the things you really need to know about life at SVU?" He smiled. "Like which sororities have the fastest women."

Todd wasn't sure if Mark was joking or not, but he didn't want Mark to think he wasn't sophisticated enough to be interested in fast women. After all, he was a college man now, and already a prized member of the basketball team that had been state champion four years running.

Todd smiled back. "Why don't I drive so you can concentrate on talking."

As she walked toward the campus coffee bar,

Jessica couldn't help thinking how lucky she was. She'd been at Sweet Valley University for only a few fantastic hours, and already she'd made friends with Isabella Ricci, one of the most popular and stupendous sophomores on campus. Jessica couldn't help smiling to herself as she strutted across the lawn. She'd been missing Lila a lot the last few days. Not just because she was concerned about Lila's whereabouts, but because though Elizabeth had Todd and Enid to talk to, Jessica didn't really have anyone to share her own excitement with. Now she had Isabella Ricci. Isabella was even more beautiful and sophisticated than Lila. And she knew *everybody* who was anybody and had dated almost every eligible man on campus.

Jessica caught sight of the clock tower at the end of the quad. It was almost six thirty. She'd promised Isabella she'd meet her at six thirty to hear a jazz trio playing in the café this evening.

Jessica was running as she came up the path that circled the café, but as soon as she turned the corner, she slowed down. When she walked through the doors of the café, it was with the step of a woman who has seen it all. She stopped just inside the entrance. She kept her expression slightly bored, but inside she was bubbling with enthusiasm. Dark and cramped, with posters and paintings on its brick walls, the café looked like something out of a French movie. The students sitting at the candlelit wooden tables, all of them nearly as sophisticated as Isabella, were talking in low, intimate voices and drinking coffee from small white cups. *You can have your gondola, Lila,* Jessica thought. *I'd much rather be here.*

As casually as she could, she looked around the room. Thank God, the trio hadn't set up yet. She would have died of mortification if she'd had to walk through them while they were playing.

Jessica shook her head, and her golden hair shimmered in the subdued light. She didn't have to look to know that she was creating a sensation. She'd spent the whole afternoon practicing making an entrance, imitating the way she'd seen Isabella walk and stand and gaze around a room, and so far it hadn't let her down once. She could feel the eyes sizing her up: the girls with envy, the guys with admiration.

At a table in the corner she saw the long white neck and tousled black hair of Isabella Ricci against the red wall of the coffee bar. She looked as though she must be thinking of something incredibly romantic. In high school Jessica would have waved, but not now. Now she was a college woman. She raised her head ever so slightly, just enough to let Isabella know that she'd seen her, and crossed the coffee bar like a model walking down a catwalk, like Isabella Ricci crossing a street.

Jessica had heard of people who went through their entire lives without ever understanding why they'd been born. There always seemed to be people in TV dramas and the kind of books they made you read in English who had no idea what their lives were about. They spent hours or hundreds of pages trudging around being miserable and wondering why their lives had no meaning. But not Jessica. She might be only eighteen, but she knew exactly why she'd been put on this earth.

So she could go to college.

There wasn't a doubt in her mind. Today had been the most wonderful day of her entire life. This was where she belonged. This was where she was meant to be. In only a few brief hours, she had not only met scores of people and made an incredible new friend but she'd been asked out by not one, not two, but four different men.

Jessica reached Isabella's table and slid into the empty seat with a sigh. "I'm sorry I'm late," she apologized. "I wanted to put my name down on the tryout list for cheerleading, and I had trouble getting out of the gym."

Isabella looked concerned. "Did you get lost?"

Jessica smiled. "No, I mean, these adorable guys kept stopping me, wanting to talk."

Isabella threw back her head and laughed. "Jessica Wakefield, you really are too much. I thought I was the only wild woman on this campus, but obviously I was wrong." Her gray eyes sparkled with mischief. "You are definitely a girl after my own heart."

"We were destined to meet," Jessica said. "If I

hadn't bumped into you in the gym, I would have bumped into you somewhere else."

One perfect Ricci eyebrow rose a fraction of an inch. "Speaking of which," Isabella said, barely seeming to move her lips, "don't look now, but there's someone headed toward us who looks as though he'd like to do more than bump into you."

Jessica kept her eyes on Isabella. "Who is it?" she asked. "Somebody I should know?"

"Somebody everybody should know." Isabella lifted her cappuccino to her lips and took a small, delicate sip. "Peter Hazlitt Wilbourne the Third, president of the Sigmas and the most powerful undergraduate on campus." A smile flickered over her lips but didn't land. "Peter thinks he's God's gift to earth. Some people think he's the gift of someone else entirely."

"Now I really am interested," Jessica whispered. "Where is he? Can I turn around now?"

Isabella raised her eyes. "Why, Peter," she purred. "How nice to see you. You're looking very well after your summer vacation."

Peter stopped beside Jessica. "I didn't come for chitchat with you, Izzy, and you know it," he said dismissively. "I wanted to be introduced to your little friend."

Isabella made a face. "Don't mind Peter, Jessica," she said with mock sweetness. "Rudeness is part of his charm." She waved an arm at Jessica and her gold jewelry flashed. "Jessica Wakefield, Peter

37

Wilbourne the Third. Peter, Jessica."

Jessica turned around to find herself looking at one of the most arrogant, self-satisfied faces she'd ever seen. It was also an undeniably handsome face, but not half as handsome as its owner seemed to think.

"Well, how do you do?" he asked, but in such a way that Jessica knew he was really saying, *Aren't you lucky to get to meet me?*

Jessica returned his insincere smile with one of her own. "How do you do?"

He leaned closer. "You know, I don't usually go out with freshmen," he said in a smooth, smug voice. "But I think in your case I might make an exception." He reached out and touched a strand of her hair. "How about going to one of the house parties with me this week? I'm pretty busy with frat stuff for the next night or two, but the Sigmas are having a party with the Thetas at their house on Friday that might interest a girl like you."

Jessica smiled sweetly. "I'm sorry," she said, her voice almost as smooth and smug as his, "but I've already got a date for the Theta party."

He ran a finger up her arm. "Break it."

Jessica's smile didn't falter. "I'm afraid I can't."

Peter looked over at Isabella. "Didn't you tell your little friend who I am?" he asked. "Doesn't she know there's no one on this campus who can't be dumped for me?"

"She told me who you are," Jessica said. "But I don't believe in breaking dates."

Isabella shook her head as Peter strode back to his table. "I'm not so sure you should have done that," she said. "Peter's a bad enemy to have. Some people even think he's the leader of a secret society on campus. You know, all very heavy and power obsessed."

Jessica shrugged. "I don't care what he leads. I really do have a date with this gorgeous guy I met at lunch."

"I just hope he's worth it," Isabella said. She lifted a tiny spoonful of froth and coffee to her lips. "What's this Prince Charming's name?"

"Danny," Jessica answered. "Danny Wyatt."

The spoon stopped inches from Isabella's blood-red lips. *"Danny Wyatt?"* she repeated. "But Jessica, Danny Wyatt's—"

"I did notice that he's black, if that's what you were going to say," Jessica cut in. She was a little taken aback that someone as worldly and intelligent as Isabella should feel it necessary to point this out to her.

"There's that, too," Isabella said slowly. "Hey, don't get me wrong," she rushed on, seeing the look on Jessica's face. "I'm not saying he's not a terrific guy, because he is. Everybody knows that. Danny's great. But everybody also knows that Peter Wilbourne is not a really big fan of interracial couples." She bit her bottom lip. "Seriously, Jess.

Peter has this thing about Danny. Up until last year, he and Danny were in constant competition, and Danny always won. Peter was used to being number one because he's rich. But Danny was smarter, he was stronger, he was better looking, he was nicer and more popular—he would probably have been president of the Sigmas, too, if he hadn't dropped out last winter. Peter will go nuts when he finds out he's been iced in favor of Danny. Peter hates him, Jess. I mean, really hates him."

Jessica leaned back as the trio came onto the small, makeshift stage. "Well, maybe he won't find out who I turned him down for."

Isabella smiled grimly. "Oh, he'll find out."

Outside room 28, Dickenson Hall was full of talk and music. Inside room 28, the only audible sound was the ticking of Elizabeth's watch.

Elizabeth, sitting on her bed with her hands folded on her lap, glanced at herself in the mirror on the back of the closet door. She knew that anyone who saw her sitting there would assume that she was about to go out to have a good time. Her hair was back in a loose French braid, she was wearing her favorite cranberry linen dress, and her bag and her jacket were on the bed beside her. Elizabeth scowled at her reflection.

"Well, they'd be wrong," she said out loud. "I'm not going anywhere. I'm all dressed up with nowhere to go."

For at least the twentieth time in the last forty minutes, her eyes turned to the intercom on the wall by the door. She couldn't bear to look at her watch again.

Laughter like gunshots echoed down the hallway. As far as she could tell, everyone who wasn't out at some special event on campus or in town was having a party in the dorm.

Probably everyone in the world but me is either out having a good time or throwing a party, she thought bitterly. *A party I'm not invited to.* She dared a quick look at her watch. It was nine. Nine! That meant she'd been sitting here, waiting for nothing, for two whole hours. Elizabeth picked up the book she'd been trying unsuccessfully to read and threw it across the room.

She'd thought that after their coffee she and Enid would probably do something together. There was a free film showing in the movie house on campus, and she'd seen a poster for jazz at the coffee bar, but Enid had other plans. "Gee, I'm sorry, Liz," she'd said. "I just assumed you and Jessica and Todd would be seeing Steven tonight, so I told some of the girls on my floor that I'd go for pizza with them."

But Jessica never came back to the room, and Todd had disappeared too. When Elizabeth came back to the dorm and couldn't reach him on the phone, she'd been sure he must be on his way to pick her up. She'd been so sure, in fact, that she'd

41

gotten dressed and gone to wait in the lobby for him. She'd waited until she got tired of people looking at her as though she were in the wrong place, and then she'd come back to her room.

One of the girls on her hall had asked her if she wanted to go to the campus pub, and a couple of other girls had invited her to the common room to watch a movie, but Elizabeth still thought Todd would show up and she didn't want to miss him.

"Well, I shouldn't have worried," she said to the empty room as she kicked off her shoes. "I could have gone to San Francisco and he wouldn't have noticed."

She lay back on her bed, imagining her parents at home, reading together in the living room. "I wonder what the girls are doing right now," her mother was probably saying. Her father would laugh. "Oh, you know them," he'd say. "Wherever they are, they'll be having a good time."

Down the hallway, several people started laughing as though they'd just heard the funniest story in the world.

But in room 28, Dickenson Hall, it was just about then that the tears began to fall.

Chapter Three

Elizabeth rolled over in her sleep, kicking off the covers. "Jessica!" she moaned. "Please let me in!"

Elizabeth was lost in the dark, bare concrete corridor of an enormous dorm. For some reason she was wearing her pink-and-white-striped pajamas and her hair was in pigtails. On her feet were blue bunny slippers; in her hand was the suitcase she'd had as a child. She couldn't find her room.

Scared and lonely, Elizabeth wandered up and down a maze of hallways. "Excuse me," Elizabeth kept saying. "Excuse me, but I'm looking for my room."

They laughed. "Oh, it can't be in this dorm," they told her. "You're just a little kid."

She began knocking on doors. Every room was filled with laughing, happy students, dressed in fashionable clothes and sipping champagne.

Growing desperate, Elizabeth shuffled along, try-

43

ing to keep anyone from noticing the tears streaming down her cheeks. And then, down at the end of a dimly lit corridor, she saw it: number 28, her room!

Through the open door she could see her beautiful sister, stretched out on a chaise longue, a crystal goblet in her hand and her head thrown back in a laugh. Jessica was wearing a red-and-gold brocaded cocktail dress, and her hair was piled on top of her head. She was surrounded by handsome men, kneeling in a circle around her.

And then Elizabeth's eyes fell on what was behind Jessica and the men. It was her old room on Calico Drive, and all her things were just as they should be. Overcome with joy, Elizabeth moved forward.

But at that instant, Jessica turned and saw her. "No!" she screamed. "You can't come in here! You'll ruin everything."

Tripping over the bunnies' ears, Elizabeth started to run. She had to get inside; her room was there, her *old* room, her real room. Once she got inside, everything would be all right again. Just as she reached the door Jessica slammed it in her face.

Crying uncontrollably now, Elizabeth started pounding on the door. "Jessica!" she called. "Jessica, let me in!"

Suddenly Elizabeth's eyes blinked open. She sat up in bed, her heart pounding. *It was just a dream,* she told herself, trying to calm her breathing.

She looked around. The sun was streaming

through the blinds, illuminating the piles of clothes on the floor, the half-unpacked suitcases, the stacks of boxes. Socks and underwear dripped off the furniture, and curtains sat in a heap on top of Jessica's dresser, waiting to be hung. A purple lace bra hung over Elizabeth's brass desk lamp.

Elizabeth swung her legs over the side of the bed. Despite the chaos around her, for the first time in the two days that she'd been at Sweet Valley University, Elizabeth was actually relieved to be in room 28.

Her eyes fell on the other bed, and a feeling of annoyance started creeping back. Jessica, in her new satin purple nightshirt, was still sound asleep. The clothes she'd been wearing last night lay in a pile on the floor, just as she'd stepped out of them. Jessica was smiling.

I'm not going to lose my temper, Elizabeth told herself as she climbed out of bed. *I'm going to be calm. I'm going to be reasonable and understanding.* She calmly picked up her sister's jacket and hung it on the back of a chair. *You see?* she said to the pale face that stared back at her from the mirror on the closet door. *You don't have to get upset. Everything's going to be fine.*

Elizabeth wasn't sure how it had happened, but in just two days, she and her twin had driven each other to the brink of insanity. Yesterday morning, Elizabeth had accused Jessica of being irresponsible, and Jessica had accused Elizabeth of being as much fun as wet socks. "You must've been asleep by *ten* last night!" Jessica had raged. "Old people go to bed at ten, Liz, not college freshmen. You better hope you die young, because you're not going to have anything to look forward to when you retire." And then she'd stormed out of the room and Elizabeth hadn't seen her again. Until now.

Elizabeth wanted to start all over. She had given it a lot of thought, and she'd decided that it was up to her to be more flexible. To give things a little time to settle down.

After all, it had worked with Todd. Instead of giving him a hard time because he'd abandoned her the day they arrived, she'd acted as though nothing had happened. She hadn't told him how she waited for him that first night, or how she'd cried herself to sleep. And things between them were almost back to normal. Yesterday they'd had a nice dinner before he had to go off to some basketball meeting. And today they were getting together for breakfast and to register for classes.

Elizabeth smoothed out the spread and stood up, smiling to herself. Jessica had done a lot of running around in the last two days, but by now she was probably ready to get down to hanging the curtains and putting away her luggage.

Taking a deep breath, Elizabeth went over to Jessica and gave her a shake. "Hey, sleepyhead," she whispered. "You better get up. We have a lot to do today. We've got to finish setting up the room. We have to register for classes. And we have to start buying our books. . . ."

Jessica rolled over, pulling the covers over her eyes. "Books?" she mumbled. "Are you kidding? I don't have time for books. I have two teas and a lunch date today. I have to get my sleep."

"Well, maybe if you hadn't stayed out till four in the morning, you'd have already had your sleep," Elizabeth answered, a little less patiently and understandingly than she'd intended.

Jessica groaned. "Oh, don't start."

"I'm not starting," Elizabeth said calmly. "I just meant that if you actually spent a little time here, you'd be able to unpack. You could even put some of your stuff away."

"I don't want to put my stuff away," came the muffled reply. "I'm too busy right now."

Elizabeth could feel her calm vanishing as she stared down at her sister's purple sheets. It wasn't fair that she always had to be the one who was flexible while Jessica did exactly what she pleased.

"You're not too busy right now," Elizabeth snapped. "Now's the perfect time to discover two wonderful inventions—drawers and closets. You'd be amazed how handy they are. They completely eliminate the problem of having to step over dirty bras and socks to get to the door. Not only that," she rushed on, "but there is a luggage room, you know. We don't have to keep your suitcases and your trunk in here for the rest of the year."

47

Jessica pulled the pillow over her head. "I wish we didn't have to keep *you* in here for the rest of the year."

"Come on, Candy, hurry up, will you? If I don't get a move on, I'm going to be late for registration."

"Has anybody seen my green bra? You know, the shiny support one? I think maybe I dropped it in the bathroom last night."

"What about you, Maia, do you shave or wax? I'm always cutting myself. On the other hand, though, I really hate the sound when you rip the hair off your legs."

"Can somebody lend me a tampon? It's an emergency."

"Men! Can you believe that cretin? He broke our date *again*!"

Hurtling out of sleep like a rabbit being smoked out of its hole, single words registered in Winston's brain. Wax. Bra. Tampon. Cretin. His first thought was: *Where am I?*

And then he remembered. He was in Oakley Hall, room 18, surrounded by girls.

Very, very slowly, Winston opened his eyes.

"Anoushka! Winnie said I could borrow his weights after you, so don't forget to give them to me before you go out."

And closed them again. His free weights. Winston had thought that suave college men were all into weights, but it was beginning to look as though it was college women. He hadn't seen his since he'd dropped them on his foot as he was bringing his stuff in from the car, and Anoushka had pounced on them like a cat on a bug. He should have left them home. He should have left himself home with them.

After two hectic days of running around from office to office trying to get the computer to admit it had made a mistake when it put him in a women's dorm, Winston was exhausted. And defeated. He had eventually found a human in the office of the dean of students who conceded that something had gone radically wrong.

"I know it's an unusual situation," Ms. Lombardi had sympathized, "but I'm afraid you're stuck with it, Mr. Egbert, at least for the time being."

"Stuck with it?" Winston had repeated. "What do you mean, stuck with it?"

Ms. Lombardi had smiled, more wryly than sympathetically. "I mean, like Super Glue. You may not have been aware of it before, but there's a severe housing crisis at the university, and I'm afraid there isn't a spare bed in any of the male or coed halls at the moment. Not even off campus."

"But I can't be stuck with it," Winston had protested. "I'm a b— I'm a man. I can't live in a hall filled with girls."

"You mean women," Ms. Lombardi had corrected him. "And I'm afraid that unless you'd prefer to sleep in your car, you're going to have to live with them until things settle down. Once a few people start dropping out or moving into the frat houses we'll be able to find you a place."

"But Ms. Lombardi . . ." Winston had leaned forward so that the other women in the office wouldn't overhear him. "You have no idea what it's like. They never stop talking. And they walk around in their . . . in . . ." It had been difficult to say the words out loud, especially when halfway through his sentence he'd realized that Ms. Lombardi, despite the fact that she must be at least forty, was a woman too.

Ms. Lombardi's lips had twitched, as though she were about to start laughing. "They run around in their *what?*"

"In their underwear! How am I supposed not to look? It's very embarrassing. I have to wait till they're all done in the bathroom, and even then I have to brush my teeth with my eyes closed in case one of them's still in the shower. Plus, I have to be dressed all the time . . ."

Her lips had twitched again. "Winston, trust me," she'd said. "You'll get used to it. After all, you're a college man now, right? I'm sure you'll handle this just fine."

The corridor had gone silent. Winston opened his eyes again.

Even if he did handle it just fine, he still had a

problem that he hadn't been able to explain to Ms. Lombardi. He was hoping to impress the frat guys with what a big man he was. What were they going to say when they found out he was living with a bunch of girls? A bunch of girls who called him Winnie and borrowed his weights?

Winston listened. He glanced at the clock. They stopped serving breakfast in half an hour. That explained it—they'd all gone to talk about tampons and men over scrambled eggs and cornflakes. Pulling on his jeans and a T-shirt, Winston warily stuck his head out the door. He looked left. He looked right. The coast was clear.

Please, he hoped as he dashed into the bathroom. *Please don't let there be anyone in here waxing her legs.*

Elizabeth's stomach growled, and she didn't blame it. She felt like growling herself. She'd been waiting nearly half an hour for Todd, and he still hadn't shown up. If he didn't hurry, the kitchen would be closed. She forced herself to look away from the door. *Three more people,* she told herself. *If Todd isn't one of them, then I'm going down to breakfast by myself and wait at the table.*

The one real advantage to being one of the last students to come for breakfast was that there wasn't any line. Elizabeth walked right up to the counter and put some fruit and cereal on her tray. Then it occurred to her to take some extra for

Todd, in case he didn't get there before the kitchen closed. She took a glass of juice, a doughnut, and a bagel with cream cheese for Todd. She also got the hot dish for Todd and an order of toast for herself. She was going to need her strength for registration, and besides, from the horror stories she'd heard, she probably wouldn't be done in time for lunch. She smiled to herself as she had her meal ticket punched. From what she'd heard, she'd be lucky to be done by dinner.

Elizabeth decided to sit in the middle of the cafeteria so Todd would see her as soon as he came in. Several girls from her dorm waved as she made her way across the room. She was smiling back at Daria Mendez, with whom she'd struck up a conversation in the bathroom last night over the cold-water faucet that wouldn't go off, when she felt someone staring at her from a nearby table. Thinking that it might be Todd , she turned—only to find herself staring into the ice-blue eyes of a boy she didn't know. His gaze was so intense that she bumped into another table in confusion.

Where *was* Todd when she needed him? Elizabeth grabbed the first empty table she came to, throwing herself into a chair with a sigh of relief.

That was another thing about college life she hadn't counted on, that other guys might start coming on to her. At Sweet Valley High everyone knew that she and Todd were a couple. But here it seemed as if every time she turned around, some guy was staring at her as though he'd never seen a girl before in his life.

Elizabeth munched on her apple while she waited for Todd. She was really looking forward to seeing him. He'd been so excited yesterday about the basketball team and all the great guys on it that she'd barely had a chance to tell him anything she'd been doing. Not that she'd been doing much. Hanging around, waiting for Jessica to turn up. Hanging around, waiting for Todd.

She tossed the apple core on her tray and started putting butter and jam on her toast.

She hadn't been doing *nothing* for the past two days. She'd talked to a bunch of girls in her hall yesterday. She'd visited the library and the arts complex, and she'd signed up for both the school paper and the news department of the campus TV station. In the evening, she'd made popcorn and nachos with a couple of people from her floor and watched an old movie. If she hadn't been thinking about Todd most of the evening, wondering where he was and if he was missing her or not, she might have actually enjoyed herself.

Elizabeth checked her watch. She lifted the plate covering Todd's breakfast. The eggs looked a little solid, but the potatoes were still warm. She broke a piece off with a fork. She might as well eat the hash browns. There was no use in letting the whole meal go to waste. Not when there were so many hungry people in the world.

Elizabeth reached in her bag and took out the registration handbook. That was the other thing she'd done yesterday. She'd spent hours combing through the course listings, picking out what she wanted and fitting it all into a workable schedule. She was excited about the result. Not everything might be going right for her at the moment, but she was looking forward to some really interesting classes. After all, that was what college was about. Even if Jessica didn't think so.

Elizabeth made a sandwich out of a piece of toast and some cold scrambled egg. She ate it slowly while she went through her schedule again. Because she'd taken advanced history and English in high school, she was able to go straight to the courses she really wanted: a creative-writing workshop, a literature course on the roots of feminism, a foundation course in classical thought and culture, the social history of the twentieth century, and Journalism I.

Elizabeth put down Todd's juice glass with a happy sigh. She was going to have to do a lot of reading, but it was going to be worth it.

"Liz!"

Elizabeth looked up. Todd had just burst through the doors and was hurrying toward her.

"Liz, I'm sorry," he was saying even before he reached her. "I'm really, really sorry."

He looked really sorry. He was probably so exhausted from all the basketball practice that he'd overslept. "It's all right, Todd," she said with a smile.

He smiled back and gave her a kiss. "You're the best, Liz." He flung himself into the chair beside her. "I completely forgot all about meeting you because of registration."

"Registration? What do you mean?"

"You have freshman burnout already?" he teased, tapping the leaflet she'd been reading. "Registration for classes, remember?"

Elizabeth stared at him. "But you couldn't have registered," she finally managed to choke out. She picked up her listing of course offerings and shook it in his face. "Freshmen whose names begin with W don't register until eleven."

Todd winked in a disgustingly supercilious way. He must have picked it up in the athletes' dorm, because he had never winked like that before.

"They do if they're on a varsity team," he said.

"Oh, do they?"

"That's right. They get to preregister before registration even begins."

Impossibly enough, his smile was even more supercilious than his wink. No wonder he had no time for her. He was too busy taking lessons in how to be a superjock.

"It was so cool, Liz. We didn't have to wait in line or anything. We just told them what we wanted, and they punched it into the computer."

Elizabeth shoved the tray away from her. "But

we were going to register together."

"I know," he said, not quite meeting her eyes. "I would've called you before I went this morning, but it was so early and rushed . . ." He shook his head. "I couldn't have done it anyway. I've got practice this afternoon. And then we've got a booster dinner."

He got to his feet suddenly. "Come on, Liz. Why don't we go to the snack bar and get a coffee? I have just enough time before I have to meet the rest of the guys."

"But what about your breakfast? I got extra food for you."

Todd laughed. "You really do have freshman burnout, don't you?" he teased. He pointed to the tray. "There's nothing there."

Elizabeth looked in disbelief. Todd was right: there was nothing left but a few spoonfuls of cereal and an apple core. She must have been hungrier than she'd thought.

"It's a good thing I already ate with the team," Todd said, putting his arm around her.

"Oh, right," Elizabeth said. "A very good thing."

Jessica had gotten into bed smiling, she'd smiled through her sleep, and now she woke up with a smile still on her lips. What a day she'd had yesterday! What a fabulous day! Isabella and Isabella's friend, Denise Waters, had taken Jessica on a

56

head-to-toe tour of the campus. She'd seen the pond where the frat boys went skinny-dipping. She'd seen the window a girl had climbed out last winter when she eloped with the new history lecturer. She'd seen the lawn where Denise's friend, Mariela Winterson, punched another girl for trying to steal her boyfriend. She'd seen Isabella's tremendous double suite in the new apartment complex. She'd been asked out by five more gorgeous guys.

Jessica stretched languidly, slowly opening her eyes. Thank God, Elizabeth was gone. If there was one thing that could stop Jessica from smiling these days, it was her twin sister.

Jessica looked over at Elizabethland, her sister's side of the room, with irritation. You'd think they were in boot camp, not college. Everything in Elizabethland was neat and tidy. The bed was made. The furniture was dusted. The few things that were out—her framed photographs, her jewelry box and brush and makeup bag, the slippers under the bed—looked as though they'd been glued in place. In fact, Elizabethland was so neat that you wouldn't think anyone lived in it.

Jessica kicked off the covers and sat up. Not that anyone did live in it. Not anyone *real*. "The Stepford Twin," Jessica muttered to herself as she got out of bed.

"Oh, geez. Where's my underwear?" Jessica asked aloud. She had to have blue underwear to go with her blue-and-white flowered leggings and blue sleeveless shirt. She shuffled through another heap of clothes and looked into a couple of suitcases, but her blue underwear was gone. "I bet *she's* put it somewhere," Jessica grumbled.

Jessica yanked open the top drawer of Elizabeth's bureau. Elizabeth *always* kept her underwear in her top drawer. And there it was. Everything, even the tights, was neatly folded.

"It must be exhausting being so neat all the time," Jessica muttered. "No wonder she never has any time to have fun."

She pulled out a sky-blue pair of bikini underwear and a matching bra, grabbed her shower stuff from the top of a box, and hurried from the room—leaving Elizabeth's top drawer open, like a hole in the perfection of Elizabethland.

"I don't know how much more of the Stepford Twin I can take," Jessica said as she bit into a croissant. What could be more sophisticated than having something you could barely pronounce for breakfast? "You should have heard her shouting at me this morning. The whole hall heard her." She took a sip of the espresso coffee Isabella had made in the tiny kitchenette of her suite. Croissants *and* espresso. If Lila Fowler could see her now, she'd be so envious! "I'm telling you, I'd rather live with my mother than with Elizabeth."

Denise put down her cup. "You have my sympathy, believe me, Jess." She was one of the most beautiful girls Jessica had ever seen, but she was so unself-conscious about it that you hardly even noticed. "Last year I got stuck with this complete dork. She dressed in nothing but brown, and all she ever ate was seeds and nuts."

"Tell her about Mommy," Isabella urged, laughing.

Denise rolled her almost-black eyes. "Oh, God." She leaned toward Jessica. "I swear, Jess, every sentence that came out of this girl's mouth started with 'Mommy says . . .' *Mommy says you should never eat anything that's been processed . . . Mommy says brown is the most harmonious color . . . Mommy says young women should never raise their voices.* God, it was a nightmare!"

Jessica laughed. "You can't be serious. She couldn't have been that bad."

Isabella was shaking her head. "She was worse. She used to play this tape of crickets all the time to relax her inner self."

"By the end of the first week, I wanted to strangle her outer self," Denise said. "I still can't believe I got through an entire semester listening to bugs."

Jessica collapsed against the sofa in hysterics. "Stop it," she begged. "You're making Liz sound almost human."

Isabella nibbled delicately on her croissant. "You know, Jessica, I just may have the solution to your roommate problem."

59

"Really?" Jessica straightened up. "What?"

Isabella nodded toward the room. "Why don't you move in here with me? Ms. Loyola, the dorm dictator, said last night that she didn't think my roommate was going to show up after all. And they're going to have to find someone to take her place anyway . . ."

Jessica couldn't believe it. Isabella Ricci, one of the most popular girls in the whole school, provider of croissants and espresso coffee, was asking *her* to share her suite.

"I don't want to pressure you or anything, Jess," Isabella added quickly. "I know you'll need some time to think it over, but we should let Ms. Loyola know before she finds someone else . . . another nut-and-bug woman."

Denise laughed. "You should do it, Jess. Your sister will be fine. She'll probably be as relieved to get rid of you as you'll be to get away from her."

"I'm not saying I'm a perfect roommate," Isabella said. "But I'm not too hard to get along with. Am I, Denise?"

Denise smiled. "Easy as instant pudding."

This was more than she'd dared hope for. Jessica was so excited she hardly trusted herself to speak.

"What's the matter?" Isabella asked when Jessica still didn't respond. "Is something worrying you? Ask me whatever you want."

Jessica took a deep breath. "Well . . . I do have one question . . ."

Isabella held out her hands. "As the gunslinger said to the sheriff, shoot."

"When can I move in?"

Six and a half hours. Six and a half hours, and for what? Elizabeth fumed as she made her way back to her room. Six and a half hours to be shut out of the class she'd wanted most, Journalism I.

She staggered through the front glass doors of Dickenson Hall with a sigh. For the first time since she arrived, it actually seemed to her like a quiet and sane place.

I'm exhausted, she thought as she started up the stairs. *I'm emotionally and physically exhausted. What I need is some peace and quiet, a nice hot shower and a nice dinner.*

She turned down her hall. The good news was that she could have all three of those things. There was no way Jessica was going to be in the room, not at five forty-five in the evening. Jessica wouldn't be back for hours.

She stopped outside the door of her room with a puzzled frown on her face. She could hear voices inside. She looked at the number again. It was definitely her room. Something heavy hit the floor. Elizabeth was just about to reach for the knob when the door flew open and two large, good-looking young men walked past her, Jessica's trunk between them.

61

"What—"

But before Elizabeth could finish her sentence, a girl Elizabeth had never seen before stepped out, Jessica's purple satchel over her shoulder and a box of shoes in her arms. She looked more like a Paris model than a California college student, except that she was wearing ripped jeans and a faded Save the Rain Forests T-shirt.

"Hi," she said. "You must be Elizabeth." She stuck a hand out toward her. "I'm Denise Waters."

Stunned, Elizabeth shook the slender white hand.

"I'll meet you guys in the car," Denise called over her shoulder. She smiled at Elizabeth again as she passed her. "See you around."

As much as Elizabeth wanted to know what was going on, she was almost afraid to ask. She stepped into the room. And into another exquisite-looking girl, this one dressed in black leggings, a tight black top, and gold jewelry, who was carrying Jessica's tape deck.

"Oh, my God, you really are twins!" she exclaimed. She looked from Elizabeth to Jessica. "It's kind of creepy, isn't it? Having somebody around who looks *exactly* like you? It's like living in an episode of *The Twilight Zone*."

Elizabeth was looking at Jessica too. Jessica had two hats on her head and was leaning over Elizabeth's desk. She turned with a big smile on the face that was exactly like Elizabeth's.

"Oh, Liz, I'm so glad you showed up!" she cried. "I was just writing you a note."

Oh? I wonder what this note was going to say, Elizabeth thought. She decided not to speak. If she opened her mouth, she might start screaming or, worse, crying.

"Have you met Isabella?" Jessica gestured toward the other girl. "Isabella, this is my sister, Liz. Liz, Isabella Ricci."

Elizabeth continued to stare at her sister in silence. *If Jessica smiles any harder, her mouth will crack,* she thought. Jessica picked up an armload of dresses from the back of Elizabeth's chair. "Isn't it wonderful?" she asked. "Isabella's asked me to be her new roommate!"

Elizabeth dug her nails into her palm. *And I wonder if you bothered to tell her that you already had a roommate.*

Jessica started toward the door. "I would've told you before, Elizabeth, but we only just thought of it."

Isabella made a sad little face. "The girl who was supposed to share with me never turned up, so Jessica's really being a lifesaver."

Jessica came up beside Isabella. "I'll drop by tomorrow, Liz, and we can work out a schedule for the Jeep."

Elizabeth nodded blankly.

"Elizabeth . . ." Jessica took a step forward. "You're blocking our way. Isabella and I have to get

63

going. We're meeting some people for dinner."

Elizabeth's voice was low but hard when she finally found it. "What about me?"

Jessica wrinkled her nose. "What do you mean, what about you? You weren't invited. It's Amber's birthday."

"What about me?" Elizabeth repeated. "You're just going to walk out and leave me on my own?"

"I don't see why you should be upset," Jessica said flatly. "You don't like living with me anyway." She hitched up the clothes in her arms. "And besides, you're not going to be on your own. They'll get you another roommate."

Isabella slipped past Elizabeth. "I'll meet you outside," she said.

"No, I'm coming with you!" Jessica pushed past her sister. "I don't have anything else to do here."

Elizabeth stood in the doorway, without moving or thinking, for several minutes. Jessica's voice echoed through her head. *I don't have anything else to do here.* . . .

And then, very slowly and calmly, Elizabeth walked over and sat down on her bed. And very quickly and angrily dissolved into tears.

Chapter Four

Elizabeth told Enid about Jessica0 moving out as the two girls walked across the campus to a sorority open house. "I was upset at first," Elizabeth admitted as they passed beneath a tunnel of palm trees. "But then I realized that it's actually the best thing that could have happened."

Enid waved at someone across the lawn. "Oh, really?" she asked, sounding slightly distracted. "Why is that?"

Elizabeth laughed. "Because now I'll be able to share with you."

Enid came to a sudden stop. "With *me*?"

"Of course with you. Who else?"

Enid shrugged. "Liz, I already have a roommate. And Trina and I get along really well. I'm not going to leave her in the lurch now."

Elizabeth couldn't believe her ears. She'd felt such a sense of relief when she realized Jessica's leaving meant that she'd be able to room with Enid, just as they'd always planned. It hadn't occurred to her that Enid might say no.

"But Enid, you *wanted* to room with me," Elizabeth argued. "You were so disappointed when I told you I'd decided to room with Jess."

"For the hundredth time, Liz, my name is Alexandra, not Enid. I really think you could make a little effort to get it right."

Elizabeth kicked a few leaves out of her way. She was beginning to feel as though she couldn't get anything right. "I'm sorry, *Alexandra*," she said, struggling to control her emotions. "I will try, I promise—but you did say you wanted to be my roommate. You said you'd always hoped we would room together in college."

Enid gave her an almost pitying look. "Oh, come on, Liz, that was last summer. Things are different now."

"Last summer was only a few weeks ago," Elizabeth protested. "And besides, I don't see how things are that different."

"Don't you?"

They turned toward the Pi Beta Phi house.

"No," Elizabeth said, "I don't. You're still my best friend, aren't you?"

"Of course I'm still your best friend," Enid said quickly. She kept her eyes straight ahead. "It's just that I don't want things to be the way they were in high school, that's all."

66

Elizabeth stopped and turned to her friend. "What do you mean?" she asked. "Weren't you happy then?"

Enid met her eyes. Her look was cautious.

"I *was* happy, Liz," she said with a sigh. "But I was also in your shadow. I was Enid Rollins, Elizabeth Wakefield's best friend."

"Oh, E— Alexandra—"

"No, it's true, Liz, and you know it. It was like you were Batman and I was Robin." She shrugged. "Your decision to room with Jess got me thinking about all this. And I decided I'm tired of being Robin. Now I have a chance just to be me, and I'm going to take it."

Elizabeth opened her mouth to say something, but there was nothing to say. Enid was right. Elizabeth had been the star in high school, and Enid had been the star's sidekick.

Enid touched her shoulder. "Come on," she said gently. "It's not the end of the world. We're still best friends. And I'll bet a little change will do you as much good as it'll do me."

Elizabeth nodded. "Um . . ." she mumbled, not really trusting herself to speak.

"Come on," said Enid, slipping her arm through Elizabeth's. "Let's go see what the Pi Beta Phis are like."

The Pi Beta Phis were not the most prestigious sorority on campus. They didn't have the most popular and wealthiest girls. None of them were models or daughters of film stars. And they certainly weren't the sorority all the "right" people wanted to join.

Pi Beta Phi was known as the sorority of eccentrics and activists. They didn't wear a sorority blazer as the other houses did. Not even today, at their get-acquainted open house. The only way you could tell the Phis from the other girls was that most of the Phis were either wearing Help the Earth Fight Back badges or AIDS ribbons or were dressed so casually that they had to be members since they obviously weren't trying to make a good impression.

Elizabeth thought they were wonderful. Unlike some of the other houses, the Pi Betas actually encouraged individualism and even a certain amount of offbeatness, which Elizabeth was starting to find very appealing.

Elizabeth took another cookie and looked around the room with a smile. Even though she was a little overdressed for the house in her glamorous new black dress, for the first time since she'd arrived on campus, she felt really relaxed. The sorority house was cozy, and the girls themselves were warm, intelligent, and interested in a wide variety of things. So far that afternoon she'd had conversations about civil rights, gothic novels, and vintage motorcycles. But even more important, she was sure that the Pi Beta Phis liked her.

"I'm taking the car, Liz. I have to go into town."

Elizabeth had spotted her sister as soon as she arrived, but Jessica was with some friends whom she hadn't made any move to introduce, so Elizabeth had ignored her, too. She'd then forgotten about her so completely that she hadn't even heard Jessica come up beside her.

"I can't wait to get out of here anyway," Jessica went on. "This place is the pits. I haven't seen this many dogs since the last time I took Prince Albert to the vet."

Elizabeth rolled her eyes. "Actually, I was just thinking how much more friendly and interesting the Pi Betas are than the usual sorority zombies," she said frostily.

"You would." Jessica made a face. "You're into saving whales and women's rights and stuff like that, but most people think it's boring." She nodded toward several Pi Betas. "I bet the most exciting thing they do is take their bottles to the recycling center."

Elizabeth could feel her temper rising. "They're a lot more exciting than the Thetas," she snapped back. "At least they have more on their minds than what people are thinking and saying about them."

Jessica was staring at her as though she'd said something outrageous. "Are you kidding?" she asked. "The Thetas are *Mom's* sorority. The Thetas are the most prestigous sorority in the whole

69

school. Isabella and Denise are Thetas."

If Elizabeth hadn't already taken a dislike to the Thetas, learning that Isabella and Denise belonged would probably have done it.

"The Thetas are a bunch of elitist snobs," Elizabeth said. "They won't even consider taking anyone who isn't pretty and doesn't dress the way they do."

"Well, that certainly isn't a problem with the Pis." Jessica cast a meaningful glance around the room. "Half of them couldn't get a date on the planet of the apes."

"Boy, what an enlightened woman you are," Elizabeth snapped. "They have more important things to think about than getting dates." Elizabeth was having trouble keeping her voice down. "They're not afraid to be different."

"They couldn't afford to be afraid to be different," Jessica shot back. "They're barely human as it is."

Elizabeth felt like kicking her sister. "They are socially aware. They contribute to the community," she told her. "The only thing your stuck-up friends might contribute is jobs for the fashion industry."

A sudden silence fell. Every girl in the room was looking at them. Elizabeth felt the blood rush into her cheeks. She'd been shouting. She'd finally found a group she liked—girls she wanted to impress—and what did she do? She shouted at her sister like a seven-year-old.

Jessica, who didn't give a used lipstick for what the Pi Beta Phis thought of her, smiled. Elizabeth could see her sister was enjoying her discomfort.

"I have to go now," Jessica said in a sweet, calm, and very audible voice. "I have to go into town and create a few jobs for the fashion industry."

The sun was shining, the radio was playing a catchy love song, and Jessica's head was filled with images of herself, dressed in something chic and sexy, stepping over the prostrate bodies of all the boys she'd refused to date as she went off into the sunset in the arms of . . .

Jessica turned the Jeep into the main street of town. She'd met dozens of boys in the past few days, one more gorgeous than the next, but she still couldn't put a face to the man of her dreams. The handsome, intelligent face of Danny Wyatt appeared in her mind. She was going shopping for her date with him, but although she was looking forward to the evening, she already knew that Danny didn't give her that special buzz. No, now that she was beginning to realize how many great-looking guys there were in the real world—and how easy they were to get—she was determined that the man who won her heart was going to be really special. The kind of man who could dine with kings but looked gorgeous in a T-shirt and jeans. Handsome . . . charming . . . witty . . . wealthy . . . sophisticated . . .

Bang!

Jessica gripped the steering wheel. *Oh, my God, where did this guy come from? I didn't even see him!*

In front of her—very close in front of her—was a blood-red 1964 Corvette in perfect condition. That was, it had been in perfect condition up until a few seconds ago. Now its taillights and back bumper were so close to the Jeep they were sort of part of it. The Jeep, though, seemed OK.

"What are you, *blind*?"

Jessica pushed open the door of the Jeep and started to climb down. "I'm sorry," she said. "I'm really, really sorry."

He was standing between the two cars, staring at the damage, shaking his head. "You're not as sorry as you're going to be." Tearing his eyes away from the Corvette's crumpled rear, he turned to face her.

Jessica was about to say she was sorry again, but the words died in her throat. Not two feet away from her was the most drop-dead handsome man she had ever seen. He was tall and lean but muscular, with dark hair and hazel eyes that looked almost golden. He was dressed in faded black jeans, cowboy boots, and a white T-shirt. His hair was longish in front and fell over his forehead in an incredibly appealing way. She didn't think she'd seen a man this beautiful on a movie screen or in a magazine. Whoever the Corvette driver was, even angry, he exerted a powerful, charismatic charm.

"I know it's my fault," Jessica said, recovering

slightly. "And I'm really sorry, I really am. But I didn't even see you."

And he was angry. He was definitely angry.

"Didn't *see* me?" The golden eyes flashed. "How could you not see me? I was right in front of you. Right behind the stop sign. The car is *red*, Princess. Dragon's-blood red. You can see it in the dark."

Half of Jessica wanted to burst into tears, and the other half wanted to check how she looked in a mirror.

How could I not have seen this guy? she asked herself. Those clean, classic features . . . those sparkling eyes . . . that sensual mouth . . . that incredible car . . .

"Well, it's not as though it's a write-off or anything," she said, trying to sound more reassuring than defensive. "I'm sure the insurance will pay—"

"You bet your blind blue eyes the insurance is going to pay," he snapped back. He pointed to the small but ugly dent in the Corvette. "Do you have any idea how much bodywork costs for a car like this?" he demanded. "Do you know how hard it is to match that color?"

Do you know how good you look in that T-shirt? she wondered. Out loud she said, "But it's possible, right? It can be matched. And I said I'll pay . . ."

"But what if it can't be matched? What if they botch it? I've spent a fortune customizing this car. It was perfect. Flawless. And now, because you were paying no attention to where you were going, it isn't."

73

Horns started honking around them.

"But it can be fixed!" Jessica wailed.

Why was he giving her such a hard time? She'd said she was sorry, she'd agreed to pay; what more could she do?

"But it might not be the same," he argued. "It may never be perfect again."

The honking grew louder. Jessica glanced around. They were causing a mini traffic jam. Pretty soon she wasn't going to have just one man mad at her, but dozens.

"Look," she said, "I'll give you my name and everything, and we can straighten this all out later." She reached into her bag and pulled out a notebook and a pen. "All right?"

"All right. Don't forget your phone number."

"I won't forget my phone number." She looked up, holding out the sheet of paper. And that was when she realized that besides the thick dark hair and golden eyes, he had a smile that could melt a polar ice cap.

"Don't think for one minute that this is the end of it," he said. He snatched the paper from her hand. "You'll be seeing me."

Jessica watched him walk away from her. She had to stop herself from shouting after him, *When?*

Winston sat back against the wall, smiling happily to himself. For the first time in days he was surrounded not by young females talking about premenstrual tension, but by young males talking about football. He was really enjoying himself. He hadn't felt this normal in days.

The first person Winston ran into when he arrived at the joint Sigma-Theta rush party was Bruce Patman. Bruce had been a year ahead of Winston at Sweet Valley High and never exactly a close buddy, but tonight they'd greeted each other like twins who had been separated in childhood. Bruce was pretty big in the Sigmas. He'd put his arm around Winston's shoulders and introduced him to all his frat brothers as "My friend, Winston, one of the funniest guys I know."

Winston smiled again. Here he was, sitting on the stairs with a couple of Sigmas, listening to the exploits of past rush weeks, being called Winston, and having a wonderful time. The Sigmas were definitely cool. There was nothing flaky or clownish about them; they had character and style. One of the juniors even had a Volkswagen Beetle a year older than Winston's. "It's about time we had another Bug in the Sigmas," he'd said.

Winston took a pretzel from the bowl on the step below. He was having no trouble picturing himself in the blue Sigma jacket, sitting on these very stairs next year, telling funny stories about his own rush week.

A Sigma named Gary was telling him about the camping trip they went on in the spring.

"It's great, Winston," he said. "We do the whole

thing: tents, wood fire, mountain climbing, white-water rafting . . ."

"Oh, listen to macho man," one of the other Sigmas said, laughing. "Gary's the guy who got treed by a wolf last year."

"A wolf?" Winston asked. "Where'd you go camping?"

The Sigmas all started laughing hysterically.

"It was a wolf named George who was with his owners in the next campsite," one of them gasped.

Gary grinned. "All right, all right, so I overreacted. But it was dark. German shepherds look a lot like wolves in the dark."

Winston was joining in the laughter when he suddenly saw something in the doorway that wiped the smile from his lips. Candy, Anoushka, and Samantha Holtzman, a girl from the floor below, were just coming into the house.

Panic grabbed Winston's heart. *Oh, man, what if they see me?* he thought. *What if they call me Winnie?* Any chance he had of being pledged to the Sigmas would be out the window. Guys who went white-water rafting weren't going to take the mascot of a girls' dorm seriously. He got up so quickly he knocked over the pretzels. "Bathroom," he mumbled, already rushing up the stairs. He was pretty sure there was a back staircase that led into the kitchen. He could get out the back door.

And if there isn't a back staircase? he asked himself as he reached the safety of the second floor. He knew the girls were near the stairs, because he could hear Candy's giggle. *Then I'll jump off the roof.*

Elizabeth nibbled on a potato chip, also wondering whether the Theta house had a back door. This was the worst party she'd ever been to. She didn't like the crowd. She didn't like the music. She didn't like the atmosphere. The only thing that met her approval was the refreshments. Even the Thetas couldn't ruin pretzels and potato chips.

Elizabeth shifted her position, trying not to look as alone as she was. Although she'd come to the Sigma-Theta party with Alexandra and some girls from Alexandra's floor, they had quickly abandoned her in favor of hanging out with a group of Thetas and their dates. Elizabeth could have gone with them if she had wanted to hear another conversation about the number of rooms in Peter Wilbourne's beach house.

"What's wrong with you, Liz?" Enid had demanded when Elizabeth had declined to join them. "Theta's *the* sorority on campus. And anyway, I thought it was your mom's sorority."

I never in my life thought I would hear Enid Rollins sound so much like Jessica Wakefield, Elizabeth said to herself.

"I don't feel that comfortable with them," she'd answered. Another time, she might have made more of an effort to fit in, but she didn't feel like it tonight.

All her life she'd been at the center of everything—beautiful and popular and part of the crowd—and it had been effortless. Now she was discovering what it felt like to be an outsider.

Elizabeth reached for another potato chip. It was awful. It was like being in a country where you couldn't speak the language. The funny thing was, though, that tonight she didn't really care. The feeling of dislike she'd had for the Thetas was even stronger now. The few brief conversations she'd had with them had been so superficial that she preferred not talking at all. Elizabeth was sure that in her mother's day they had been wonderful, but now they were stuck-up snobs whose greatest concern was how they looked and how much money everyone had. Joining the Theta Alpha Thetas would be like living with a houseful of Lila Fowlers. Elizabeth smiled to herself. Even Lila's familiar face would almost be a welcome sight here.

She looked around the room and saw the next-best thing: Bruce Patman. Bruce was in a corner, holding court to a bunch of freshmen. He was just as handsome and arrogant as he had been at Sweet Valley High. *I'm not desperate enough to inflict the Patman ego on myself,* Elizabeth decided.

Jessica was dancing with her date and hadn't looked in her sister's direction all evening. And Winston, who was a friendly face, had suddenly disappeared from the staircase.

Elizabeth checked her watch again. *Not much*

78

longer, she told herself. In a little while she'd have to leave to meet Todd, who'd gone to a party with the team. Elizabeth reached for another chip. There was just one question: Was being with the new Todd Wilkins, superjock, going to be any better than being here?

Danny's arms were around her, and her eyes were staring out at the crowded room, but all Jessica could see was the man with the '64 Corvette. She'd wanted to kick herself a thousand times since this afternoon when she realized that although she'd given him her name and address, she hadn't thought to ask him for his.

It's all right, Jessica told herself as she swayed to the music. *He'll call; he was flirting with you.* She smiled wryly to herself. *And besides, you dented his car.*

Suddenly the thought of what her sister was going to say when she found out about the accident pushed the dark hair and golden eyes from her mind, and Jessica found herself staring at Elizabeth instead. Only this wasn't her imagination—this was the real Elizabeth, standing at the edge of the room like an uninvited guest.

Leave it to Liz, Jessica thought. *This has got to be one of the best parties the world has ever seen, and my sister looks like she's at a lecture on the life cycle of the earthworm.*

Jessica had always known that her twin could be

incredibly boring, but at least in high school she'd always had fun at parties. She'd always talked with everybody and danced a lot. But now that they were in college she'd gotten even more boring. Pretty soon she probably wouldn't bother going out at all. *Not that anybody would notice,* Jessica thought. *For all the effort she's making, she might as well have stayed in her room.*

The music stopped and Danny put a friendly arm around her. By now it was somehow unspoken but clear that their relationship wasn't really going to be romantic. But Jessica felt as though she had made a friend. Not only did he have a good sense of humor and know how to dance, but he loved pineapple pizza. The lovers of pineapple pizza, Jessica had discovered, were few and far between.

"Did I tell you my sister actually prefers the Pi Beta Phis to the Thetas?" she asked as she leaned against him.

Danny smiled. "Come on, Jess. The Pi Betas are okay. Everybody rags them because they're always on some crusade, but most of them are really cool."

"Oh, *please* . . ." Jessica made a face of disbelief combined with nausea. "It's like preferring oatmeal to caviar."

He laughed. "To tell you the truth, *I* prefer oatmeal to caviar. Who wants to eat fish eggs? Yuck."

"Oh, stop it." Jessica gave him a playful shove. "You're just being difficult."

"And you're just feeling guilty for walking out on your sister like that. That's why you jump on everything she does."

Somehow, although she hadn't meant to, she'd found herself telling Danny about moving out of the room with Elizabeth and in with Isabella.

Jessica scowled. It was a good thing Danny was in no danger of becoming her boyfriend. He already knew her too well. "Okay," she admitted, "I do feel a little bit guilty. But you don't know what it's like rooming with someone who drives you crazy. You've got Tom."

Danny looked over to the other side of the room, where his best friend, Tom Watts, was getting ready to leave.

"I know I'm lucky," he said as the music started and he took her into his arms again. "Tom's a great guy."

"I'll bet he says the same about you," Jessica said, but she was already staring dreamily at nothing, thinking about those hazel eyes again.

Jessica was just imagining her first ride in the Corvette, out by the ocean under a moonlit sky, when she realized that the face of the man of her dreams had been displaced by the face of Peter Wilbourne III.

"I believe this is my dance," he was saying, his hand on Danny's shoulder.

To her amazement, Danny started to pull away, but Jessica stopped him. "I believe it's Danny's," she said evenly. And then, remembering Isabella's warning about Peter, she smiled and said, "You can have the next dance if you'd like."

Peter Wilbourne III smiled back. The long white fingers didn't move from Danny's shoulder, and the hard blue eyes focused more intensely on her. "But I don't want to have the next dance," he said softly. "I want this dance."

Jessica suddenly felt cold, as though someone were pouring ice water down her spine. "Well, I'm sorry—" she began.

His look was as cold and sharp as the blade of a knife. "And I'm sorry too," he said, cutting her off. "I can't tell you how disappointed I am in you, sweetheart. When I saw you with Izzy, I thought you looked promising, really promising. 'There's a freshman who can go places,' I said to myself. 'There's a girl who could be a real star.'"

Jessica was trying so hard not to show the nervousness she was feeling and so caught by the intensity of his eyes that she didn't notice Peter edging his way between her and Danny. Not until Danny's hand slipped from her own and she felt Peter Wilbourne's breath on her forehead did she realize what had happened.

He laughed, a sound as pleasant as the rattle of a snake. "It never occurred to me that you would turn me down for scum like this," Peter said, clearly and sharply. He shook his head sadly, raising his voice. "I never dreamed for one second that you were just another piece of white trash. That you were the sort of tramp who would rather dance with our black brother here than with me."

Jessica felt her face go red with fury. "Don't talk to me like that," she hissed, stepping around him to get back to Danny.

"I'll talk to you any way I like," Peter answered. "You're beneath my contempt, sweetheart. I'd sooner take orders from the maid than from a little traitor like you." He laughed again as she moved closer to Danny. "Don't expect *him* to help you," he scoffed. "He's just a cowardly black boy, aren't you, Danny?"

Seeing the sneer on Peter's lips as his eyes fell on Danny, Jessica suddenly remembered what Isabella had told her. Peter didn't hate Danny just because he was black; there was something more there. Peter hated Danny because he was Danny.

Jessica turned to Danny herself, expecting this last insult to finally cause an outburst of anger. After all, Danny was bigger and looked stronger than Peter. But he wouldn't even meet her eyes.

"Leave us alone, Peter," he said in a half whisper. "Nobody wants any trouble—"

"You don't want any trouble, Danny . . ." Peter reached out and pulled Danny's tie, drawing him forward. "I know you don't. You just want to hide behind this white girl here, don't you?" He gave the tie a yank. "Maybe you'd like her to fight your battles for you since you won't do it yourself."

Jessica was suddenly aware that a crowd had gathered around them. She felt so afraid that she couldn't move, couldn't think. Some of the Sigmas started to urge Peter on.

"Get him, Pete," they muttered.

Very low, almost like a hum, Jessica could hear the beginnings of a chant. *Fight fight fight fight . . .*

"Danny," she whispered, reaching out for his hand.

But Danny kept stepping backward, his body rigid, his eyes empty.

"What's the matter, Aunt Jemima?" Peter taunted. "Don't you come with a spine?"

"Don't you come with a brain?"

Jessica spun around as an anxious silence fell over the crowd. A tall, dark-haired boy, lean as a snake but broad and muscular as well, was standing behind Peter. There was nothing empty about the look in Tom Watts's dark eyes; it was furious and cold.

Peter turned slowly around. "This isn't your fight, Watts," he said, sounding distinctly nervous despite his smooth smile.

"It isn't anybody's fight," Tom said. He placed a hand flat against Peter's chest. "Unless you want it to be," he said softly. "And in that case, I'm making it mine."

Peter's smile became even smoother, but his eyes darted nervously at his friends. "Look, Watts," he said, backing off. "I'm not going to bust up a good party for you to play hero for your scared little friend." He turned away. "He isn't worth it." He joined his frat brothers. "Let's party," he ordered.

Jessica moved over to Danny. "Come on," she said. "Let's get out of here."

Tom wanted to get out of there too, but every time he tried, somebody else came up to tell him what a good guy he was. He hated the attention. If it had been anybody but Danny, he probably would have kept right on walking out the door and let what was going to happen, happen.

But he couldn't. He'd gotten halfway across the room, and he knew he couldn't just turn his back. He didn't care about any of these people or the stupid things they did and said, but he cared about Danny. Danny had stood by Tom when his whole world had fallen out from under him, and he never asked any questions or made any demands. He was just there when you needed him. It was only right that Tom should be there when Danny needed him, too.

Tom had just disengaged himself from the embrace of a girl he used to go out with and was pushing his way toward the door when he heard an angry female voice behind him.

"Just a minute," the voice was saying, quietly but forcefully. "I want to tell you something."

Tom and just about everyone near him turned around. He blinked. It was the girl Danny had been with, Jessica something, staring Peter dead in the face. Tom shook his head. This girl looked exactly like Danny's date, but it couldn't be; hadn't he just seen them leave together?

The Sigma president, having recovered himself, smiled smugly and raised one disdainful eyebrow at her. "And who the hell are you?"

The girl didn't hesitate for a second. "It doesn't matter who I am—"

"Well, it matters who I am," he cut in. "Maybe you don't realize it, but I'm Peter Wilbourne the Third."

The girl made a face. "You mean they tried twice before you and they still didn't get it right?"

Some of the onlookers sniggered. Tom let himself smile. This girl was really something. She cared about impressing these people about as much as he did.

Peter Wilbourne III looked as though he was trying to think of some suitable reply to this, but before he could open his mouth the girl went on.

"I'm leaving," she said, "but I wanted to tell you I think you're disgusting. I thought people who went to college were supposed to be at least semi-intelligent. But I was obviously wrong. I'm ashamed to be in the same room with you." She tossed her hair over her shoulder. "You can be sure that it won't happen again."

No, Tom told himself. *That definitely isn't the girl Dan was with. This girl isn't like anyone I've ever met before.*

"You better hope it doesn't happen again!"

Peter Wilbourne shouted after her. "For your sake, you really better hope so."

Tom tried to catch the girl's attention as she stormed past him, but she didn't look right or left.

Watch out, Watts, Tom warned himself as his eyes followed her through the door. *There goes trouble.*

And he didn't need trouble. He'd had enough trouble for one life already.

Elizabeth was still seething when she arrived at the coffeehouse to meet Todd as they'd arranged. She barely registered the cozy, intimate atmosphere and the candlelit tables. In her mind she was still looking into the Sigma president's smug, smiling face.

"Liz! Liz! Over here!"

Elizabeth stopped at the front of the café and saw Todd waving to her from a corner table. Just the sight of him made her feel better. Everything was all right. There was strong, supportive, sensitive Todd waiting to comfort her, just as he always had. Forgetting the experiences they'd had the past few days, Elizabeth hurried to join him.

"God, you won't believe what happened at the Sigma-Theta rush party," she said as she slid into the chair across from him.

"And wait'll I tell you what happened to me today, Liz," he countered. "I've had the most unbelievable day—"

"The president of the Sigmas called my sister trash and tried to pick a fight with her date," Elizabeth began in a rush.

Todd waved one hand dismissively. "Never mind the Sigmas," he said, obviously not hearing a word she was saying. "The Zetas want me on board, Liz! Isn't that terrific?"

Elizabeth, about to describe the scene between Danny and Peter, could only stare at him.

"The Zetas, Liz. Do you know what that means? The Zetas are *the* fraternity for athletes, and at the dinner tonight the president himself basically told me straight out that they want me on board."

She gave herself a little shake. Todd was justifiably proud and happy. She should put her own distress aside for a few minutes to congratulate him. Elizabeth reached across the table and took his hand. "That's great, Todd," she said sincerely. "It really is. I know how much you—"

"I knew you'd be happy," Todd said as the waitress brought them their menus. "I mean, it's been so great having all the guys on the team be so friendly, but to be a Zeta, too. You should've seen them at the dinner, Liz. These are really good guys . . ."

Elizabeth listened, a smile on her face.

Her smile faded slightly when, having described the Zeta dinner in minute detail, he began to tell her how the other guys on the team had reacted to his good news.

"Bryan said he knew the Zetas would want me

on board," Todd explained, "because Sinclair Ash, the vice president, had told him I was just the sort of guy they were looking for."

By the time their order arrived, she was ready to strangle him. What was all this *on board*? What normal, intelligent person said *on board* every other sentence?

"Can I tell you what happened at the Sigma party now?" she asked, when he finally stopped talking long enough to put a forkful of carrot cake in his mouth.

Todd nodded. "Sure, Liz. I didn't mean to do all the talking." He lifted his coffee cup to his lips, looking at her expectantly.

Elizabeth started telling him about Peter Wilbourne's attack on Danny and Jessica and how Danny had refused to confront him. "And then this amazing guy suddenly appeared from nowhere," Elizabeth continued. "You should've seen him, Todd. He was incredibly well built, you know, and I guess he knew no one was going to try and fight him . . ."

"Is he an athlete?" Todd asked.

The spoonful of triple-chocolate mousse Elizabeth was holding stopped in midair. "What?"

"Is he a jock?"

"I have no idea," she answered, wondering how much of what she was saying was actually going into Todd's head. "I don't even know his name."

Todd shrugged. "I just thought I might know

him," he said. "He sounds like the sort of guy the Zetas would want to have on board too."

Elizabeth leaned against Todd as they walked back to his dorm in the moonlight, their arms around each other. It had taken a while, but eventually the warm atmosphere of the coffeehouse had helped her to relax. Todd had wound down a little himself and stopped getting "on board" everything. At last, it had started to feel as it used to between them.

"I can't believe this is the first time you're seeing my room," Todd said as they took the elevator to the twelfth floor. He leaned over and kissed the top of her head. "I've been waiting to get your opinion on what I should put on the walls," he whispered. "I don't have your sense of style."

Feeling better than she had in days, Elizabeth raised her lips to his. "All you had to do was ask," she whispered back.

Todd laughed nervously as he unlocked the door to his room. "I feel like I should carry you over the threshold or something."

Elizabeth gave him a squeeze. "That's when you get married," she joked. "Not when you move into a jock dorm."

"Yeah, I know that," he said, not turning on the light as they floated into the room. "But this is the first time I've had my own place."

The lights of the campus shone like stars outside Todd's window as Elizabeth melted into his arms. It felt so right, getting lost in his kisses, that she didn't realize things were going farther than they usually did until she felt the urgent way he was trying to pull off her blouse and bra.

"Todd . . ." she whispered as her clothes fell to the floor. The sensation of his hands on her body in the dark room made her skin tingle.

"Elizabeth . . ." His voice was thick and seemed to be coming from more than one direction. He pulled her to the floor.

Part of her knew that things were going too fast and wanted him to stop. But another part—a part that couldn't believe his hands could make her feel like that—didn't. "Todd . . . Todd, please . . ."

"It's all right." His mouth was against her ear. "I don't have a roommate. We're all alone."

She was willing her body to push him off her, but instead it insisted on pushing itself closer. "Todd . . ." With an enormous effort, she managed to pull herself to a sitting position. "Todd, what time is it?" she asked desperately. "I'd really better get back to my dorm."

It took him less than a nanosecond to pull her back down. "You don't have to leave," he said, his voice a purr. "You can stay here tonight."

For a moment she actually thought that he meant that because it was late and he was tired and didn't feel like walking her back to Dickenson Hall, she should crash with him. But as his hands

91

moved down her body she realized the truth. He wanted to make love to her. The part of her that wanted him to stop started shouting louder than the part of her that didn't.

"Todd!" Elizabeth jerked herself away from him so quickly that he landed on the floor with a thud. "We've talked about this. We said we'd wait for the right time."

"But we did wait," he said, pulling her to his chest again. "And this is the right time."

Shaking with something that was anger and something that was more like desire, Elizabeth managed to get to her feet. "It may be the right time for you," she said, practically shouting so she could hear herself against the roar of her heart. "But I don't think it's the right time for me yet."

"But Liz—"

"I mean it." Only by keeping her voice hard and cold could she hide the confusion she was feeling. It would be so easy to fall back in his arms; so easy to stay the night. Too easy. She took a deep breath. "I want to go back to my room now, Todd. Right now."

The light went on so suddenly, she felt as though someone had punched her in the face.

"Sure," Todd said, in a tone she had never heard before. "Whatever you want."

Chapter Five

The first word that came into Elizabeth's head when she woke up on Saturday morning was: *Enid*.

She opened her eyes. "Alexandra," she corrected herself. "Not Enid, Alexandra."

But it didn't matter. Enid or Alexandra, she was still the best friend Elizabeth had ever had, the person she could talk to about anything, the one who supported her through good times and bad.

Elizabeth rolled over. These were certainly bad times. She wasn't upset about the scene at the Theta-Sigma party. Everything she'd said to that smug creep Peter the Third was true. And it didn't matter if she'd blown her chances with the Thetas, either, because if that was what the Greeks were like, then she didn't want any part of them. She'd come here to get smarter, not more stupid.

But Todd did matter. A heaviness fell over Elizabeth at the thought of him. She'd heard of couples drifting apart once they got to college, but she and Todd were separating at a rate of knots.

She felt lonely and isolated; he'd already found a tight group of friends. She'd gone from being *the* Elizabeth Wakefield, one of the brightest stars of Sweet Valley High, to being a nobody; he was well on his way to becoming *the* Todd Wilkins, the gorgeous basketball star. She wasn't ready to take their relationship any further; Todd definitely was.

Elizabeth climbed out of bed with a sigh. That was what she had to talk to Enid about. There was no one else she could confide in.

The walk back from Todd's dorm last night kept playing itself over in her mind. They hadn't spoken or touched the entire way. Todd had walked beside her, inches that might have been miles between them, his hands in his pockets, as though he hated even the idea that he might brush against her. Seeing them pass by, no one would have thought that they had laughed together, or cried together, or shared so much as a stick of gum.

Elizabeth started going through her dresser, still seeing the expression on Todd's face as he said good night. Cold and remote, it had been the face of someone she didn't know; someone who didn't want to know her. She pulled out a pair of jeans and a black T-shirt to match her mood.

Elizabeth glanced at her watch. If she didn't hurry, she'd be late for breakfast with her best friend.

* * *

Enid threw herself on the still-made bed with a sigh. Was any girl as lucky as she was? Was any girl as happy? "I'm so happy!" she shouted out loud.

She kicked off her shoes and closed her eyes, going over the events of last night for at least the twentieth time. She'd had a blast at the Theta-Sigma party. The Thetas really liked her, and the more she'd known they liked her, the more she had sparkled. It used to be that no one really noticed her at parties because they were too busy looking at Elizabeth, but it wasn't like that anymore. Now she was a star in her own right.

The thought of Elizabeth caused a slight shadow to fall over Enid's happiness. She decided not to think too much about the part where she had lost track of Elizabeth at the party last night. And anyway, although she knew that Elizabeth hadn't seemed to be having a good time, she was still there when Enid and her friends went on to the after-dinner party at Zeta house. Enid had seen her, standing by the food table and looking at her watch.

Enid hugged herself. It was the Zeta party that she wanted to remember in detail. Walking in and seeing Todd over by the window, noticing that he was talking to an absolutely gorgeous sophomore with a stop-traffic smile. Todd looking up and beckoning her over, saying, "This is my friend Alexandra Rollins. We went to high school together." Todd nodding to the dark-haired man with the crooked grin. "Mark Gathers, backbone of the SVU basketball team. Mark, Alex."

"Alex?" he'd said. "That's great. I love girls with boys' names. I think it's so sexy."

Enid opened her eyes, giving herself another hug. *I think it's so sexy.* In four years of high school, no one had ever said the name *Enid* and the word *sexy* in the same breath. Not even by mistake.

Humming happily, she began to undress. She didn't have time to shower before meeting Elizabeth for breakfast, but she was going to have to change. Not only had she been wearing this dress since last night, she'd actually wound up sleeping in it.

Enid caught her reflection in the mirror and gave that pretty, sexy, glowing face a big smile. Who would have thought that after only a week at college, *she* would be spending the night with one of the most popular guys on campus? She, good, old reliable and slightly dull Enid Rollins, shadow of the spectacular Elizabeth Wakefield, had sat up half the night with the most handsome, intelligent, and interesting man she'd ever met.

They'd talked about everything from cereal to politics. She couldn't remember talking so much; certainly not to a guy. And they'd made each other laugh. In fact, they'd talked and laughed so much that when they finally checked the time, it was three in the morning and they didn't feel like coming all the way back across campus to her dorm. "You might as well stay here," Mark had said. "You can have the bed and I'll sleep on the floor." So she had.

Enid pulled on a clean shirt and gave herself another smile. Somehow, sleeping in Mark's bed while he slept on the floor, even though nothing had really *happened*, was the most romantic, grown-up thing she'd ever done.

She ran a brush through her long, wavy hair. She couldn't wait to tell Elizabeth.

Maybe Todd's right, Elizabeth told herself as she hurried to breakfast. *Maybe we should sleep together. I mean, it's not like we only just met or something. We love each other. We've been together for years.*

"Hey, look who it is!" someone shouted as she cut across the green. "It's the Martin Luther King fan club."

"Uncle Tom's friend," someone else said.

Not realizing whom they were talking to, Elizabeth glanced over.

Two Sigmas from the night before were leaning against the hood of a metallic blue Toyota, leering in her direction.

"Hey, Little Miss Equal Opportunity," the first one called to her. "Why aren't you out protecting the less fortunate?"

"Somebody should be protecting her," the other one said with a laugh. "After that little scene last night, I think she'll need it."

Elizabeth bit her lip. Was that a threat of some kind? Were these clowns trying to scare her? She turned away quickly. She had too many things on her mind to waste her time worrying about them.

But I'm really not ready, Elizabeth argued as she walked through the cafeteria door.

There was no sign of Enid, so she joined the two or three people getting their food. Saturday breakfast was the one meal you could be pretty sure you wouldn't have to stand in line for. Most people preferred sleeping late to eating.

Just because we're in college now doesn't mean we should immediately jump into bed together. He wasn't asking me to sleep with him two weeks ago. What's the big difference between then and now?

Faced with the usual wide choice of foods, Elizabeth realized that she wasn't really hungry. She was too hyped up over what had happened last night. She put a grapefruit, a muffin, and a cup of coffee on her tray and went out to find a table.

Of course I'm right, Elizabeth assured herself as she stirred milk into her coffee. *Just being in college is no reason to go back on what we decided.*

She looked up to see Enid hurrying toward her. Elizabeth couldn't remember ever seeing her friend look so pretty. It wasn't just her clothes or her makeup, either. In fact, she didn't really look as though she was wearing makeup. No, it was something else. She almost seemed to be glowing from inside.

"Elizabeth!" Enid shrieked. "Wait till I tell you what happened!" She put her tray down and slid into her seat.

Elizabeth was dying to confide in her about Todd, but she put on an interested smile. "What? Tell me!"

Enid shook her head and made a distraught face. "I don't know where to start," she said breathlessly. She giggled. "It's too wonderful, Liz. You just won't believe it! It's so great!"

"Well, go ahead," Elizabeth urged. "Don't keep me in suspense." She made her smile more encouraging.

It wasn't necessary. One minute Enid was sighing and not knowing what to say; the next she was giving Elizabeth a nanosecond-by-nanosecond account of her night with Mark Gathers.

Elizabeth listened in silence, at first with interest, but then with growing concern.

By the time Enid reached the end of her story, she wasn't just glowing, she looked as though she were lit by a klieg light.

"Wait a minute," Elizabeth said. "Are you honestly telling me that you spent the *entire* night with a—a stranger?"

Enid grinned, thinking she was teasing. "He wasn't a stranger, Liz. He was a friend of Todd's." She put down her cup. "And he certainly isn't a stranger now."

Elizabeth stared at her. "You're right," she said, "I don't believe it. I don't believe you spent the night with somebody you don't even know. You must have lost your mind."

Enid held the smile on her face for another instant, and then her mouth went hard. "Oh, come on, Liz. We're in college now. It's not that big a deal."

We're in college now . . . We're in college now . . . Was that the only thing anyone could say anymore? "Maybe you don't think it's such a big deal," Elizabeth snapped, half arguing with Enid, half arguing with Todd. "But I do. I thought we came to college to learn and grow, not to jump into bed with the first guy who asks us."

Enid stared at her angrily. "It's not all that easy to learn and grow when your best friend criticizes you every time you try."

There was something as frighteningly final as a gunshot about the way Enid scraped back her chair. "And for your information, Ms. Morality, we didn't sleep together. We hardly kissed. But even if we had, my sex life is none of your business."

Elizabeth watched the girl she used to know so well, the best friend she'd ever have, march out of the cafeteria in a rage.

Great, she thought. *My boyfriend's mad at me, my sister's deserted me, and my best friend isn't speaking to me anymore.*

Elizabeth picked up her tray and went back to the food counter. All of a sudden she was starving.

"I wanted to thank you for . . . uh . . . dealing with Wilbourne last night."

Tom looked up. Danny was sitting on his bed,

hunched over as he put on his shoes, his eyes on the floor. Even someone who didn't know Danny as well as Tom did would have been able to tell that though he really was grateful, Danny didn't want to talk about what had happened.

"It's all right," Tom said, returning his attention to ironing his shirt. He didn't want to talk about it either. He wanted to put the whole thing out of his mind and leave it there. "You don't have to thank me. That's what friends are for."

"Well, thanks anyway," Danny muttered. Slowly and meticulously, he began to tie the lace of his running shoe. "I know you figured I—"

"You don't have to explain, man," Tom cut in. "I understand."

Tom understood that the trouble between Peter Wilbourne and Danny went back a long way. Peter had always surrounded himself with sycophants and yes-men, people who did whatever he said, but Danny stood up to him.

Until last winter, that was. Last winter something happened to Danny. It made him stop standing up to Peter. And that was the thing Tom didn't understand. He knew that something had happened at home—something with Danny's older brother—but he didn't know what. And some part of him didn't want to know.

"I don't think I could explain, even if I wanted to," Danny said slowly.

Tom kept his eyes on the iron. "I told you," he

said quickly. "You don't have to explain."

They were best friends, as close as brothers, but they never pried. If Danny wanted him to know something, he'd tell him; if Danny didn't want him to know something, he wouldn't tell him. And vice versa. It was a simple arrangement, and one that worked. There were things, like why Danny had stopped standing up for himself and why Tom had changed so much since they were freshmen, that they never discusssed—and never would discuss. It was enough for Tom to know that Danny wouldn't fight, not even a bastard like Peter Wilbourne. He didn't need to know why.

He turned his shirt and picked up the iron again. Another hiss of steam hid Tom's sigh.

There was one thing about last night that wouldn't stay out of his mind, no matter how hard he tried. Ever since she stormed out of the Theta house, crackling like a fire, the image of the girl with the gold-blond hair and the blue-green eyes kept appearing to him. It followed him back to the dorm, it hung around the lounge while he was trying to watch TV, it kept drifting in and out of his dreams. And here it was now, distracting him while he was trying to get those annoying little creases out of his collar.

Tom looked over at Danny again. *What the hell,* he decided. *There's no harm in just knowing her name.* He gave a little cough. "So, that girl you were with—what's her name, Jessica?—she has a twin sister, doesn't she?"

Danny nodded, getting to his feet. "Elizabeth Wakefield." He grabbed his sweater from the bed. "Did you see her?" he asked, shaking his head. "It's incredible; the two of them look exactly alike, but from what Jessica says, they have about as much in common as a taco and an ice-cream sundae."

Elizabeth. Elizabeth Wakefield.

"No kidding?" Tom started ironing one of the sleeves. "Your girl seemed really nice," he went on, hoping he sounded casual.

"She is really nice." Danny grinned wryly. "Only, she's not my girl. I think we're going to be what's described as 'just good friends.'" He shrugged. "The spark wasn't there. Sometimes it is, and sometimes it ain't."

Tom turned off the iron. "So what's the sister like?" he asked as Danny opened the door.

Danny turned around. "I'm not really sure. According to Jess, she's very serious, a straight-A student, and about as exciting as a cold potato." He winked. "Sounds like she's just your type, Tombo. You want me to ask Jessica to introduce you?"

Tom pulled out the plug. "Oh, right," he said with a laugh. "Do me a favor." But he was still staring at the door after Danny had left.

Elizabeth, he was thinking to himself. *What an ordinary name for such an extraordinary woman.*

"You can't say I didn't warn you about Peter,

103

because I did," Isabella was saying as she put the coffee cup down on the table. "Though maybe I should have been a little more adamant."

Jessica, only half listening, brought the toast to the table. Although she'd decided that she wasn't going to tell anyone about Mr. Corvette, that didn't mean she was going to stop thinking about him. While she'd been waiting for the bread to pop up, she'd been fantasizing that with his cool good looks and immaculate sense of style, he must be some sort of spy.

Isabella sat down, stretching her long legs. "He's a nasty piece of work. I'm sure the rumors about him being the head of the secret society are true. I bet he's had plastic surgery done so you can't see the 666 tattooed on his forehead."

Jessica set the warm plate on a woven mat. *Of course, he might be a rock musician or a movie star,* she mused, still deep in her fantasy. She frowned. But then she would have recognized him; then she'd probably know his name.

"Jessica!" Isabella was waving a slice of toast in front of her face. "Are you listening to me? This could be really serious. Peter Wilbourne the Third is no one to make an enemy of. Especially when it's obvious that Danny isn't going to protect you. Just think what could have happened if Tom Watts hadn't been there last night. You should've just danced once with Peter when he asked you. You could've saved a lot of trouble."

Jessica spread some jam on her toast. It was hard to get herself all worked up about an egomaniac like Peter the Terrible when her mind was already so occupied. "I don't care about Peter and his prejudices," she said flatly. "And anyway, most of the people at the party were on our side. It was just his pals who were egging him on." She reached for the coffee. "I'm sure the whole thing will blow over by the time classes start."

"Maybe," Isabella said. "But I'd be cool about being seen too much with Danny if I were you. Especially if you're planning on any public clinches."

More like her sister than she might imagine, Jessica raised her head and flicked her hair over her shoulder. "I'll be seen with whoever I want," she said firmly. "But you don't have to worry about any public clinches between me and Danny. It's strictly platonic."

Isabella lifted her cup to her lips. "Well, I'm glad to hear that. You don't want to start your college career on the wrong foot if you can help it. And being beaten up by Peter's henchmen would definitely be the wrong foot." She took a long, slow sip of her coffee, a mischievous look in her beautiful eyes. "Now all we have to do is find the perfect nonplatonic man for you."

"Ummm . . ." Jessica smiled, imagining her own reflection in that pair of golden eyes. "I wonder who he could be."

*   *   *

"Morning, Winnie!"

"Good morning, Candy!" Winston called. It didn't even bother him that she called him Winnie. Why shouldn't she? The entire British nation had called Winston Churchill Winnie, and he'd won the war.

"Hey, Winnie, dig that robe!"

Winston smiled back. "Morning, Sophie. I like your hair like that." Why should he wind himself up just because she was wearing only cycling shorts and a sports bra? He was a man now, not a boy. Men took that kind of thing in stride.

"Hi, Win! I've fixed your hair dryer for you. You can pick it up whenever you want."

"Thanks, Luce. You can borrow my weights anytime." Luce fixed small appliances, Kate was practically a professional mechanic, and there was a girl on the floor above who did radios and stereos. Living in Oakley Hall was going to save him a fortune in repair bills. He would have been too embarrassed to admit to a bunch of guys that his own mechanical skills were pretty much expended by turning on a light switch, but girls didn't care. They didn't laugh at you and make you feel like a jerk; they just smiled and maybe asked you to do them a favor in return, like pick them up after a late meeting or open a jammed window.

Winston strode into the bathroom, a towel over his shoulder and his toilet kit under his arm. It was

106

Saturday morning and he was in a wonderful mood.

I'm in a wonderful mood, he told himself as he stopped in front of the last sink in the row and put his stuff on the shelf. *Maybe living with girls is like living with cats. Maybe they just take getting used to.*

That's what it is, he thought as he eyed himself in the mirror. *I just had to get used to them. Now I'm fine.*

Winston grinned at his reflection. His reflection grinned back. After all, how could he not be fine? The Sigmas loved him. There were a few tricky moments at the party last night when one of the frat guys asked him where he was living, and then when the girls arrived—but those were tiny clouds in an otherwise bright blue sky.

Since the bathroom was empty except for him, Winston risked striking a few poses in the glass as he imagined himself strolling around campus in his Sigma jacket and his RayBans.

Maybe he'd take up skiing or wrestling or even white-water rafting. After all, Sigmas were very athletic guys. Winston hunched in front of the sink, his arms back, his expression stern as he flew down the giant slalom at a speed that had the onlookers breathless, the wind and sun in his face, his body taut and agile. The crowd was going insane. *Go, Winston! Go, Winston!* they chanted. *Go, Winston! Go—*

"Winnie!"

His toothbrush still in his mouth, Winston dove to the floor, pretending to be looking for something that he'd dropped. The door opened and Anoushka slid into the room.

"Winnie! There are a bunch of Sigmas downstairs, asking about you. What do you want us to say? Candy thought you might be a little shy about living here, after the way you snuck out of the party last night as soon as we arrived."

Winston stifled a groan. *Women.* They never missed anything. Why wasn't every cop in the world a woman?

He removed the toothbrush from his mouth. "Anoushka," he whispered, trying to maintain as much dignity as possible, considering that he was on all fours. "Anoushka, I didn't sneak out. I had to—"

"Shhh!" Anoushka yanked the door open and stuck her head out. She slammed it closed again. "It's them!" she announced. "Do you want me to tell them you'll be right out?"

"No!" He scrambled to his feet. "Tell them there's been some mistake. Tell them the Winnie Egbert who lives here isn't me. Tell them it's my twin sister."

Anoushka smiled. "Is there something in this for me?" she asked sweetly.

How could someone look like such an angel and have such a scheming mind? Winston wished Anoushka were a boy so he could hit her.

Winston calculated quickly. How much was not being found in the girls' bathroom by the Sigmas worth? Probably about a million.

"What do you want?"

"I want to borrow your car to go shopping later. Benny was going to take me, but you know Benny. He'd rather play football than go shopping, and I hate to take the bus—"

Did she have no mercy? He didn't want to hear about Benny now. "You can have the car!" Winston grabbed her by the shoulders and turned her around. "Just tell them they've got the wrong Egbert and that I live over in Marsden."

Anoushka gave him a shrewd look. "You'll never beat them over there," she said. "Not since you have to wait for them to get out of sight."

He gave her a shove. "I will if you lend me your bike."

Todd stood motionless, the tension easing out of him as the hot water ran down his body. He couldn't get over the way Elizabeth had acted last night.

At first he'd thought she was kidding. After all, it wasn't as though they didn't know each other. It wasn't as though their feelings hadn't been tried and tested over the years.

Todd closed his eyes and raised his face to the spray. He knew they'd never said it in so many words, but he'd thought that once they were living away from home, their relationship would go into the next phase. Why did she think he'd worked so hard to get on the varsity team? Aside from the fact that basketball meant a lot to him, he'd wanted to get a single room so that he and Elizabeth could spend more time together.

But Elizabeth didn't want to spend more time with him. And the time she did spend with him wasn't exactly quality. She'd become so quiet and distant since they'd been on campus that it was hard to believe she was the same girl.

Until last night, he'd thought she was just having some trouble getting used to college life, but now he wasn't so sure. Maybe it had nothing to do with college. Maybe it had to do with him. Everything had been fine when they were in high school. But now that he wanted a real commitment—an adult relationship—she was refusing to give it. All of a sudden nothing he said or did was right. All of a sudden her kisses didn't have enough fire to toast a marshmallow.

Todd turned off the faucet and reached for his towel. Maybe he shouldn't take it so personally. He wasn't the only thing she complained about. She complained about the Greeks, about her sister, about her best friend.

Enid. Todd wrapped the towel around himself and walked out of the shower stall.

This morning, after a fitful night's sleep, he'd gotten up early and gone for a walk. Just as he was returning, he'd seen Enid coming out of the front door of his dorm, looking like she was floating on air.

Elizabeth certainly hadn't been walking on air when he took her home last night. She'd held her-

110

self rigid and untouchable, just inches away from him, and hadn't said a word until they reached Dickenson Hall. Then she'd said "Good night." That was it—no kiss, no hug, no "I'll see you tomorrow," no "I'm really sorry, let's talk about it later"—just "Good night."

"A good night was the last thing it was," Todd muttered as he marched into the hall.

Mark was just coming out of his room. He still looked tired, but it was the tired of someone who'd had a wonderful night, not the tired of someone who couldn't sleep because his long-term girlfriend didn't want him to touch her.

Mark's face lit up. "Yo, Wilkins! I've got to thank you for introducing me to Alex. That was the greatest night I've had in a long time."

Todd smiled in the jokey but suggestive way he'd seen the other guys on the team smile when they started talking about girls. "Oh, yeah? And how great was that?"

Mark grinned back. "I'll have you know, Wilkins, that I'm not that kind of guy." He punched him in the arm. "Anyway, I'd never make a move on a girl like Alex. I like her too much. I'd be afraid she wouldn't respect me in the morning."

"Oh, yeah?" Todd gave him a knowing look. "Then who was it I saw coming out of here this morning? Alex's double?"

Mark raised an eyebrow. "Boy, you were up early. Were you walking Elizabeth back home?"

Rather than answer, Todd just kept smiling and looking knowing. If Mark thought he was sleeping with Elizabeth, that was all right with him.

"It's okay for you guys who've been going out with the same girl for half your life," Mark said. "But we jocks who have always played the field have to go slow in this relationship game." He punched him again. "Anyway, I'd better get going or I'll be late. But thanks again, Todd. You may just have changed my life."

Todd went back to his room, wondering if his life was changing too. If guys like Mark were slowing down, maybe guys like him should start speeding up. Mark might have been joking, but he was right. There were an awful lot of women on this campus who liked jocks.

Todd pulled on his jeans and a T-shirt and gave himself a once-over in the mirror. He looked good. That wasn't vanity, that was the truth.

He brushed back his hair. And some of those women were older women, women with experience. Women who weren't afraid of a little more experience, either.

Chapter Six

As Jessica left History 101.8 on Monday morning and headed to her second class, she couldn't help thinking that having to take classes was a major bore—the big cloud in the silver lining of college life. She didn't want to be stuck in a room listening to someone drone on about people who were dead and things that had happened hundreds of years ago. She wanted to be out experiencing life and buying clothes to wear to that experience.

Jessica checked her schedule again. At eleven she was supposed to be in room 25 in Denton Hall for introductory philosophy with Professor Malika.

Who wants to be introduced to philosophy? Jessica wondered glumly as she climbed the stairs of Denton. *I'd much rather be introduced to Mr. Corvette.*

Jessica entered room 25 with a martyred sigh. She hadn't even meant to sign up for philosophy, but the adviser at the philosophy department desk had been so cute that before she realized what had happened he was handing her back her computer card and telling her he hoped she enjoyed the class.

Jessica headed for a seat in the middle of the large, crowded classroom. Experience had taught her that if you sat in the front, teachers would notice when you weren't paying attention, but that if you sat at the back, they expected you not to be paying attention and would always ask you questions to make sure you were still awake. If you sat in the center, they hardly knew you were there.

Professor Malika shut the door and walked to the front of the room. He was not the cute adviser at the philosophy registration table. He was a balding, middle-aged man with glasses and a slight stoop. Settling as comfortably into her chair as possible, she opened her notebook, faced the front of the room, and began to think about young men who drove expensive cars.

She couldn't understand it. Here it was, the first day of classes, and she still hadn't heard from him. Why had he taken her name and number if he didn't intend to call? Every time she replayed their conversation after the crash, she became more and more convinced that he'd been flirting with her. What about that glint in his eyes? What about that smile? Sure, he'd pretended to be angry and upset, but he wasn't really. She'd seen enough men angry in her life to know the difference—especially when she was the one who had made them angry.

114

And besides, he hadn't even contacted the insurance company yet. Her mother had made both her and Elizabeth promise to call every Sunday, and though Jessica had dreaded making the phone call last night because of the lecture she was sure her father would give her about automotive safety, Mr. Wakefield hadn't said a word.

Jessica shifted in her chair. Sunlight was falling across the trunk of the Corvette, and in its deep shine she could see the reflection of a tall, dark man with an enigmatic smile. Who was he? Why hadn't he called?

The boy next to Jessica nudged her arm. Jessica looked around in annoyance, about to give him a piece of her mind, when she realized he was gesturing toward the front of the room. Professor Malika must have been trying to get her attention. She turned with one of her sweetest smiles.

Professor Malika smiled back. "Thank you, Miss, ah—"

"Wakefield." She sat up a little straighter, wishing she knew what was going on. "Jessica Wakefield."

"Wakefield," he repeated. "Now, if you'd be good enough to answer my question . . ."

I'd love to answer your question, Jessica thought. *If only I knew what it was.*

"Of course," she said. She gave him one of her three-hundred-watt smiles and looked at him expectantly. It was a technique that used to work in high school.

There was half a second of silence while she smiled at the philosophy professor and he stared back at her like a rabbit in the headlights of an oncoming car. And then he said, "What is the purpose of philosophy?"

The phantom image of Mr. Corvette shimmered in front of Professor Malika. Jessica's smile went up to six hundred watts. Maybe the cloud in the middle of her silver lining wasn't as large or as dark as she'd feared. "To discover the truth," she said confidently.

"Truth!" cried Professor Malika, looking surprised but pleased. "Truth is the purpose of philosophy. Very good, Miss Wakefield. I'm glad someone has a basic understanding of the subject."

Jessica fell back into her daydreams. College was going to be even easier than she'd dared hope.

Tom stopped in the doorway of his film class, checking out the room. The film majors, looking intense and superior, were gathered at the front. The kids who were taking the course because it was the only thing they could fit in their schedule were bunched up in the middle. And at the back were a couple of big-league jocks with the usual cluster of admiring girls around them, listening to them discuss bombs and squib kicks as though they were the most fascinating things in the world.

Tom stepped into the room and walked over to a second-row seat at the side. In the old days, if he'd decided to take a course on Hollywood comedies of the '30s and '40s it would have been because he figured he could skate through it without too much trouble. Anybody could watch a movie, right? And in the old days he'd be sitting at the back with the campus heroes, feeling like a big man because he knew how to throw a ball.

He read through the assigned text while he waited for the instructor to arrive. These were not the old days. Now he was taking film because he was interested; he was interested in everything. Life was too short not to get all you could out of it.

And he sat at the front with the film freaks because they still thought of him as Wildman Watts, superjock, and left him alone. In the old days, all Tom wanted was a good time and to be surrounded by people who told him how great he was. Now he'd rather be on his own than have a bunch of insincere good-time friends. Life was too short to waste.

The two people sitting beside him started arguing about who was better, Frank Capra or Howard Hawks.

Tom closed his book and looked out the window. *Who cares who's better?* he asked silently. *They're both dead now. Being better won't do either of them any good.*

He watched the students hurrying to their classes and thought about crowd scenes. You saw these people all the time, but you never knew them; they just walked back and forth in your life. *And for all I care they can keep walking,* Tom thought as a flash of golden yellow caught his eye. He turned. It was Jessica Wakefield, striding down the path by herself.

He missed a breath. It wasn't Jessica; it was her sister, Elizabeth. Identical as they were, he was sure it wasn't Jessica. Jessica moved like someone who was sure of everything, just as he used to. But Elizabeth moved like someone who'd learned that you couldn't be sure. Tom leaned forward, watching Elizabeth disappear into the English building.

Something about Elizabeth Wakefield made him wonder if he really wanted *everyone* to walk by.

Jessica was the first one on her feet when the class finally ended. She wasn't going to have any problem getting a good grade out of Professor Malika as long as she kept smiling.

She glanced at the clock tower as she fled the philosophy hall. If she hurried, she could dump her books in her room before she met Denise for lunch.

"It's just me!" Jessica called as she pushed open the door of the suite. She hadn't expected Isabella to be home, but the door was unlocked.

"I thought you said you'd be out all—" she began, but the words shriveled up in her throat. There was someone stretched out on the couch, reading a magazine, and it wasn't Isabella Ricci.

Slowly, as though he'd only just realized someone had come into the room, he turned toward her.

118

"I was hoping you'd come back before lunch."

How could anyone have such an insolent and yet such a charming smile? Today he was dressed in jeans and a faded flannel shirt, with dirty old black high-tops on his feet. Jessica stood silent for a few seconds, trying to get her heart back to its normal beat.

He dropped the magazine and sat up. "You're not a very good hostess, are you?" he asked. "You haven't even offered me a cup of coffee. If you're not nicer to me, I might not come back."

Play it cool, Jessica told herself. *Don't let him rattle you. Play it cool.*

She forced her legs to carry her to the table and threw down her books. "I don't remember inviting you in the first place," she said, keeping her face impassive. "Just how did you get in here?"

"These locks aren't exactly high security, you know." Insolent smile; face of an angel. "And anyway, you did invite me when you rammed into my car." He got to his feet, his hands in his pockets. "You didn't think I'd forgotten, did you? You didn't think I got home and the Corvette had miraculously healed itself?"

She wasn't going to let him intimidate her just because she found it so hard to look at him and think at the same time. Jessica raised her chin. "I thought you were going to contact the insurance company. I told you they'd take care of it."

He came toward her, stopping only a few feet away. "I changed my mind about that." A smile as sweet and slow as molasses appeared on his face. "It's not insurance money that I want."

She felt as though the air had suddenly been drained from the room. There were flowers on the table and traces of her and Isabella's perfume in the air, but all she could smell was him.

"What do you want?" she asked, surprised to discover she could still speak.

"Don't worry," he said, brushing a strand of hair away from her cheek. His touch was as gentle as a butterfly. "I'll let you know when I'm ready."

He was gone before she'd quite absorbed the fact that he was there. As she picked his magazine off the floor to stick it in the rack with Isabella's, a plain black card fell out. Across it he'd written his name in silver ink. *Michael McAllery.*

"Michael McAllery," Jessica read out loud. "Well, how do you do?"

Enid made her way through the lunch line, talking to Elizabeth in her head. *If you can't accept me as I am, then maybe you're not the friend you thought you were,* she was saying. *I'm not going to stay in your shadow just to make you feel better.*

She dropped a sandwich and an apple onto her tray.

If you can't see me as anything but good old Enid, maybe I should stick to people who never knew me then, she continued.

She smacked down a bag of potato chips and a

Diet Coke. *I'm sorry, Elizabeth,* she said as she banged her tray down next to the register, *but I think you and I have come to a parting of the ways. You want to stay just where you are, and I want to move on.*

Ever since their argument on Saturday morning, Enid hadn't been able to think about much else. The trouble was that although she was no longer speaking to Elizabeth Wakefield in the flesh, she couldn't stop arguing with her in her head. Emerging into the dining room, she turned left and walked purposefully to the window table where Shaun, Jan, and Delia were sitting. They were still talking about Friday night.

"I really, really hope I get pledged to Theta," Delia was saying as Enid took the seat beside her. "They are just the coolest."

Shaun giggled. "Plus the fact that they're paired with Sigma doesn't hurt. Those guys are gorgeous."

"I still think it's too bad about your friend Elizabeth," Jan said. "I hear that Peter Wilbourne's going around bad-mouthing her."

"I'm sure it's just a bunch of lies," Shaun said.

Jan shrugged. "Maybe. But nobody makes Peter look like a fool without paying for it. I've heard that when he doesn't like someone, things just have a way of going wrong for them."

Enid was busy unwrapping her sandwich and didn't look up. She had already left the party by the time Elizabeth caused the scene everybody was

121

talking about. She hadn't heard about it until Saturday. Even as angry as Enid was with Elizabeth, she had to admire her for standing up to Peter like that. She knew Elizabeth had been right—even if she secretly thought she'd been pretty foolish to throw her college social life away like that. After all, Danny Wyatt was built like a tank; he didn't need Elizabeth to defend him.

Delia shook her head. "I wouldn't want to be her for anything," she said. "Jan's right. From what I hear, Peter Wilbourne can be brutal."

"And from what I hear, he's not the only one," Jan said.

The others all looked at her quizzically.

"What are you talking about?" Shaun asked.

Jan lifted a forkful of rice salad into the air. "I overheard some girls in my art class talking about this psychic in town who's predicting some brutal murderer will strike here on Halloween night."

"Oh, come on!" Enid cried, happy to get the conversation away from her ex–best friend. "What are you talking about, 'Nightmare at Sweet Valley U'?"

"Hey, it's not *my* prediction," Jan said. "I'm just telling you what I heard. These girls said this psychic really knows his stuff. They say he predicted the earthquake in San Francisco, and that hurricane in Florida."

Shaun smirked. "Oh, yeah. And he probably predicted the assassination of Lincoln, too."

Enid laughed. "I agree with Shaun. The thing with these psychics is that they always tell you when they got something right, but they never tell you all the thousands of times they were wrong."

Delia put down her glass. "I don't believe in any of that stuff," she said. "As far as I'm concerned, if you can't eat it, wear it, or put it on the wall, it doesn't exist."

Jan pointed her fork at Delia. "There's more in heaven and earth, Delia Thomas, than is dreamt of in your philosophy."

"Oh, ha ha ha." Delia put on a haughty face. "I know you're quoting Shakespeare, Jan. I *am* in college now."

That's right, Enid thought. *We are in college now.* And the phrase suddenly sent Enid's mind back to the same subject it had been with all day: Elizabeth Wakefield.

Elizabeth had arrived at lunch in a buoyant mood. She couldn't wait to see Todd, to tell him how much better she was feeling. Not only was she looking forward to the arrival of her new roommate, but she was feeling excited now that classes had begun. Even though she hadn't gotten all the courses she'd wanted, she really liked the teachers. Just settling down to schoolwork again cheered her up. She sighed to herself. Unlike people, with schoolwork you knew where you stood.

But after having waited for twenty minutes, Elizabeth's mood was beginning to sour. She swallowed the last spoonful of pudding and put down the spoon. She hated eating alone, but the other option had been to sit here by herself with a full tray, staring expectantly at the door while she waited. At least eating had given her something to do.

Elizabeth glanced toward the entrance. *Why don't you just face the truth?* she asked herself. *He's not coming. He's got something better to do.* Her eyes fell on a crowded table across the room. Sitting in the middle, smiling radiantly and looking even prettier than she had in high school, was Enid. *Alexandra,* Elizabeth corrected herself.

She started stacking her dishes. Todd had been busy all weekend with the team, but they had managed to have a cup of coffee together last night. The atmosphere between them had been stiff and awkward, but not unfriendly. And it *was* Todd who suggested having lunch today.

Maybe he had to make a change in his schedule or something, Elizabeth told herself. *I'll give him ten more minutes. I'll go get another dessert, and if he's not here by the time I'm done, then I'll leave.*

In the end, she gave him fifteen minutes and twenty-three seconds, then picked up her books and left the cafeteria. She avoided passing Enid and her friends, but she couldn't help feeling that everyone was watching her. Watching and wondering what was wrong with her, because she had no friends.

*   *   *

By the time she reached her dorm, Elizabeth wanted to get inside her room, lock the door, and never come out. Not only had she just experienced one of the most depressing lunches of her life, but as she was coming across the campus she'd run into two Sigmas who'd given her a hard time about Friday night. They'd blocked her path and refused to let her pass. Even though it was broad daylight and they'd pretended they were just fooling around, Elizabeth had sensed a menace in their smiles.

All I seem to do around here is make enemies and lose friends, she told herself unhappily as she hurried down her hall.

She stopped in front of room 28, fumbling in her pocket for her key. But before she could put it in the lock, the door swung open suddenly.

Elizabeth blinked in surprise. Standing in front of her was a strikingly beautiful girl with masses of honey-blond curls and the reddest lips and most heavily made-up eyes Elizabeth had ever seen on anyone who wasn't acting in a play. Behind her, boxes and furniture were piled so high that the beds had disappeared.

"Hi," the girl drawled in a soft southern accent. "I'm Celine Boudreaux, your new roommate."

The door shut behind Elizabeth with a thud. Celine looked up from the drawer she was filling with silky underwear and lacy bras. Her pretty mouth curled unattractively and her eyes narrowed.

"I'd appreciate it if you didn't smoke in our room," she mimicked in a babyish voice. "I hope you don't mind, but I like to keep things neat."

She got up and took a cigarette from the pack on her dresser, lighting it with her brushed-gold lighter.

"My God," Celine said in her own voice. "I can't believe I've escaped Granny Boudreaux and the Simeon Academy for Girls, only to wind up living with Little Miss America."

She opened her roommate's closet, scattering ashes as she began looking through Elizabeth's clothes. "At least she won't have to worry about me borrowing her things," Celine muttered.

She pulled out several skirts and blouses and a pink cotton dress. "Lord help us," she cried, her mouth pinched in distaste. "I didn't think they made things like this for girls over twelve."

She went over to Elizabeth's dresser. "Now, what have we here?" she asked, taking up the photograph of Elizabeth and Todd with their arms around each other. "What's a sweetheart like you doing with a boring princess like this?" she asked the image of Todd. "I'd dump her if I were you. Start having some fun."

After rummaging through the things on top of the dresser, she started going through the drawers themselves.

"This girl doesn't even have a secret life," Celine drawled as she lifted slacks and shirts, looking for love letters and some form of birth control.

She held a pajama top up between two fingers. "Bless my granny's gout," Celine said. "I'll bet the princess is a virgin."

Celine lit another cigarette, closing her eyes while she inhaled deeply.

The one thing she wanted right now was to leave the past behind. Celine's pale blue eyes opened again as a shudder ran through her slender body. No, she wanted more than that. She wanted to set it on fire and scatter its ashes over the ocean.

That was why she had chosen Sweet Valley U. She couldn't have gotten farther from Louisiana and its nightmare memories than here. And after all those years with Granny Boudreaux breathing down her neck and all those horrible boarding schools with their regulations and stuck-up prisses, she had also been hoping to find someone like herself here. Someone with life, spirit, and a sense of fun. Someone who didn't live by the rules.

And instead she'd been given a person for whom the rules were made in the first place. Someone who didn't take any risks, who did what she'd been told.

Celine looked at Elizabeth's desk. Elizabeth's notebooks were neatly stacked on one side, her textbooks on the other, and her pens and sharpened pencils were neatly collected in a glass jar. There was no dust, no piles of papers, no stray stockings or trails of ash. It didn't look like a real desk to Celine; it looked like a desk in a magazine ad. Just as Elizabeth was like a girl in a magazine, perfect and bloodless.

She blew a smoke ring across the room. "Well, we'll just have to shake you up a little, honey," she said, her voice sweeter than syrup.

It's impossible, Elizabeth was telling herself as she marched across the quad. *You can't totally loathe someone after only fifteen minutes.* She pictured Celine's face with its pouty red mouth and its long, fluttering eyelashes. She recalled the heavy, flowery smell of her perfume. She heard her soft, sticky-sweet voice. "I know there are rules in the dorm, sugar, but rules are there to be broken, aren't they?" Elizabeth shuddered. "I hope you don't mind," Celine's voice went on, "but I'm going to need a little more closet space."

Elizabeth stopped in the middle of the quad, wondering what to do next. She had nearly two hours to kill before her next class. "You know what, sugar?" Celine's voice was still going in her head. "If you could just move your dresser against your bed, then when the rest of my things finally get here, I'll have a place for my granny's chair."

Snack bar, Elizabeth decided suddenly. Even though she'd just had lunch, she was going to

128

need a cup of coffee and maybe a brownie to calm her down enough to be able to study.

As soon as she stepped through the door, Elizabeth began to feel better. The snack-bar smells of coffee, fries, and burgers put the smells of powder, perfume, and menthol cigarettes out of her mind.

Maybe Celine isn't as bad as she seems, she told herself as she got in line. *You really shouldn't judge people by first impressions. And she is friendly.* Elizabeth put a peanut-butter brownie on her tray.

Friendly was an understatement. Celine had only been in Dickenson for a couple of hours and already she knew half the girls on the floor. Elizabeth felt her blood pressure rising again. She took a chocolate-chip cookie, too. Not only did Celine know half the girls on the floor, but she had loaned one of them Elizabeth's camera and another the pen Elizabeth's grandparents had given her for graduation.

Elizabeth paid for her food and found a table in a corner by the window. *Maybe you're being a little petty,* she scolded herself. *After all, Celine had no way of knowing how expensive that pen is. And you'd more or less already told Lilli that she could use your camera.* Elizabeth bit into the brownie, her irritation over Celine fading away. *Once you get to know her a little better, everything will be fine.*

Winston entered the cafeteria warily, standing in

the doorway for a few seconds, just looking around. Most of the Sigmas lived and ate in the frat house, but once in a while one turned up in the cafeteria. He saw a few of his dormmates, but no blue jackets. He took a deep breath and strode in.

Winston grabbed a tray with a sigh. *I'm only eighteen. I shouldn't have to live under all this stress.*

On Saturday morning he'd managed to beat the Sigmas to Marsden by avoiding roads and riding Anoushka's bike across the lawn. He was a little breathless as he strolled out of the hall and into the frat guys, but they didn't seem to notice. They'd been looking all over for him, they said. One of the brothers had a printout of the freshman housing list, but the only W. Egbert they'd found lived in Oakley. They'd laughed heartily about that. "You must think we're a bunch of idiots, looking for you in a girls' dorm," Bill Montana, the sky diver, had said. Winston had laughed the loudest. They'd all gone to breakfast then, and the Sigmas had invited him to a rush dinner that night. By the time he got back to his room, he'd been feeling pretty pleased with himself. *Clever Winnie,* he'd told himself as he drifted off to sleep. *You're made.*

Sunday he'd woken up in a cold sweat. All of a sudden he realized that he wasn't quite as clever as he thought. What if the Sigmas *called* Marsden? What if a couple of his new buddies decided just to drop by? Winston had felt his heart crawl down to his toes. His name wasn't even on the dorm directory. No one there had ever heard of him. *I'm dead*, he thought. *I might as well go buy myself a coffin and get inside.*

It was Maia who came to the rescue. She remembered that Betsy Spuma on the second floor went out with a guy who lived in Marsden. For the loan of the Beetle for the next four Fridays, Betsy's boyfriend was willing to write Winston's name on the room list and field all calls. But that, of course, hadn't been the end of his problems.

Winston decided to go for the hot meal. He needed his strength.

First thing this morning, there'd been a call from Betsy's boyfriend saying that Bill had left a message that he and some of the other guys would pick him up to go to breakfast. Winston barely had time to brush his teeth so that he could be waiting outside Marsden when the Sigmas arrived.

"Do you think I could have just a little more of the chicken?" Winston asked the server. He was sure he'd read somewhere that protein was good for stress.

"Don't tell me," the girl behind the counter said, "you're a growing boy."

Growing old, Winston thought as she handed him his plate.

Chapter
Seven

Elizabeth came out of the bathroom, a towel wrapped around her just-washed hair, and her shower things in her arms. At the door to her room she stopped to listen. *Please let her be asleep,* she silently prayed. Elizabeth's heart hit the floor as the sound of a relentless drumbeat drifted through the door. Celine was the only person Elizabeth had ever known who liked to wake up to incredibly loud heavy-metal music. But then, Celine was the only person Elizabeth had ever known who lived on coffee and cigarettes, kept a fifth of bourbon in her hair-dryer case, and couldn't discuss the weather without managing to bring up sex.

In fact, three weeks of sharing a room with Celine had convinced Elizabeth that Celine was like no other human she had ever encountered. She was so arrogant and self-centered that she made Lila Fowler, seem humble by comparison.

132

Elizabeth closed her eyes and counted to ten. *Please be dressed,* she begged. *Please be dressed and on your way out of here.*

Taking a deep breath, she opened the door. Celine was sitting on Elizabeth's bed, smoking a cigarette and polishing her nails.

"Um, Celine," she said as calmly as she could manage. "It's eight in the morning. Do you think you could turn that down?"

Celine didn't look up.

Elizabeth went straight to Celine's expensive sound system and turned it off.

That got her attention. "What'd you do that for?" she demanded.

"It's eight A.M., Celine," Elizabeth repeated. "I'm sure everybody on the hall would appreciate a little peace and quiet."

Celine gave her a dismissive look. "You know what my granny always says. You'll get all the peace and quiet you want when you're dead."

Elizabeth ground her teeth together. She was almost as sick of Celine's granny as she was of Celine. No matter what Elizabeth suggested—that Celine hang up her clothes, that she not smoke in the room, that she stop using Elizabeth's shampoo and borrowing her towels because she was too lazy to do a load of laundry—Celine had some stupid saying from her granny as an answer.

"Could you do that on your own bed?" Elizabeth asked as she started to put her things away.

133

Celine blew on her nails. "No can do, sugar."

"No can do?" Elizabeth stopped searching for the hair dryer Celine always borrowed. "What do you mean, 'No can do'?"

Celine turned to her with one of her more radiant smiles. "That bedspread cost a fortune," she answered sweetly. "My granny would just kill me if I got any polish on it."

"And I'll kill you if you get any on mine," Elizabeth said, mimicking Celine's syrupy voice.

"Oh, don't go gettin' your underpants all in a twist." Celine got up, scattering cotton balls over the floor. "I'm all done, sugar. And anyway, I have to hurry; I'm meeting the most gorgeous guy for breakfast. I swear his backside looks better than the one on the lead singer of Lethal Substance."

"I'm so happy for him," Elizabeth mumbled.

But Celine was already out of the room, the door banging shut behind her.

Elizabeth grabbed one of Celine's shoes that was under her desk and threw it after her. Giving up on the hair dryer, she went over to her bed and stared down at the open box of cookies, the used cotton balls and emery boards, and the full ashtray Celine had left there. "Death's too good for her," Elizabeth said in a voice close to breaking. "It would have to be slow torture."

Not only had Celine been doing her nails and smoking on Elizabeth's bed, she'd been eating Elizabeth's food as well. Furious, she started dumping everything in Celine's wastebasket—the only space Celine never filled.

When she was through brushing the crumbs onto the floor, she collapsed on the bed herself. Not for the first time, Elizabeth wished that she hadn't let Jessica talk her out of bringing her stuffed animals with her. She could really use something soft and blue to hug this morning.

"I don't know how much more of this I can take," she said as she reached into the wastebasket and took out the box of cookies.

Celine leaned across the table, her beautiful mouth in a pout, her blue eyes troubled. "You have no idea what I have to put up with. I'm just not used to being treated this way."

The boy, whose name was either Jeff or Joe, she wasn't quite sure which, nodded sympathetically. "Roommates can be a real drag," he agreed. "Yours really sounds awful."

Celine arched one perfect eyebrow, shuddering delicately. "Awful? All she does is moan and nag all the time. It's like rooming with somebody's mother." She put on her Elizabeth Wakefield voice, which was not sweet and hushed like her own but loud and slightly whiny. "Don't do that, Celine. Don't do this, Celine," she mimicked. "Celine, where's my shampoo? Celine, did you leave the light on? Celine, don't forget to lock the door. What time are you coming back tonight, Celine?" Her foot accidentally brushed against his ankle. "That's why I'm having so much trouble in physics," she said forlornly. "I can't even work in our room, she makes me so unhappy."

Jeff or Joe, or perhaps it was Jason, smiled. "Don't worry about that. I'll give you all the help you need. I've always been good in science."

Celine looked deep into his eyes. "You're so sweet," she purred. "I don't know what I'd do if it weren't for you."

He stared back, looking like a man about to drown. The sudden alarm on his watch made him jump. "Wow. I'd better get going or I'll be late for math." He gathered up his books. "So, I'll meet you after dinner to do the homework, right?"

Celine was in the middle of nodding when a look of devastation came onto her face. "Oh, no," she gasped. "I can't tonight! I'm so far behind in everything because of *her* that I have to try to catch up in history tonight." She sighed so heavily that the gold C around her neck heaved up and down. "Oh, what am I going to do? I'll never get my physics homework done in time."

Jeff, Joe, or Jason got to his feet. "I'll tell you what," he said. "Why don't I meet you in the morning and you can copy mine this one time? Then tomorrow night or the night after we can work together and I'll show you what to do."

"Why, what a brilliant idea. I do believe you're

136

a genius." She grabbed his hand. "And an angel. An absolute angel."

Jeff, Joe, or Jason blushed. "Well . . ." he said. "Well . . . I . . . Maybe you . . ."

Celine gave him a gentle shove. "You'd better go," she said. "I'd hate to think I made you late for math." She smiled. "I'll see you outside the library at ten, how's that?"

"That's great," he said, bumping into someone coming along the aisle as he backed away. "Thanks, Celine. I'll see you then."

Celine leaned back in the booth, watching him dash out of the snack bar. *Well, that takes care of physics,* she thought happily. Some skinny boy with acne and glasses was doing her history, and a fat sophomore with bad breath was doing her English. Now that her work was taken care of, Celine looked around the room for someone she knew.

She was just about to go back to the dorm and take a nap when a tall, handsome boy stepped through the door. A tall, handsome boy she recognized but didn't know. *You'll do,* Celine said to herself. *You'll do just fine.*

The aroma of hamburgers and french fries assaulted Todd as soon as he opened the snack-bar door. He hadn't realized how hungry he was. He and Mark had had a few free hours and decided to play some ball, but they'd gotten so engrossed in their game that they played through lunch.

Todd joined the line. Lately he was so completely caught up in basketball and the team that he was always forgetting everything else. Especially Elizabeth. A pang of guilt even stronger than his pang of hunger hit him. Out of the maybe twenty times in the last two or three weeks that he and Elizabeth had arranged to meet, he must have forgotten at least half of them.

He ordered a double cheeseburger and a double order of fries and leaned against a poster for the Halloween dance taped to the wall. Of the ten plans with Elizabeth he hadn't forgotten, at least five had had to be canceled because of something that came up with the team.

Elizabeth blamed him, of course. Everything was his fault. He wasn't making enough of an effort. But how much of an effort did she expect him to make when all she did when they were together was complain or sulk? Or ice him. She was always accusing him of not loving her anymore, but when he said that he did love her, that he loved her so much he wanted more than anything to spend the night with her, she froze up completely.

I'm in a no-win situation, Todd told himself as he watched the guy at the grill flipping burgers. *And I'm beginning not to care*. If there was one thing he was learning at college, it was that there were a lot of pretty girls around. Girls who were cool and smart and a lot of fun, the way Elizabeth used to be. Girls who weren't afraid of getting close, the way Elizabeth was.

Something incredibly light and warm touched his arm. "A penny for your thoughts, Todd Wilkins," said a female voice as gentle as a caress. "A brand-new, bright shiny penny."

Todd turned to find himself staring into the face of one of the most beautiful girls he'd ever seen. Her perfume had not only obliterated the smell of the hamburgers, it made him want to bury his face in her hair. "Excuse me?" he said. "Do I know you?" He was sure he didn't. She wasn't the kind of girl you forgot.

"No, you don't. But I know you. I look at your picture every day." She laughed. "I guess you could say I've been admiring you from afar."

Todd shook his head. "I don't think I—"

She laughed again, extending her hand. "I'm Celine Boudreaux. I share a room with Elizabeth." Her grip was firm and lingering. "She talks about you all the time."

"Double cheese and fries!" the guy at the grill shouted, banging a plate down on the counter.

"Oh, right." Todd hoped he was hiding his shock. From the description of Celine he'd had from Elizabeth, he'd expected her to look like the Wicked Witch of the West. "Celine. Of course. Elizabeth talks about you, too."

"Oh, isn't she sweet . . ." Celine smiled. "I just love rooming with Elizabeth. I come from Louisiana, as you may have guessed, and I don't know

139

anyone here. I don't know what I'd do without her. It's not always easy to make new friends, is it?"

Todd picked up his lunch, feeling even more annoyed with Elizabeth than he had before. *This poor girl,* he was thinking. She was grateful to Elizabeth, and all Elizabeth ever did was complain about her.

"I know," Todd said. "It can be tough adjusting to college. Especially when you come from another state and everything. You must be lonely."

"I'd be devastatingly lonely if it weren't for your girlfriend," she answered. "It would be just too awful to bear."

Todd was sure he'd never seen a blue the color of her eyes before. "Are you sitting with anyone?" he asked as he moved down the line.

Celine shook her head sadly. "No, no. I'm on my own."

"Well, what do you know?" Todd said. "So am I."

Celine brushed against him as she poured herself a soft drink. "I can't tell you how happy I am that I bumped into you."

Todd smiled. He was feeling pretty happy about it himself.

"Yuck," Jessica said, pretending to shudder. "This is revolting." She pushed her history textbook away from her. "I don't know why they think showing you pictures of dead bodies is going to help you remember what happened back then."

"You'd better get used to looking at dead bodies," said Isabella. She pointed to the photograph in Jessica's book with her pen. "Because according to Barnabas Montoya, that's exactly what this campus is going to look like on Halloween."

Jessica groaned. "Oh, not you, too. What is it with everyone in this school? How can you believe a silly rumor like that?"

"How do you know it's a silly rumor?" Isabella leaned forward, her eyes bright with excitement. "How do you know it isn't true that on Halloween night a blood-crazed psychopath is going to go on a killing rampage in a college building shaped like an X?"

Jessica put on a gullible face. "Oh, gee," she said. "I wonder which building that could be?" She widened her eyes. "It couldn't be Xavier Hall, could it? Where the big dance is being held?"

Isabella flicked a paper clip at her. "You can scoff, Ms. Wakefield, but remember, he who laughs last laughs best. And this time he who laughs last may be holding a very sharp ax."

Jessica laughed and got up. "How about a cup of coffee? I'm exhausted from studying."

"Jessica . . ." Isabella gave her a mocking smile. "We've been sitting here for only an hour, and most of the time we've been talking."

Jessica looked over her shoulder. "Does that mean you don't want coffee?"

Isabella laughed. "No, I want coffee." She leaned back in her chair. "So what's this new interest of yours in vintage cars?" she asked. "Your sister's not going to be too pleased if you turn in the Jeep for a Thunderbird, you know."

Jessica poured water into the espresso machine. "What are you talking about? I'm not into vintage cars."

"Then whose magazine was that I found in with my fashion magazines?" Isabella asked, following her into the kitchenette.

Jessica was glad that she had her head bent so that Isabella couldn't see she was blushing. As close as she and Isabella had become over the last few weeks, she still hadn't mentioned Michael McAllery to her. If it had been any other guy, Jessica would have told Isabella everything right away. But Michael was too important. He wasn't just another guy to be dated and cast aside when the next one came along. He was special. Every chance she got, Jessica went into town, hoping to catch sight of him again. That was why she was afraid to talk about him, because she thought that if she did, she would jinx herself and then she'd never see him again.

"A friend of mine left it," Jessica mumbled, fitting the filter into place.

"A friend of yours?" Isabella's voice was shrewd. Jessica didn't have to look over to know that those gray eyes would be shrewd too. "You

142

don't have any friends who are into classic cars. Unless you count that guy Winston with his Beetle."

"That's who it was," Jessica said quickly. "It was Winston."

"Jessica Wakefield!" Isabella grabbed her and pulled her so they were face to face. "You're lying! I can hear it in your voice. Come on, you can tell me. Whose magazine is it?"

Jessica was torn between the part of her that wanted to keep Michael McAllery a secret and the part that wanted to talk about him incessantly. The part that wanted to talk about him incessantly opened its big mouth.

"It's just this guy I ran into." Jessica made a face. "Actually, I ran into him literally. I bashed into his car when I was driving the Jeep."

Isabella leaned against the counter with a wicked smile. "And?"

"And not much," Jessica admitted. "He gave me a hard time when I hit him, but he never made a claim on the insurance. And then one day I came back to the room and he was lying on the couch, reading his magazine."

"What?" Isabella was still smiling, but her eyebrows shot up. "What do you mean, he was lying on the couch? How did he get in?"

"I don't know. He doesn't say much." Somehow, talking out loud about his behavior made it seem even weirder than it had before.

Isabella frowned. "Just who is this guy, Jess? Do you know his name?"

Jessica gave her an offended look. "Of course I know his name. It's Michael." At least his name was normal. You couldn't get any more normal than Michael.

"Not Michael McAllery," Isabella said.

Jessica looked at her sharply. "How did you know that?"

"There aren't that many mystery men around here who are into classic cars and good at picking locks." She made a face. "In fact, I'd say that Mike McAllery is probably it."

Jessica couldn't hide her excitement. "You mean you know him?" She grabbed Isabella's arm. "Tell me! Tell me everything you know. He isn't married or anything, is he?" She closed her eyes and groaned. "Oh, I knew it. I knew someone that gorgeous couldn't be unattached!"

"Hold on a minute, Jessica," Isabella said. "You're not actually interested in Mike, are you?"

There was something in Isabella's tone that Jessica didn't like—something serious—but she chose to ignore it.

"Interested?" she shrieked. "Are you kidding? How could I not be interested? He's the most incredible man I've ever met."

"He's gorgeous," Isabella agreed. "I'm not saying he isn't, but he's out of your league, Jess. Believe me. Michael McAllery is bad news."

144

"I don't believe it." Jessica took two mugs out of the drainer. "How can someone who looks like that be bad news?"

Isabella turned off the coffee maker. "How can someone who looks like that *not* be bad news?" She poured the coffee. "Really, Jess, this is not the kind of guy you want to get involved with. Mike McAllery left town right after high school because of some sort of scandal. I don't know if anybody remembers what it was, but it was huge at the time. Anyway, he went to L.A. and became a very successful photographer, and that was it. But then his father died a few years ago and he came back. He was the only child, and he inherited a fortune. But he's been in and out of trouble ever since. If it isn't drinking, it's women, and if it isn't women, it's fast cars."

Jessica felt herself go cold at the mention of women. "Maybe he's in mourning," she said. That would explain the drinking and running around. He hadn't gotten over his father's death.

"What?" Isabella started laughing. "Mike McAllery in *mourning*? For what?"

"For his father, obviously."

Isabella took a sip of coffee. "Oh, brother, do you have a lot to learn. Depending on who you hear it from, either Mike McAllery missed his father's funeral because he was out at the beach getting drunk, or because he was fooling around with his best friend's wife."

It was grief, Jessica told herself. *Isabella's wrong.*

That's the way people act when they're overcome with grief. "Those are just rumors," she said out loud. "People love spreading rumors about someone like that."

"Maybe." Isabella shrugged. "But I still think you should set your sights on someone a little more house-trained." She set her cup down. "I'll tell you what. Why don't I set you up with my friend Mark Gathers? He's a big basketball star and he's very dishy and very cool."

"Sure," Jessica said. "What's the difference? It isn't like Mike McAllery's interested in me or anything. I don't even know if I'd go out with him if he did ask me. He has been pretty rude."

"You should thank your guardian angel if he isn't interested in you," Isabella said. "She's saving you a load of trouble." She went over to the coffee table and picked up the student directory. "Now, let's just give Mark a call and see what he has to say for himself."

Jessica stared into her coffee cup. *Not only is Mike gorgeous and sexy,* she was thinking. *But he's misunderstood.* She smiled at her reflection in the dark liquid. Maybe their meeting had been destiny. Maybe she, Jessica Wakefield, was the one woman who could finally understand him.

The old Tom Watts had always done well enough in school, but he had been no scholar. If there was a choice between playing a little touch football and hitting the books, the old Tom Watts would have chosen running across a field with sweat streaking down his body any day of the week. What had mattered to him was being Wildman Watts, all-state champion and national record breaker, the college quarterback to watch. He could have anything he wanted; the world was his.

The new Tom Watts leaned back in his seat in the library study room, rubbing his eyes. The new Tom Watts knew that if there was something you wanted, you had to work for it; work hard and make it yours. He knew that the gifts the world gave you, the world took away.

Tom folded his arms on the tabletop and rested his head on them. He was tired. After his morning classes, he'd spent all afternoon and part of the evening at the university TV station. The station had become a huge part of his life. Tom didn't get into campus activities or the college social scene. He got A's in his classes, but it was without really participating, and the only friend he had was Danny. But he was involved in being an investigative reporter. That was what Tom Watts cared about: discovering the truth and making it known. He'd learned the hard way that fame and money and adulation were nothing to hold on to when things fell apart, but the truth was. The truth was one of the few things that might even be worth dying for.

Tom was drifting off into a half-dream where he

was tearing down a dark runway with a news camera over his shoulder when he was disturbed by a low, unpleasant male voice nearby.

"Well, whaddayaknow?" the voice was saying. "If it isn't Little Miss Equality."

Tom's eyes blinked open, and he felt his whole body tense.

A second male voice joined the conversation. "How about going to the movies with me some night, sweetheart?" it wheedled. "Or is this white girl reserved for black guys?"

"Hey, don't tell me you've gotten shy all of a sudden," said the first voice. "You had plenty to say at that Theta party."

"You're not very nice, you know," the other one said. "You don't stick up for your own kind, and you don't talk to them either. I think we're going to have to do something about that."

And then a girl spoke, her voice quiet but sharp. "Why don't you leave me alone?" she asked. "I'm trying to study."

Tom recognized her immediately. He remembered her voice so clearly and vividly that it seemed impossible he had heard it only once before.

"Because we think there's something you should learn here besides English." The taunting had become a threat.

"I'm serious. Go away."

"Oooh, I'm really scared . . ." They both laughed unpleasantly.

"What if we won't go away, honey? What are you going to do then?"

"She's not going to do anything." Tom barely spoke above a whisper, but the effect was as though he'd fired a gun. The two Sigmas had been bending down on either side of Elizabeth, but they straightened up immediately. Tom kept his eyes on them, not on the lovely face that had turned to him with relief.

"Hey, Watts," the larger one said. He smiled.

Tom didn't smile back. "I believe I heard Ms. Wakefield ask you to leave her alone," he said, his voice still hushed. "And I believe that would be a very good idea."

They both shrugged.

"Sure. Whatever."

"You're losing your sense of humor, Watts," the tall Sigma said. "We were just having some fun."

It wasn't until they'd left the study room that Tom finally looked at Elizabeth. For just a second their eyes met; and for just a second he thought about losing himself in them.

"Thanks," Elizabeth said.

The second passed. "Don't mention it," Tom said, and he turned his back on her and returned to his books.

"You guys watch too many soap operas," Jeff Cross was saying. "There's not going to be any bloodbath in Xavier Hall on Halloween. It's just a

149

practical joke." He winked at Winston. "I wouldn't be surprised if old Win here had a hand in it."

Winston put down his coffee cup, shaking his head. "Not my style," he answered. "I'm strictly a jumping out of closets and impersonating the principal over the phone kind of guy."

A group of girls from Winston's dorm waved to him as they left the coffeehouse.

"You also seem to be the kind of guy who knows an awful lot of women," Bill said. "How did you meet so many so fast? You studying nursing or something?"

Winston smiled his new nonchalant, big-man-on-campus smile, while under the table he wiped his sweating palms on his jeans. No matter where he went with his Sigma buddies, he seemed to run into girls from his hall. He could hide in the men's bathroom and they'd find him.

"It's the old Egbert charm," he said. "Handed down from father to son." He put on a pained smile. "Believe me, guys, it's not a gift, it's a curse."

"Yeah, right." Andy Hoffer stuffed a last forkful of chocolate cake in his mouth. "You look like you're suffering."

If you only knew, Winston thought. His heart missed a beat as he noticed Candy and Anoushka walk through the door.

Oh no, they're coming over! He put a hand on his heart, less as a gesture of honesty than to keep it in his chest. "We Egberts are martyrs to our sense of duty," he managed to choke out as the girls approached.

Candy reached them first. She gave him a big, friendly smile. "Hi, Win—"

He couldn't let them call him Winnie. "Candy!" He got to his feet so quickly that he knocked his fork off the table. "Anoushka, great to see you! It's been a while."

Candy looked puzzled but smiled. "What are you talking about, we just saw you—"

Winston cut her off. "Do you guys know Candy and Anoushka?" He gestured to the Sigmas. "Candy, Anoushka . . . this is Bill, Andy, and Jeff."

"Hi," Candy and Anoushka said.

Winston wasn't the only person to be impressed by Candy's eyes and Anoushka's smile. The Sigmas were grinning back as though they'd been put in a trance.

Candy shook his arm. "We came over to ask you something."

Winston held his breath. *Please,* he silently begged. *Please don't let her ask if I still want to try her mango shampoo.*

"Debbie wanted to know if—"

Winston breathed again. Debbie wanted to know if she could borrow either his car, his weights, or one of his tapes. "Sure, sure," he said quickly, "tell her it's fine."

Candy was staring at him in bafflement. "Don't you even want to know what she wants?"

151

Winston started shoving the two of them along the aisle. "It's fine. Whatever she wants is fine."

"Hold on a minute, Win," Jeff said from behind him. "Why don't you ask your friends if they'd like to join us?"

Bill and Andy were both nodding.

"Yeah, there's plenty of room. You sit here; I'll get another chair," Bill said to Anoushka.

"No! She can't." Winston gave Anoushka such a shove that she bumped into Candy. "They're very busy people," he went on, ignoring Candy's and Anoushka's strange glances. "They don't have time to eat; they're probably on their way to some important meeting or something . . ."

He knew he was gibbering, but he couldn't stop. "Maybe another time when they aren't in such a hurry." He grabbed Anoushka's elbow. "That would be nice, wouldn't it? We could all get together sometime for coffee when you and Candy aren't so busy . . ."

"What is wrong with you?" Anoushka shook him off. "Remind me to lend you some of my herbal relaxer when we get back to—"

The end of Anoushka's sentence was obliterated by the sound of breaking glass as Winston knocked a lemonade off a nearby table.

"Oh, I'm so sorry," he said, grabbing a napkin and mopping up the floor as Candy and Anoushka, with one last puzzled look, finally went away.

Chapter Eight

I've been on some boring dates in my time, Jessica was thinking as Mark Gathers went through the lineup for the varsity basketball team, *but this has got to be one of the worst*. She was grateful that the coffeehouse was dark. As long as her face was in shadow she wouldn't have to pretend to be smiling the whole time.

She was so bored that the sight of Enid Rollins coming through the door actually cheered her up for a second. Jessica sat up straighter and tried to catch her eye. If she could get Enid to join them, at least she'd have someone to talk to. Enid's eyes fell on their table, and Jessica gave her a big smile. But instead of smiling back, Enid swung around and practically ran out the door.

Maybe she's already met Mark and heard about the team, Jessica thought. She looked back at Mark and felt guilty when she realized he thought she'd been smiling at him. The problem wasn't Mark. He was really a pretty nice guy; it was just that he wasn't Michael McAllery.

Somehow, as the days passed and she heard nothing from her mystery man, not being Mike McAllery had become something to hold against every other man on the planet. Whenever Jessica saw or talked to a guy, all she could think was, *He's okay, but he isn't Mike McAllery.*

"So, how are your classes?" Mark asked. Every few minutes he would notice the silence and make some comment about the university, or basketball, or the standard of food in the cafeteria, but the truth was, his mind seemed to be somewhere else too. "Are you taking anything you really like?"

She looked up at him. Mark was attractive. He was intelligent. He was a big basketball star and one of the most popular guys in the school. Jessica stifled a yawn. But he definitely wasn't Michael.

"It's okay," she said. "I like my music class." She didn't explain that the reason she liked music was that since they mostly listened to recordings, it gave her time to think about Michael.

Mark nodded. "Music," he said, fiddling with his coffee spoon. "Yeah, music's good."

Jessica nodded. "Yeah, it is."

Mark looked over at her, both worried and wary. "Look, Jessica, I know I'm a little distracted tonight, and I'd really like to apologize . . ."

She smiled blankly. "I'm having a wonderful time," she lied. "Really."

Mark smiled back, but his smile was rueful. "You don't have to be polite," he said. "This isn't exactly the date of the century. And I don't want you to misunderstand what I'm going to say, but the truth is that I came only as a favor to Isabella."

For the first time all evening, Jessica's attention was entirely focused on Mark. And she wanted to throw something at him. Every day another gorgeous guy was begging her to go out with him, but she turned them down. And for what? To go out with someone who "only came as a favor to Isabella"?

"Is this some new kind of line?" she asked coolly. "Wow her by making her think you don't like her?"

"I didn't mean that the way it sounded." He looked embarrassed. "All I meant was that though I *do* like you and find you very attractive, I'm actually interested in somebody else."

Jessica sipped her espresso. Although part of her was still annoyed, another part was grateful he'd let them both off the hook. "Well . . . to tell you the truth," she said as she put down her cup, "I'm interested in someone else too." She made a face. "I came only because Isabella wouldn't take no for an answer."

"Leave it to Isabella . . ." For the first time since he'd picked her up, Mark laughed a warm, genuine

155

laugh. "What a relief, though. Now we can relax and have a good time. The group playing tonight's supposed to be really great."

Jessica picked up her bag. "Maybe I'll go to the ladies' room now, before the band starts."

"Good idea." Mark gestured to where some members of the basketball team were sitting. "I'll go say hello to the guys while you're gone."

Mark was still crouched between Todd and a guy Jessica didn't know when she came out of the rest room. Her eyes scanned the crowded room, looking for someone she knew. She spotted a guy from her science class . . . a girl who worked in the snack bar . . . a girl from her dorm . . . Jessica stopped suddenly. She felt as though a giant vacuum cleaner had sucked her heart right out of her chest. There, sitting on a stool at the counter, all by himself, was Michael McAllery. *He's not a student here,* she told herself. *Could he be following me?*

Afraid to move, Jessica watched as he lit a cigarette and exhaled a small cloud of smoke. When the cloud cleared, he was looking straight at her.

He wants me to go over, she decided, already walking toward him. *That's why he came tonight, to see me.*

She stopped only inches from him. After all these days and nights of imagining what it would be like to be kissed by him, being so close made her catch her breath.

"I knew I'd see you again," she purred in her sexiest voice, "but I didn't expect to see you here."

The gold eyes gave nothing away. "No?" Another cloud of smoke drifted around her.

She tossed her head. "No. I didn't think you'd be interested in this kind of scene."

"I'm not," he said. He pointed his cigarette at the tiny stage as the band started setting up. "The keyboardist is a friend of mine."

Jessica watched the keyboardist checking her amp. At that moment she looked up and winked in their direction. *He said friend,* Jessica reminded herself. *And that's what he meant, friend. He probably only came because it was an excuse to be on campus and run into me.*

"Oh." She wasn't quite sure what to say next. He wasn't exactly talking up a storm. "You know, I'd really love to take a ride in your car sometime," she said.

He glanced at her. "I think your boyfriend's wondering what happened to you," he answered, as though she hadn't spoken. He indicated Mark sitting at their table, looking around for her. She opened her mouth to explain that Mark wasn't her boyfriend, but he didn't give her a chance.

"You'd better sit down," he said. "The band's about to start."

"Am I the only person in this entire college who does any work?" Elizabeth threw down her

157

pen and picked up the last cookie in the box as another song started on the stereo across the hall.

Shrieks of laughter rolled down the corridor. "They won't be laughing when they flunk out," Elizabeth told her desk lamp.

The door to the room opened suddenly, letting in more laughter and a blast of music. Elizabeth put her head on the desk. If Celine was already back, she'd never get her work finished.

"Is Celine here?"

Elizabeth looked up to find one of Celine's many friends, a large, loud girl who lived on the floor above, staring at her almost accusingly.

"She's on a date," Elizabeth said flatly. *Now just go away,* she added to herself.

But the girl didn't go away. Elizabeth watched in speechless amazement as she walked into the room, stepping over the pile of Celine's dirty clothes that had been left in front of the door.

"That's all right." The girl headed straight for Celine's dresser, rummaging around among the heap of makeup and toiletries on top. "I just wanted to borrow a couple of cigarettes." She held up a half-empty pack and stuck it in her pocket. "Tell Celine I'll pay her back tomorrow."

Elizabeth recovered her voice as the girl reached the door. "Maybe next time you could knock," she snapped. "I am trying to work."

The girl threw her a disgusted look. "They sure don't call you dull for nothing, do they?" she

158

asked. The door slammed shut behind her.

Dull! Elizabeth could feel her face flushing with anger.

The music got louder as a second stereo joined the first. Dull! She wasn't dull, she was responsible. Let Celine, Jessica, Todd, and Alexandra throw all their energies into their social lives—she was going to do well in college. That's why she'd come, wasn't it?

Slamming her book shut, Elizabeth got to her feet. "That does it!" she shouted to the empty room. "I'm going to the library where I can concentrate."

As she steamed down the corridor, two girls carrying bags of chips and bottles of soda passed her.

"Where's *she* going?" one of them half whispered.

The other laughed. "Nowhere we'd want to be."

Tom stepped out of the television studio and into the night. His co-workers always joked that he was a workaholic. "You don't have to be here every spare minute," Professor Sedder, the head of the communications department, was always telling him.

He hurried across the quad. Sometimes he wondered if there might be some truth to the jokes. Especially now that Professor Sedder was threatening to get him a freshman trainee. "Even you can't do everything yourself," he'd told Tom that afternoon. "What happens if you get sick? What happens if NBC gives you a special award and sends you to Europe for a month?"

Tom looked at his watch. He'd arranged to

meet Danny for pizza half an hour ago.

He'd talked to enough psychiatrists and psychologists in the months right after the accident to know that he was overcompensating. "You think if you're always busy, you won't have to think about what happened," one doctor had told him. "But you're only fooling yourself."

Tom cut across the lawn, heading for the science building, where, hopefully, Danny was still waiting for him.

He wasn't fooling himself, though. Maybe he worked more than normal, but it wasn't because he was trying to stop himself from thinking about the accident. He never stopped thinking about the accident. Not a day went by that the memory of it didn't hit him like a sledgehammer. Not a night went by that it didn't replay itself in his dreams. It was with him every second of every minute of every twenty-four hours, and it always would be. He didn't work the way he did because he wanted to forget what had happened. He worked like that because he remembered; because he wanted to do something worthwhile with his life. It was his way of paying them back for what had been lost.

Tom slowed down as he noticed a girl with long, straight blond hair taking the library steps almost at a run. *Why is she always in there?* he asked himself. *Doesn't she have a room?* He stopped to watch her until she disappeared through the heavy oak doors. *Now what's* she *overcompensating for?* he wondered.

He might have stood there thinking about Elizabeth for the next hour if he hadn't spotted Danny, waiting under a palm tree. Danny was easy to pick out even from a distance or in a crowd because of his height and broadness. Tom waved.

Danny had just stepped onto the lawn when two figures came up behind him. One of them said something, and Danny stopped. *They probably just want to know the time,* Tom thought, but he stood up straighter, tense and watchful.

Danny started to walk again. One of the men reached out to grab his shoulder, but Danny was too fast. He kept walking, heading straight for Tom.

They were close enough now that even in the dim light, Tom could recognize them. One was Peter Wilbourne III, and the other was his yesman, Simon Amerring. Their voices carried in the stillness of the night.

"What's the matter, Wyatt?" Peter was saying as they followed Danny. "You yellow as well as black?"

Simon found this pretty funny. Danny didn't say a word.

"He's just a lousy coward who needs some white guy to fight his battles for him!" Simon shouted.

Tom held himself in check. It wouldn't help Danny if he stepped in now.

Though they continued to taunt and poke at Danny, they stopped short of actually attacking him. Tom could only guess that Wilbourne and Amerring, aware of Danny's strength, weren't

161

quite sure how far they could push him. They had to know that if he wanted to, he could take on the two of them without any trouble.

As soon as Danny approached, Tom stepped away from the building and walked beside him.

"I'm sorry I'm late," he said, acting as though he didn't know the white guys were behind Danny, as though he didn't know what had been going on.

"It's all right," Danny said. "I figured you lost track of time."

He could hear the Sigmas drop back as they came out onto the lighted path.

Tom glanced at his friend. Even though he'd sworn to himself that he'd never ask, there were times when he couldn't help wonder why. Why did Danny let those idiots push him around like that?

"You think I'm a coward too?"

Danny's voice was so normal, and the question so surprising, that for a second Tom wasn't sure he'd heard him right. "What?"

"Do you think I've gone soft?" Danny came to a stop under a streetlamp and turned to face him. "Come on, I know you must've thought about it. Why do you think I won't fight anymore?"

"Of course I've thought about it." Tom jammed his hands into his pockets, but looked straight into Danny's eyes. "It doesn't matter, man. You don't have to explain yourself to me."

"I know." Danny shrugged. "Maybe that's why I will."

162

Tom didn't interrupt him once. The two of them stood on opposite sides of the streetlamp, looking out across the campus, and Danny told him about his brother. His big brother, Thad.

All his life, Danny had looked up to Thad and tried to emulate him. Thad was a leader, so Danny became a leader. Thad was a fighter, so Danny became a fighter. "Don't let anybody push you around," Thad always told him. "Not anybody." And Danny didn't. But last winter, Thad had taken things a little too far. He'd gotten into an argument with some guys from L.A., and one of them had a knife.

"So now he's in a wheelchair for the rest of his life," Danny said. "It was a stupid argument, Tom. A stupid argument over parking a car. None of them could even remember how it started." He shook his head. "Can you figure that out? A stupid argument over a car, and now Thad will never walk again. I never thought something like that could happen," Danny said, his voice as dead as his brother's legs. "But now I think about it all the time."

"There are some things that are worth fighting for," Tom said, his eyes still on the moon. "But not that many."

"No," Danny said. "Not that many at all."

It was after midnight when Elizabeth followed the path back to Dickenson Hall. Exhausted, but relieved to have finished her work, she looked for a crack of light under the door of her room. It was dark. As late as it was, she knew Celine probably wasn't in bed. Celine slept so little at night and so much during the day that Elizabeth sometimes seriously wondered if she might be a vampire. Elizabeth slowly opened the door. *And she certainly has a taste for blood,* she thought ruefully, remembering the fight they'd had that morning.

Elizabeth crossed to her desk and turned on the light. Celine's bed was unmade, as usual, and empty. She threw down her books with a sigh of relief. All she wanted to do was get into her own bed and sink into a deep sleep before the Vampire Queen came home. She sat down for a minute before getting into her pajamas, just to relax. She kicked off her shoes. She closed her eyes.

"All work and no play makes Elizabeth a real bore," Jessica was saying. "That's why I didn't want to room with you, Elizabeth, because you're just so *dull.*"

"I'm not dull!" Elizabeth shouted back. She was standing in the center of a ring of people. Besides Jessica, Celine, Todd, and Alexandra, there were a bunch of Thetas and Sigmas. Everyone was pointing at her. "I'm very interesting. I—I'm—"

"No, you're not!" Alexandra shouted as the circle started skipping around her. "You're a boring old prude."

"I'm not!" Elizabeth was near tears, spinning around, trying to keep up with them.

"Little Goody Two Shoes," Celine drawled. "You're about as much fun as my granny's dentures." She laughed.

"Not everything in life has to be fun," Elizabeth protested.

Loose, high-pitched giggling rose above the taunting. Someone put a spotlight on Elizabeth.

"Look at her!" shrieked Celine in a loud whisper. "She even looks boring when she's sleeping."

A boy laughed. Elizabeth turned, trying to see who it was.

"Shhh!" Celine hissed. "You'll wake it up."

"We're going to wake it up anyway," the boy spluttered. Something thudded to the ground.

Shielding her eyes against the light, Elizabeth turned again and again, but the ring was fading.

"Maybe we should turn off the lamp," the boy whispered.

"I've got a better idea," Celine said between giggles. "Bombs away!"

Something soft and warm and smelling of tobacco fell over Elizabeth's head.

She opened her eyes to darkness and laughter. There was something over her face. She could smell whisky as well as tobacco. *I'm awake,* she told herself. *I'm awake, the light is on, and there's someone else in the room.* She flung Celine's sweater from her head and sat up, blinking.

Celine and a strange boy were sitting in a heap in the middle of the floor. Celine, her makeup

165

smudged and her hair tousled, was slumped against him, her arms around his neck. Even in her dazed state, Elizabeth knew where the smell of liquor was coming from.

"Uh-oh," said Celine in a stage whisper. "I think we've been caught."

Don't let them get to you, Elizabeth told herself, grateful that at least she wasn't in her pink pajamas.

She got to her feet with as much dignity as she could muster. "Get this guy out of here, Celine," she ordered.

Celine struggled to a sitting position, hanging on to her date. "He's not going anywhere, Little Miss Priss! He's staying here tonight."

"In *my* room?"

Celine staggered to her feet. "It's my room, too," she yelled. "I can have whoever I want stay."

Someone from the room next door pounded on the wall. "Shut up! We're trying to get some sleep."

"Well, we're not!" Celine screamed back. "And we'll make as much noise as we want!" She slid back to the floor, her arms around the boy again. "Won't we, honey?" she asked.

Elizabeth was already out the door, her bag and her jacket in her arms, and didn't hear his reply.

Blind with tears, Elizabeth raced out of the dorm. She didn't care how much noise she made, she just wanted to get as far from room 28 and Celine as she could.

It wasn't until the front door of the building locked behind her that she stopped abruptly, gasping for air. What was she doing? Where could she go? The night was cold now; cold and moonless with only a scattering of stars.

I'll go to Todd's, Elizabeth told herself, pulling on her jacket. She started up the path, but the farther she got into the darkness, the less this seemed like a good idea. What if he wasn't there? Or, worse, what if he was and didn't want her around? She didn't even want to consider the possibility that he wasn't alone. She slowed down. It had been so long since they'd really spent any time together she couldn't be sure of her welcome anymore.

The image of her sister flashed through her mind, but she couldn't be sure of her welcome there, either. She imagined barging in on Jessica and her new crowd, her clothes rumpled and her face streaked with tears. She could hear Jessica saying, *Oh, grow up, will you, Elizabeth? We're in college now. It's no big deal to have a guy stay in your room one night.*

Something scurried through the bushes. Elizabeth picked up speed again. *Enid,* she decided. *I'll go there. No matter what's happened in the last few weeks, she'll be there for me. She's still my best friend.*

Almost running now, Elizabeth headed toward Enid's dorm. Memories of all the times Enid had stood beside her and comforted her filled her mind as she raced across the lawn.

167

But when Elizabeth finally got to Enid's dorm, she realized she'd made another mistake. Enid wasn't here. The Enid she'd been hurrying to no longer existed. The girl whose light shone through a third-floor window of Parker Hall was someone else. Someone called Alexandra who was pledging the most popular sorority, who had no time for Elizabeth anymore—someone who might have a guy in her own room tonight.

Elizabeth shivered. Except for the occasional campus patrol car passing by, she might have been the only person left on the grounds.

She turned away from the dorm and headed toward town. There must be an all-night laundromat or even a diner where she could sit until morning.

It was only as she reached the outskirts of town that she realized that there was in fact one person from her old life who wouldn't turn her away. A responsible, kind, caring, and generous person who lived in an off-campus apartment only a block or two from where she was now.

"Steven!" Why hadn't she thought of him before? Steven would help her. Steven would make her feel as comfortable and loved as she used to feel.

Elizabeth ran to her brother's, almost feeling as though she were going back to Sweet Valley, going home.

*　　*　　*

"What are you doing here? What's wrong?" Steven was standing on the landing, the door to his apartment open behind him, wearing a T-shirt and a pair of old sweatpants that had obviously been thrown on quickly, since they were inside out.

Elizabeth didn't care. She'd never been so happy to see anyone in her life. "Oh, Steven," she sobbed, hurling herself into his arms. "I've had the most terrible night."

"What is it?" a soft, gentle voice asked. An equally soft and gentle hand touched Elizabeth's shoulder. "What happened?"

Elizabeth pulled herself away from her brother's embrace. Steven's girlfriend, Billie, was standing beside them in the doorway, a robe pulled around her, her feet bare. Elizabeth had been so upset that she'd forgotten about Billie. She wiped the tears from her eyes and forced a smile. "It's nothing," she apologized, trying to keep her voice from wobbling too much. "I'm really sorry for bothering you. I . . . it's just . . ."

As the tears streamed down Elizabeth's face, both Steven and Billie slipped their arms around her and steered her into the apartment.

"Why don't I fix us all a cup of tea?" Billie asked. "Would you like that, Elizabeth? Some tea and cookies?" She gave her a squeeze. "It'll give you a chance to talk to your brother," she added in a whisper.

Elizabeth collapsed onto the sofa. Across from

169

her the bedroom door was open, the bed unmade, clothes thrown on the floor. She must have interrupted Steven and Billie; they'd obviously already gone to bed. Suddenly Elizabeth felt like an intruder. Why hadn't it occurred to her that her brother would be busy too? That he had his own life and it didn't include her?

Steven sat down beside her, resting one arm along the back of the couch. "What is it, Elizabeth?" he asked.

In the kitchen, Billie turned on the faucet to fill the kettle. "You take milk, Elizabeth?" she called.

Steven answered for her while Elizabeth snuffled back tears. He moved a little closer. "Come on, Elizabeth, tell me what's wrong."

Was it concern she heard in his voice or impatience? *Oh, stop it*, she scolded herself. *Of course it's concern. He's your brother. Just because he has a girlfriend doesn't mean he's stopped caring about you.*

Haltingly and in a voice choked with sobs, Elizabeth told Steven what had happened. But because she could hear Billie opening cabinets and getting out cups, and because she could still see the waiting bedroom out of the corner of her eye, she didn't talk about anything but Celine and her date.

Billie came in just as she'd finished, setting a tray filled with steaming mugs and a plate of chocolate-chip cookies on the coffee table.

Elizabeth caught the look Billie gave Steven. It was the sort of look she and Todd might have exchanged when they were close. It said, *Well? What's wrong?*

Steven started explaining as he handed Elizabeth her tea. "Elizabeth's roommate came back drunk with a guy tonight and refused to make him leave."

Billie sat beside Steven, leaning against him. "Oh, you poor thing," she said. "I know exactly what it's like, believe me. The first girl I shared with when I came here was like that." She laughed. "It got so bad that one time I actually barricaded the door so I could get a whole night's sleep."

Steven passed her the plate. "I think this is part of what they call the college experience," he said. "I could tell you stories about some of the people I've roomed with that would curl your hair."

Elizabeth smiled weakly, helping herself to a cookie. All of a sudden she was starving. "I know—" she began, hoping to explain that it wasn't just Celine that had her upset, that everything about college was wrong for her, that her entire life seemed to be falling apart.

But Steven cut her off. He started telling her a story about a roommate of his who used to bring his friends in through the window at all hours of the night to play cards and drink beer.

Elizabeth ate while Steven talked and Billie tried to keep her eyes open.

What he's telling me is that it's no big deal, Elizabeth thought. *What he's saying is that I'm overreacting and I should go back to my room.*

When Steven had finally finished his story and she'd finished her tea, Elizabeth put down her cup. "I guess I'll go now," she said, getting to her feet. "I'm really sorry I bothered you. I'm feeling much better now."

She turned to Steven just in time to see Billie nudge him.

"You don't have to go," he said quickly. "You can sleep here. We have a spare room."

Elizabeth shook her head. "No, it's all right. I have an exam first thing in the morning, anyway."

With a look at Billie, Steven stood up too. "I'll drive you back."

After Steven let her off, Elizabeth went back to Dickenson Hall, but not to room 28. Instead she went into the common room and huddled in one of the armchairs, dozing fitfully and wondering how the world had started moving so fast that it seemed to have left her behind.

Chapter Nine

It's not really true that I have no friends, Elizabeth consoled herself as she entered the study room. Since she came here every night, she'd begun to recognize the faces of the regulars. At the front carrel was Nina Harper, a girl from her floor at Dickenson. The man who had come to her aid the night the Sigmas were hassling her—Tom something—was sitting to one side, and behind him was a pale, sharp-featured guy with longish blond hair who often stayed late reading books of poetry.

Maybe they weren't technically friends, but just seeing these people made her feel she wasn't completely alone. She smiled at Nina as she passed her desk, and Nina smiled back.

Maybe I'm not the only one with roommate problems, Elizabeth thought. She had to go almost to the back to find an empty carrel. As she walked up the aisle, she could feel the ice-blue eyes of the blond boy on her face. Sometimes, walking across campus, she would feel someone watching her and look up to find it was him. Elizabeth couldn't decide whether she liked this attention. Before she came to college, she would have thought nothing of an attractive guy noticing her, but her confidence was so low now she wasn't sure what it meant. She tried never to let him catch her looking back.

It was Tom's nod she responded to as she walked by. They hadn't spoken since he'd stepped in for her with the Sigmas, but they always acknowledged each other. And sometimes, when she looked into his face, she felt as though he really could be a friend.

Elizabeth chose a carrel behind Tom. *My home away from home,* she thought as she sat down. Her relationship with Celine had deteriorated rapidly after the night she'd fled the dorm. She and Celine never said a word to each other. Not one. Sometimes Elizabeth would come into the room and find Celine deep in conversation with one of her friends, but as soon as they saw her they clammed up. She figured they couldn't *always* be gossiping about her.

She took her pens, a notebook, and a chocolate bar out of her bag and began to go through her notes. A flier fell out from between the pages. It was for the big Halloween dance. COME TO THE ZOMBIE BALL! it said. BRING THE GHOUL OF YOUR CHOICE! Elizabeth jammed the paper back into her notebook. Todd hadn't asked her yet. Maybe he

174

thought she wouldn't want to go, because of all the rumors about the psychopath.

Elizabeth sighed. Or maybe he thought she wouldn't want to go with him. If she did, what would she go as? A wallflower? A letter stamped return to sender? The invisible girl?

Something made her turn around to catch another glimpse of the man with the high cheekbones and the piercing stare. If he went to the party, he would probably go as Dracula. She could easily picture him in a black cape and a blood-red tie. *Which means that Celine, Vampire Queen, would be his perfect date.* Even as the thought crossed her mind he looked up again, his eyes almost seeming to reach out and catch hold of hers. Blushing, she turned back to her work.

Anoushka made a serious face at her reflection in the bathroom mirror. "You know what I think?" she asked, her eyes shifting to glance at Winston painfully shaving himself. "I think you should go to the Halloween dance as a girl."

Winston winced as the razor took off more than whiskers. "I may have to go as the victim of a brutal murder if you don't shut up and let me shave in peace."

"Oh, don't get touchy. I'm serious." She turned, looking at him closely. "You've got the right kind of face for it, and you must have picked up a lot about being a girl from living in Oakley."

"I won't argue with that," Winston answered. "I know so much about feminine-hygiene products I could probably walk out right now and get a job selling the stuff."

"You just have no sense of humor sometimes, do you?" She scooped up some water from the sink and splashed him. "I think it'd be great if you went in drag. You could go with me and Debbie; we don't have dates. I bet everybody would wonder why you weren't wearing a costume."

Winston put down his razor and turned to face her "Anoushka," he said in a patient voice. "Do you think you're bolstering my sense of self by saying I'd make a good woman? Do you? Because if you do, you're wrong. You're undermining my sexual identity."

"Oh, please . . ." She pulled out the plug.

Winston dabbed at his bleeding neck with a tissue. "You wouldn't catch me dressing up as a girl on Halloween, not when everybody's saying a psychopath's going to be on the loose."

Anoushka scooped up her things. "Why not?"

"Why not? Don't you read the papers?" Winston looked at her in the mirror. "Because most serial killers go for women."

She slapped him on the rear with her towel as she headed out the door. "In that case, maybe I'm the one who should go in drag."

"Alexandra! Alexandra, over here!"

Enid stood at the entrance to the stands, her eyes moving across the noisy crowd of students.

Delia nudged her. "Up there! See? Where that big Get 'Em Vanguards banner is."

Enid found the banner, and beneath it a large group of Thetas and their boyfriends. "Alex! Come sit with us!" one of the Thetas was shouting.

Why are you hesitating? Enid told herself. *The Thetas are calling you. You've done it! You've completely changed your image.* But her eyes continued to wander across the fans who had come to cheer on the Sweet Valley football team, the Vanguards, in their first home game.

Enid knew why she was hesitating. Because Jessica Wakefield was sitting at the end of the group and because Mark Gathers was nowhere around. She'd seen them together in the coffee house a few nights ago, and it had upset her so much that she'd turned around and left immediately. If Mark preferred Jessica, there was nothing she could do about it, but still she scanned the stands, searching for the guys from the basketball team, half hoping Todd might spot her and call to her to join them.

"Alexandra Rollins!" Delia hissed at her. "If you don't start moving, I'm going to drag you up there."

Enid knew when to give in. There wasn't any point in trying to avoid Jessica just because she'd gone out with Mark. Jessica was as likely to be pledged to the Thetas as Enid was. If they were going to be sorority sisters, they would at least have to pretend to get along.

Enid laughed. "Okay, okay."

"Now remember," Shaun said as they climbed the stairs. "I sit next to the guy in the blue sweater if humanly possible."

"That's fine with me," Delia said. "I've got my eye on one of the Vanguards." She made a face. "I just wish I could remember what his number is. It's pretty hard to tell them apart with their helmets on."

"So, what does everybody think?" Enid said with a big smile as she squeezed into a seat beside Kimberley Schyler and her boyfriend, Tony. "Are we going to wipe the field with them or what?"

Tony shook his head. "We'll be lucky if they don't wipe the field with us," he said. "Our team hasn't been the same since Watts quit."

Enid nodded, squinting at the end of the bleachers, hoping for a glimpse of a familiar face.

"Oh, come on," the guy sitting behind Tony said. "It's not that bad. Watts was a genius, but we've still got some good players."

Kimberley groaned. "Give us a break, you two. Alexandra doesn't want to hear about the legend of Wildman Watts and how the future of the Vanguards was ruined the day he quit the team."

"Yes, I do," Enid said, even though she was a lot more interested in basketball players than football players at the moment. "Who was this guy Watts? What happened to him?"

Nick smiled at her in a way that reminded her that she really wasn't Enid anymore. "Tom Watts was a phenomenal quarterback. He made himself a legend in his freshman year, and then he just dropped out completely."

"You mean from football?"

Tony shrugged. "From football, from his friends . . . from everything."

"Where is he now?" Enid half expected them to say he'd gone to live in the desert by himself.

Nick pointed to the field. "Down there," he said. "With the camera. All he does now besides go to classes is work for the campus TV station."

"The regular guy must be sick or something," Tony put in. "Tom's a reporter, not a cameraman."

Nick put his head close to hers. "You see him? The big guy in the black shirt?"

Enid nodded, but she didn't see Tom Watts at all. Far away as he was, she had suddenly recognized the man standing beside the cameraman, talking and nodding. It was Mark.

She sucked in her breath. *This is my chance,* she thought. *Somehow or other, I have to talk to him before the end of this game.*

"See who I mean?" Nick was still pointing.

"Oh, yes," Enid said, her eyes on Mark. "I see."

"It can't just be a story," Denise was saying. "There are too many details. The psychopath will be dressed in black. He'll use a knife. The first victim will be a beautiful blonde . . ."

The guy she was talking to, Ben Somebody, groaned in exasperation. "Cripes, Denise, those aren't details; they're the little extras people put in every time they tell the story again."

Denise gave him a withering look. "Oh, sure. And I suppose naming Xavier Hall as the site of the murders is a little extra too."

Ben ran his hand through his hair in exasperation. "But that's just it," he argued. "Whoever started these stupid rumors chose Xavier Hall because it would make the stories seem real."

Jessica had been half listening to this conversation while she idly scanned the bleachers for a familiar face, but the only one she'd found was "Alexandra" Rollins's. How ironic could you get? Here she was at her first college football game. She wasn't on the cheerleading team yet because they'd had only two openings, and she was sitting with a group dominated by Enid the Drip.

She turned to Denise. "Well, it worked, then. Everybody believes something horrible is going to happen at the Halloween dance." She yawned. "That's all anybody talks about anymore."

Denise laughed. "Don't tell me Jessica's bored," she teased. "Are serial killers so commonplace in your part of Sweet Valley that you're already tired of ours?"

"It's not that we have that many psychopaths."

Jessica smiled sweetly. "It's just that we don't talk about them so much."

Ben laughed. "I'm with Jess. I'm sick of everybody talking about the Halloweeen Horror all the time. If they're that worried, then cancel the dance."

"Cancel the dance?" Both Denise and Jessica stared at him as though the killer had suddenly materialized behind his head.

"Are you crazy?" Jessica demanded. "Cancel the dance just because of a little bloodbath?"

Denise gave him a shove. "This is the first big social event of the year, you moron. Nobody's going to cancel it just because of a few rumors."

Ben shook his head. "Women," he muttered. "I wish I could understand them." He shrugged. "But since I can't, I think I might fight my way down to the snack van. Anybody want anything?"

Jessica was about to say no when she suddenly felt her heart drop into her stomach. The one thing she did want was disappearing out the exit two aisles away.

Mike! She got to her feet so fast she knocked Ben back into his seat. "I'll get it," she said quickly. "I have to go to the ladies' room anyway."

"That's all right, Jess—" he began, but she climbed right over him.

"Hot dog?" she asked, backing down the stairs. "Fries? Soda?"

As she raced toward the exit she heard Ben call after her, "Two large fries and a cheeseburger!"

With the determination of an explorer, Jessica fought her way through the crowd to the refreshment vans parked behind the stadium. What if he wasn't there? What if he wasn't going for food? What if he was leaving?

Don't be silly, she told herself as she shoved several people out of her way. He didn't buy a ticket just to leave before the game even started.

But Michael McAllery wasn't buying food. She pushed on. He wasn't in line for the men's room, either. Jessica stopped. There wasn't anywhere else he could be. He really must have been leaving. She looked around as the crowd began to thin out. The game would be starting soon. She might as well give up and go back to her seat.

"What's the matter, blondie?" asked a voice directly behind her. "Did you forget where you're sitting?"

Jessica was so surprised that she jumped.

Michael McAllery was standing so close to her, she could smell the soap he'd used that morning. He was grinning at her.

"What's the matter?" he asked, his voice unusually gentle. "Did you think I was the psychokiller, making an early appearance?"

Jessica gazed up at him. "I'd think you'd be more the type to save me from him," she said, pouting sexily. "I didn't think I was in danger from you."

He reached out and twisted a strand of her

golden hair between his fingers. "Don't kid yourself, sweetheart," he whispered. "You're always in danger from me."

Todd glanced at his watch again. What had happened to Mark? He'd gone for sodas at the beginning of halftime, and now the second half was about to start and he still hadn't come back.

"Well, hello, stranger," said a voice sweeter than honey and twice as smooth. "You saving this seat for me?"

Todd turned. It was Celine, dressed in something tight and blue-green, her hair and eyes and lips all sparkling in the sun.

"Sure," he said immediately, shifting over. "Sit down." Now he found himself hoping that Mark wouldn't come back after all. "You just get here?"

Celine squeezed in next to him. "No, I've been here since the beginning." She pointed toward the field. "I was down there with some of the girls from the dorm when I noticed you sitting here on your own." She held out a box of candy to him, smiling shyly. "If there's one thing I can't stand, it's a handsome man all by himself."

Todd blushed. He'd never met a woman who was so direct with a compliment. "I'm not supposed to be alone," he said. He meant that he was supposed to be with Mark, but Celine misunderstood him.

"Elizabeth is busy as usual?" she asked gently.

Something in the way she said "busy as usual" made him look at her closely. Todd had been under the impression that he was the one who was always busy, not Elizabeth. According to Elizabeth, all she ever did was study.

"Elizabeth had a paper to do today," he said. "I'm seeing her tonight."

"Oh, I'm so glad to hear that, Todd, I really am." She looked uneasily at the ground. "It's just that I do won—worry about Elizabeth, you know. She's never in our room anymore. She's gone by the time I wake up in the morning, and she doesn't get back until I'm already asleep." She sighed, looking up at him out of the corner of her eye. "Of course, I *know* she works in the library all the time, but you can understand why I'm concerned."

Todd couldn't exactly understand. "Well, Elizabeth has always been a very serious, hardworking person," he said. "She's always had her priorities straight, I guess."

Celine touched his wrist. "There are priorities and there are priorities. I was hoping that when Elizabeth said she couldn't come with us today, it meant she was coming with you." Her hand was warm and reassuring on his arm. "I guess things are different where I come from," Celine went on, her voice making him think of sultry nights and Spanish moss. "But I was raised to believe that a woman always makes time for her man."

He hadn't quite thought of it like that before,

184

but she was right. Ever since they'd gotten to college, Elizabeth had made no time for him, no effort. She wasn't happy about his success and popularity, and she certainly didn't want to share in it. What Elizabeth Wakefield wanted was to lock herself in the library.

Celine gently squeezed his arm. "It's like my granny always says, If you have no time to ride your horse, then maybe you shouldn't have one."

"Hey, Gathers!" Todd threw his towel across the bathroom. "What happened to you this afternoon? It's a good thing I wasn't waiting for you to bring back a doctor—I would've died."

Mark turned from the sink with a slightly shy smile. "I'm sorry, man, I really am. But I got sort of distracted at the snack bar."

Todd put his shaving kit down. "Oh, really? And do I need to ask by what?"

Mark's smile brightened. "No, but you might want to ask by whom."

Todd turned on the faucet. "Well, it's not Jess, I know that. You look too happy." He took another look at Mark, who had started shaving again. "Do I detect a hot and heavy date?"

Mark waggled his eyebrows in the mirror. "You do, my man. You definitely do. In fact, Wilkins, you may very well be watching a man preparing for the date of a lifetime."

Todd snapped his fingers. "Enid!"

"Alex," Mark corrected him. "The incredibly intelligent, beautiful, and sexy Alex Rollins." He rinsed his razor in the sink. "I can't believe how close I came to blowing it. Do you know, Alex *saw* me with Jess the other night?" He faced his friend. "What was I thinking, going out with someone else when I knew I wanted to be with her? Even as a favor, it was a stupid thing to do."

Todd laughed. "Did you two even bother to stay for the second half?"

Mark's good-natured grin returned. "We decided the coffee was better in the coffeehouse." He splashed water on his face. "What about you? You seeing Elizabeth tonight?"

Todd nodded, concentrating on putting lather on his face. Ever since that afternoon he'd been thinking about what Celine had said. "Yeah, we're having dinner together."

"Nice, Wilkins. I'll be sure not to barge in to tell you what a good time I had when I get back. But expect me right after breakfast."

Don't worry about it, Todd thought as he watched Mark saunter out of the bathroom. *You could bring the Marine marching band in with you and you probably wouldn't be disturbing us.*

It was wrong from the start. As excited as she was to be having a real date with Todd—and to be out of the room for the night and not in a carrel in the study room—Elizabeth was nervous about what to expect from the evening. As she walked across campus she couldn't shake the idea that what happened tonight might determine the fate of her and Todd's relationship forever.

What if after so many weeks of hardly speaking they couldn't find anything to talk about? What if, next to his new friends, he found her as dull as Jessica and Celine claimed she was? What if all his big-jock conversation annoyed her as much as it had before? What if he pressured her again?

And when he'd opened the door to his room, his body was so tense and his eyes somehow so suspicious that she'd immediately known she'd been right. It was going to be wrong.

"So," he said as she sat down in the armchair. "Did you get all your studying done?"

Elizabeth nodded. No matter which direction she looked, her eyes seemed to fall on the bed. "How about you? Was it a good game?"

Todd shook his head. "Not really. We lost twenty to zero." He handed her a glass of soda and sat down across from her. "Celine was there."

"Oh, really?" Her grasp tightened on the glass. "I didn't know you knew her."

Todd stretched his legs. "You know, Liz, in all honesty I don't know why you dislike Celine so much. She's really nice. She's sensitive, she's—"

"She's a two-faced witch." The words were out of her mouth before she'd realized they were even in her head.

187

Todd's expression was surprised and irritated. "Celine really likes you a lot, Liz. She's as concerned about you as I am."

"Concerned? You're concerned about *me*?"

Todd nodded. "Of course I am."

Elizabeth banged her glass down. "And how do you show this concern?" she demanded. "By talking about me behind my back to Celine?" The weeks of frustration and loneliness and feeling abandoned all rushed through her like a very fast train. "That's supposed to mean that ever since we've been here, you haven't paid as much attention to me as you pay to your basketball shoes."

"*I* haven't been paying any attention to *you*?" Todd got to his feet. "You're the one who hasn't been paying any attention to me. You won't even let me touch you."

She stood up too. "Since when does our relationship depend on how much I let you touch me? Since when does my not sleeping with you mean I'm not paying any attention to you?"

"That's not what I said!" he shouted. "Stop trying to put words in my mouth."

"All right!" she shouted back. "You tell me what you're thinking. You tell me what you want."

He collapsed on the bed, his head in his hands. It was such a sudden movement that she almost thought he was in pain. "All right," he said, his voice muffled. "All right, I'll tell you what I think." He raised his head, looking straight at her, his eyes full of sorrow. "I think this just isn't working. I think maybe it's time you and I went our separate ways."

I'm okay, Elizabeth told herself as she silently picked up her bag and her jacket. *Todd's right, it isn't working. It isn't working and it hasn't been working, and the quicker I get out of here, the better off we'll all be.*

Todd buried his face in his hands again. "I'm sorry, Liz. His voice was thick and muffled. "I'm really, really sorry."

Elizabeth didn't answer. She was already running down the hall, hoping to reach the safety of the elevator before the tears began.

"Isn't it a small world?" Celine asked. "Imagine us both ending up at the same school. I had no idea you went to SVU." She slipped her arm into the arm of the man beside her as they walked across the parking lot of Dickenson to his silver convertible Karmann Ghia.

"We're not walking on ice, Celine," he said, his voice itself like ice. "There's really no need to hold on to me."

Celine ignored his rudeness. If there was one thing she'd learned in her eighteen years, it was that you got nowhere in this life by doing as you were told.

"Don't be like that, William," she chided coyly. "After all, our families have known each other for generations. And we did have that date in New York last spring, didn't we?"

"You may call it a date, honeychile," he drawled, crudely imitating her accent. "But I call it an exercise in genteel blackmail." He came to a stop, extricated his arm, and opened the door.

A dark look came into Celine's face as she slid into the passenger seat. It was true that she'd had her father arrange for William White to be her escort to the debutantes' ball last June, but she hadn't realized at the time how much of an ordeal William had found it. He had been less than gracious, but then, he was a Yankee; she hadn't expected manners. It wasn't his manners that attracted her to him. It was his sensuous good looks and his slightly jaded, untamed air. Her instincts told her that he wasn't just unique and mysterious; he was dangerous. In fact, of the things that had made her choose SVU, William Barrington White's presence here was one of the most important. She'd been sure that once he realized she was nearby, he'd be all over her like flies on a picnic.

She was smiling again by the time he shut the driver's door. "Then what do you call this?"

He started the engine. "I call this a ride to the Sigma party." He put the car in reverse and backed out of the space. "And if I hadn't been so surprised that you had the nerve to ask me to take you, you can be sure that I would never have said yes."

Celine pushed back a tangle of curls. She wasn't

190

used to rejection, not from men. Men usually found her irresistible. She glanced over at William, his sharp, clear features, his piercing eyes, his longish blond hair. She was as attractive as he was, or nearly, and her family had just as much money as his. Why was he so impervious to her charms?

She ran her finger over the gearshift. "You know what I've always found amusing about you, William?"

"Don't touch, Celine." He pushed her hand away. "I know all about your weird sense of fun. One minute you're fondling the shift, and the next you're steering us into a ditch."

She leaned back, gazing up at the sky, her hair blowing around her face. "I've always thought it was amusing that your name's White, but you dress all in black."

They stopped at an intersection.

"Don't you think that's amusing, William?" she purred. She waited for his usual sarcastic response, and when it didn't come, she straightened her head. William was staring to the right.

"What's the matter?" Celine snapped. "Why aren't we going?"

"Shut up," he ordered. "Someone's coming."

She followed his gaze. Just reaching the crossing was a blonde in a prim, long-skirted white cotton dress. She didn't stop at the corner to check for traffic but hurled herself across the road.

"Oh, I don't believe it." Celine groaned. "It's

191

like being followed by your own tail."

William was now looking to the left. "What is?"

Celine pointed to the fleeing girl. "That is." She sighed melodramatically. "And of course she's crying. I have never seen one woman cry so much in my life."

For almost the first time since he had picked her up, William was looking at her. "You know that girl?"

Celine fished a cigarette out of her bag. "Of course I know her. I live with her." She struck her lighter. "If you want to call it living."

The car glided into motion again. "What's her name?"

Celine turned her head, her eyes as sharp as a cat's. Could it possibly be true? Had the handsome, wealthy, and enigmatic William White rejected *her* only to be interested in Little Goody Two Shoes? "Elizabeth," she answered tonelessly.

"And you're her roommate." He looked over at her. "I guess it is a small world after all," he said with a smile.

I am going to get you for this, William White, Celine decided. *Just you wait. I am going to make you fall in love with me if it's the last thing I do.* She blew smoke in his face. *And then I'm going to break your ugly little heart.*

Chapter Ten

Jessica was sitting on the living-room floor, surrounded by sewing materials, hemming the skirt of her Halloween costume. She was amazed to discover that her classes weren't a total waste of time. After all, if it weren't for her freshman humanities course, she wouldn't have heard about the *Odyssey,* and she wouldn't have thought of going to the dance as Penelope.

She sighed, thinking once again of Mike McAllery—not that she thought about much else lately. Somehow Penelope, weaving by day and unweaving by night while she waited for the return of Odysseus, the husband she loved, seemed perfect. Penelope, like Jessica, was madly in love, steadfast and true. Like Jessica, she was separated from the man of her dreams by almost insurmountable obstacles. In Penelope's case a war; in Jessica's the fact that the man of her dreams wasn't particularly interested in her. But the best part about Penelope was that at the end of the story, she got Odysseus back.

Jessica leaned against the sofa, thinking about Penelope, running to meet her husband's ship, all her years of sacrifice and loneliness finally over. But when Odysseus stepped out on the deck, she saw Michael in black jeans and a rust-colored silk shirt, and instead of Penelope, she pictured herself running into his arms.

The ringing of the telephone disrupted the passionate kiss between her and Michael. Jessica's heart banged against her chest. Maybe it was him. *Don't be stupid,* she scolded herself as she reached for the phone. *You always think it's him and it never is.* She lifted the receiver, part of her still whispering, *Yeah, but maybe this time it really is.*

It was Steven. Her brother's voice was as warm and friendly as ever, but she knew him well enough to know after a few minutes that this wasn't just a casual call. Every time he finished one sentence, he started the next with "So." It was a dead giveaway.

"So," Steven said after she told him about her costume. "I saw you at the game the other day."

"Really?" She picked a piece of thread from the carpet. "Why didn't you come over and say hello?"

Steven's voice lost a little of its warmth. "You seemed pretty busy." He swallowed hard. "You were talking to Mike McAllery at the time."

The Jessica Wakefield early-warning system told

her that this was it. She kept her own voice casual. "I didn't know you knew Mike."

Usually her brother's laugh was a pleasant sound, but this one wasn't. "Jessica, everybody within a hundred-mile radius knows Mike McAllery. Especially if they're female or work for the police force."

Jessica stiffened. She'd had enough lectures from Isabella on the subject of Michael McAllery to be able to guess what was coming. "What are you trying to say, Steven? Is this your way of giving me a little brotherly advice?"

"I'll tell you exactly what I'm saying, Jess. Mike McAllery is bad news. He's wild, he's a womanizer, and though nobody's quite sure what he does for a living anymore, you don't have to be Einstein to figure out that he isn't selling Girl Scout cookies."

She was holding the receiver so hard that her hand was sweating. "What you're saying is that you know nothing about the man, but you've already judged him."

"No. What I'm saying is that you better stay away from him. This isn't advice, it's an order."

Enraged, she sat up on her knees, her face flushed. "You can't order me, Steven. I'm an adult now. I can see anybody I want."

"You may be an adult, but you're still my little sister!" He was shouting now. "I'm not going to sit back and watch you throw yourself at a piece of scum like Mike McAllery."

195

"How dare you!" She'd always been able to shout louder than he could. "How dare you say that! You don't even know him. You're just jealous because you could never be the man he is."

"I wouldn't want to be the man he is!" Steven shouted back. "And I don't want him hanging around my sister."

"Well, that's just too bad, isn't it?" she thundered. "Because, really, Steven, there isn't one little thing you can do to stop it." She slammed the phone down so hard that it fell off the table.

Jessica slumped against the couch, tears of rage filling her eyes. It wasn't bad enough that Mike didn't want her. Nobody wanted her to want him. She reached into the magazine rack and took out the one he'd been reading the day she found him lying on the couch and held it against her. "I'm not giving up," she said out loud. "I don't care what anybody says. I'm not giving up." Another small gray rectangle of paper fell out. Wiping her eyes on the sleeve of her blouse, she reached down and picked it up. How had she missed this the first time? It was his card. *Michael McAllery, 555-4343.*

"I don't believe this," Jessica whispered. "I've had his number all the time. He left it for me!" All the unhappiness and anger were instantly replaced with euphoria.

Holding the card against her heart, Jessica sank into the couch. "You just try and keep me away from him, Steven Wakefield," she said. "You just try."

         *   *   *

Tom was bent over the editing table, doing the rough cut of his feature about the psychic's predictions for Halloween night. He was dimly aware that the snack bar and the coffeehouse had been decorated with orange and black streamers and jack-o'-lanterns. He'd even noticed the paper skeletons in the cafeteria and the black cat taped to the door of his dorm. In classes he overheard people talking about masquerade parties and the Halloween dance, but none of that really meant anything to him. All Halloween meant to him was the final chapter in his mini-documentary: *What Happened That Night.*

Tom leaned back, rubbing his eyes. He was pleased with what he had so far. He'd interviewed the psychic, Barnabas Montoya, and several people who regularly consulted him, including the chief of police. Then he'd done an overview of the campus, intercutting interviews with students in which he'd asked them whether or not they believed the predictions, and ending with Tom himself standing in the empty gym of Xavier Hall, wondering what October 31 might bring.

He ran a hand through his hair. With a little luck, he might even get one of the local stations to pick up his story. "Some luck," he muttered to himself as he slid off his chair in search of a cup of coffee. "Guaranteed a local will take it if something awful does happen."

197

Not that Tom thought anything was going to happen. He'd spoken with a lot of people, and as far as he could tell, old Barnabas was no more than your average lucky guesser—and not always that. Tom had a hunch that the psychic was trying to drum up a little extra business for himself. In fact, when Tom actually sat down and talked to Montoya, his predictions for Halloween night were a lot more vague than those of the students at Sweet Valley University.

All over the campus people were saying that the killer would carry a knife, that his first victim would be a beautiful blonde, and that he'd strike just before midnight. One kid Tom talked to even described the psychopath in detail, saying he'd be dressed all in black with a black ski mask over his face. "What color shoes?" Tom had asked, but the kid hadn't seen the joke.

No one else saw the joke, either. They were all too busy egging each other on. That was why he'd wanted to do the documentary, to show how rumors get started and take on a life of their own.

Tom stared thoughtfully into his steaming mug of coffee. Doing the edit, he'd realized there was something about the whole business that was disturbing him in a real way, but he couldn't quite put his finger on what it was. Just a feeling. He didn't believe in Barnabas Montoya's killer, but he did believe something was going to happen—something nasty.

When Tom separated the actual prediction from the fantastic stories that had built up around it, there was one strand of rumor that gave him a chill. The blonde. Barnabas swore he'd never said anything about victims at all, but everyone had heard about the beautiful blonde. And no one remembered exactly where.

Tom put down his coffee and went back to the editing board. Maybe it was because when he thought of the blonde, he thought of Elizabeth Wakefield, but it disturbed him that this one detail should be so specific.

Tom glanced at his watch. He didn't have much time. Professor Sedder, the station adviser, had arranged for him to spend the rest of the afternoon training the new intern who had been recommended by the English department.

He hadn't even bothered to disguise his anger about this. "I can't believe we're getting a freshman," Tom had raged. "How can you expect me to waste my time training a freshman? Are you crazy? We hardly ever take on even sophomores." But Professor Sedder wasn't interested in Tom's complaints. He'd had the assurance of the head of English that this guy was really hot, a seasoned journalist with real style and flair.

Soon Tom was deep in his work again, his worries about blondes and his complaints about freshmen forgotten. He was so engrossed that he didn't know someone had come into the room until he felt a hand on his shoulder.

"Geez!" he snapped. "Why don't you knock?"

"I'm sorry," said a delicate female voice. "I didn't mean to startle you. Professor Sedder said I should just come in."

Tom turned around. And found himself staring into the beautiful blue-green eyes of Elizabeth Wakefield.

She smiled, and it was as though someone had turned up the lights. "It's you!" she said.

"You took the words right out of my mouth," Tom answered.

Elizabeth was in a good mood as she hurried back to the dorm, the package her mother had sent her tucked under her arm. In fact, she was in a great mood—the best she'd been in for weeks. And she had Tom Watts to thank. Since she'd started working with him at the TV station, she'd rediscovered the excitement she used to feel working on the *Oracle*, the Sweet Valley High paper.

How could I have forgotten how much I love reporting? she wondered as she opened the door to her room. How could she have forgotten how nice it was to work with someone who was funny, intelligent, and as excited about a story as she was?

Elizabeth sat down on the bed to open the parcel. She hadn't planned to go to the Halloween dance, but she was feeling so much more confident these past few days she'd asked her mother to send her the costume she'd worn last year, just in case she decided to go after all.

She lifted out the multicolored silk skirt and peasant blouse. Gypsies weren't supposed to be blond, but she knew she looked good in this outfit. Todd had certainly thought so last year. She remembered him grabbing her and pretending to run off with her.

Elizabeth quickly shook off the memory and stepped into the silk skirt. Something was wrong; she couldn't get it to close. Elizabeth stared at herself in the full-length mirror. She gave another tug on the waistband.

"I don't understand it," she said to her reflection. "Last year it fit me fine." She tried holding in her stomach, but still she couldn't get it to fasten. "But I've always been a perfect size six," she wailed. *"Always."*

Elizabeth turned to the side. Not anymore. If she was a perfect anything, it was an eight. Maybe even a ten. Now that she was looking, she could see that her hips and breasts were a little heavier; even her cheeks seemed full. She felt like one of those Before and After photographs in a women's magazines. Only, she was becoming Before.

"It's misery," she told herself. "I've been comforting myself with cookies and potato chips." She twisted around to get a look at her bottom. No, she decided, she hadn't been comforting herself. She'd been eating herself into a coma.

201

Elizabeth faced the mirror again, wondering if crying burned up any extra calories.

"Gypsy," Elizabeth mumbled as she stepped out of the skirt. "If I go as anything, it'll be a pumpkin." She picked up the skirt, flung it into the bottom of her closet, and threw herself on her bed.

Something crackled beside her. She looked over and saw the half-empty box of peanut-butter cookies she'd been eating while she studied last night. A sudden pang of longing attacked her.

Elizabeth reached for the box. What was one little peanut-butter cookie? She wouldn't have any more after that. Ever. And tomorrow she'd think about going on a diet. But right now she needed something to make her feel better.

Just as she put the cookie to her lips, a voice inside her head started screaming. *Drop that! Have you completely lost your mind? If you hadn't eaten so many boxes of cookies in the last few weeks, you wouldn't need to feel better. You'd still be a size six!*

Elizabeth sat up. The voice was right. Tomorrow was too late to start her diet. She'd been letting herself slide since she got to college, and it was time she stopped. It wasn't until she'd started her internship at the television station that she realized how bored she'd been. She'd been burying herself in her classes, thinking that because she was busy she was all right.

But her afternoons with Tom Watts had made her realize she was wrong. The thrill she used to

202

feel at *Oracle* meetings had come back to her, the buzz she got when she was working on a story.

Elizabeth put the cookie back in the box and stood up. Maybe it was time she faced things honestly. She tossed the box into the wastebasket.

Starting with her hips.

"But it doesn't make sense," Danny said over the din of the snack bar. "Why would the Sigmas start a rumor like that?"

Tom pointed a french fry at him. "You're the one who used to be a Sigma. You tell me."

Danny shook his head. "I can't. It doesn't make sense. When I was in the Sigmas, they were into climbing mountains and working out, not spreading psycho stories."

"When you were in the Sigmas, Peter the Horrible wasn't their president," Tom pointed out.

"You think that has something to do with it?"

Tom shrugged. He'd followed his feeling about the Halloween rumors and spent an afternoon in the cafeteria, asking everyone who came in what they'd heard and where. Most people had no idea, but a few of them said they'd heard about the blonde at a Sigma party. "If I'm right and it is the Sigmas who started all this, then you can bet Wilbourne's at the bottom of it."

Danny chewed thoughtfully on his burger. "If Wilbourne's at the bottom of it, then you can be sure it's not just a practical joke. You know what he's like. He did it for a reason, and you can bet your tape machine it won't be pleasant."

"You know him better than anyone." Tom picked up another fry. "You've outguessed him before. What do you think it could be?"

Danny laughed. "Well, that's easy. Peter only does anything for one of three reasons:ego, jealousy, or revenge."

"Ego, jealousy, or revenge," Tom repeated. "Now I just have to figure out which one it is."

"Sit still," Samantha ordered. "I can't do your eyes if you're wiggling." She shoved him back against the chair. "And stop blinking. You're going to be crooked."

Winston blinked as the eyeliner came toward him again. "You mean I'm going to be blind."

He couldn't understand how women put up with so much torture. So far he'd had his eyelashes curled, his eyebrows tweezed, his nails manicured—he felt as though he'd spent the last two hours on the rack. He'd always thought that women went to beauty parlors to relax and indulge themselves; now he realized they went to toughen up in case they were ever made prisoners of war.

Candy looked up from the sink, where she was putting her manicure set away. "Those nails are still tacky, Win. Don't go getting fluff on them."

"Winnie!" Debbie kneed him in the back. "Will you please relax? If I don't get this wig combed out right, you're going to look more like Harpo Marx than Shirley Temple."

"The only way I'm going to relax while Samantha's trying to dig my pupils out is if you knock me unconscious."

Shirley Temple had been the Sigmas' idea—and his dormmates had immediately taken it to their hearts. They all thought Shirley Temple was really cute. It could have been worse, he supposed. One of the other Sigma hopefuls had to go as Marilyn Monroe. At least Shirley Temple didn't wear heels.

"Men . . ." Debbie sighed. "You really are overly delicate, aren't you?"

"You mean they really are babies," said Candy.

"We are not babies," Winston said, trying hard to keep the pain out of his voice. Why did he spend half his time defending the entire male sex? "We're just not raised for self-mutilation, that's all."

Candy laughed. "No, guys like mutilating other people instead."

The bathroom door flew open with a bang. "I found it!" Anoushka came charging into the room. "I knew I had it somewhere."

"Watch it!" Winston whimpered as Samantha started glueing his lashes together.

This time she kicked him. "Sit still, Win. It wouldn't hurt if you'd cooperate a little."

"Sam's right." Debbie smacked him on the head with the comb. "Don't turn."

"Watch those nails!" Candy yelled.

"I want to see what Anoushka found."

"I've got the dress! I've got the perfect Shirley Temple dress!" Anoushka held up something short and white with red polka dots.

Good Lord, Winston thought. *She can't seriously think I'm going to wear that!*

"Isn't it perfect?" Anoushka demanded. "It's a good thing I brought some of my ice-skating costumes with me or we would have had a hell of a time finding the right dress."

"My middle name must be Lucky," Winston mumbled.

Anoushka grabbed his hand. "Come on!" she ordered. "Let's try this on you."

"Watch out for his hair!" Debbie shouted.

"Wait for me!" Denise Waters charged into the bathroom with a pair of red patent-leather shoes and white ankle socks in her hands.

Winston, almost on his feet, collapsed back onto the chair. He could not let Denise Waters see him in a skating dress. It was bad enough that she was seeing him with his face made up and blond sausage curls covering his head. Denise Waters was possibly the most beautiful girl he'd ever seen. There was no way he was putting on a dress designed for Minnie Mouse in front of her.

"Come on," Anoushka said. "Up!"

Denise winked at him. "I like your knees, Winnie. They're very attractive."

I'm not going to faint, Winston told himself.

I'm not going to be sick to my stomach. I'm going to act like this is fine. Like it's perfectly normal for the most stupendous girl on the continent to compliment my knees.

Anoushka tugged the dress over his head. "There!" She stepped back, Samantha and Debbie on one side of her, Denise and Candy on the other. "Well? What do you think?"

"Fantastic," Samantha said.

"You look great," said Debbie.

Candy blew him a kiss. "I've always liked guys in polka dots."

Denise put her arms around him. "I think I may have to stand guard over you tonight," she said. "If the psycho really is going to go for a blonde, I sure wouldn't want it to be you."

Isabella flicked her tail. "I don't really know Geoff Gordon," she said as she admired herself in the mirror. "He's one of those guy's guys, if you know what I mean. He's always riding something too fast or gunning something else down, but I guess he's all right." She fiddled with her whiskers. "Anyway, it's only one date, right? And he is a Sigma, so I guess that counts in his favor."

Jessica adjusted her robe with a sigh. "Yeah, I guess so." If she couldn't go to the Halloween dance with the man of her dreams, then she didn't really care if she went with King Kong. Or Geoff Gordon. Although Geoff was cute enough, Jessica's secret feeling was that he had less charisma than a stick insect.

Isabella raised one eyebrow, causing her to look even more like a cat than she already did. "And he isn't Mike McAllery," she added, as though reading Jessica's thoughts. "So that's another five points for him."

"I wish everybody would stop being so down on Mike," Jessica grumbled. "None of you have given him a chance."

Isabella pulled on her paws. "Giving Mike McAllery a chance if you're a woman would be like giving Davy Crockett a chance if you were a bear." Her expression became unusually serious. "I mean it, Jess, I could—"

Jessica jumped up as the phone rang. She didn't want to hear what Isabella thought about Mike. All she wanted to hear was his voice, asking her out, telling her how beautiful she was. She paused for just a second before picking up the receiver, praying that this time it would be him.

"Hello?" She held her breath.

There was the crackle of static and then, from somewhere that sounded very far away, a familiar voice. "Jess? Is that you?"

"Lila?" The last letter she'd had from Lila had arrived two days ago, saying she was fine but had been held up because of some business of her mother's and would be back in California within the next two weeks. "Lila, where are you?"

"I'm here." Lila laughed as though someone near her had said something funny. "Here in Italy."

Even though Lila was thousands of miles away and the connection was bad, Jessica could tell something was up.

"But why?" she demanded. "I thought you'd be on your way home by now."

"I thought so too." Lila laughed again. "But I guess I was wrong."

"What do you mean, you *guess* you were wrong? Lila, what's going on?"

The line crackled and Lila giggled. Jessica could just make out another voice, a man's voice, talking close to the phone in Italian.

"Are you ready?" Lila said. "Maybe you should sit down for this, Jess."

"Lila!"

There was another wave of static and then, almost drowning beneath it, Lila's screaming. "I got married, Jess! I got married yesterday!"

Jessica was certain she hadn't heard her right. Her best friend, a girl her own age, couldn't possibly have gotten married. *"What?"* she shrieked. "You did *what* yesterday?"

"I got married, Jess! He's wonderful. He's a count. His name's Tisiano Mond—" She broke off and Jessica could hear the other voice, the Italian voice, again. "I've got to go, Jess, they just announced our plane. We're on our way to Paris."

"But Lila . . ."

"I'll write, Jess, I promise I'll write. As soon as we get back from our honeymoon."

She heard a click and the line went dead. Jessica stood there for several seconds, staring at the receiver, trying to catch her breath, trying to take in what she'd just heard. Her best friend, Lila Fowler, was a married woman. A married woman living in Italy with a count.

"Jess?" Isabella was slipping on her jacket. "Get moving, will you? We're supposed to be meeting the guys downstairs in three minutes."

Jessica didn't move. Lila was flying to Paris on her honeymoon with an Italian count, and she was going to a Halloween dance with a guy who had the foot of a rabbit he'd shot hanging from his rearview mirror. Lila was a real woman now—a real woman with a real man. And Jessica was still a kid going to dances.

"Earth to Jessica!" Isabella boomed. "Let's go!"

A pang ran through her as she realized how much she'd missed Lila. Lila would have been on her side with Mike. She wouldn't have tried to turn Jessica against him; she would have helped her get him.

Slowly, Jessica put down the phone and picked up her bag. "I'm ready," she said. *I am ready,* she thought as she followed Isabella out the door. Ready to get what she wanted, just as Lila had.

Chapter
Eleven

The Xavier Hall gym was draped in jack-o'-lanterns and skull lights and black-and-orange paper chains. Waterfalls of colored cellophane dripped from the ceiling, and ghosts and witches dangled in midair. Celine stood in the doorway like an actress about to take the stage. Although she'd had several invitations to the dance, she'd decided to go by herself. She didn't want some guy who thought he owned her cramping her style.

Across the room, dressed as Count Dracula, she could see William White, looking so handsome and smug that he stood out against the crowd like a moon against a black sky. No, she definitely didn't want anybody getting in her way tonight.

Celine's bracelets jangled as she adjusted one of her thin silk scarves across her breasts. She had chosen her costume with care. She'd wanted to make a statement. She moistened her lips with her tongue and shook out her hair as she slowly began to make her way across the gym. She'd wanted something that would melt every man at the dance, even the cold-blooded Mr. White. She could feel the male eyes following her as she walked, her scarves trailing, her bracelets tinkling, and her movements tempting. A satisfied smile appeared on her beautiful face. That was what she'd wanted, and that was what she'd achieved.

Or almost achieved. Even Celine could see that the look William gave her as she came up to him was not exactly the look of a man helplessly melting with desire.

"Let me guess," he said. "Salomé."

She let one of her scarves fall carelessly across his arm. He was bluffing. Even he couldn't be so immune to her. He was human, wasn't he? He was made of flesh and blood. "How clever of you," she said. "You got it in one."

His eyes moved from her gold sandals to the beads woven through her hair. "Subtlety has never been your strong point, Celine," he said. "Whose head is it you're planning to serve on a platter?"

Celine laughed, brushing against him. "You don't need to worry," she said softly. "I like your head just where it is."

He picked up his glass of punch. "I wasn't worried," he said as he turned away. "You're the last person I'd lose my head over."

She watched her scarf fall from his arm. Did he

really think she would give up that easily? Did he really think he could resist her forever? Celine took a step to follow him, but then she saw Peter Wilbourne III, dressed as a skeleton, coming toward her. Peter might not be William White, but he was handsome and powerful and wealthy. And she could tell from the smile on his face that he appreciated her costume in the way she'd intended.

You'll do for now, Celine decided as she looked his way. What William needed was a little competition. A challenge. She knew he was enough like her to want what he thought he couldn't have, to want something that belonged to someone else. Celine looked straight into Peter's eyes. *Yes, you'll do just fine.*

I should have stayed in the dorm, Elizabeth decided as she entered the dance behind a clown, a flower, and a box of cornflakes. *I was crazy to come.* She tugged at her costume. In the end she'd decided to dress as Justice. She'd made a scale out of cardboard painted gold and a blindfold from an old white scarf with eyeholes cut in. For the gown, she'd wound herself in a white sheet. She'd thought that it might hide the fact that she was no longer as slender as she used to be, but she had the suspicion that the effect was more like Frosty the Snowman without the hat and scarf.

You don't have to stay, she told herself as she hovered at the edge of the dance. *You can just check it out and leave.* Her eyes searched the

213

crowded room. Deep in her heart, she knew exactly why she'd come. She was hoping to see Todd.

"I really am crazy," she mumbled to herself as she pushed her way a little farther into the room. What was the use of running into Todd? He was right: things weren't working between them; they were better off apart. But then she felt someone staring at her, and her heart began to race. *Todd*, she thought. *He's here. He's looking for me, too.*

Unable to stop herself, she turned to see who it was. It was a guy in a black bodysuit and hood, skeletal bones painted on it in pale blue, luminous paint. His black half-mask was hanging around his neck, so she could see he was watching her intensely, but not with yearning or regret; he was watching her with loathing. Elizabeth raised her chin and stared back. She wasn't going to let a creep like Peter Wilbourne III intimidate her.

Swinging her cardboard scales of justice, Elizabeth marched toward a group of girls she recognized from one of her classes. She'd hang out with them for a few minutes, then go home.

When she reached them, however, they were so engrossed in their own conversation that she felt too shy to interrupt. Elizabeth stepped back against the wall, trying to give the impression that she was waiting for someone. Her eyes started scouring the room again. Winston, dressed as Shirley Temple, was doing a tap dance for a bunch of laughing Sigmas. Jessica was in the middle of the room, locked in the embrace of a large guy also dressed as a skeleton. Elizabeth gave her sheet another tug. Jessica, too, was wearing a white sheet, but on her it looked svelte and seductive. Feeling spectacularly unattractive, Elizabeth turned her gaze in the other direction.

I don't believe it! Elizabeth stared across the room. The man from the library, the one with the piercing eyes and the cool good looks, really had come as Dracula. But what was even more amazing was that he was talking to Celine. At least, Celine was talking to him. *What could an intelligent guy like that see in her?* Elizabeth wondered.

Very little, apparently. Elizabeth felt a small zing of joy run through her as he suddenly stalked away, leaving Celine standing by herself. Elizabeth just couldn't resist a tiny smile. *That's better,* she thought. The smile grew when Peter Wilbourne materialized beside Celine. *That's much better.* Celine and the Sigma president were a perfect couple. They were both arrogant and they were both stupid. It should give them plenty to talk about.

Elizabeth's eyes sought out Dracula again. "I'm glad you don't like Celine," she whispered to herself. But she didn't ask why.

"Is Elizabeth dancing with that oaf Geoff Gordon?" Mark asked as he handed the gypsy beside him a glass of punch. He frowned. "Talk about going for the wrong person on the rebound.

215

Geoff Gordon's got to be at least two rungs behind the chimp on the evolutionary ladder."

Enid shook her head. "That's not Elizabeth, that's Jessica." She nodded toward the other side of the room. "That's Elizabeth over there." *By herself,* she added silently, feeling a slight twinge of guilt. "I'd think you'd be able to tell them apart," she teased. "After all, you did spend a whole evening with Jessica."

"Two hours and twenty-six minutes," Mark corrected her. "And two hours and twenty-five of those minutes were spent thinking about you." He slipped his arm around her shoulders. "Anyway, you must admit that their costumes are almost identical. Anybody would have trouble telling them apart."

Enid leaned against him. Even though she didn't want them to, her eyes kept going back to Elizabeth. Enid's life had been so busy and exciting since school began that it had been easy not to think about Elizabeth. But now she couldn't help wondering what had gone wrong. How could so many years of closeness disappear so quickly?

"It's a shame about Elizabeth and Todd, isn't it?" Mark asked, obviously thinking similar thoughts. "From what I understand, they really went through a lot together. They really loved each other." He rested his head on hers. "They had the kind of relationship I could imagine having with . . . with someone like you."

Enid turned to look in his eyes, Elizabeth and her problems fading once again. "Maybe we should dance," she said. "I think this punch is going to your head."

A lean figure, all in black from his boxer's shoes to his knit cap, moved unseen through the night, circling Xavier Hall as silently as a bat. When he reached the rear entrance he stopped, listening.

Tom had chosen his costume carefully. He couldn't risk anything bright or flamboyant, or anything that could be easily spotted in the dark. Tom hadn't come to the Halloween dance to have a good time. He'd come to keep an eye on Elizabeth. Maybe he was crazy, but if there was going to be a beautiful blond victim tonight, he was going to make sure it wasn't her.

Satisfied that there was no one in hiding outside, Tom slipped soundlessly through the door. As soon as he reached the gym, his eyes began to search the crowd for the pale figure in the flowing white robes, but all he seemed to see were skeletons. There were skeletons by the refreshment table. Skeletons by the front door. Skeletons dotted across the dance floor. Tom frowned. *And they're all Sigmas*. Obviously, he wasn't the only one who wanted anonymity tonight.

All at once his eyes caught a flash of white and gold in the center of the room. Tom's stomach knotted and his heart did a double flip. Her back

217

was to him, but there she was, in the arms of one of the Sigma skeletons.

"What's she doing with Gordon the Moron?" Tom muttered. Talk about dicing with death; there was Elizabeth, dancing with it. It was a good thing he wasn't the type to get involved, or he'd just go over there and drag her away from Geoff.

While Tom watched, his heart pounding and his jaw set, the couple turned. "It's not her!" he whispered aloud. He'd made a mistake. That wasn't Elizabeth, that was Jessica. For the first time all evening, Tom smiled. *I knew she was too smart to go out with a dork like that.*

Almost laughing with relief, Tom resumed his search. And then he saw her, standing all alone at the other side of the gym. Tom's heart did another flip. How could he mistake Jessica for her? They might be identical twins, but there was something about Elizabeth that made her stand out from everyone else, even from someone who looked just like her.

Tom stared at the face that seemed to have been burned into his memory. He'd assumed that Elizabeth would have a date tonight and that he'd just watch her from afar. But she clearly didn't. *It's not like I'm trying to pick her up or anything,* Tom told himself as he slowly started to cross the room. *But it'll be a lot easier to keep her safe if I'm right beside her.*

Halfway across the gym, Tom saw something that

made him stop in his tracks. Three skeletons were slipping out one of the exits, and Tom was pretty sure that the one in the lead was Peter Wilbourne. *Now what are they up to?* he wondered, torn between going to Elizabeth and following them.

Whatever the Sigmas were up to, he knew it was trouble. Tom looked around for Danny. If he was going to follow the Sigmas, maybe he should at least have a little moral support.

Suddenly the lights started flickering. A few nervous shrieks rose above the general din. Winston looked at his watch. It was getting close to the bewitching hour, when the psychic had predicted the killer would strike.

"What's the matter, Win?" Bill asked, giving him a playful shove. "You think the psychopath's coming to get you?"

Winston grinned back. "Of course not. I don't believe those stories."

"Well, some people do," Bill said with a laugh as the lights flickered again.

Winston looked toward the far exit. Three guys masked and dressed as skeletons were slipping through the door. A vaguely curious thought raced through Winston's brain. There were quite a few skeletons at the dance—in fact, most of the Sigmas, including Bill, seemed to have come as skeletons.

"That wasn't Peter Wilbourne and his pals leaving, was it?" he asked, hoping he was making it sound like a joke. Peter Wilbourne didn't seem like the type to be scared by a few rumors.

Bill winked. "Maybe."

For the first time Winston seriously wondered if the prediction might come true. After all, if a bunch of macho guys like the Sigmas left because the lights were flickering . . .

"Maybe?" he repeated.

Bill laughed. "Chill out, Win," he said. "It's Halloween, remember? Haven't you ever heard of trick or treat? Maybe the brothers are going to play a little trick on someone."

Winston pushed a curl out of his face, hoping his relief wasn't showing. "Oh, right," he said. "I figured it must be something like that."

Bill put a hand on his shoulder. "Sure you did, Win."

"No, I did, really," Winston protested. Suddenly Bill tightened his grip.

"Do my eyes deceive me?" Bill asked. "Or is the beautiful Anoushka heading our way?"

"Anoushka?" Just when he'd thought it was safe to hang out in public, along came Anoushka to ruin everything. Panic galloped through Winston at an alarming rate. "Where?"

Bill released him. "Right here."

She was dressed as a gunslinger in a black suit, a black cowboy hat, and black cowboy boots. She looked incredible.

"Winnie!" She hurled herself into his arms.

"Don't you think he looks wonderful?" she demanded, turning to Bill. "I was watching him shave the other morning, and I decided he'd make a wonderful girl."

Bill frowned. "Are you two . . . uh . . . together?" he asked, looking from one to the other.

"Sure. We live together." Anoushka started giggling. "Let me tell you," she said, rolling her eyes, "it took hours to get him ready for tonight."

"What?" Bill's smile stayed on Anoushka, but his eyes shifted over to Winston.

"Oops!" Anoushka clapped her hand over her mouth. "I think maybe somebody spiked my punch. I seem to be talking too much."

Bill brought his eyes back to her.

Winston put a hand on Anoushka and tried propelling her away. "You heard her," he said. "She's drunk."

"Oh, please, Winnie, I'm hardly tipsy." She pushed him off. She gave Bill a conspiratorial wink. "Winnie has this big thing about living in Oakley Hall," she told him. "He wants to keep it a secret."

Winston felt his entire blood supply rush to his feet.

Bill turned to him. "*You* live in Oakley?"

As far as Jessica was concerned, the psychic's prediction had come true. There was a psychotic loose at the Halloween dance. Only his weapon wasn't a knife, it was probing hands and a filthy

221

mouth—and he happened to be her date.

"You know what I like best about you, Jessie?" Geoff's voice was thick and low in her ear.

Jessica tried to pull away, but he was holding her tightly.

"Your body." His hand slid down her back again, trying to find a spot not protected by folds of sheet. "That was the first thing I noticed about you, that body."

She reached for his hand and wrapped her own around it. "The first thing I noticed about you is that your ears are very close together," she whispered back. He wasn't listening.

"Not that you can see much of your body in that costume," he was saying. "What are you supposed to be, some Greek god or something?"

"Or something," Jessica mumbled, willing the music to end. At least she had a good idea now of what Penelope had to put up with while she waited for Odysseus to come home: dozens of Geoff Gordons trying to get her to dance too close.

"You know what you should've come as?" His voice was husky. "You should've come as a harem girl. You know, one of those belly dancers? You would have looked great."

And you should have come as Jack the Ripper, Jessica thought. Maybe she could say she was going to the ladies' room and sneak back to her room. She'd be better off sitting by herself in the dorm watching some Halloween horror movie than being here with this goon, living a Halloween horror of her own.

His tongue, a fat, sluglike thing, started twisting its way into her ear. "Why don't we go somewhere you could take that stupid costume off?" he half whispered, half moaned.

This time, by applying a little discreet pressure with her knee, Jessica managed to put a few inches between them. "I don't want to go. I want to stay here." She pressed her arms against his chest.

"But I don't." The music stopped, but instead of stepping back he put his hand flat on the base of her spine. "I want to go somewhere and take that sheet off you." His tongue darted for her ear, but she dodged it.

Jessica's temper finally exploded. *I want to go somewhere and take that sheet off you? Was he kidding?* This time she gave him such a fast, hard shove that he lost his balance and staggered backward a few steps. "I'm not going anywhere with you," she informed him. "I wouldn't go anywhere with you if you were the last guy on the planet."

He lunged forward, grabbing her wrist hard. "Oh yes, you are," he leered. "And you're going now. I'm tired of this stupid dance. I want to have a private party. Just you and me."

She tried to free her hand, but he was twisting the skin so hard that it hurt. "You can have your private party by yourself," she hissed. "How clear can I make it? I don't want to have anything to do with you."

223

The music started up again, and his arm wrapped around her like the tentacle of an octopus. "I don't care what you want. You came out with me, and you're leaving with me." He pushed against her. "You've been leading me on all night, Jessie. You can't stop now."

His mouth was to her neck, which meant that her mouth was to his neck. But she wasn't going to waste her breath telling him again that her name was Jessica, not Jessie. Instead, she bit him as hard as she could. With a cry of pain he released her, and she started pushing her way through the crowd.

He was right on her heels. "So you like to fight, do you?" he asked, grabbing her from behind. "I like a girl who likes to fight. Let's go outside where we can really get down to it." Holding her so she could barely breathe, he started steering her toward the exit.

Suddenly Jessica was really frightened. Once he got her away from the dance, she would have no chance of escape. She searched desperately for a face she knew. Or even a face she didn't know. Why was there never a knife-wielding psychopath around when you really wanted one?

Geoff shoved her out the door, into the lobby of the gym, mumbling obscenities all the while, his hand trying to find a way into her sheet.

She would scream, that's what she'd do. She'd start screaming like crazy. There were enough people milling around that someone would hear her and realize she wasn't just fooling around. The closer they got to the front doors, the more panicked she felt.

Jessica opened her mouth to let out a wail, but suddenly Geoff let go.

"I don't think she really wants to go with you," a deep, strong voice said right behind her.

Jessica swung around. Danny Wyatt was standing beside Geoff, holding him by the arm.

Geoff pulled himself free. "It's none of your business, Wyatt." He smiled slyly. "We're just having a little lover's argument." The slyness eased into menace. "If you know what's good for you, you'll just go back to whatever hole you crawled out of and leave me and Jessie alone."

Danny looked at Jessica. "Is that true, Jess? Do you want me to go away, or is this guy giving you a hard time?"

Jessica moved toward Danny. "He's giving me a hard time, Danny. He's—"

"Don't listen to her . . ."

Geoff made a grab for Jessica, but Danny stepped between them.

"Jessica doesn't want to go with you, Gordon," he said calmly. "So maybe you should leave."

"Don't let him talk to you like that," said another voice from the side.

Jessica looked around, her panic rising again. She'd been so focused on Geoff and Danny that

225

she hadn't noticed they'd been joined by several other skeletons. She looked around at the faces, expecting to see Peter Wilbourne's, but didn't.

"Don't worry about Danny," another skeleton said. "He's not going to do anything."

Danny eyed them uneasily. Jessica studied the side of his face. It was fear that she saw there, but somehow it wasn't the fear of getting hurt in a fight. It was something worse.

She touched his back. "Let's just go, Danny."

Danny nodded. "I'm taking Jessica home now," he said quietly. "You and your friends can just step aside."

The Sigmas started laughing. "Oooh. You're scaring us."

Jessica slid her hand into Danny's.

The punch was so sudden that Danny staggered back, losing his grip on her.

Jessica screamed.

The skeletons laughed again.

This time, Geoff managed to get hold of Jessica and yanked her to his chest. "I'm warning you, black boy," he hissed. "If you don't mind your own business, you're really going to be sorry."

One of the Sigmas gave Danny a shove from the side. "Wyatt's not black, he's yellow."

Jessica couldn't look into Danny's eyes because she was afraid of what she would see there, so she looked at his hands instead. They were so tightly clenched his knuckles were white. He was going to back down again, she could sense it. The Sigmas could sense it too.

Geoff patted her hip. "Let's get out of here, baby." He smiled at Danny. "I think your savior would rather go back to his room and play solitaire."

Jessica looked at Danny, her eyes filled with tears.

"Let her go," Danny said.

One of the Sigmas reached out and ruffled his hair. "You're scaring us," he taunted.

"Let her go."

The Sigmas just laughed.

Winston stared back at Bill, every cell in his body as frozen as a bar of ice cream. It was all over. It was done. He was back to being Winston the loser, the clown. In about ten minutes, as soon as Bill stopped laughing and went back to his friends, the Sigmas would all know that Winston Egbert lived in a female dorm with a bunch of girls who borrowed his stuff and called him Winnie.

"You live in Oakley?" Bill asked again.

Winston nodded, waiting for the laughter. *Come on, Bill. Let's get it over with.*

It took several seconds for Winston to realize that Bill wasn't laughing. He wasn't even smiling.

"Winston," Bill prodded, "is Anoushka saying that *you* live in Oakley Hall with two hundred girls?"

Winston looked up in astonishment. The tone in Bill's voice wasn't ridicule, it was awe. And the

227

look on his face wasn't mocking, either. The look on his face was pure envy.

Winston stood up tall. Suddenly he had an incredible, wonderful realization. The other guys wouldn't think he was a sissy because his dorm-mates shaved their legs and rarely played contact sports. They would think he was as lucky as a fox in a henhouse. Why hadn't he thought of this?

Winston slipped a companionable arm around Anoushka and smiled. "A hundred ninety-eight, actually, Bill." He winked. "Not that I've had the time to count them all personally, of course."

Tom stopped abruptly in the lobby. He'd found the Sigmas. A bunch of them anyway. And he'd found Danny, too. He'd walked in upon a scene so charged he could feel the violence in the air. Geoff Gordon held Jessica Wakefield by the wrist, and he and his fellow Sigmas surrounded Danny.

"Danny!" he heard Jessica cry as the Sigmas closed in. "Oh, God!"

Tom felt his body tense, poised for a fight. He knew this could get ugly. They weren't just threatening Danny this time. He studied Danny's face and saw there was a strange look of calm.

And then Danny's face changed. Before Tom knew what had happened, Danny had hauled off and punched Geoff with such force that Geoff staggered back against the wall and fell to the ground.

The other Sigmas were even more surprised

than Tom was. They seemed to be frozen. Danny, ready to strike. "Does anybody have anything else they'd like to say to me?"

Nobody did.

He turned to leave, giving a last look at Geoff, who was getting shakily to his feet, his nose and mouth already grotesquely swollen. "Don't mess with me, man. Ever."

Danny spotted Tom at the door. Their eyes met and Danny just shrugged. "It's not that those morons are worth fighting," Danny explained, as the two of them walked out into the cool night. He smiled a small, crooked smile. "But if my brother saw the way they were messing with me, he'd take them all himself. And the man can't even walk."

Jessica knew she should stop and thank Danny, but all she really wanted was to get away from the dance and Xavier Hall as quickly as she could. She fled, not even bothering to try to hide her tears.

Just as she burst through the doors of Xavier and into the black night, she thought she heard someone whispering urgently, but then the night was silent again.

Looking neither left nor right, Jessica ran down the path that led to the dark parking lot. At the bottom she stopped, thinking she heard someone talking again. "Hello? Is somebody there?" The only answer was the rustling of the wind through the trees.

Out of the corner of her eye, Jessica thought she saw something move in the bushes.

"Elizabeth," she heard a voice hiss, so low it was almost inaudible.

"Who's there?" she demanded, trying to keep her voice from shaking. She peered into the dark. "I know someone's there," she bluffed. "I—"

The arm was around her neck, choking off her air before she knew what had happened—before she had a chance to scream.

Elizabeth looked at her watch again, trying to pretend she hadn't been standing against this wall, completely alone, for the past hour.

Why had she ever come to this dance? Just because a few hours of working at the TV station had made her forget how awful things really were? Just because she thought Tom Watts would be here and they'd be able to talk and joke the way they did at the studio? Just because, way at the back of her mind, she'd half hoped that with everyone in disguise she might lose some of her inhibitions, that it might be possible to patch things up with Enid, or Jessica, or even Todd?

Well, she'd been wrong. Neither Enid nor Jessica had given any sign that they saw her, even though she'd tried to catch their attention. Eventually, she'd stopped trying. She didn't need to torture herself by seeing how radiant and happy Enid was with her new boyfriend. And as for Todd, neither he nor Tom Watts seemed to have come to the dance at all.

It was time to give up. Elizabeth moved toward the exit.

And that was when she saw him. It was a sight that chilled her to the bone. Todd was deep in a kiss with a willowy redhead. A girl named Lauren Hill, who Elizabeth recognized from her writing class. They were oblivious to the party around them—and anyone who might be watching them.

For a second Elizabeth felt nothing, and then it was as though a herd of cattle had stampeded through her heart. Throwing her paper scales to the ground, she rushed toward the exit.

I hate college. I hate it here. I wish I'd never come. Her eyes flooded with tears as she pushed her way across the crowded gym. *I just want to go home.*

"Well, what have we here?" a high, threatening voice demanded. "Could this possibly be the blonde of my dreams?"

Jessica struggled fruitlessly against him. "Let go!" she gasped. "Let me go!"

His laugh was high and threatening too. "Oh, I don't think so. I don't think that will be possible. First I need to teach you a little lesson about respect."

She thought she saw the glint of steel in the hand that wasn't pressed around her throat. *Oh, God. It was him, the psychopath!* The psychic's prediction had been true after all.

"Please . . ." she begged, almost speechless with terror. "Please, I—"

"Blondes are so troublesome, aren't they?" he cackled. "And you're the most troublesome of all." He tightened his grip.

"Elizabeth! Elizabeth, wait!"

At the sound of Tom's voice, Elizabeth started running faster. The sight of Todd kissing someone else had brought all the loneliness and misery she'd felt in these first disastrous weeks of college right to the surface. Her heart lay in shreds.

She didn't want to talk to Tom now. She didn't want anyone to come near her. She wanted to be alone, in the dark, where she could cry herself into a blank, numb sleep. She threw her weight against the heavy exit door and came out into the cold, black night.

"Elizabeth!" His grip was so strong and so sudden that she had to stop. "Elizabeth, please. I don't think you should go out there by yourself."

Keeping her back to him, she tried to shake herself free. "Tom, don't. I—I have to get out of here."

"Just let me walk you back to your dorm. I just want to make sure that you're safe."

Elizabeth broke free, walking away from him as quickly as she could, her white robe flapping around her ankles. "I'll be fine, Tom. I can get across campus on my own."

"Listen to me for a minute, will you? I'm worried the Sigmas are up to something. It's no secret that Peter Wilbourne's had it in for you since the night of the Theta party. He's not the kind of guy to forgive and forget."

How ironic life was. Her best friend, her sister, and the boy she thought was her one true love hadn't given her a thought in weeks, and here was a virtual stranger worrying about her. The odd thing was that instead of making her feel better, it made her feel worse. Instead of making her feel gratitude, it made her feel even sadder.

"I have to go," she gasped, trying to keep her voice from breaking.

Tom grabbed her shoulders and held her. He looked into her face, and she saw more compassion and care in his eyes than she had seen since she got to college. "Please, Elizabeth, tell me what's wrong. I want to . . . I—I—"

The tears were about to come. And when they did, she knew she wouldn't be able to stop them. They'd go on forever. She broke away. "Please just leave me alone."

Elizabeth ran as fast as she could. All the way back to Dickenson Hall and room 28, tears streaming down her cheeks, her chest heaving.

At the entrance to the dorm, she turned back. She heard a rustling noise and saw a figure like a shadow disappearing into the trees. It was Tom. He had followed her all the way home to make sure she was safe.

She called out her thanks in a shaky voice, but he was already gone.

Jessica tried to scream, but the hand over her mouth muffled the sound. *Please. Oh, God, somebody help me.* Her terror had made her body numb.

And then she heard another voice. A calm, confident voice. "Leave her alone, you bastard."

Jessica felt as though she were being hurled from a nightmare to a dream. Maybe terror was making her hallucinate. Maybe he'd already killed her and this was the afterworld. Because she was sure that was Michael McAllery's voice. She'd recognize it anywhere. There couldn't be two men in the world who sounded like that.

The grip around her neck tightened, and she felt herself being dragged into the woods. *Michael! Is it you?*

Suddenly her attacker staggered backward as Mike pulled him off her. It broke the spell of Jessica's fear. She kicked back at her attacker as hard as she could and freed herself of the arm around her neck. She watched as Mike pulled the man in the ski mask to face him and punched him so hard he fell backward to the ground.

Jessica was feeling so many conflicting emotions, from shock and relief to hatred and love, that she couldn't think to speak, but her heart was shouting *Mike! It really is you!*

She wasn't dead and she wasn't hallucinating.

She was alive and Michael McAllery had come to her rescue, just as he had in her dreams.

"Don't touch her again or I will kill you," Michael said calmly. "And tell that to your buddies out there in the bushes." He stepped back slightly, his handsome face in an easy smile.

And suddenly Jessica felt Michael's arms around her, holding her close as he led her down the path back into the light. "It's all right," he kept whispering in her ear. "I'm here. Nobody's ever going to hurt you again."

Jessica wiped tears from her eyes, the terror in her heart replaced by joy. She wrapped her arms around him.

If she'd had any doubts about why she'd come to college, they were gone now. This was why: this man, this moment; the future they promised.

"Come on, Jess." Mike brushed the hair back from her face. "Let's get out of here. Let's go home."

She closed her eyes as the lips she'd been dreaming of for so long touched hers at last. *This is it*, she thought. *This is my destiny*.

SWEET VALLEY UNIVERSITY

Love, Lies, and Jessica Wakefield

Written by
Laurie John

Created by
FRANCINE PASCAL

BANTAM BOOKS
NEW YORK · TORONTO · LONDON · SYDNEY · AUCKLAND

For Mia Pascal Johansson

"How can you sit there, gazing into space like that?" Isabella Ricci demanded, groaning dramatically. "It's Friday night. Gorgeous, sophisticated young college women like us are supposed to be out partying on Friday night, not sitting in their dorm twiddling their thumbs."

Does she think I don't know that? Jessica wondered. She had started her countdown to the weekend on Monday morning. But she couldn't trust herself to answer her roommate right away. She wasn't sure she could speak without bursting into tears. Here it was Friday—a night when no one even *pretended* to do any work—and she, Jessica Wakefield, was staring at a wall. As much as she liked Isabella, she was not the person Jessica wanted to be spending the evening with. The person she wanted was tall, dark, and dangerously handsome. The person she wanted was Michael

1

McAllery—but at the moment it didn't seem as though Michael McAllery wanted her.

Isabella was looking at her expectantly. "I'm not twiddling my thumbs," Jessica finally said. *I'm torturing myself,* she added silently, *wondering where he is right now.* And wondering whether or not he was alone.

"Oh, no?" Isabella raised one perfectly sculpted eyebrow. "Maybe you're right. Twiddling would be too much activity. You haven't moved at all. You've been sitting there for almost an hour, staring at the wall."

"Thinking," Jessica said by way of explanation. Much to Jessica's relief, Isabella didn't ask her *what* she was thinking. Because Isabella wouldn't have approved. Isabella didn't know much more about the enigmatic Mike McAllery than Jessica did, but insisted everything she did know was bad.

"Well, I was thinking too," Isabella said, shaking her dark, tousled hair. "I mean, what's wrong with the guys on this campus? Have aliens cut off their testosterone supply? How can two of the sexiest, most sophisticated, most desirable women at Sweet Valley University not have dates on a Friday night?"

I wish I knew, thought Jessica. *I wish I knew how he could say he'd call and just not. Not even to make up some excuse.* Her attention went back to the wall. Was it something she'd said? Something she'd done? Had he met someone he thought was pret-

2

tier, sometime between Wednesday and today?

"Jessica! Are you listening to me?"

Jessica dragged her mind back to her roommate. She put on one of her best cheerleader smiles. "You could have had a date," she reminded Isabella. "In fact, you could have had two dates, if I remember correctly. Didn't that hunk on the wrestling team ask you out? And the graduate student who works in the bookstore?"

Sexy, sophisticated Isabella stuck out her tongue. "The hunk has muscles where his brains should be, and the guy in the bookstore wears mohair." She gave Jessica a critical look. "Anyway, what about you? A different guy called you every day this week."

In the past Jessica had been interested in every good-looking man she met. If three different guys had asked her out for the weekend, she would have gone out with all of them. But now there was only one man Jessica wanted to see.

"They were all dorks," Jessica said dismissively.

"You mean you didn't want to go out with any of them." Isabella's look became serious. "You'd rather sit around here waiting for the mystery man, Mike McAllery, to call."

Jessica scowled. Isabella hadn't been fooled after all. It was bad enough when Jessica's identical twin sister, Elizabeth, knew what she was thinking without being told, but having Isabella do it was too much. They weren't even related.

3

"What makes you think I'm waiting for Mike?" she asked innocently.

Isabella made a face. "Oh, give me a break, will you, Jess? Ever since he rescued you from that goon at the Halloween dance, you've been moping around like Mike McAllery's water and you're dying of thirst."

"I have not."

"Oh, yes, you have." Isabella hurled herself from the sofa. "I'm not saying I'm much better, turning down someone who looks like a body double for the Terminator just because I'm hoping Tom Watts will ask me out. But at least Tom is a nice guy. He's not a drinking, womanizing—"

"Stop it!" Jessica put her hands over her ears. "Stop it, Isabella. I mean it. I'm sick of you and my brother, Steven, trying to turn me against Mike. You're wrong about him. He's kind, and caring, and thoughtful. If you could have seen the way he handled that thug who tried to scare me you'd know that you're wrong." *If you could feel how he kisses me, you'd know you're wrong,* she added silently. She scowled at Isabella. "For all you know, Isabella, Mike's had an accident or something, and right this minute he's lying in a hospital too hurt to call and tell me what's happened."

Isabella rolled her intelligent gray eyes. "You really are too much, you know that?" She came over and sat down on the arm of Jessica's chair. "Jess," she said, her voice suddenly gentle. "I'm not trying

4

to turn you against Mike. I mean that. And neither is Steven. We're just concerned about you, that's all. Mike McAllery's out of your league. Why can't you see that? This guy's like Jesse James. He's wild and romantic, but you wouldn't want to depend on him to pick up the milk on his way home." She put a hand on Jessica's shoulder. "And anyway, if he's so caring and thoughtful, why are you sitting here waiting for the phone to ring?"

In her mind, Jessica played back the end of her last date with Mike. His arms were around her, his lips were on hers, his breath was warm against her skin. *I'll see you,* he had said. *I'll call.* She fought back the threat of tears. "He didn't say exactly when he'd call, Isabella. He is busy, you know. He's not just a college kid. He's got other things to do."

"I'm sure he does," Isabella said knowingly.

"Business," Jessica snapped, her eyes flashing.

Isabella held up her hands. "All right, all right. I don't want to fight about Mike; he's not worth it." She stood up. "What say you and I go out and get a pizza? Just because we don't have dates doesn't mean we can't go out and have a good time."

Jessica looked up at Isabella in disbelief. *Go out now? What if he calls? What if he decides to stop by?* a voice in her head was screaming.

"You go," she said calmly. "I'm not really hungry."

Isabella put her hands on her hips. "Not really hungry? Jessica, you haven't eaten anything since breakfast. Since when can't you be tempted by a pineapple pizza with two kinds of cheese?"

"No, really." Jessica yawned, not meeting Isabella's gaze. "I'm tired. It's been a long week. I just want to stay here and relax."

"Jessica," Isabella said, enunciating each syllable. "You cannot spend the rest of your life in this room, waiting for Mike to show up. You can't let him call all the shots. You have to—"

"I'm not letting him call all the shots, Isabella," Jessica cut in. "Really. I just don't feel like going out. I'm exhausted."

"Snack bar," Isabella said. "That isn't as far as the pizza parlor. You can take the phone off the hook so he thinks you're talking to someone, and leave a note on the door in case he does come by."

But what if he calls the operator and finds that the line isn't busy? What if he thinks I left the phone off the hook because I don't want to talk to him? What if he doesn't come to the door? What if he comes to the door, but the note's fallen off and he doesn't see it? What if he's insulted that I left him a note?

"Isabella, it's not because of Mike. Really. I'm just not hungry, and I don't feel like going out."

Isabella picked up her jacket from the sofa. "Okay, fine. Suit yourself. If you change your mind, I'll either be at the snack bar or at Vito's."

Jessica kept her eyes straight ahead as Isabella walked past her. "I won't change my mind."

Isabella stopped at the door and looked back.

6

"No," she said with a sigh. "I don't think you will."

Elizabeth and Jessica Wakefield might have looked identical, with their blue-green eyes and their long blond hair, but that was where the resemblance ended. Inside, the twins couldn't have been more unalike. Jessica had always been the frivolous, fun-loving sister, and Elizabeth had always been the hardworking and dependable one.

Which is why Jessica is probably at some wild party being asked out by twenty-five different guys, and I'm headed to the library to finish my English paper, Elizabeth thought as she pulled a baggy black hooded sweatshirt over her Save Our Planet T-shirt. She knew that everybody else in the world had a date or a party to go to that night and that she'd probably be the only person in the library, but she didn't want to stay in her room. Even though Celine Boudreaux, Elizabeth's roommate, wouldn't be back for hours, Elizabeth disliked Celine so much that she spent as much time out of the room as she could. Just the smell of Celine's perfume and the sight of her clothes thrown all over were enough to make Elizabeth's blood pressure rise.

As she turned from her desk, Elizabeth caught a glimpse of herself in the mirror. Recently, a new difference between her and her sister had appeared. Now only one of the Wakefield twins was a perfect size six, and it wasn't Elizabeth.

The truth was, she'd been having a difficult

time adjusting to college life. Not only did she have to live with Celine, the Scarlett O'Hara of SVU, who had come all the way from Louisiana just to make Elizabeth's life miserable, but in just the first few weeks of school she'd broken up with her long-standing boyfriend, Todd Wilkins, and had grown apart from both her sister and her best friend, Enid Rollins. It seemed as if the only thing she hadn't lost was her appetite.

"That's what you get for turning to food for comfort," Elizabeth told her reflection, giving a tug at the tight waistband of her jeans. "Discomfort."

Her stomach growled.

"No," she told it. "You're on a diet. You've had your fifteen hundred calories for today, and that's all you're getting."

Her stomach gave another plaintive rumble. Not that Elizabeth blamed it. Ever since she had started this diet, she was hungry all the time. The funny thing was that even though she hadn't cheated once, she didn't seem to be losing any weight. The book she was using said it was because she was on a plateau, but to Elizabeth it felt more like a valley.

Her eyes fell on the open bag of nacho chips on Celine's bed. Celine could stuff her face with junk food from morning till night and never gain an ounce. It was just another thing to hold against her. Elizabeth's stomach moaned.

"Library!" Elizabeth commanded, snapping off the light and practically fleeing the room.

Nonetheless, as she marched purposefully across campus, Elizabeth's mind was not on the nineteenth-century British novel, where it was supposed to be. It was on food. Everything she saw made her hungry. Soda cans, candy wrappers, a pizza box, even a poster outside the new arts complex advertising a performance of *The Cherry Orchard* by the student theater group.

At the edge of the quad she froze. There, coming toward her from the other side, was her ex-best friend, Enid Rollins, eating what looked suspiciously like a burrito grande.

This was the one time since they had arrived at the university that Elizabeth wished Enid would just walk right by her. *Please don't stop,* she silently prayed. *Be in a hurry. Don't see me.*

"Hi, Liz!"

Enid stopped close enough for Elizabeth to see that it was a jumbo chicken burrito with guacamole and sour cream.

"Hi, Enid."

Enid sighed. "Alex, Liz, not Enid. How many times do I have to tell you? It's like you have this pathological—"

"I'm sorry, Alex," she apologized quickly. The last thing Elizabeth needed was a half-hour lecture on Enid's new name while she watched her eat. "My mind was somewhere else." Most of the time

9

she did manage to remember that Enid wanted to be called Alex or Alexandra now that she was at college and had a new image, but the burrito had made her forget. There was salsa on it besides the guacamole and the sour cream. Enid took another bite. And melted cheese.

Chewing slowly, Enid nodded at the books in Elizabeth's arms. "Where are you going? Don't tell me you're studying tonight."

Enid used to be the person Elizabeth told everything to. She was the one person to whom Elizabeth could have admitted how miserable she was, and that the only things she liked about college were her classes and her apprenticeship at the TV station. But things had changed so much between them since they arrived that she couldn't bring herself to tell Enid the truth: that she was working on a Friday night because she had nothing else to do.

"I've got an English paper due on Monday," Elizabeth said with a groan. "The professor's a real tyrant. I think he must have been Louis the Fourteenth in a former life."

Enid laughed. "My sociology teacher's like that. We're all afraid to breathe too loud."

Elizabeth sighed with relief as Enid swallowed the last of her burrito. "So, what are you doing on your own on a Friday night?" she asked. "I thought you'd be out with Mark."

Enid had been dating campus basketball star

Mark Gathers, a friend of Todd's, almost since school started. They were already quite an item.

"I thought so too." Enid made a face. "But you know those jocks. There's always somebody wanting to give them a dinner or take them out or something." She giggled. "It's a good thing he gets the grades he needs without having to work too hard, because with practice and everything he doesn't have that much time left to study."

Elizabeth felt a pang that wasn't hunger. She used to know exactly what those jocks were like, but she hadn't seen Todd in weeks. Occasionally she'd catch a glimpse of him, striding across the campus like a young god, and once again feel amazed that someone she had been so close to could now be so far away.

Enid didn't seem to notice that she was upset. "The way athletes are treated on the campus really is unbelievable, isn't it?" Enid continued. "Sometimes after a game I have to wait forever before Mark can get away from his admirers to take me out." She made another face, but Elizabeth could tell that Enid was secretly proud to be the girlfriend of one of the biggest jocks at school.

Elizabeth used to know what that felt like. She felt another pang sear her heart.

"Well," she said, already starting to move forward. "I'd better get to work or I'll be up all night."

Enid nodded. "Right. I've got to go too. Mark's picking me up for a late date after his din-

11

ner, so I want to get a nap before then. I'll see you around, Liz."

"Sure," Elizabeth called over her shoulder. "I'll see you around."

That's the one good thing about having someone turn a knife in your heart, Elizabeth told herself as she raced up the library steps. *It makes you forget all about your stomach for a while.*

Danny Wyatt's heavy footsteps echoed as he walked down the corridor of the campus television station. During the day and on weekends there was always a lot of activity in the WSVU offices—camerapeople, soundpeople, and reporters running in and out, everyone shouting and behind schedule—but on a Friday night there would be only one or two people in the studio, running music videos of local bands.

Danny made a left turn into a silent, empty hall. There *should* have been only one or two people in the studio, but Danny had a hunch that he might find an extra person in the newsroom, working overtime as usual.

Danny stopped at the door marked NEWS, and listened. Nothing, not even the faintest of sounds. *I know he's in there,* Danny told himself. Shaking his head, he opened the door without knocking.

The room was dark and the desks were empty—except for the desk in the farthest corner, where a light was shining and a tall, broad, dark-haired young man was hunched over, reading so intently that he didn't even look up when Danny shut the door behind him.

"Hey, what a surprise."

Without turning around, Tom Watts held up one finger. "Hold on," he ordered. "I've just gotten to the good part."

Danny came up behind him. "What are you doing, man? It's Friday night. Nobody works this late on a Friday night." He put a hand on his roommate's shoulder. "And besides, I've been waiting for you for two hours. We were supposed to play some tennis tonight and go out for Thai food."

"I don't feel like playing tennis," Tom said. His eyes didn't move from the page he was reading.

Danny laughed. "Well, neither do I. *Anymore*. But I do feel like eating. Or has your reporter's brain cut off all communication to your stomach again?"

"This is incredible, Danny. Really incredible. If half of this is true, we're really onto something here."

"What is it? More on the Halloween hoax?"

A few weeks before Halloween, a local psychic had predicted that a psychopath would make an appearance at the university's Halloween dance. Rumors had built up to an almost hysterical pitch. Like the good investigative reporter he was, Tom had set about interviewing everyone from faculty and students to the psychic himself, following his own instincts. In the end, there had been two unpleasant events at the dance—one a racial incident involving Danny and the other an attack on Jessica Wakefield. Tom was not only sure that the attack on Jessica had been meant for her sister, he was also sure that Peter Wilbourne III, president of the Sigmas, the most prestigious fraternity on campus, was behind both. Tom had been working on a follow-up ever since.

Tom shook his head. "No, I still haven't found anything solid on Wilbourne. This is something completely different. Something I stumbled on by accident."

Danny leaned over Tom's shoulder, his eyes scanning the typed page. It was a letter to the co-captain of the basketball team, canceling repayment on a student loan. When he got to the bottom, Danny whistled. "This is dynamite, Tombo. They let Howser borrow five thousand dollars to top off his scholarship and then they just let him have the money because he's so valuable to the team." He whistled again. "They never did anything like that for me when I was on the wrestling team."

Tom laughed. "They never did anything like that for me when I was their star quarterback, either. But then, they didn't have to work hard to recruit me." He took two more pieces of paper from his desk and handed them to Danny.

"Marotta's grade transcripts," Danny said. Marotta was Tom's replacement on the football team.

Tom leaned back and spun his chair around so he was facing his friend. "Look at them closely."

Danny frowned, puzzled. "One semester he was flunking everything, and the other he was doing C's and B's."

Tom gave him a slow smile. "Look again, amigo."

"I don't believe it." Danny's eyes moved from one paper to the other. "They're for the same semester."

"That's right." Tom's voice was tight with excitement. "Obviously somebody was supposed to throw out the first transcript, only they forgot."

Danny stared back at him in amazement. "But how did you get hold of it?"

"Pure chance. I just happened to be in the athletics office, doing some background on the basketball team for a special we're doing on the new season, and I found the letter about the loan mixed in with some clippings and stuff like that. At first I didn't think anything of it. I mean, I thought it was strange, but I figured there was something I didn't know. Like, maybe somebody else, some alumnus for instance, had paid off the loan. Then all of a sudden I thought of Marotta." Tom grinned. "Not only isn't he as good a quarterback as I was, but he isn't as smart, either. And I remembered there was a lot of talk about whether or not he'd be able to keep up his average. So I just thought I'd look in his file while I was there. You know, see how he was doing."

15

Danny laughed. "Remind me not to leave anything unlocked around you." He nodded at the other papers on the desk. "What else have you got?"

"Not much, really." Tom shrugged. "I've got a letter from a kid who went somewhere else, thanking the coach for bringing him out here from New York to see the school and putting up him and his family. And I've got a picture of the captain of the basketball team riding around Florida in a rented Porsche when they went there to play Miami. And I've got some notes of my own about how the jocks are housed and stuff like that. It's all pretty much hunches and supposition, but I think the pieces are going to fit."

"So what happens next? You don't sleep or eat for the next three weeks? I forget I have a roommate?"

Tom laughed. "I'm afraid you're out of luck this time, man. I'm not going to be able to do the digging on this one. I'm too well known, especially in the athletics department. As it was, Coach Sanchez was looking at me funny when I left. If I start hanging around there, he'll know something's up."

Danny gave his best friend a skeptical look. "You're not trying to tell me that you're going to forget about this, are you?"

"Are you nuts? Forget about this?" Tom laughed. "No, someone else is going to get the story. I'll just be the presenter."

16

"Who?" Danny asked, not hiding his surprise. "You're not exactly a born delegator, Tom. You never trust anybody else to do anything."

Tom turned back to the desk, locking the papers in his top drawer. "There's one person I trust enough," he said over his shoulder.

Danny stared at his back. "Who?"

"Elizabeth."

Tom's voice was so low and so fast that Danny wasn't sure he'd heard him right. "Elizabeth? You mean Elizabeth Wakefield?"

"Yeah." Tom glanced over at him. "You know I'm training her to work at the station."

Danny continued to stare. "And you know that her boyfriend is one of the big jocks on the basketball team."

Something locked in Tom's dark eyes. "Ex-boyfriend."

Danny knew that there was something going on with Tom, something concerning Elizabeth Wakefield. But he also knew that Tom wasn't going to tell him what it was. Not without a struggle. Tom was the best friend Danny had ever had, but not because they talked a lot. He kept his own counsel, just as Danny did.

"Right," Danny said calmly. "Ex-boyfriend." He grinned. "So, does that mean we can eat?"

Elizabeth spent so much time in the library that by now she usually found a few familiar—even

17

friendly—faces in the study carrels. Tom Watts, Elizabeth's boss at the TV station, was often there, working late. So was Nina Harper, who lived on her floor in Dickenson Hall. She seemed to be one of the few girls on their hall who hadn't completely fallen under Celine's spell. And then there was the coolly handsome blond man with the glacier eyes, William White. At least two or three times a week Elizabeth found him sitting at the back when she arrived, watching her as though he'd been waiting just for her.

But none of them were in the library tonight. The only students bent over the desks were people who, like Elizabeth, obviously had nothing else to do. The losers of Sweet Valley U.

Stop feeling sorry for yourself, Elizabeth scolded, trying to concentrate on what H. F. Mullerman had to say about the wit and irony of Jane Austen. But she couldn't stop feeling sorry for herself. Meeting Enid had upset her too much.

Elizabeth stared blankly at the page in front of her. It wasn't really meeting Enid that had upset her. She was relieved that she and Enid were at least speaking again. It was because talking about superjocks and the basketball team made her start thinking about Todd again.

Sometimes Elizabeth almost thought that she was over the breakup. It had been her decision as much as his. Todd had wanted to take their relationship further than she was prepared to go. He seemed to think that now that he was a Big Man on Campus, Elizabeth should automatically want to sleep with him, but Elizabeth hadn't wanted to. She'd wanted to get used to her new world, with all its new experiences and feelings, before she made a commitment like that. A vision of Todd and her, holding each other as they were in the photograph she kept on her bureau, covered the page of Professor Mullerman's flawless prose. Elizabeth sniffed back a wayward tear. Sometimes she thought she was over him, and other times she knew she wasn't.

Unable to concentrate, Elizabeth checked her watch. It was getting late, but not late enough to go back to the dorm. Elizabeth couldn't do that until she was sure that she'd fall asleep right away. The last thing she wanted was to be awake when Celine got back. Celine sober in the middle of the day was bad enough, but Celine after she'd been partying all night was unbearable. They almost always wound up having a fight.

It was an off-campus party, filled with loud music, laughter, and handsome men, but still Celine Boudreaux was bored.

Idly playing with the miniature white rose she'd taken from the vase beside her, she stared back at the very attractive but exhaustingly dull young man in front of her. His name was either Darren or Daryl and he was a philosophy major. For some reason he was trying to seduce her by explaining

Aristotle's ethics to her. Celine wasn't interested in anybody's ethics. Ethics were like rules: they cramped your style.

"Excuse me," she said in her soft, sexy drawl. "But I just want to go refill my glass."

Even though he'd been in the middle of a sentence, he smiled back at her.

That was the advantage of having a Southern accent among Yankees. No matter what you said, they thought it must be something nice.

Without a backward glance Celine floated out of the room, her perfume drifting behind her like a train of blossoms. She could feel the eyes on her. Celine considered her granny to be a first-class witch in many ways, but she had to admit that her granny often gave good advice. Always make an entrance and always make an exit, her granny had told her. And that's what Celine always did.

Coming into the kitchen, she caught her reflection in the window over the counter. *You look gorgeous,* she told herself, pouring another drink. *You look stunningly, devastatingly, eat-your-heart-out gorgeous.*

Behind her, in the window, she could see other reflections. There was a drippy guy from her English class and Nina Something from her hall.

And suddenly there appeared someone she'd been looking for all night. The reflection showed a young man wearing an expensive black linen suit.

He was as beautiful as a fairy-tale prince. And he looked as bored as she felt.

A shadow crossed Celine's heart. She was extremely good at manipulating people. There were very few people she couldn't get around. One was her ghastly roommate, Elizabeth Little Goody Two-Shoes Wakefield. And the other was standing behind her, talking to a guy who looked as if one of his parents must have been a tank.

Celine took a deep breath and swung slowly around. She was also good at getting what she wanted. And she wanted the young man in black like she had never wanted anyone—if only because he didn't want her.

"William!" she gushed, gracefully sliding between him and the tank and tapping the flower against his chest. "I didn't know you were here. What a nice surprise!"

He looked from her to the rose. For just a second the bored expression in his eyes was replaced with something else: disdain. Then he took the flower from her hand and went on talking as though she weren't there. He sounded just a little bit drunk.

"It sounds to me like your friend went to the wrong part of Mexico," he said to the tank. "It's too bad you didn't tell me he was going. I could have recommended an incredible beach."

Celine's smile grew brighter. "Oh, Mexico." She sighed. "I love Mexico. Isn't it just the most romantic place?"

William continued to ignore her, but the tank began to speak. "Um . . . uh . . . William," he said, his eyes on Celine. "I don't believe I've met your friend."

William looked at him blankly. "My friend?"

It was at times like these that Celine wished her granny were a real witch. If she were, Celine would be able to put a spell on William White that would destroy his happiness for the rest of his life.

She turned toward the tank. "Celine," she said, her voice as soft as velvet and as sweet as pecan pie. "Celine Boudreaux."

The tank grabbed her hand so roughly she thought he was going to shake it loose from her wrist. "I'm glad to meet you, Celine," he said. He sounded glad. "I've been wanting to meet you since the beginning of the year. I'm Steve Hawkins." He grinned at her mindlessly. "I've seen you around."

Well, I haven't seen you. She looked down for a second, so he would think she was blushing modestly. *And if I had, I would've run.*

"You mean you noticed me?" she whispered. "You noticed little me in a school this big?"

Impossible though it seemed, the grin became even more mindless. "I'd notice you anywhere."

"Did you hear that, William? Your friend's been wanting to meet me." Celine glanced over her shoulder.

William White was gone.

Celine stared at the space where William had

been, her pretty mouth set in a smile as hard as industrial steel. The fact that she hadn't been able to turn William White into a horned toad or a hunchback with black teeth and b.o. wasn't really important. She was going to destroy his happiness anyway. Totally and completely. It was just going to take her a little longer to do without the help of witchcraft, that was all.

Elizabeth pushed her notebook aside with a sigh. Maybe she'd just lean back and close her eyes for a few minutes, try to re-energize herself. All she needed was to relax a little. From somewhere behind her cellophane crackled.

Her eyes snapped open. *I don't believe this. Somebody's eating!* If it wasn't her broken heart that was giving her a hard time, it was her stomach. She was sure she could smell garlic-and-onion potato chips.

This is really unfair, she said to herself. *You're not supposed to eat in the library. It's against the rules.* There was another crackle of a wrapper being torn, this one from the other side of the aisle. Now she was sure she could smell chocolate. The only thing that could make this moment worse would be if Todd Wilkins walked in right now with another girl on his arm and a cheeseburger in his hand.

I'm not going to be able to put up with this. I'll have to go get a cup of coffee. Elizabeth started gathering her things.

23

"I knew I'd find you here."

Every thought in Elizabeth's head drained away. She had never heard that voice before—not this close, not speaking to her—but she knew before she raised her eyes whose voice it was. She looked up to find herself staring into a pair of blue eyes so light they looked like ice.

He had a smile that was as secretive as it was dazzling. Elizabeth could never decide whether she thought the secrets it hid were good or bad.

He leaned against the carrel. His eyes might be cool, but his breath was warm. Warm and smelling faintly of wine.

"Tell me one thing," he whispered. "What's someone like you doing in the library on a night shot through with stars?"

She said the first thing that came to her mind. The truth. "Jane Austen."

"Well, I certainly wouldn't want to deprive Jane Austen of your company." He lifted his hand. "But I got this for you."

Elizabeth took the delicate white flower and sat there staring at it for several seconds, not quite knowing what to say. When she looked up again, William White was gone.

Chapter Two

Jessica opened the door to her twin's room with uncharacteristic caution, standing in the entrance for a second and looking around. Elizabeth was sitting at her desk with her back to her, her head bent over something she was writing.

Leave it to Liz, thought Jessica in exasperation. *Forty-five minutes till the big Theta tea and my sister's studying. It's a good thing she isn't Cinderella. She'd be too busy finishing her English assignment to get to the ball.*

"Psst . . ." she called in an exaggerated whisper. "Where's the South's Revenge?" Jessica was one of the few people in the world who hadn't been fooled by the charm Celine used to fool everyone else. The first time Jessica met her sister's roommate, Celine had mistaken her for Elizabeth and treated her viciously.

Elizabeth looked up and smiled. "It's okay, Jess.

25

Celine's out shopping." Elizabeth glanced meaningfully at the heaps of clothes around the room and at Celine's closet, crammed so full that the door wouldn't close. "Apparently she has nothing to wear to the Homecoming dance."

Jessica, who also had a room heaped with clothes, a bulging closet, and nothing to wear to the Homecoming dance, made no comment. Instead she gave her sister a stern look and shut the door behind her. She crossed the room and sat on Elizabeth's bed.

"Why aren't you dressed yet?" she demanded. "We have to be at the Theta house by three o'clock. *Today.*"

Elizabeth chewed on the top of her pen. "To tell you the truth, Jess, I'm not so sure I want to go."

"You what?" Jessica gazed at her sister in disbelief. How could they have come from a single egg and have so little in common? "What are you talking about, Elizabeth? This is the last Theta rush event. This is where they start to make their final decisions on pledges. You *have* to go."

"Not if I don't want to join their sorority, I don't," Elizabeth answered.

"*Not* join Theta?" Jessica squealed. "Elizabeth Wakefield, have you completely lost your mind? Theta was Mom's sorority. It's practically thanks to her that it's the most important sorority on campus today. Mom's a legend there, Liz. You not joining would be like Prince Charles of England deciding to move to Detroit and work at the Ford plant."

Elizabeth gave her one of her tolerant smiles. "I know it was Mom's sorority, Jess, but I'm not really sure it's right for me." She pushed her chair away from the desk. "If I do join a sorority, I think I'd like to join the Pi Beta Phis."

Now Jessica knew for sure that she and Elizabeth weren't really related at all. It was obviously some sort of weird cosmic accident that they looked exactly alike, had the same parents, and had been raised in the same house.

"The Pi Beta Phis?" Jessica screeched. "*You* want to join the Pis?" She sat up, leaning forward earnestly. "Elizabeth, nobody who wants a social life at SVU joins the Pis. The Pis eat soy burgers and crusade to save South American tree toads. They think a party is sitting around singing *Guantanamera!* while some girl who's never heard of makeup plays the guitar. They do nothing but study and take up causes, Liz. They're boring. They're dull and—" The words froze on Jessica's lips. The more she described the Pis, the more obvious it was that they were just like her sister. Boring. Dull. More interested in studying and recycling their bottles than in having fun.

"You mean they're just like me?" Elizabeth asked, but she was smiling and there was a humorous glint in her eye.

Jessica got up suddenly, grabbing her sister's hand and pulling her to her feet. "But you don't have to be dull and boring, Liz," she said sincerely.

27

"You could be one of the most popular girls on campus if you just tried a little harder. After all"—she smiled brightly—"you look exactly like me."

"But Jessica—" Elizabeth protested as Jessica dragged her over to her closet. "Maybe I don't want to be one of the most popular girls on campus anymore. Maybe I think other things are more important."

Jessica gave Elizabeth a "you would" look and opened her closet. She was determined that this was one argument she was going to win. After all, you never could tell about sorority politics. If Elizabeth turned down the Thetas, they might turn down Jessica. Or—worse yet—if the Thetas realized how dull and boring Elizabeth really was, they might think Jessica was the same way.

Jessica rummaged through Elizabeth's clothes, looking for something sophisticated enough for the Theta tea. She finally pulled out a slinky pink sheath and held it up to her twin. "You owe me this," she informed her sister. "You owe it to Mom. You were born to be a Theta, Liz, and that's all there is to it." She shoved the dress into Elizabeth's hands. "Here. Put this on."

Reluctantly Elizabeth got out of her jeans and T-shirt and put on the dress.

Something was wrong. Jessica took a step backward, eyeing her sister critically. She remembered when Elizabeth bought this dress, because she'd bought one just like it. They'd caused quite a sensation at the spring fling last year. Everyone had said they looked like models. She took another step back. Elizabeth didn't look like a model in this dress anymore; she looked like a sausage.

Elizabeth turned to the mirror. "Really, Jessica. I don't feel comfortable in this dress. I'd rather wear something more casual."

You mean you'd rather wear something bigger, Jessica thought, realizing that her sister had not only become more boring since she'd arrived at college but that she'd put on weight as well. A strange, unpleasant sensation crawled through Jessica's heart. She and Elizabeth had always been different, but they'd always looked the same, and they'd always been close. All at once the differences between them seemed enormous. Elizabeth wasn't just like her. Not anymore.

"I have that nice peasant skirt," Elizabeth said. "I could wear that with my—"

"Give me a break, will you, Liz?" Jessica said. "You can't dress like a peasant for the Theta pledge tea." She put her arm around Elizabeth and smiled at their reflection. For the first time in eighteen years they didn't look completely identical.

It was a perfect California Saturday afternoon. The sky was blue, the air was warm, and the sun was shining. Everyone was outside—playing softball, riding bikes, or just lying in the sun on the beach. Everyone, that was, except Winston Egbert.

Winston was lying under his bed in Oakley Hall, trying not to breathe too loudly. Outside his room, three of his Sigma pals, Bill Montana, Tony Calavieri, and Jeff Cross, were pounding on the door.

Winston groaned silently. Ever since the Sigmas had discovered that Winston was the only male living in an all-girl dorm, they wouldn't leave him alone. They were always dropping by, or taking him out, or following him around, hoping he'd introduce them to girls. Winston had enjoyed this newfound popularity at first, but he was getting tired of it.

And the Sigmas were making it hard for him to get a date himself. The only time he could talk to a girl without some Sigma suddenly looming over her shoulder was when he was in the Oakley Hall bathroom. Winston groaned again as he imagined asking Denise Waters, the most fantastic girl in the entire world, to go out with him. "What about Saturday night? I thought we could hang out in the bathroom for a couple of hours."

Winston checked his watch again. It was two thirty, two thirty on a Saturday afternoon. Somewhere on the SVU campus there was a softball game with his name on it. Winston's stomach growled. Somewhere in the SVU snack bar there was a double chili cheeseburger wondering where he was.

The door shook as the Sigmas started knocking again. "Yo, Win!" called a voice Winston recognized as Bill's. "Win, are you in there?"

Go away! Winston yelled silently. *What are you, stupid or something? Can't you see I'm not here?*

The banging stopped suddenly.

Winston's heart did a double flip of joy. They'd given up. They'd given up and gone away.

The door opened. From beneath the hem of the bedspread, Winston could see three pairs of Nikes enter the room. His heart froze in mid-flip.

"I guess he's not here," Bill said.

Winston choked back a sigh and closed his eyes. Bill was one of the most popular guys in the fraternity, but it wasn't because he was smart.

"Where do you think he went?" Tony asked.

"Maybe he had to go into town for something," Bill suggested.

"His Beetle's outside," Jeff said.

"Maybe he got a lift with someone," said Tony.

"Can I help you guys?"

Winston opened his eyes. A fourth pair of feet, these in black-and-red cowboy boots, had appeared in the doorway. It was Maia, the dorm monitor of Oakley Hall. Winston felt like kissing the mattress. Maia was tougher than the entire NFL put together. She'd get rid of them.

"We were looking for Winston," Bill said, putting on the smooth, ingratiating voice he always used when he was near a pretty girl.

But his charm was lost on Maia. "Winnie's not here," she said shortly. "And in the future I'd appreciate it if you were a little more quiet when you looked for him. Some people are trying to study."

The Nikes started to shuffle toward the door.

"Sure," Tony said.

"We're really sorry we disturbed you," Jeff said.

"You busy tonight?" Bill asked.

"I'll tell Winnie you dropped by," Maia said.

Very slowly and very carefully, Winston lifted the bedspread and peered out.

"Maia!" he hissed. "Are they gone?"

Maia, just about to close the door behind her, turned around. "Winnie!" She seemed surprised to see him crawling out from under the bed. "What are you doing under there?"

"What do you think I was doing?" He pulled himself to a sitting position. "I was hiding from those guys."

Maia's surprise was replaced by amusement. "But I thought you loved them. I thought your only wish in life was to be pledged to the Sigmas and be a big man on campus."

"You didn't read enough fairy tales when you were a kid," Winston said, brushing dust balls from his hair. "Or you'd realize that every wish comes with a curse."

A high, familiar laugh bounced across the room. Elizabeth looked over to the circle of giggling Thetas with her sister at the center of it. All of them were so fashionably dressed that they could have been models posing for an ad. And all of them were stuffing cake and cookies into their mouths as though they might not eat again for a week.

How is it they can eat without gaining weight and I can't? Elizabeth wondered as she sipped her cup of black tea.

Elizabeth sighed, checking her watch for the third time in the last half hour. To make Jessica happy, Elizabeth had agreed to come to the Theta tea and to wear the uncomfortable pink dress. To make Jessica happy, she'd been making an effort to be sociable and outgoing, even though most of the sorority sisters were so superficial and snobby that it was almost impossible to find anything to talk about. In the hour that she'd been here, Elizabeth had said just about all there was to say about the weather and its effects on the skin and hair, and the importance of accessories in getting the most out of your wardrobe. Elizabeth stifled a yawn. But she couldn't pretend to be having a good time, not even to make Jessica happy.

Elizabeth's thoughts were interrupted by an oily voice right behind her.

"I can't believe it," the voice was saying. "I mean, I knew you and Jessica must be related, but I never realized you were supposed to be twins! Identical twins!"

Elizabeth turned around. The owner of the oily voice was a tall brunette, so astoundingly immaculate she looked as though her clothes had been washed and ironed on her body. Elizabeth recognized her immediately. She was Alison Quinn, vice president of the Thetas.

Elizabeth put a smile on her face as insincere as the one on Alison's. "We're not only supposed to be identical twins," she said sweetly. "We *are* identical twins. You can ask our mother."

If Alison noticed the sarcasm in Elizabeth's voice, she did an excellent job of disguising it. "Well, you could have fooled me," she said. Her gray eyes narrowed. "I guess it's because you have such different personalities." Alison nodded toward Jessica as a fresh wave of laughter rolled across the room. "Jessica's so outgoing . . . so gregarious . . . so—"

"Much fun," Elizabeth filled in.

"Exactly." Alison showed her perfect teeth. "Though, of course, I'm not suggesting that just because a person's quiet she can't be interesting or exciting." She looked as though she were about to yawn.

Elizabeth tightened her grip on her teacup. Would her mother and sister ever forgive her if she threw her cold tea down the front of Alison Quinn's champagne-colored silk blouse?

"Of course, you're not always so quiet, are you?" Alison went on. "You were pretty outspoken the night of the Theta-Sigma house party, if I remember right."

"You remember right," Elizabeth replied.

The joint Theta-Sigma party had been one of

the first big social events at school. Elizabeth had gone alone, and Jessica had gone with Danny Wyatt. Peter Wilbourne III, the smug, self-opinion-ated president of the Sigmas, was angry that Jessica had gone with Danny rather than with him, and had made a racial attack on Danny. Only the inter-vention of Tom Watts had stopped Peter from actu-ally trying to rough Danny up.

After Jessica and Danny had left the party, Elizabeth had gone up to Peter Wilbourne and told him exactly what she thought of him and his frater-nity. It didn't surprise her that the Thetas hadn't forgotten the incident. What surprised her was that they were still willing to consider her as a pledge. The name Alice Wakefield must have even more in-fluence with them than Elizabeth had thought.

"Still," Alison said, her voice edged with barbed wire, "I'm sure you didn't realize what you were doing at the time, publicly attacking someone like Peter."

Elizabeth put down her cup.

"And I'm sure you're really very interesting," Alison added, sounding bored.

Elizabeth gave the Theta vice president her most dazzling smile. "You're wrong," she said, her voice as pleasant as the afternoon outside. "I *did* realize what I was doing, and I'm not very interesting at all."

Jessica had given Elizabeth an accusing look when she caught her leaving the pledge tea early,

35

but Elizabeth didn't really care. She couldn't have stood one more minute of Alison Quinn and her sorority sisters.

As she strode across the campus, Elizabeth couldn't help smiling to herself. A few weeks ago an afternoon like the one she'd just spent would have depressed her and made her feel totally inadequate. She would probably have skulked back to the dorm and eaten half a box of cookies. Now it had just made her feel angry. She smiled again. But she still wouldn't mind at least a quarter of a box of cookies right now.

"Let Jessica live her life the way she wants, and I'll live mine the way I want," Elizabeth told herself as she marched down an unfamiliar path. She'd decided to try a shortcut because she couldn't wait to get back to her room to take off the stupid pink dress.

"There isn't anything wrong with me just because I don't want to fit in with people like that," Elizabeth said as she kicked a stone down the path in front of her. "They're wrong for acting as if everyone *should* be like them."

Elizabeth slowed as she came to an outdoor basketball court where a group of shouting, whooping guys were playing a fast pickup game. She hadn't changed so much that the sight of a basketball game didn't make her think of Todd. She still had trouble believing she'd really lost him.

Elizabeth stopped before she reached the court. The guys were all tensely watching the basket. The ball was balancing precariously on the rim, threatening to fall back to the ground. Suddenly it fell through the net. One voice stood out above the general roar that followed. "Way to go!" it shouted.

Elizabeth felt her blood turn to ice water. Todd. That was Todd's voice. Yes, there he was, wearing his old blue sweatpants and a white T-shirt soaked with sweat. His hair was damp and his face was flushed. How many times had he rushed up to her after a game, looking just like that, and taken her into his arms? Too many times. Even from here she knew exactly what he smelled like at this moment; the thought of it made her feel weak.

Elizabeth watched Todd as he darted and wove across the court, his movements quick and supple. She couldn't seem to take her eyes off him. She couldn't seem to stop her heart from pounding. Elizabeth wiped her moist palms on her dress.

When Todd had wanted her to sleep with him, she'd told him she wasn't ready.

Maybe I'm changing even more than I thought, Elizabeth told herself as she reluctantly turned away from the game before anyone saw her. *Because I certainly feel ready now.*

Enid had been so lost in her thoughts of the Theta tea and what a great time she'd had that she hadn't realized at first who the figure rushing away from the basketball court was.

"Liz!" Enid called. She hadn't even seen Elizabeth leave the sorority house. One minute Elizabeth had been there, talking to Alison Quinn, and the next she was gone. "Liz!" But Elizabeth was already out of sight.

Enid laughed, remembering what she'd heard about the scene at the Theta-Sigma party when Elizabeth told Peter Wilbourne off. Elizabeth seemed to be making a habit of leaving places abruptly lately.

"Alex! Over here!"

Instantly forgetting all about Elizabeth, Enid looked toward the court. Her boyfriend, Mark Gathers, was jogging toward her, a smile on his handsome face.

"I was beginning to worry that you weren't coming," he said as she ran to him. "I was afraid one of those Sigma creeps the Thetas hang out with had stolen you away."

Mark's clothes were wet and rivulets of sweat ran down his face, but she didn't hesitate for a second. She threw herself into his arms for a long, deep kiss.

"It would take an army of Sigmas to steal me away from you," she whispered when they finally pulled apart.

"It better," he said. He brushed a strand of hair away from her face. "So, how was it? You have a good time?"

Enid nodded. "It was terrific. They're such a great bunch of girls." She leaned against him as he

38

wrapped his arm around her waist. "And it's unofficial, of course, but I'm definitely going to be pledged. Magda Helperin, the president, told me herself."

Mark gave her another hug. "In that case, Ms. Rollins, I think we should go out tonight for a special celebratory dinner. Just you and me, a quiet corner table at Da Vinci's, a candle, and one red rose."

She couldn't hide her surprise. "Da Vinci's? You can't be serious. Da Vinci's is the most expensive restaurant in town."

"My grant's just come through," he said, smiling at her worry. "You can even have two desserts."

She hugged him back, but then the worried look returned. "Oh, no . . ." she wailed. "We can't go out tonight. You have a big physics test on Monday, remember? You said yourself you can't afford to do badly on it."

"Don't you worry about me." He winked. "I'm a superjock, right? I'll be fine."

Enid frowned. "But I don't want to distract you from—"

He put a finger to her lips. "No buts, Alex. You don't distract me; you make me concentrate. And what I want to concentrate on is you."

I can't believe how perfect my life is, Enid thought, holding tightly to Mark's hand. *It's almost too good to be true.*

Mark turned back toward the court as they started to walk away. "See you later," he called.

"See you later," one of the other players called back.

At the sound of the other guy's voice Enid turned too. It was Todd. She'd been so glad to see Mark she hadn't even noticed Todd. That was why Elizabeth was watching the game when Enid arrived. And why she left so abruptly.

It's too bad everyone's life can't be perfect, Enid thought as she and Mark headed back to his dorm.

Cheddar-cheese potato chips, an insistent little voice was whispering in Elizabeth's head. *Forget about the Thetas. Forget about Todd. What you want are cheddar-cheese potato chips. They sell them in the snack machine in the common room. You can buy two bags.* Against her will, Elizabeth imagined locking herself in her room, closing the curtains, and snuggling up on her bed with a bag of cheddar-cheese potato chips and a good book, safe and far away from sorority teas and a sweaty man who used to call her his. It was such a comforting image that she could practically taste the salt on her lips.

Elizabeth quickened her pace as she caught sight of Dickenson Hall, rising in front of her like a desert oasis. Potato chips or no potato chips, all she wanted was to get inside.

"Elizabeth! Wait up!"

If it had been anyone else, Elizabeth would have kept on walking, but she recognized the voice immediately and stopped. It was Tom Watts. She

40

turned around. He had a smile on his face that made the day look dull.

"How can you walk so fast in that dress and those shoes?" Tom asked, falling into step beside her.

For the first time all afternoon, Elizabeth found herself laughing. "It's genetic," she told him. "Boys get the Y chromosome and facial hair, and girls get two X chromosomes and the ability to run in heels and clothes as tight as a bandage."

He looked her up and down. "So, where have you been? Some sort of masquerade party?"

Not even an hour ago laughing seemed like the last thing she would do today, but here she was doing it again. "Is that your diplomatic way of telling me you hate my dress?"

"No, I don't *hate* your dress." He looked over at her as they walked along. "I just don't think it's very . . . uh . . . you." His voice went almost to a whisper as he added, "I like the stuff you usually wear."

Elizabeth felt herself blushing and turned away. "I guess I don't have to ask you where you've been," she said, relieved that she didn't sound as rattled by him as she felt. "Working at the station, right?"

He held up his hands in a gesture of surrender. "Guilty!" he said with a laugh. "Actually, that's what I wanted to talk to you about, Elizabeth," he went on, suddenly serious. "I think I've stumbled

41

onto something really major, and I want you to work with me on it."

The tone of his voice made her stop and face him. "What is it?"

Elizabeth listened quietly but intently while Tom told her about looking through the files of the athletics office for some background material on the basketball team, finding the letter about the loan, and becoming curious about Marotta's grades. Her eyes widened as he explained the theory he was forming that the jocks got special perks and privileges.

All the while two thoughts were going through her mind: *This guy is really sharp* and *Todd*.

"So, what do you say?" Tom asked when he'd finished.

Elizabeth shook her head. "I'd say that the police force lost a terrific detective when you decided to be an investigative reporter."

Tom didn't take compliments well, but for a second he looked really pleased. "What about you, though?" he pressed. "I can't do the groundwork myself because of my reputation here. I need somebody really good who I can trust completely. Will you work with me on this?"

As hurt as she was by what had happened between her and Todd, Elizabeth knew in her heart that though Todd might have some special privileges as a varsity athlete, he would never take any kind of bribe. And she also knew that Todd understood how much journalism meant to her. He would want her to do what she'd always done: tell the truth.

Tom touched her arm. "Look, Elizabeth, I know you and Todd Wilkins—"

"Of course I'll work with you," Elizabeth said, cutting him off. "If your hunch is right, then it's our duty to prove it."

She almost thought he was going to take her into his arms, he looked so happy. But he didn't take her into his arms. He shook her hand.

"Hey, blondie! Want a ride?"

Jessica stopped right in the middle of something she was saying to Isabella and Denise Waters as though someone had pulled out her plug.

Mike! her heart screamed. *It's Mike! He's right there beside you! It's him!*

Trying not to show the ecstasy she was feeling, Jessica turned to the blood-red Corvette and the dark, handsome man sitting inside it. The passenger door opened as if by magic.

"What were you saying, Jess?" Denise asked.

But Jessica was already in the Corvette—and in Michael McAllery's arms.

"I think your friends are trying to get your attention," Mike whispered when they finally broke for air.

"Um . . ." Jessica murmured, her mouth against his neck. This close to Mike, the only thing she could think of was him—holding him, kissing him, inhaling his scent, melting under his touch. Isabella and Denise could be doing headstands for all Jessica cared—she wasn't going to miss one second of this.

Someone was knocking on the window. "Jessica!" Isabella called. "Do you want to meet us at the café or what?"

Mike slipped a hand under her jacket and around her waist. "You going somewhere with the girls?" he asked, his voice as soft as the line of kisses he was tracing up and down her face.

"Um . . ."

"Jessica! Do you want us to meet you at the café? Denise has to go back to her room and change anyway. We could meet you in about an hour."

"Because if you want to go with your friends, I won't try to stop you, baby. I don't want to ruin your plans."

"Jessica!"

"You're not ruining anything," Jessica managed to say despite the shivers running through her body. "I don't have any plans."

"Because if you're not going with your friends, maybe we could go someplace a little more comfortable."

"We're leaving, Jess." It was Denise's voice. "We'll see you later. Nice talking to you, Mike."

"That sounds great," Jessica answered, her voice low.

His hands moved across her body. "Don't you

44

want to say good-bye to your friends?"

"What friends?" Jessica asked as he leaned down to kiss her again.

Celine was sitting in a dark corner of the campus coffeehouse, watching William White the way a cat watches a bird.

Look at him, she said to herself. *Rich, conceited, attractive as sin* . . . Her eyes moved from the handsome, unsmiling face to the lean, muscular body slouched against the booth he was sitting in alone. But it wasn't really his wealth or his looks that attracted Celine, and she knew it. It was *him*. William White was the person Celine Boudreaux wanted to be. She wanted to have that effortless arrogance, that casual contempt for everybody else. She didn't want to have to constantly prove to herself that she was beautiful and desirable; she wanted to know it the way William White knew it, with every cell he possessed.

Celine's eyes narrowed. *Can it really be true?* she wondered. *Can someone like William have a crush on the Little Princess?*

Celine sipped her espresso. She'd observed William watching Elizabeth Wakefield now and then, but she hadn't really taken it seriously. If Celine couldn't tempt him with her lush, sensuous looks and wild nature, what could he possibly see in Little Miss America with her boring prettiness and golden-girl perfection? If Celine was a challenge,

Elizabeth was a tranquilizer.

She scraped her long, gold-colored nails along the table. No, she hadn't taken William's interest in Elizabeth seriously until this morning. But this morning when she woke up, there was a single miniature white rose in a soda bottle on Elizabeth's desk. It had taken Celine a few minutes to remember why the sight of the flower, brilliant in the sunlight, disturbed her so much.

And then it had come back to her. Last night at the party she'd been holding a rose when she tried to talk to William, and he'd taken it away from her. There must, of course, be more than one small white rose in Southern California, but there wasn't a doubt in Celine's mind that the one on Elizabeth's desk was the one William had been holding when he disappeared last night. He'd iced her completely, and then gone out to find Princess Pill. Celine's nails dug into the worn wood. Someone was going to pay for that. Two someones.

She could take care of that stupid Elizabeth easily enough. It was so much fun to spread stories and rumors about her. William was trickier. She couldn't tell him many lies about Elizabeth because he knew Celine too well; he wouldn't believe her. She was going to have to get at him some other way.

Pushing her empty cup across the table, Celine got to her feet. She picked up the shopping bags on the floor beside her chair, and slow and graceful as a cat moving in for the pounce, crossed the coffee-house.

"Why, William," she purred, sliding into the booth beside him so quickly that he couldn't stop her. "Imagine running into you again so soon. Where did you get to last night? I turned away for one minute and you were gone."

"Did somebody ask you to sit down here, Celine, or have you started hearing voices?"

Celine rested her chin on her hands. "I wouldn't be too rude to me if I were you, William White. Because it just so happens that I know something that you don't know. Something you might like to know." She touched his wrist. "Something you might like to know very much."

He raised his eyebrows, his mouth a smirk. "Oh, really? And what's that?"

Celine smiled, as a cat smiles after it's caught its prey. "The name of my roommate," she said.

*Chapter
Three*

"I hope you don't mind me dropping in like this," Alison Quinn said. "But Isabella said you were here."

"Oh, of course not," Jessica said. She smiled her brightest and most enthusiastic smile.

It was a lucky thing she was ready for this. She had been lying in her bed, the covers over her head, remembering every detail of last night with Mike. Dreaming of what their next date would be like. Waiting for his call. But then she'd heard Isabella leave, and she'd decided that even a girl who was madly in love could use a cup of coffee. And that was when she found Isabella's note: *Alison Q. phoned. She needs to talk to you. Will be over soon. Love, Isabella.* Jessica had just enough time to get washed and dressed before Alison was knocking on the door.

Alison sat down on the couch without waiting

to be asked. "I guess you're wondering why I had to see you so urgently."

"Well, yes . . . I am . . ." Jessica lied. She'd actually been too busy thinking about Michael McAllery to give Alison Quinn much thought at all. The smile vanished from her face as something truly awful occurred to her.

Alison smiled regally, reading her thoughts. "Don't worry, Jessica, it isn't about you and the Thetas. Not specifically, anyway."

"Thank goodness." A sigh of relief escaped Jessica as she sat in the chair across from Alison. "You had me worried for a second."

Alison's smile became a little less comforting. "It does *concern* you, though, I'm afraid," she said, smoothing out a tiny wrinkle in her skirt.

Jessica looked into Alison's chilly gray eyes. For the first time in nearly twenty-four hours every thought of Mike went out of her head. "Liz!" she blurted. "It's Elizabeth, isn't it?"

This time the smile was approving. "Got it in one." Alison leaned back, her expression suddenly serious. "Let's not play games, okay, Jessica? You know and I know that the Thetas are practically obligated to pledge you and your sister because of your mother. Not that we don't want to pledge *you*, of course. *You* we love. But Elizabeth . . ." Alison shrugged, as though the problems with Elizabeth were so many and so awful that she didn't know where to begin.

49

"Elizabeth's been going through a difficult time," Jessica said quickly, her brain rushing ahead, creating traumas for her twin. "She—"

"Just isn't Theta material," Alison filled in. "You are. You are exactly what we look for. But Elizabeth . . ." Again she trailed off, defeated by the enormity of Elizabeth Wakefield's shortcomings. "We were very unhappy about the incident with Peter Wilbourne. You could be forgiven. You didn't know how much Peter dislikes Danny. And no one's saying that Peter wasn't out of line, attacking Danny like that, because he was. But Elizabeth made a spectacle of herself." Alison crossed her legs, flicking an invisible piece of lint from her sleeve. "Still, we were willing to overlook it. After her behavior yesterday, though—walking out in the middle of the tea like that—I'm not sure we can overlook it anymore."

"You mean you're not going to pledge her?" Jessica had warned her twin that this might happen, but still it came as a shock. More and more she seemed to be leaving her sister behind. The sensation made her feel unexpectedly lonely and vulnerable.

Alison made a sour little face. "We can't *not* pledge her," she said crisply. "Not unless we don't pledge you. I mean, I suppose she could turn us down . . ." Alison smiled as though this idea was so ridiculous she was almost embarrassed to mention it. "But there is no way we can pledge you and not pledge Elizabeth. You're seen as a package deal."

50

"But that's not fair!"

"Life's not fair." Alison shook her head. "That's why I'm here, Jessica. Magda and I have discussed it thoroughly, and if we're going to pledge your sister, she's going to have to assure us of her loyalty."

Jessica's stomach clenched. Elizabeth had no loyalty to the Thetas, and it wasn't going to be easy to get her to pretend she did. There were times when Elizabeth was too honest for Jessica's good. "How?" she asked bleakly.

Alison got to her feet. "We haven't quite worked that one out yet, but I'll let you know as soon as we do. In the meantime, though, I thought maybe you could have a word with Elizabeth. Tell her what I've told you. Get her to shape up a little."

"Sure," Jessica said, with an optimism she didn't feel. If Elizabeth wasn't careful, she could wind up a fat failure, but it was going to take more than Jessica to convince her of that. "I'll speak to her. As I said, she's been having a hard time. Her boyfriend—"

"I'm glad we had this talk." Alison held out her hand. "I know I speak for all the Thetas when I say that we'd really hate to lose you."

Jessica shook Alison's thin white hand. *I'd really hate for you to lose me too*, she thought.

Elizabeth marched into the television room, wondering if there was anything in the snack machines that wasn't fattening. She'd spent the after-

51

noon going over the material Tom had given her that morning, making notes and working out the way she thought the story should be handled.

She'd gotten so involved that she'd actually forgotten to go to dinner. If she didn't want to starve to death or trek all the way across campus to the snack bar, she was going to have to find something to eat here.

Elizabeth looked at the machines with a sinking heart and a growling stomach. Cookies, chocolate, tortilla chips . . . There was nothing that wasn't guaranteed to make your thighs swell. Why hadn't anyone ever thought of selling carrot sticks and cottage cheese in vending machines?

"How am I supposed to stay on my diet when I'm surrounded by candy bars and potato chips?" Elizabeth asked aloud. "It just isn't fair."

"You can say that again."

Elizabeth flushed. She'd thought she was alone.

"If you ask me, it should be illegal to have those things in a female dorm. Everybody knows that at any given time three out of every six women are on a diet."

Elizabeth turned around. The pretty face of Nina Harper was looking at her from over the back of the couch. Only, for the first time Elizabeth could remember since she'd met Nina, her face wasn't serious, it was grinning.

Elizabeth laughed. "Don't tell me you're on a diet too! You don't need to lose weight."

"Neither do you," Nina said. She smiled wryly. "I'm sort of on the lifer's diet. You know," she said, seeing Elizabeth's puzzled look. "If I weren't on a diet, I would have to lose weight. All you have to do is put me near a pepperoni pizza and I'm a lost woman."

"Potato chips," Elizabeth said, giving the snack machine a kick. "I've been resisting those cheddar-cheese potato chips since yesterday, but now I'm so hungry I may have to succumb. I've been working all afternoon."

Nina studied her for a minute. "I'm always seeing you in the library. You work almost as hard as I do. Do you have parents with enormous expectations too?"

Elizabeth shook her head. "No, I just don't have much else to do." She smiled ruefully. "*And* I have a roommate who drives me out of my mind."

"Celine, right?"

"The one and only." Elizabeth glanced toward the ceiling. "Thank God."

Normally she wouldn't complain about someone behind her back, but Celine was the exception to every rule. And things between them were just getting worse. Yesterday morning Elizabeth had found the rose William White had given her in her wastebasket, its petals not just plucked, but crushed.

"Roommates can be difficult," Nina said mildly. "Mine's okay, but we don't really have much in common. It's bad enough that she doesn't like my music, but she even complains that my hair makes too much noise."

"You must be kidding," Elizabeth said, trying not to choke with laughter. Nina's hair was in dozens of thin braids, each one held by a wooden bead at the end. "I love your hair. I think it looks great."

"Yeah, well, my roommate says it wakes her up in the night. And she goes nuts if I just shake my head when she's trying to study. That's why I go to the library so much. I can't study with her sighing and moaning all the time. And I guess the truth is, I'm a workaholic. It runs in my family." She shrugged. "What about you? Why do you want to lose weight?"

"Because I've gained some weight since school started," Elizabeth answered immediately, surprising herself. She hadn't even discussed her weight gain with Jessica, and here she was telling a stranger. "I used to be a perfect size six."

Nina stood up. "I haven't been a size six since I was ten." Nina was tall and big boned, but solidly built. "You're not going to get anything decent to eat from that machine," she said as she came over to Elizabeth. "I'm supposed to be studying for a psych test, but I could use a break. Why don't we go over to the coffeehouse? They make a great vegetable salad. If we split one, we could have enough spare calories to have some bread with it."

Elizabeth was tempted to say no. She really should go back to work. She really didn't feel like trudging across campus in the rain. She really shouldn't eat anything. A little starvation would do her good. She looked at Nina Harper's smiling face. It was one of the friendliest faces she'd encountered all semester.

Elizabeth smiled back. "Only if you promise not to let your hair make too much noise."

"You must have come home pretty late last night."

Jessica looked up from the history reading she was trying to do to kill time while she waited for Mike to call. Isabella was leaning against the wall, watching her with an expression that reminded Jessica of her mother. Jessica bit her lip. The last thing she needed right now was a lecture.

"Since when are you my mother?" she asked, laughing to keep her tone light.

"Since you've started making a public spectacle of yourself with Mike McAllery," Isabella replied, not sounding light at all. "What were you thinking yesterday? Leaving me and Denise standing there like a couple of idiots." She strode into the room, sitting at the table across from Jessica. "What time did you get in, anyway? You didn't spend the night with Mike, did you?"

Jessica couldn't hide her surprise. "Is this Isabella Ricci, the wild woman of SVU, talking?"

"No, this is Isabella Ricci, your best friend at SVU, talking." She grabbed Jessica's hand. "Listen

55

to me, Jess, you have got to get a grip. How many times do I have to tell you? Mike is not just some college kid with a crazy streak. He's dangerous. This guy should come with a government health warning tattooed across his forehead: *This man could seriously damage your heart.*" She gave Jessica a sarcastic look. "Not to mention the damage he could do to your reputation."

"My reputation?" Furious, Jessica pushed back her chair and jumped to her feet. As good a friend as Isabella had become since school started, Jessica sometimes wished that Lila Fowler, her best friend from high school, had come to college as planned, instead of staying in Europe and marrying an Italian count. Lila wouldn't have been critical. Lila would have been supportive.

"You don't seem to understand something, Isabella," Jessica said calmly. "I'm in love with Mike. He's the man of my dreams."

"You may think he's the man of your dreams now," Isabella said ominously. "But if you're not careful, he's going to turn into the man of your nightmares."

Jessica glared back at her. "I don't have to listen to this!"

"Yes, you do!" Isabella got to her feet too. "Jessica, will you please stop thinking with your hormones? It's not just that Mike drinks and fools around with lots of different women. No one has any idea what he does for money. He might be a drug dealer, for all you know."

"You said he was a photographer," Jessica said, feeling cornered. Somehow, she'd never gotten around to actually asking Mike what he did for a living. He wasn't the kind of man who encouraged personal questions.

"I said he *used* to be a photographer. But that was a long time ago."

Jessica's cheeks were burning. "What about his father? You told me he inherited a lot of money."

"Look at the car the man drives!" Isabella shouted. "The way that guy lives, he could have gone through at least three inheritances by now."

"I don't care!" Jessica screamed. "I don't care about any of that!"

"Well, you should care. You should—"

The ringing of the telephone drowned out Isabella's words. *Saved by the bell*, thought Jessica, making a dive for the phone.

"I've been thinking about you, baby," the voice said, as smooth and supple as a snake. "I was afraid I missed you. I was afraid you might have gone out with your friends."

I may never go out with my friends again. "No, I'm right here." She lowered her voice. "I was hoping you'd call."

"I'm coming by to get you. Wait downstairs."

Jessica hung up the phone, her anger of a few minutes before replaced by joy. *I'm coming by to get you. Wait downstairs.* Without another word to

Isabella, she picked up her jacket and ran out the door.

There she was! *Be still, my catapulting heart,* he told himself. *Don't make so much noise, she'll hear you!*

Half hidden by a large potted palm, Winston Egbert gazed across the snack bar to where a beautiful young woman sat by herself, reading a novel while she ate a plate of onion rings. Winston couldn't help sighing. Watching Denise Waters eat onion rings was like watching poetry in motion.

He held his breath, trying to figure out his next move. It hadn't been easy following her here. He'd had to hang around in the lobby of Oakley Hall for hours, pretending to be waiting for someone, till she finally came out. Then he'd had to trail her from the dorm. He'd never known anyone with so many friends. They barely managed to walk a couple of yards before Denise would run into someone else she knew and stop to talk. And the whole time, of course, he'd had to keep his eye out for the blue jackets of the Sigmas.

Winston's eyes scanned the room again. Not only had he made it across campus without seeing one Sigma brother, but, miraculously, there weren't any in the snack bar, either.

This is it, Win, he told himself. *This is your chance. Go over and ask her if you can sit down. She'll say yes. She likes you. She always laughs at your jokes.*

Denise took another onion ring from her plate,

dipped it in ketchup, and lifted it to her lips. Winston thought his heart might break. It was like watching a Shakespearean sonnet eat, only better. No sonnet in the world looked or sounded or smelled like Denise Waters.

Go, Winston urged himself. *Go now. Good grief, you're her buddy. She borrows your hair dryer. She lends you tapes. She shared her popcorn with you when you watched the television movie Wednesday night. She even told you when it was all right to look. This woman isn't a stranger, Win, she's a friend.*

Winston took a deep breath and stepped from behind the palm. Nothing happened. Because a large, meaty hand had suddenly locked itself onto his shoulder.

"Win, old pal!" Bill was shouting. "Win, we've been looking all over for you. Where've you been?"

Winston laughed nervously. "Oh, around. Just around." It wasn't easy, but he forced himself to smile.

Bill's arm slid around his shoulders. "Let's go get a burger, pal," he said as he propelled Winston toward the line. "My treat."

"Your treat?"

Two other Sigmas followed, making their usual racket. Winston glanced over at Denise. There was no way he could approach her now. After seeing Winston with these guys, Denise would forget what a nice, normal human being he was. She'd think he was one of them.

"You know, this is a very fortuitous meeting," Bill was saying as he picked up a tray. "Really fortuitous, Winston. Because I've been meaning to ask you for a little favor, and the object of that little favor happens to be right over there."

A chill, dank suspicion engulfed Winston's heart. It couldn't be. It just couldn't be. Bill couldn't be interested in Denise. Winston hadn't done anything to deserve it. Surely the gods wouldn't be this unkind to him. Winston stared into Bill's big-man smile. It was a good thing he'd been so preoccupied with waiting for Denise today that he'd forgotten to eat lunch, or he'd probably throw up about now.

"Oh, really?" he croaked. "What's that, Bill?"

Bill leaned so close, Winston could smell the grape bubble gum he was chewing. "I was wondering if you could introduce me to Denise Waters. I mean, I know her by sight and everything, but she's always been really standoffish to me. I thought that maybe you and I could go over there and sit with her. You know, once she got to see what a good guy I am, she might warm up."

Winston could only stare at Bill in horror. A girl like Denise might incinerate a guy like Bill, but she wasn't going to warm up to him. And she wasn't going to warm up to anybody who tried to set them up, either. Even if Winston could impersonate Donald Duck singing the telephone jingle, she would never go out with him after that.

"She's a friend of yours, right?" Bill asked. He

winked. "She's in your dorm, right? You two wash your faces together. You've seen her with goop in her hair. Be a real pal, Win. Just give me an intro."

For weeks Winston had been thinking of Denise. He even dreamed about her. She was intelligent, she was beautiful, she was nice. They made each other laugh. She was everything he'd ever wanted in a woman. For weeks he'd been working up enough courage to ask her out, and here he'd finally gotten himself to the brink—and what happened? Bill happened.

Winston's fantasies were disintegrating in front of his eyes. He looked over at Denise. She was leaving! Her guardian angel must have whispered in her ear that Bill was on his way over to put the moves on her. She was definitely on her way out.

"Oh, gee, will you look at that!" Winston said, his voice filled with disappointment. "She's going, Bill. We're too late."

Bill watched Denise disappear through the door. "Well, you can forget about that hamburger then, Win."

"What did she ever see in him?" William asked. "He looks like he should be dating Barbie."

Celine followed William's gaze across the jammed living room of the Zeta house to where Todd Wilkins and his basketball buddies were demonstrating a play for a circle of admiring girls. *You mean, what did he ever see in a wet towel like*

61

Elizabeth, Celine thought. She shrugged. "I really don't know, William." She gave him a meaningful look. "It's a mystery to me what attracts certain people to certain other people."

He wasn't paying attention. "You're sure they've broken up?"

"Sure as the Mississippi is wide," Celine said. She pointed to the attractive redhead at Todd's side. "That's his new girlfriend, Lauren Hill. I hear they're very close." She lit a cigarette, blowing a thin stream of smoke past William's handsome face.

William choked. "I wish you'd give those things up, Celine," he snapped. "Next to your personality they're one of the most unappealing things about you."

"Why, William White," Celine drawled, floating a perfect ring of smoke in front of him. "Are you trying to turn my head with flattery?"

"I'm going to go get another drink before you asphyxiate me. I'll be back."

Celine watched him cross the room. Aloof and apart, he stood out in the crowd of normal, average students like a diamond in a bag of peanuts. Celine blew another smoke ring into the air. For all his aloofness, people were drawn to him. She watched them stop him as he moved toward the refreshment table. Celine moistened her lips with the tip of her tongue. She knew he'd be back. It didn't matter how much he insulted her; the important thing was that he was no longer pretending she didn't exist. Now that William knew she lived with Elizabeth, he needed her. They were allies. Partners. Celine smiled to herself. William, of course, thought that he was using *her*.

She knew it was the other way around.

Jessica sat behind Mike on the customized lowrider as they sped through the night, the lights of the buildings flashing past them like stars. She felt as though she were flying.

If my parents could see me now, they would have a fit. The Wakefields hated motorcycles because of the accident Elizabeth had had her junior year, and they'd forbidden the twins ever to ride on them again. But Ned and Alice Wakefield couldn't see Jessica now. They stopped at a light and Jessica put her lips to the cracked leather of Mike's jacket, trying to commit the smell and feel of it to memory. It didn't really matter if her parents could see her. She wasn't a child anymore, after all. She was a woman. If she wanted to ride behind Mike on his motorcycle, there was no way in the world anyone could prevent her.

At last the bike pulled to a stop in a parking lot and she jumped off. "That was fantastic!" she cried. "Absolutely fantastic! That's the most incredible machine I've ever seen." She laughed, throwing herself into his arms. "I didn't even know you owned a motorcycle."

He smiled. "There's a lot you don't know about me."

Jessica rested her head against his chest with a happy sigh. And then her eyes fell on the building in front of them. She'd thought he was taking her out for a late-night snack, but she'd been wrong. It was an apartment building: a large, white apartment building with a green door and cacti out front. A building Jessica had seen many times before.

"What's this?" she asked, trying to hide her surprise.

"I thought it was about time you saw where I live." Mike put his arm around her and started leading her up the flagstone path.

"You could have told me this was where we were coming," she said, sounding a little more petulant than she'd intended. This was the building where her brother, Steven, and his girlfriend, Billie lived. It wasn't a happy coincidence.

"Well, now you know." He gave her a squeeze. "I'm tired of making out with you in the car, Jess. It wrinkles my clothes and it cramps my style." He opened the front door. "And besides, I'm not a teenager, even if you are."

Jessica followed him up to his apartment, the exhilaration of the ride forgotten. She hated it when he teased her about her age. Just because she was young didn't mean she wasn't grown up. She was a woman.

"Well, this is it," Mike said. He unlocked the door and ushered her inside. "My humble home."

"My God!" Jessica tried to be extra cool when she was around Mike, but this time she couldn't hide her shock. "This place is unbelievable. I've never seen anything like it in my life!"

Mike's apartment was the exact size and layout of Steven's, but all similarities ended there. Steven's was just a run-of-the-mill student apartment, furnished with bits and pieces people had given him or he'd found in secondhand stores. But Mike's was a state-of-the-art bachelor apartment, so expensively and perfectly decorated it looked like a movie set. It didn't look like a place where a real person lived. Jessica looked over at Mike. And Mike wasn't a real person. He'd stepped right out of a dream.

"So you think it's okay?"

"*Okay?* Yes, I think it's okay."

Jessica stood at the entrance to the living room for a few minutes, just looking at the highly polished wood floors scattered with afghan carpets; the oversize sofa and armchairs, upholstered in silk, the slatted wooden blinds in the windows; and the large, old-fashioned green fan that looked like a propeller hanging from the ceiling. One wall was lined with shelves filled with books, and another was taken up by a large-screen television, a VCR, and a black-and-chrome music center. The lighting was subtle and indirect.

Isabella's voice started yammering in her ear. *How does he get his money, Jess? What does he do? A*

'64 Corvette . . . a custom-made motorcycle . . . this apartment . . . He must do something, Jess. He didn't win it all in a game show.

Mike's arms encircled her, causing Isabella's voice to vanish back into the air. "I'm glad you like it," he whispered. "I want you to feel at home here, baby. I want you to feel relaxed."

Jessica leaned into him. If she felt any more relaxed, her bones would dissolve. "I do feel at home," she whispered back. "I love—I love it here."

He kissed her ear. "Then why don't we lie down on the couch, put a video in the machine, and not watch it for a couple of hours?"

She didn't have to answer. He'd already lifted her in his arms and was carrying her across the room.

Later, when a second video was playing unnoticed and they were lying on the couch in each other's arms, exchanging small, personal details about themselves, Jessica remembered Isabella's questions. Mike's breath was as warm as sunlight on her face. His body was so close, she could hardly tell where hers ended and his began. The mood between them was so close and so intimate that she felt she could ask him now.

She ran her fingers through his long, soft hair. "What is it you said you do for a living?" she asked in a near whisper, straining to make her voice casual and easy.

Mike flicked off the movie, tossing the remote

across the floor. He moved so that he was over her, his mouth a kiss away, his eyes staring into her heart.

"I didn't say."

Sometimes, when Celine was in a really good mood and was feeling wanted and at peace with the world, she would come into the dorm quietly late at night. She would unlock the door to her room softly. Instead of turning on the overhead light, or even the lamp on her desk, she would undress by the tiny night-light Elizabeth had put in the outlet by the door. She wouldn't throw her shoes across the room. She wouldn't bang into things. She wouldn't turn on the radio or light up a cigarette.

Tonight, however, Celine was not in a good mood. It had been a terrific party, full of laughter and music—the sort of party that made you feel as though you had a million friends and would always be beautiful and young.

But in the end, William had spoiled it for her. She'd been charming and funny and full of conversation, yet the longer the evening wore on, the more sullen and silent he'd become. Celine was certain that if she could get close enough to him, she could make William White fall in love with her. That was her plan. To make him fall in love with her and then to break his heart into more pieces than there were grains of sand on the

California shore. But to make him forget Elizabeth and fall for her was going to be harder than she'd thought.

"You're thinking about *her*, aren't you?" Celine had finally asked, only just managing to keep the jealousy and revulsion out of her voice. "You haven't stopped thinking about her all night."

He'd turned to her, his skin so white, his mouth so soft, his eyes so hard. "And who else would I be thinking of?"

Remembering that moment and the way William had looked at her, as though she were some form of pond life and not a beautiful young woman herself, Celine marched down the corridor of Dickenson Hall, a lighted cigarette in her hand, and threw open the door to her room with a bang. She snapped on the desk lamp and hurled herself onto her bed.

The effect was instantaneous. A blond head rose up from the opposite bed, squinting and rubbing the sleep from her eyes.

"Celine?" The blue-green eyes slowly opened. "What do you think you're doing?"

But Celine wasn't going to listen to one of Elizabeth's lectures tonight. Tonight wasn't a night for arguing. Tonight was a night for claws and blood.

"You missed a great party, Lizzie," she said sweetly. "A really great party. One of your favorite people was there."

Elizabeth was sitting up, anger replacing sleepiness. "Celine, are you out of your mind? What do you—"

"Todd," Celine said. "Todd was there. With that lovely girl, what's her name? Lauren? Lauren Hill?"

Elizabeth was staring at her now, her expression a mixture of hurt and disbelief.

Celine's smile grew. "They certainly have gotten very close very fast, haven't they? But then, she is so very, very lovely." Celine's eyes flashed. "Slender . . . pretty . . . vivacious . . ." Celine blew a cloud of smoke across the room.

"By the way," she said, feeling much better all of a sudden. "Todd was asking about you. 'How's Liz?' he asked."

Celine's smile grew even bigger and brighter. "You don't have to worry, Lizzie," she purred. "I didn't tell him you were still sulky and putting on weight. I told him you were fine."

Chapter Four

Even as Jessica gradually gained consciousness, she wondered where she was. She could tell from the sounds outside and the feel of the air that she wasn't where she was supposed to be. When she opened her eyes she wasn't going to see the deep-raspberry walls of the room she shared with Isabella, or Isabella herself in the opposite bed, lying flat on her back on her paisley sheets. The question was, What was she going to see?

Slowly Jessica opened her eyes. The room was dark, only a few determined shafts of light managing to struggle through the blinds. She looked around. Books . . . television . . . fan . . . Mike's apartment! She was still at Mike's. She was on the couch, still wearing the clothes she'd been wearing the night before, though now they were rumpled and her blouse was unbuttoned. And there, his head resting between her arm and her breast, was Mike, still wearing his jeans and a T-shirt. His dark hair fanned over her skin, his sensuous lips parted in a smile.

Jessica had no memory of falling asleep. She remembered snuggling against him, intoxicated by his smell. She remembered the room melting away as she lost herself to his hands and his lips. But she didn't remember closing her eyes. They must both have passed out, exhausted from so many passionate kisses. She leaned over and rested her cheek on the top of his head.

I can't believe it! she thought as she stared down at him, almost hypnotized, just watching him sleep. *I can't believe I spent the whole night with a guy!*

What more proof did she need that she really was a sophisticated woman of the world? There was nothing she couldn't do now. Wait till she told Lila! Wait till she told Lila what a wonderful, incredible night she'd had.

A frown appeared on Jessica's face. Lila wasn't here anymore. Lila was in Italy, married to a count. Isabella was here. And Isabella wasn't going to think it was wonderful or incredible at all. Isabella was going to think it was shocking. She was going to be full of more warnings and lectures and tales of gloom. Jessica sighed. She would have to tell Isabella something else. That she'd stayed with Steven, or even with Elizabeth.

She would save the truth for a letter to Lila. The frown deepened. Lila wasn't going to think Jessica's night was so wonderful and incredible either. What was so wonderful about sleeping on a couch in your jeans and a flannel shirt? Lila was a married woman.

"Morning, baby."

Jessica looked over. That smile was more dazzling than any sunny morning. "Morning, yourself."

He nuzzled against her, his mouth in her hair. "You sure are a nice thing to wake up to," he said, his voice still fuzzy with sleep. "But I guess all the guys tell you that."

She gave him a shove. "What are you talking about? I never woke—"

Mike laughed, lifting himself up on one arm to look at her. "Chill out, Jess. I know you're still a little girl. You made that pretty clear last night."

She hadn't thought it was possible to get mad at him, but she was almost mad now. What was it with men? If you weren't a virgin, they wondered if you slept around, and if you were a virgin, they accused you of being a little girl.

"Hey!" Seeing the expression on her face, he leaned over and kissed her on the tip of her nose. "I'm just teasing you, baby. Don't get yourself all wound up."

Jessica smiled back, but she couldn't help wondering if Lila's husband called her "baby."

Mike got up and stretched. "How about some coffee? I could use a whole pot of it poured over my head. I feel like I slept in a box."

Jessica laughed. "I'd love a—" She shook her

72

wrist. Could it really be eight thirty? "Oh, my God! I've got a philosophy seminar in forty-five minutes that I can't miss. I've got to go!"

Mike turned in the doorway. "Why don't you blow off your classes today? Hang out with me. We can take the bike up the coast. I know a beautiful little beach. . . ."

Jessica was already on her feet, pulling on her shoes. "I can't, Mike, I really can't. I'm not doing so well in my classes right now. I can't afford to cut this seminar. It's going to figure a lot in our final grade." She didn't need to mention that she wasn't doing so well in her classes because she spent all her free time thinking about him.

"Suit yourself. There's a brand-new toothbrush in the medicine cabinet. It's yours if you want it."

"I don't have time." It was bad enough that she was going to have Isabella on her case for spending the night with Mike; she didn't need to miss class, too. She snatched up her bag and her jacket. "I'll just have to have gorilla breath for one morning."

Jessica opened the door, but before she could rush through it, two strong arms wrapped themselves around her.

"Hey," Mike whispered. "What sort of a guy do you think I am? I don't want people saying my baby's a gorilla. Go brush your teeth and then I'll run you to school."

My life has fallen into a routine, Steven Wakefield

was thinking as he threw the garbage into the black plastic can in front of his building. Monday mornings he emptied the trash. Tuesday evenings Billie had a class and he picked up pizza on his way home. On Wednesdays, Billie cooked and he did the laundry. Thursdays he had late classes and she picked up something for supper. Fridays he cooked and they usually rented a video and stayed in.

Steven looked up at the cloudless, blue morning sky. *But it's a nice routine,* he told himself. Peaceful. Secure. There were no major problems to be overcome, no major traumas to adjust to. He had Billie, he had school, everything was going well for him.

I'm a lucky guy, Steven was thinking as he turned back to the front door.

The smile shriveled on his lips. Standing there on the stoop, for everyone to see, was Mike Mr. Attitude McAllery, locked in a passionate kiss with his very own sister.

Steven clenched his fists as his blood began to churn. He was used to seeing Mike McAllery with women. Mike McAllery had more women coming in and out than the local beauty parlor. Steven was also was used to seeing Mike kissing his women in public. But he wasn't used to seeing him kissing his little sister. Not at eight thirty in the morning!

"What the hell is going on here?"

The couple on the stoop didn't look over. They were too involved in mashing their mouths together to even have heard Steven's roar.

74

"Hey! McAllery! I'm talking to you, you low-life. What the hell do you think you're doing?"

Very slowly, like an elephant who thinks an ant may have just walked over its foot, Mike McAllery pulled back, his arms still around Jessica, and turned to Steven. Jessica had the decency to look horrified and embarrassed. But Mike didn't even blink.

"I live here," Mike said. "That's what I'm doing. I'm living here. What are you doing?"

"I'll tell you!" Steven shouted, already up the path and grabbing hold of Jessica to pull her away. "I'm going to hit you so hard in the mouth it'll be a year before you kiss anyone again!"

"Steven!" Jessica shrieked. She pushed him away. "What are you doing? Have you lost your mind?"

"Me? Have I lost *my* mind? Jessica, what are you doing with this creep? What are you doing at eight thirty in the morning kissing this creep?" He reached for her again.

Mike McAllery stepped in front of Jessica, laying one hand flat on Steven's chest. "Before I make this guy part of the fertilizer, Jess," he said in his slow, calm way, "you want to tell me who he is?"

Steven knocked his hand away. "I'll tell you who I am, you piece of garbage. I'm her brother."

McAllery smiled. "Is that true?" He looked over his shoulder at Jessica. "Is this vigilante really your brother?"

Jessica nodded. Steven noticed that though she

75

was looking at him, she was holding on to Mike.

Mike turned back to Steven. "Well, let me tell you who *I* am, Superbrother. I'm Jessica's boyfriend. And that gives me top billing, as I see it." He stretched out his arm and Jessica stepped into it. "Come on, baby," he said, giving Steven an arrogant smile. "Let's get going before big brother here makes you late for school."

Steven felt as though his blood had been freeze-dried. Not long ago, Elizabeth had turned up on his doorstep in tears in the middle of the night. Elizabeth had always been popular and sure of herself in high school, but college had thrown her, and she was miserable with loneliness and insecurity. Billie thought that all Elizabeth needed was some time to find her feet, but Steven couldn't stop worrying about her. And now this. Now Jessica had turned up on his doorstep in the middle of a passionate kiss with a creep. What was it with his sisters? Were they trying to drive him nuts?

Steven was still standing in front of the building, staring down the street in the direction the motorcycle had gone, when Billie came looking for him.

"Steven! What are you doing out here, gazing into space? I was getting worried."

He turned to her. Her pretty face was drawn with concern. "You should be worried," he said, shaking his head. "My sister Jessica just left here with Mike McAllery."

"What?"

76

"You heard me. Jessica is seeing that ape Mc-Allery. She was here. With him. Kissing. They just left."

The concern on Billie's face disappeared. "I think you're overreacting a little, Steven. Mike McAllery may be a character, but he is not an ape."

Steven stared at her as though he'd never seen her before. "What? Are you saying that you approve? Are you saying that you think it's just fine for my sister to hang around with a womanizing cretin like that?"

She was smiling. Billie was actually smiling.

"Oh, come on, Steven." Billie took his hand. "I'm not saying it's fine; I'm just saying it's not really any of your business. Jessica's a woman now."

He pulled his hand away. "And what's that supposed to mean?"

Billie gave him an exasperated look. "It's not supposed to mean anything. It just—"

"Are you suggesting that Jessica might actually be *sleeping* with that delinquent? Is that what you're suggesting?"

She looked as though she might start laughing. "College people do sleep together, you know, Steven. It has been heard of."

Steven glared at her. As much as he cared about Billie, there were times when she baffled him. He knew what she was getting at, of course. She thought that it was hypocritical of him to live with her and then be so outraged that his sister might be

77

having a serious relationship. What she didn't seem to understand was that there was no connection between his and Billie's relationship and Jessica and Mike McAllery's. How would she like it if it were *her* sister running around with a man with a vintage Corvette and no visible means of support?

"They sleep with responsible, trustworthy people they can have a real relationship with, Billie," Steven said stiffly. "Not with bums who have more girlfriends than Ford has cars."

She touched his shoulder. "Steven," she said patiently, "don't you think that you may be exaggerating just a little? I know he gets around, but—"

"No, I don't think I'm exaggerating. McAllery is a man of the world and Jessica's still in her teens." He could hear his voice getting louder, but he couldn't stop it. "What if he hurts her, Billie? Have you thought about that? What if he winds up breaking her heart?"

"Stop shouting at me, Steven!" Billie turned back to the door and yanked it open. "It's not your heart he'll be breaking," she said, standing halfway in the building. "It's Jessica's. Why don't you let her worry about it?"

"Muesli, skim milk, one small apple, black coffee . . . Well, what do you know? You and I are having the exact same breakfast. I guess this meeting of the SVU Diet Till You Drop club can now begin."

Elizabeth, who had been staring vacantly into

her muesli, looked up to see Nina putting her tray down on the table across from her.

"You have no idea what willpower it took not to have frosted cornflakes and a doughnut this morning," Elizabeth said with a laugh. "I slept so badly last night I could use a massive dose of sugar."

Nina flopped into her chair. "You don't look so good, now that you mention it." She tilted her head, scrutinizing Elizabeth's face. "What's wrong? Dreams of pepperoni pizza and triple chocolate mousse keep you awake?"

Elizabeth sighed. "I wish."

"What's the matter, Elizabeth?" Nina's face was filled with genuine concern. "What could have happened between yesterday afternoon when we had such a good time together and this morning to make you look so miserable?"

"Celine went to a party."

"Yeah? And then what? She brought the band back with her?"

Elizabeth shook her head. "I almost wish she had. She woke me up to tell me that Todd was at the party."

Nina's eyebrows went up. "Oh. I get it." Nina poured skim milk over her muesli and dug in her spoon. In the course of a very long evening, one of the things that Nina and Elizabeth had discussed in some depth was Todd. "Let me guess. Todd wasn't alone."

"He was with Lauren."

79

"How nice of Celine to tell you," Nina said through a mouthful of cereal. "I don't suppose she went into any of the gory details, did she? I'm sure she'd want to spare your feelings."

Elizabeth smirked. "How did you guess? She also made sure she mentioned how slim and vivacious Lauren is." She pushed her cereal bowl away. "I may never eat again."

Nina pushed it back. "Cut it out, will you, Liz? You may have put on a few pounds, but you're still pretty slim and vivacious yourself. You've got a lot more on the ball than Lauren Hill, that's for sure." She chewed another spoonful of muesli.

"It's not that so much," Elizabeth said miserably. "It's that I really miss Todd. I'm beginning to think I was wrong to let the relationship just end like that, but it's too late."

"Maybe, maybe not." Nina gave her a thoughtful look. "I wouldn't let Celine wind me up if I were you," she said slowly. "Celine loves to cause trouble, especially for you." She pointed her spoon at Elizabeth. "Believe me, if that girl's mouth were a gun, it would be an uzi automatic."

Something in Nina's tone made Elizabeth look at her closely. "What do you mean, *especially for me*?"

Nina shrugged. "Let's just say that until I actually talked to you yesterday, it would have been easy for me to assume that the person with roommate problems was Celine, not you."

"What?"

80

"Look," Nina said, the beads on her braids clicking as she leaned forward. "I didn't know whether or not I should mention this, but Celine goes around telling the wildest stories about you. . . ."

Elizabeth wasn't even sure why she should feel so surprised or so betrayed. She should have known Celine would be gossiping about her behind her back. "And do people believe her?"

Nina made a face. "I think a lot of people believed her at first. You know how sweet and charming she can be. And you were so quiet and reserved. . . ." She turned her attention back to her cereal. "To be completely honest, Liz," Nina went on slowly, not meeting Elizabeth's eyes, "I believed her myself at first. Until I started seeing you in the library all the time and noticed you around campus. Then I started to suspect that Celine wasn't being too economical with the truth. I think other people are beginning to catch on too. I saw her at a party last week, and the only people who would talk to her were guys who see better than they think."

Elizabeth groaned. "Oh, great. I'll bet she's been telling Todd stories too."

"That's what I'm trying to say," Nina explained. "You don't know. Maybe it would be worth talking to Todd. Even if it is just for your own peace of mind."

Elizabeth picked up her coffee cup. "Maybe," she said. "Maybe it would."

*   *   *

Jessica saw them as soon as they came around the corner. Isabella and Denise were standing on the pavement outside the lecture hall where her seminar was being given, deep in conversation. At the sound of the bike's engine, they broke off and turned around. Then again, everyone on the sidewalk was staring at the bike as it rumbled to a stop in front of a No Parking sign.

Jessica leaned over Mike's shoulder as he turned off the ignition. "You certainly know how to make an entrance," she whispered.

Mike grinned. "It's not me, it's the killer Kawasaki engine."

She pulled off her helmet and shook out her hair. "Well, whatever it is, it sure is effective. Everybody's gaping at us."

Mike turned and slipped his arm around her. "Why don't we give them something to talk about?"

Pressed against him, his mouth on hers, it was as though the rest of the world just stopped. Nothing mattered—not Steven, not school, not her friends, not what people might think or say. She wouldn't have cared if the entire state of California were gathered on the sidewalk beside them, watching them kiss. All that mattered was that she was in Mike's arms, and that was where she wanted to stay.

The clock in the lecture-hall tower began to chime and students began to disappear.

Jessica pulled back, glancing toward the curb

again. Isabella and Denise had not disappeared. They were still standing there, staring at her with open disapproval.

Mike's eyes followed hers. "What do you say, Jess?" he asked. "You want to stay with your snobby friends? Or you want to go to the beach with me?"

"We'll have to stop by the dorm first," Jessica said. "So I can pick up my bikini."

"Strike while the iron is hot," Elizabeth mumbled to herself as she hurried across campus to the athlete's dorm where Todd lived. "Seize the moment. She who hesitates is lost."

What Elizabeth had told Nina was true. After Celine woke her up last night, taunting her about seeing Todd with Lauren, she had tossed and turned all night. Every time she drifted off to sleep, images of herself and Todd haunted her dreams. She missed him. Now that the insecurity she'd been feeling when she first got to college was beginning to fade, she could see that he'd been right all along. It was time that their relationship changed. It was time to grow up.

Nina was right. Elizabeth owed it to herself to talk to Todd. What did she really know? Just because he was seen around campus with Lauren Hill didn't mean he didn't miss Elizabeth. He might be laughing and having a good time on the outside, but inside he could be nursing a broken heart just as she was.

83

The ultramodern glass-and-steel dorm came into view. Elizabeth slowed down. "Nothing ventured, nothing gained," she told herself as she entered the building.

"You're doing the right thing," she assured herself as she got into the elevator. She knocked on Todd's door. "I'm *sure* you're doing the right thing." She knocked again.

"Liz!" He must have just gotten up. His shirt was unbuttoned, and he held a tube of toothpaste in his hand. "I—I thought you were Mark."

"I'm sorry to just show up like this," she said, her words coming out in a rush, "but I really have to talk to you."

He stared back at her as though she'd suggested they go bungee jumping. "Now?"

Elizabeth nodded. "I know this is sudden, and you probably have a class to go to—I do too—but I don't want to put this off any longer. We keep avoiding each other, like there's nothing left to discuss, but you just don't end a relationship like ours in ten minutes. . . ."

He didn't nod. He didn't speak. He just continued staring at her, his face wary and his body tense.

"Do you?" Elizabeth persisted.

Apparently he thought you did, if the expression on his face was anything to go by.

"Todd—" Elizabeth took a step forward. "Couldn't we just talk for a minute? There are a couple of things I really have to say."

He glanced over his shoulder, as though he'd heard something. "Maybe later, Liz. Why don't we meet later in the student center? My last class ends at five today. We could meet up then. Have a cup of coffee or something—"

"But I don't want to wait till five. I want to talk to you now."

Desperation was making her voice whine. Somehow, when she'd imagined this scene, she hadn't been whining and pleading. She'd been strong and clear. But when she'd imagined this scene, Todd hadn't been standing there like the Great Wall of China, stony and silent and blocking her way. He'd been welcoming her with open arms.

She'd come too far to stop now, though. She had to see it through. "Todd, please . . . I miss you so much. You were right and I was wrong. It was time our relationship changed. It was—"

"No, you were right, Liz. That side of things is over for us. We shouldn't be any more than friends. It would have been a mistake to go any further."

"Todd, I–I—"

"No, Liz, I really think—"

The bathroom door opened suddenly, sounding like the shot of a gun.

Elizabeth knew instinctively that she should turn and run, but she didn't. Instead, she looked over Todd's shoulder. Lauren Hill was standing framed in the doorway of the bathroom, wearing only Todd's practice jersey and looking sleepy and rumpled.

"Todd?" Lauren said. "Do you have the toothpaste?"

What a dream, Tom was thinking as he and Danny left the cafeteria. Just the thought of it made him smile.

"What's with you this morning?" Danny asked, giving him a curious look. "Either there were strange chemical pollutants in my tea this morning making me see things, or you're actually happy."

Tom slung his backpack over his shoulder and gave his friend an innocent "Who, me?" look. Ever since Danny had come to terms with his own fears and stood up to Peter Wilbourne at the Halloween dance, he had been on a minicampaign for Tom to come to terms with *his* feelings as well. Tom wouldn't have stood for it from anybody else, but Danny was the nearest thing he had to a brother—now. As terrified as Tom was of being close to anyone, there was too much between him and Danny to pull away.

"Happy?" Tom repeated. "I'm not happy, Daniel. I'm just hyped up because of the sports scandal piece. Elizabeth is as excited as I am, and I have a hunch this one is really going to come gold."

Danny stopped at the top of the stairs. "Sure," he said. "You're hyped up. God forbid Tom Watts should ever feel happy."

86

Tom gave him a playful shove. "Don't you have a class to go to or something?" he asked with a laugh.

"Yeah, yeah, I'm going." Danny gave him a slap on the back. "See you later, Tombo. Only, you better stop grinning to yourself like that or everybody on this campus is going to think you're happy. Then your reputation as Mr. Ice Man will really be shot."

Tom headed toward the television studio to check on the rundown for the day. So, maybe he did feel a little happy. Last night in his dream he'd felt happier than he had in years. In two long years, to be exact, since he was a freshman.

And he'd even known he was dreaming—he'd known the whole time—but he'd still felt happy. *This is a dream*, he kept telling himself. *This is only a dream*. But it sure had felt good.

Up ahead of him, a couple was saying goodbye. The girl leaned over and kissed the guy as gently as a butterfly lands on a flower. Tom stopped for a second, stunned. He could feel that kiss. He could feel it because he remembered it. That was the way Elizabeth had kissed him in his dream. In his dream, he was taking her to the Homecoming dance and he'd arrived at her door with a single red rose. Red for passion.

Next to the way Elizabeth had looked, the rose had looked like a weed, but she'd taken it as though it were the most beautiful gift in the world. And then she'd kissed him. Softly. Tenderly. As though her lips had always been intended for his.

Giving himself a shake, Tom started to move forward, but once again he was stopped in his tracks. Just coming out of the athletes' dorm was Elizabeth herself. She must have been working on their story. The happiness he'd felt in his dream was nothing compared to the way the sight of her in the flesh made him feel.

Danny's words came back to him. *God forbid Tom Watts should ever feel happy.* Maybe Danny was right. Maybe a little bit of happiness wasn't out of the question. Maybe he really should ask Elizabeth Wakefield to the Homecoming ball.

"Hey, Elizabeth!" Tom called. "I just—"

She steamed right past him. If she'd been going any faster, he might not even have noticed the tears in her eyes. Instantly he knew that she hadn't been in the dorm because of the story. She'd been there because of her ex-boyfriend, Todd Wilkins. There was no other explanation; not at this time of day, not in a state like that. How could he have fooled himself, even for just a few minutes? He wouldn't have had much of a chance with a woman like Elizabeth anyway. What chance did he have when she was still in love with someone else?

If he'd been alone, Tom would have banged his head against a wall. What a jerk he was to get suckered in by happiness—by hope. There was no such thing as being happy. You were happy for a few minutes, and then something went wrong and it was

88

taken away. He should have learned that by now.

I was right all along, Tom thought as he gloomily resumed his walk to the station. *It's me. I don't deserve to be happy. Not anymore.*

Winston stood in the kitchen area of the Oakley Hall common room, studying the instructions on a container of instant bean soup.

"Just add boiling water," he read, "and in two minutes you will have a nutritious and delicious meal."

He put a pan of water on the stove and turned it on. He opened the container and gave it a sniff. It didn't smell either nutritious or delicious. It just smelled dry. He knew that the cafeteria was serving one of his favorite meals tonight, fried chicken and corn bread, but he couldn't face it. It was Candy's birthday and everyone on the floor had chipped in to buy a cake and ice cream. The girls expected him to eat with them tonight, but if he did, every Sigma in the room would want to eat with them too. They didn't wait to be asked anymore; they just pulled up a chair and joined right in. *Love me, love my frat brothers,* Winston thought sourly.

The worst thing, though, was that he'd really been looking forward to Candy's birthday dinner, because Denise would be there. He'd lain awake half the night, wondering how he could engineer it so he could sit next to her. But just as he was imagining Denise leaning against him, helpless with laughter at his sparkling wit, he'd imagined Bill and a posse of Sigmas squeezing in between them, monopolizing the conversation for the rest of the night and annoying all of his dormmates.

"This is what I'm driven to," he muttered to himself as he waited for the water to boil. "Eating dehydrated beans all alone."

"Do you always talk to yourself, or is it just because none of your frat buddies are around to keep you company?"

Winston's heart turned to dehydrated beans. He knew that voice. He heard that voice in his dreams. That was Denise. Hoping he still had the power of speech, he turned slowly. Denise wasn't at the birthday dinner. She was standing in the doorway, dressed in old sweatpants and a flannel shirt, with a container of instant noodles and a bowl in her hand. She looked a little pale.

"What are you doing here?" he asked, too surprised not to show it. "I thought you'd be at Candy's birthday bash. They've got three kinds of ice cream."

Denise made a face. "And I've got three kinds of cramps. I feel like a squad of kick boxers are practicing in my abdomen."

Cramps. Winston knew about cramps. In the days before he lived in an all-female dorm, he hadn't understood about things like cramps and PMS and cellulite, but he'd learned fast. It didn't even embarrass him to talk about it in public any-

90

more. "Gee, that's too bad," he said sincerely. "Maybe you should be lying down. I know Anoushka recommends a heating pad and Mozart."

Denise laughed. "I've been lying down since I got back from my logic class." She held up the plastic bowl. "I thought eating something might make me feel better."

It astounded him. Even though he was alone with Denise, he was still capable of thought. "Why don't you sit down and I'll fix it for you?" He took the container out of her hand. "The water's already boiling," he said, pointing to the stove. "I made more than enough for two."

"You are a sweetheart," Denise said, sitting down at the table with a grateful sigh.

A sweetheart? Winston practically spilled water all over the counter in his excitement.

"You know, I was really annoyed with you the other night, Winnie," Denise said. "I thought we were friends. I couldn't believe you'd rather sit with the Sigmas than sit with me."

The foil lid on the noodles didn't come off as easily as the foil lid on the black beans had. A small explosion of white, wormlike things and yellow powder landed on the stove. "Me?" Winston squeaked, trying to sweep them back into the container without her noticing.

"Yes, *you*. Did you think I didn't see you? I was sure you were going to come over, but then when Bill and his pals showed up, I figured you must have been waiting for them. Some dormmate you are, letting me eat all alone just so you could talk about football with those guys."

"You're wrong, Denise," Winston protested, wincing in pain as scalding water splattered his hand.

She laughed. "Are you trying to tell me that you boys don't talk about football all the time?"

He turned, carrying the two steaming containers, about to tell her that he'd much rather sit with her than sit with the Sigmas. But even in old sweatpants and a flannel shirt Denise Waters was so beautiful that his body went into meltdown—and instant soup went all over the table. Denise screamed.

"That's why I sat with them," Winston babbled, trying to mop up the soup with the sleeve of his shirt. "I didn't want to ruin your meal."

Denise leaned over and plucked a few noodles from his arm. "I've got beef chop suey and lentil soup in my room," she said. "Should we try this again?"

Chapter Five

It was the sound of Isabella running the shower that woke Jessica up. In her dream, it had still been yesterday and she was lying on the warm sand, beside a warm, gorgeous man, dizzy with love. In reality, it was today and she had to make some excuse to her philosophy professor about missing the seminar, attend three of the most boring classes ever created, *and* talk to Elizabeth about the Thetas. Jessica groaned out loud. As if that wasn't enough, Mike had some sort of business tonight and wouldn't be able to see her. *If only I could just sleep until tomorrow,* she thought as she dragged herself out of bed. *Then tomorrow wouldn't seem so far away.*

She heard her stomach growl and was suddenly aware that she was starving. She'd been so wrapped up in Michael yesterday, she hadn't really eaten anything. Jessica decided to eat before she got dressed. While one Wakefield twin was putting on weight, the other seemed to be shrinking away, she thought as she passed the mirror.

"Cereal," she chanted as she padded into the kitchenette, "toast, coffee, juice, and condoms."

Condoms? Jessica froze with her hand on the refrigerator door. What had made her say condoms?

Slowly her eyes focused on the shining white enamel in front of her. There were the usual magnets and notes on the door . . . And taped right in the center was a page from a magazine. A young couple, obviously in love and obviously very happy, was smiling at her. Above their heads in large, bold letters was the caption: SEX: IF YOU'RE GOING TO HAVE IT, MAKE IT SAFE! CONDOMS ARE FOR YOU, TOO!

It was incredible. Absolutely incredible. Isabella was still in the bathroom, and already she was getting on Jessica's case.

Jessica snatched the clipping, tossed it into the garbage, and wrenched open the fridge. This day was going to be even longer than she'd thought.

"Have a nice day yesterday?" Isabella asked, squeezing past her to start the coffee.

Jessica kept her head in the refrigerator. "Very nice, thank you."

"And the night before?" Isabella went on. "Was that nice too?"

Slowly and carefully, Jessica loaded bread, butter, milk, and jelly into her arms. "It was perfect," she said, matching Isabella's flat, polite voice. "Absolutely perfect."

Isabella noisily emptied the coffee filter. "Your brother called three times yesterday. He seemed upset. And your sister called twice last night. She seemed pretty upset too." She noisily poured water into the coffee machine. "I see you got my message."

Jessica straightened up. "If you mean the rather crude advertisement that you stuck on the refrigerator, yes, I got it."

"And what are you going to do about it?" Isabella asked, her eyes meeting Jessica's for the first time.

Jessica swung her golden hair over her shoulder. "I'm not going to do anything about it." She glided past Isabella and put the food on the counter. "It's not any of your business, of course, but for your information, Mike and I are not having sex. The only use we have for condoms is if we decide to have a party and we run out of balloons."

"You're funny, Jess," Isabella snapped. "You're very funny. But it won't be funny if Mike gets you pregnant or gives you AIDS."

Jessica stuck two pieces of bread into the toaster. "We're not sleeping together, Isabella," she explained again with exaggerated patience. "He can't give me anything."

"You spent the night with him, Jess. Maybe you didn't sleep with him this time, but that doesn't mean you won't next time. Believe me, Mike

McAllery doesn't have women spend the night because he's too cheap to buy a teddy bear."

Jessica felt her neck go cold. She wished Isabella would stop referring to Mike's "women" all the time. "But it doesn't mean I'll sleep with him, either."

Isabella sighed. "Jess, get real, will you? *I* saw you two together yesterday. Practically everybody saw you yesterday. It was like Romeo and Juliet meet *The Wild One*."

Jessica reached over Isabella's head for a bowl. "I have kissed people before, you know," she said, jerking the cabinet open. "My boyfriend Sam and I were very passionate and we never had sex."

"You and Sam were in high school, Jess," Isabella snapped back. "You were both kids. And at least one of you was sensible. But this isn't high school, and Mike McAllery isn't a kid." She reached up and slammed the cabinet shut again before Jessica could. "And quite frankly, Ms. Wakefield, I don't think you're being very sensible at the moment!"

Steam hissed out of the coffee machine.

Jessica concentrated on pouring out her cornflakes. "I know what I'm doing, Isabella."

"Do you?"

"Yes," Jessica answered between gritted teeth. "I do."

Isabella came over to her. "Well, just in case you don't know what you're doing as well as you think you do, Juliet, let me give you this with my compliments." She pulled something out of her pocket

96

and dropped it into Jessica's cereal bowl. "My advice is, don't leave home without it."

Jessica looked down as her roommate sailed past her. Sitting on top of the cornflakes was a packet of condoms. Extra strong.

"I mean, really, Isabella," Alison said as they walked across the quad, "you should see some of the girls who can't understand why we don't pledge them. Droids, Isabella. Girls who can't tell silk from viscose." She flicked a microscopic speck of dust from the sleeve of her jacket.

"Gee," Isabella mumbled.

"Girls who *shave* their legs instead of waxing. Girls who aren't even *attractive*!" Shuddering was too violent and obvious an action for Alison, but she wrinkled her nose in distaste.

"Ugh."

"I mean, assuming that they're capable of thought, what do they think, Izzy? We're probably the most prestigious sorority in the entire state. Do they think we got there by taking *dross*? It makes me laugh, Isabella. It just really makes me laugh." To prove that it made her laugh, Alison made a sound somewhere between a toilet backing up and a goose choking.

Isabella nodded and smiled. All Alison needed was a grunt, or a nod, or a smile every minute or so and she was happy to prattle on by herself. And Isabella was happy to let her. This morning, Isabella didn't really feel like talking. She wanted to think.

Despite the lecture she'd given Jessica that morning—and despite the fact that she really did think Mike McAllery was worse news than an outbreak of cholera—seeing her roommate's state of excitement had Isabella thinking of love. Isabella was personable, intelligent, attractive, mature . . . Why hadn't she found someone to fall in love with?

They turned toward the science building and Alison changed the subject. "Did I tell you about my dress for the Homecoming ball?" she asked. "It's going to be stupendous. I mean, not just stunning, not just drop-dead gorgeous, but totally stupendous."

Isabella, who had heard about Alison's dress for Homecoming in some detail every day for the past week, shook her head. She'd been out with some of the most eligible and desirable men at school, but not one of them had made her feel more than mildly interested. Not one of them had made her heart pound, or her body shake, or her mind forget about everything but his smile. The only man who had ever done that was the one who wouldn't give her the time of day.

"Don't you think that's a stupendous idea?"

Isabella looked over to find Alison smiling at her, waiting for an answer. It was so rare for Alison to ask a direct question or expect a direct answer that Isabella had completely lost track of the conversation. Did she think what was a good idea?

Diamond earrings? Dyed-to-match shoes?

"What?"

"Making Elizabeth Wakefield go out with Peter and publicly apologize for being so rude to him at that party." Alison smiled contentedly. "I think even I could accept her commitment to the Thetas if she agreed to that."

Isabella could hardly hide her surprise. "To tell you the truth, Alison," she said calmly, "I don't really think it is such a stupendous idea. Peter behaved like a thug that night. And you know as well as I do that he had something to do with frightening Jessica at the Halloween dance. I really don't think—"

Alison waved aside her objections with one elegantly manicured hand. "I know why you're attacking Peter, Isabella. Don't think I don't."

Isabella bit back a smirk. "You mean aside from the fact that he behaved like a thug?" she asked sweetly.

"It's because of *him*, isn't it?" Alison said. "He and Peter hate each other. You'd be bound to be on *his* side."

Isabella frowned. She was lost again. Now who was Alison talking about?

"You've always been a sap for *him*," Alison continued, sighing at the irrationality of this. "I really don't know why. He's handsome, of course. And such a maverick. But really, Izzy, he is *so* moody and such a troublemaker."

All at once she realized whom Alison was talking about. The one man who had ever really inter-ested Isabella. The one man who had ever dis-turbed her sleep. And she realized, too, that he must be nearby.

Isabella looked to the left. Tom Watts was just coming out of the WSVU office.

"And of course he isn't really interested in women, is he?" Alison asked, not losing one beat of her conversation. "He isn't really interested in anything except his TV station."

Isabella raised her hand. "Hi, Tom!" she called.

Tom nodded. But his eyes didn't even meet hers.

What I need is some firsthand information, Eliza-beth was thinking as she crossed the quad. *Someone who was actually offered money or gifts . . . or some-one who knows who was . . .*

Elizabeth had spent most of the morning in the morguelike basement of the journalism building, looking for any information she could find on the teams. She hadn't found any hard proof yet, but she had found suggestions of some pretty suspi-cious dealings. Illegal presents and arrangements. Unfair privileges. Special exemptions and excep-tions made for players. Now she was headed to the station to sort out what she'd found. Knowing how nosy and prying Celine was, she had no inten-tion of leaving anything important in her room.

"Liz! Hey, Elizabeth!"

Elizabeth had been so deep in thought that it

took her a minute to realize that someone was calling her. She looked up. Jessica was running toward her, her eyes sparkling and her cheeks glowing.

"Liz!" Jessica gasped, catching her breath as she drew alongside her. "I can't tell you how happy I am to see you. I've been looking all over for you. In the library . . . in the bookstore . . . I was just going over to Dickenson to see if you were in your room. I really have to talk to you!"

All morning, Elizabeth had been thinking of nothing but the sports scandal. But the sight of her sister put it completely out of her mind. "I really have to talk to *you*," Elizabeth said. "I left two messages for you last night, but you never called back."

Jessica flicked her hair over her shoulder. "That Isabella," she said with a laugh. "She really is one of the worst secretaries I've ever had. Remind me to fire her first thing in the morning."

Elizabeth's expression remained stony. She knew her twin too well to be taken in by the *That Isabella* routine. "Somehow I don't think it's Isabella's fault that you didn't return my calls," she said coolly. Elizabeth had promised herself yesterday that she wasn't going to start shouting at Jessica. That would only make her defensive. They were practically adults now, after all. "I think it's much more likely that the person I have to thank is Mr. McAllery," Elizabeth said.

If Jessica wanted to be an actress, there wasn't a doubt in Elizabeth's mind that her twin could be a star. She was good, there was no denying it. Only the slightest movement in those sea-green eyes gave any indication that she even knew who Mike McAllery was.

"I need to talk to you about the Thetas," Jessica said, as though Elizabeth hadn't even spoken. She slipped an arm through her sister's. "I had a very interesting talk with Alison Quinn the other day, and—"

"And today you're about to have a very interesting talk with me," Elizabeth said, pulling them up short. She could feel her temper rising. "I don't want to talk about the Thetas, Jessica. I want to talk about you and Mike McAllery."

Jessica pulled her arm out of Elizabeth's. Her smile became accusing. "Who told you? Big-mouth Isabella Ricci?"

"No, big-mouth Steven Wakefield." Elizabeth's smile was accusing. "He saw you leaving Mike's apartment at eight thirty in the morning, Jess. He said that Mike McAllery isn't the kind of guy you'd let take your dog out, never mind your sister. He said—"

"What's Steven all of a sudden?" Jessica demanded. "The secret police?" She raised her voice several decibels. "I don't care what Steven says, Elizabeth. It's my life, and I'll do what I want!"

Several people were turning back to look at them as they passed.

"Steven says that Mike threatened him," Elizabeth hissed, trying to shove her off the path so that they could talk more privately.

"Get off me, Liz!" Jessica shoved her back. "Mike did not threaten him. Steven was acting like he was in some macho thriller. Mike was just straightening him out."

Elizabeth dropped her backpack and grabbed Jessica by the arm. "Steven's worried about you, Jess. And so am I. We don't want you to do something you'll regret—"

"Like what?" Jessica yelled, pushing her away. "Like sleep with the man I love?"

"Jessica!" Elizabeth wished she could understand why it was *her* face that went red and not her sister's. She made another grab for Jessica's arm, but Jess was already stalking away. "Jessica, you can't love this man. You don't even know him."

Jessica stopped dead and turned around. Several people bumped into each other trying not to bump into her.

"Then you and Steven can't hate him, Elizabeth," Jessica said in a loud, clear voice. "Because you don't know him, either."

Jessica had felt confused already about whether or not she should sleep with Mike; the last thing she needed was Elizabeth getting into the discussion. She knew her sister too well to think that the argument would stop here. Isabella Ricci might tape condom ads to the refrigerator, but Elizabeth

Wakefield would follow her around like a guilty conscience and never let up.

Maybe I should just go ahead and sleep with him, Jessica was thinking as she stormed back to her suite. *Everybody's already treating me like I'm some kind of fallen women. Everybody acts like it would be such a crime.*

Music was blaring out of dorm windows; people were shouting and laughing as they basked in the sunny afternoon. But Jessica hardly heard it. Instead she heard the disapproving voices of her family and friends. *Don't make love to him,* the voices were saying. *Whatever you do, don't let him touch you.* Except Isabella's voice was saying, *Take the condoms, Jess. If you won't say no to sex, then at least make it safe.*

Eyes blazing, Jessica steamed across the lawn of her dorm. She'd always known that there were two kinds of people in the world. There were people like her sister, who were reliable and cautious, who obeyed the rules and did what they were told. And then there were people like Jessica, who wanted to live life, not just follow the instructions. People who didn't do what they were told. People like Mike.

Everyone thought Mike was no good for her, that she should give him up. Isabella, Denise, Steven, Elizabeth . . . Jessica flew past a gardener trimming the hedge outside her dorm. If she asked him, he'd probably tell her to dump Mike too.

But what did any of them know about Mike?

Nothing. Nothing at all. They looked at him and saw a hard-edged, street-wise guy with a wild streak that scared them.

Jessica entered the suite like a hurricane, throwing her books on the table with a crash. She was confused about whether or not she should sleep with Mike, but she wasn't confused about what she felt for him. He was tough on the outside but gentle on the inside. He could make her laugh and also make her cry. Mike's wild streak didn't scare Jessica; it made her feel alive.

She marched into the bedroom and flung herself on her bed. The voices were getting louder, and the loudest was Isabella's. *What about the other women?* Isabella's voice was saying. *He's a womanizer, Jess. God knows what else he does, but I do know that. He's not a one-woman man. He'll break your heart.*

"You're wrong," Jessica said out loud. "If he's had a lot of women, it's just because he hadn't found the *right* woman yet."

Suddenly another voice drowned out Isabella's. It was Mike's. *You're my baby,* Mike said tenderly. *My little girl . . . And I'm your man . . .*

Her heart pounding, Jessica reached under her pillow and removed the package of condoms. Maybe Mike had finally found the right woman.

She knew she'd find him here. Celine stood in the doorway of the coffeehouse, her eyes fixed on a figure sitting at the back by himself. Other people went to the snack bar or the student center during the day; places where it was light and full of noise, but not William White. He liked it here, where it was dark and subdued. He was the man who was always in the back room at parties and meetings; in the corners, in the shadows.

Celine studied his fine, pale face and those secretive eyes. If she were the kind of girl who believed in the devil, she would have no trouble believing that William was at least his cousin.

She saw the ice-blue eyes flicker as he lifted his cup. He'd seen her. He'd seen her, but of course he wouldn't show that he had. He wouldn't wave to her or beckon her over like a normal person would.

That's all right, William, Celine said to herself. She took a deep breath and hugged her books against her chest. *Because you are not only about to see me, you are about to invite me to the Homecoming ball.* She knew that he was planning to ask Elizabeth. Not because he'd said as much to her, of course. But because he'd asked where Elizabeth had been the last day or two; he hadn't seen her around. He thought she might have gone away. Celine, remembering the rose, took this to mean that he'd been looking for Elizabeth. He was getting ready to ask her out.

William didn't look at her until she was sitting beside him. "Oh, I can't tell you how happy I am to see a friendly face!" Celine gushed, flashing him one of her biggest smiles.

106

He actually smiled back, a thin-lipped smile that curled at one corner. She wasn't sure if he was smiling because he was glad to see her or if he was smiling at some private joke.

"I just couldn't stand it in that room one more minute," she hurried on. "That girl is driving me crazy with talk about the Homecoming ball."

One blond eyebrow rose a fraction as he sipped his espresso.

"Who should she go with? What should she wear? What should they do after the dance? I finally had to say to her, 'Elizabeth, honey, I am *not* your fairy godmother. You are free to do as you please.'" Celine heaved a long-suffering sigh. "Thank heavens she's finally decided who she's going with. At least I don't have to listen to the list of her admirers anymore."

Something that could have been emotion flashed through the dead blue eyes. He put down his cup so softly it might have been made of tissue. "So is this your roundabout way of letting me know that Elizabeth has a date for Homecoming, Celine?" His voice was as soft as tissue as well.

Celine was all innocence. "I thought you might like to know, William," she said. She beckoned for the waitress. "I thought that was our understanding. That I . . . let you know."

"And with whom would this date be?"

Celine shrugged. "I don't have a telepathic mind, Mr. White. I can't even keep track of all the names. It could be one of several."

He stared into the dark depths of his cup for several seconds, considering.

"And what about you?" he asked at last. "Do you have a date for the Homecoming ball?"

Celine laughed. "Of course I do. As it happens, I'm going with—"

"Cancel it." He pushed back his chair and got to his feet.

She looked up at him, her eyes flashing in outrage. "But William, I can't just—"

"Cancel it," he repeated. "You're going with me."

There was a satisfied smile on Celine's beautiful face as she watched him leave the coffeehouse. William White might be the cousin of the devil, but that didn't mean he was the only one with relatives in hell.

I'm Alex, now, not Enid. I'm beautiful, I'm popular, I'm going to be pledged to the biggest sorority on campus, and I have the most gorgeous, generous, and incredible boyfriend in the entire universe. She looked around the exquisite new bistro where Mark had insisted on taking her, Todd, and Lauren to lunch to celebrate passing his big physics exam. It was a little weird, hanging out with Todd and Lauren when she was so used to hanging out with Todd and Elizabeth, but it was a weirdness she was getting used to. After all, things changed and people changed. She'd changed too. *I have to be dreaming,* she thought. *This can't be my life.*

"The sky's the limit as far as I'm concerned," Mark said. He squeezed Enid's hand under the table. "The four of us are going to have the greatest time at the Homecoming ball since man invented parties."

Todd laughed. "I'm with you, Gathers. The sky's the limit. This is the first college Homecoming I've ever been to, and I want to have the time of my life."

"Then it's decided," Mark said. "Dinner at Da Vinci's first, and then on to the dance." He grinned. "With a little bit of luck, my new Explorer will have arrived by then and we can really go in style."

Lauren turned to Enid. "What are we going to do with these guys, Alex?" she asked. "I think they're spoiling us."

Enid thought so too. She knew that Todd's family was pretty comfortable, though not so comfortable that they could put Todd through college without noticing how much it was costing. But she hadn't thought that Mark was particularly well-off at all—not new car and expensive restaurants well-off. She looked from Mark to Todd. They didn't look worried. Their athletics grants must be better than she'd thought.

Enid leaned across the table and gave Mark a kiss. "I think we're going to have to find some way of spoiling them back," she said with a laugh.

*   *   *

"Winston Egbert! We know you're in there! Open this door!"

Winston stared warily at the door as the knocking became harder and more insistent. Why did he always find himself hiding from people?

"Winnie! What do you want us to do? Break down the door?"

Winston groaned. This was even worse than being harassed by the Sigmas.

"If you don't let us in, we're going for Maia. She'll be on our side in this. She's got the key!"

With the enthusiasm of a man about to open the cage of a starving tiger, Winston forced himself up from the bed.

On the other side of his door were Anoushka and Debbie, and they were mad. They'd been chasing Winston around campus all day, trying to tell him just how mad they were, but he'd been able to give them the slip each time. When they'd seen him coming out of English, he managed to duck into the boys' gym. When they'd spotted him in the cafeteria, he'd abandoned his meal and slipped out while they were still getting their lunch. They'd almost had him cornered in the snack bar, but he'd cleverly escaped through the window of the men's room, even though it had meant tearing one of his favorite shirts.

But now there was no escape. If he jumped out this window he wouldn't just rip his clothes, he'd break both his legs. How was he going to run away from them with two broken legs?

Winston counted to three and opened the door.

The two of them were standing there with their arms folded across their chests and disgusted expressions on their faces. Winston's mother was neither incredibly beautiful nor a college student, as Anoushka and Debbie both were, but for an instant they reminded him an awful lot of Mrs. Egbert.

Winston smiled. "Noush! Deb! What a pleasant surprise."

"Cut the crap, Winnie," Anoushka ordered, sweeping past him. "You know why we're here."

"That's right," Debbie said, stepping on his foot as she marched into the room. Normally the most polite of girls, she didn't even bother saying she was sorry.

"We'd like an explanation, Winnie," Anoushka said, turning to face him.

"And then we'd like an apology," Debbie added. "Preferably public."

Winston looked from one to the other. "Explanation? Apology?"

"Don't try to get out of this, you little weasel," Anoushka snarled.

"Weasel?" Winston was genuinely shocked. "Anoushka, how can you call me a weasel? You like me. I'm your friend."

"That was before you told Tony Calavieri I'd go out with him." She shuddered. "Tony Calavieri!

111

Winnie, how could you? He's practically a Neanderthal. He doesn't think women should have the vote."

Winston shut the door. There was a good chance that he'd end this conversation on his knees, begging for forgiveness. He didn't need an audience.

"Anoushka, I swear to you, I never told Tony you'd go out with him. He asked me if I thought you'd go out with him, and I said maybe."

Anoushka was glaring. "You expect me to believe that?"

Winston ran his fingers through his hair. "Okay, okay. So that wasn't exactly how it happened. That's not the exact, literal truth." He looked to Debbie for some sympathy, but she was glaring at him too.

"So what is the exact, literal truth?" Anoushka demanded.

He looked at the floor. "Tony asked me to ask you if you'd go out with him, and I sort of said that you said you would."

"You see!" She grabbed an eraser from his desk and threw it at him. "And you call yourself my friend!"

"You hypocrite," Debbie growled. "You arranged to meet me in the library this morning and then you never showed up. Jeff Cross showed up! I can't believe you played a cheap trick like that on me, Winston. Jeff isn't even a Neanderthal. He's the missing link. He couldn't open a milk carton if it didn't come with instructions!"

"Ladies! Ladies! Please, I can explain."

They plopped down on the bed as though they'd been dropped. "So, go ahead. Explain."

Winston explained. He explained about the pressure the Sigmas were putting him under because he lived in a female dorm, how they used subtle threats to make him do favors for him. How they dogged his footsteps. How they wouldn't leave him alone.

"At first I thought it was just that they liked me, you know. They were so friendly and everything. But it's gotten worse and worse. Now I'm afraid that if I don't go along with them, they'll not only dump me from the fraternity, they'll probably dump me over a cliff, too."

"So what if they dump you from their stupid fraternity?" Anoushka demanded. "You don't need them. They're a bunch of morons."

Winston wasn't so sure. Maybe the girls in his dorm had a low opinion of Sigma brothers, but they were still the big men on campus to everybody else. And a big man on campus was what he wanted to be. Besides, there was the other consideration.

"What about the cliff?" Winston asked. "It doesn't upset you that you might have to visit me in the hospital?"

A look passed between the two girls. Anoushka shrugged. "We'll think about it," Debbie said.

113

Chapter
Six

Elizabeth looked at her watch as she left the athletics office. She'd gotten so involved in listening to Coach Sanchez's reminiscences that she'd completely lost track of the time. Coach Sanchez might not want Tom Watts hanging around asking questions, but he didn't seem to mind Elizabeth Wakefield. As soon as she'd said that she was thinking of doing a piece for the school paper about the importance of sports in campus life, he'd leaned back, put his feet on his desk, and started talking.

He talked about what a loss it had been to the school when Tom Watts quit football. "When I got here, Tom was the best SVU had," Coach Sanchez said. "Heck, he was the best anybody had. The rest of the athletes here were no better than second string. When Tom left, it demoralized everyone, not just the football players. That's when I knew I had to get tough." He told her how he and his staff had turned the SVU athletics department from a third-rate embarrassment no professional scout worth his expenses would even bother to look at into a seedbed for the major teams in every field and every division. "Not that I did it alone," Coach Sanchez kept saying. "I like to give credit where credit is due. This has been a team effort in every sense of the word."

He was full of amusing stories and colorful anecdotes. "Don't forget to mention the time Quemada left his new camera on the bus in Dallas. Chased it five blocks before he caught it." He leaned over to make sure she was getting it down. "You know who I mean, right? He's the one everyone's betting will be snatched up by the NFL when he graduates."

He had lots of useful advice for anyone wanting to put together an award-winning athletic department. "Go for the gold, that's the secret. Just go for the gold. Don't fool around with guys who might be *good* if you work their butts off. Concentrate on the guys who will be *great* if you work their butts off. Then you have a chance."

He kept calling her "angel." "You should try out for the cheerleaders, angel," he'd said more than once. "You've got the sort of looks that really gets the boys' blood moving."

"I'd like to get *his* blood moving," Elizabeth mumbled to herself as she cut across the grass. She was supposed to have met Enid for lunch ten minutes ago.

115

Once she'd reached the main quad, she started to run. *I don't understand why the pounds aren't falling off me,* she was thinking as she raced along. *Never mind how hard I'm working right now and the fact that most of what I eat tastes like cardboard. Between the stress of living with Celine and worrying about Jess, I should be burning up calories by the millions.*

But she wasn't. Elizabeth pounded down the path toward the coffeehouse. This morning she'd weighed herself on Nina's scale and she'd actually put on half a pound. Half a pound! Nina said it must be water. "Water doesn't weigh all that much," Elizabeth had said.

She was still thinking about that half pound when she plowed into someone coming from the opposite direction. They crashed to the ground in a shower of papers and books.

"I'm so sorry," Elizabeth apologized, pulling herself up with as much dignity as she could manage. "I'm really sorry. I didn't even see you. I guess I wasn't paying attention—"

"I guess you weren't." He pulled a leaf from her hair. "It isn't exactly flattering, though, that you didn't even see me."

Elizabeth flushed. She might not have noticed him before, but she noticed him now. He had been almost this close when he handed her the rose in the library, but that hadn't been in daylight. In daylight everything about him looked too perfect to be real—especially that smile.

"On the other hand," he went on, "'there is no such thing as accident, there is only will and chance.'"

"You're quoting," Elizabeth said, smiling back. There had been a time when the way he looked at her made her nervous. It wasn't making her nervous now, but it was making her wish that she'd worn something a little nicer today. It was definitely making her wish that she hadn't gained that half a pound.

"Maldono," he said, picking up one of the books she'd dropped. *"Poem to a Lover."* He turned the thin volume over. "It's not in this collection. It's in *Memories and Dreams.* You reading this for a class?"

Elizabeth shook her head. "No, for pleasure."

His eyes went from the book to her. "Not many people read Maldono anymore," he said. "Especially not for pleasure." He smiled. "I think they find her poems a little too much work to be considered fun, but she's always been one of my favorites."

"Mine, too." She couldn't seem to stop looking into those glass-blue eyes. "I like that she's so hard to pin down."

"'I saw you that first morning, walking with your friends. I stopped in the middle of doing something. There was sunlight on the trees and on your hair. Maybe you laughed and looked my way. Maybe you spoke. Maybe it was only a dream.'"

"'Remembering,'" Elizabeth answered immediately.

"I see you know your stuff." He extended his hand. "And I'm William. William White."

"Elizabeth Wakefield," she answered, but she had the feeling he knew that already.

"Maybe you'd like to go for a coffee or something," he said, still holding her hand. "It is lunchtime."

She almost said yes—and then she remembered. "Oh, no! Lunch!" She yanked her hand away and started frantically retrieving her things. "I'm late. I'm sorry, I really have to go."

When they were both on their feet again, he gave her back her book. "Nice bumping into you," he said. "Maybe we can do it again sometime."

"Don't jump down my throat, man." Danny reached into the bag he'd brought into the news office and handed Tom his sandwich. "All I wanted to know was whether you were thinking of asking Elizabeth to Homecoming. It wasn't armed assault; it was just a question."

"And I gave you an answer."

Danny grinned. "No, you didn't, you gave me an attitude."

Tom refused to look into that concerned and friendly smile. He concentrated on unwrapping his sandwich. It was beginning to seem to Tom that no matter how hard you tried to keep people at a distance, there was always one or two who had a way of sneaking up close.

118

He could feel Danny watching him.

"So why don't you ask Elizabeth to Homecoming?" Danny persisted. "You know you like her. You're always telling me what a terrific reporter she is. How much you enjoy working with her."

Just because Tom had made a few positive comments about Elizabeth, Danny was always bringing her name up lately. Why couldn't he understand that the only passion between Tom and Elizabeth was for the truth?

"Working is the key word here," Tom said. He picked a shred of lettuce from his shirt. "We work together and that's it. Just because Elizabeth and I make a good team at the station doesn't mean I want to dance with her, Danny."

Danny bit into his burger. "So what happened? You asked her and she turned you down?"

Tom felt like banging his head on his computer. He used to be so good at hiding his feelings, but ever since his first glimpse of Elizabeth Wakefield he'd been getting less good. He might as well hang his heart around his neck on a piece of ribbon.

Tom gave up and looked at his friend. "No, Daniel," he said with mock patience, "she did not turn me down."

"So what, then? She's already going with somebody else?"

Tom helped himself to a handful of Danny's french fries. "What are you all of a sudden, Miss Lonely Hearts?"

"No, I'm just your best friend. And I sense a new restlessness and moodiness in you lately, Tombo. Different than your usual restlessness and moodiness." Danny picked up his iced tea. "So if she's not going with somebody else, why don't you ask her?"

"Because she probably is going with somebody else, all right, Danny? Is that good enough for you? Can we stop now?"

"But you don't know for sure that she has a date—"

"Danny!" Tom threw his sandwich down on the desk. "Has it ever occurred to you that Elizabeth might not want to go to the dance with me?"

Danny took his second burger out of the bag. "Has it ever occurred to you that she might?"

"So what have you been up to, Alex?" Elizabeth asked as the waitress set her salad plate in front of her.

She shrugged. "Oh, not much. You know, the usual."

Enid almost wished that she'd given up waiting for Elizabeth and left the coffeehouse when she had the chance. Elizabeth seemed distracted, and anyway, what were they supposed to talk about now that they'd drifted so far apart? They'd already gone through classes and the weather and the latest movies. The things that Enid really wanted to talk about—Mark and her wonderful new life—all in-

120

volved either the Thetas or Todd. And she couldn't mention those things to Elizabeth without starting an argument or hurting her feelings.

"Not much? What about Homecoming? You must be getting ready for that. It's practically all anybody talks about anymore."

Enid perked up. Maybe this wasn't going to be so difficult after all. Maybe Elizabeth had a big date for the dance and wouldn't even notice that Alex and Mark were doubling with Todd and Lauren.

"It is pretty thrilling, isn't it?" she asked, letting her excitement show. "I mean, our first college Homecoming! Mark's taking me to Da Vinci's for dinner first and everything. I just know it's going to be the best night of my entire life."

Elizabeth gave her a quizzical look. "Da Vinci's? That's pretty fancy, isn't it? I thought a family of South American peasants could eat for a week on what a bowl of soup costs at that place."

Enid used to admire Elizabeth for her seriousness and sense of purpose, but at the moment she found it slightly annoying. She didn't have to worry about world starvation *all* the time, did she?

"What about you?" Enid asked, hoping to change the subject. Her mind was on party dresses and romantic evenings, not poor people. "Who are you going to Homecoming with?"

"Me?" Elizabeth stabbed a lettuce leaf. "I'm not going to Homecoming, Alex. I don't think I

121

could stand spending the whole night watching Todd with someone else."

Enid grabbed her fork. It was time to put something in her mouth besides her foot. "Did I tell you Mark's getting a new car?" she asked, racing for yet another subject. "An Explorer. It is so neat, Liz. Wait'll you see it. He's having it custom painted and ground lights put on and everything."

The quizzical look came back. "A new car?"

There was something about the way Elizabeth said *A new car?* that Enid didn't like. Any second now she was going to tell her that a family of South American peasants could buy shoes for the next two years with what it cost Mark for an oil change.

"But did I tell you the best news?" Enid asked, racing on. "Mark thinks he can take me with him when the team goes on their winter break. Won't that be wonderful? Last year they went to—"

"Santa Fe," Elizabeth said. "To a dude ranch."

As eager as she was to keep the conversation going, and going away from South America and Todd Wilkins, Enid paused. "How did you know that?"

"I don't know." Elizabeth bit into a carrot stick. "I guess somebody must have told me."

"But it's great, don't you think?" Enid steamed on. "Mark thinks they might even go to New Orleans this year. Don't you think that's wonderful? New Orleans?"

Elizabeth chewed thoughtfully. "I'll tell you what I think, Alex," she said at last. "I think it's pretty amazing."

Maia banged on the desk. "Okay, ladies and Winston, settle down, will you? We want to get this floor meeting started before dawn if we can."

There was a flurry of activity as the latecomers found seats.

"Winnie, what *are* you doing?"

Winston, the latest of the latecomers, had been just about to sit down next to Candy when he saw Denise on the other side of the crowded room.

"I just—I was—" Every eye was on him. He couldn't very well say that he'd changed his mind, he wanted to sit next to Denise. "I forgot something in my room—"

"Winnie!"

Maia was giving him a look his mother sometimes gave him. It wasn't without affection, but it wasn't without violence, either.

Half up and half down, Winston stared back at her. "What?"

"Don't you think it would be nice if you just sat down and let us get started, since this meeting is about you?"

"What?"

There was a ripple of laughter around him. Suddenly Winston wished he'd gone to the movies with Bruce Patman and a couple of the other

Sigmas after all. Was she serious? This meeting wasn't supposed to be about *him*, it was supposed to be about keeping the bathroom clean and noise down and stuff like that.

"But I thought this was just a regular floor meeting," Winston said. "Anoushka said—" He glared at Anoushka.

"If I told you the truth, you would have come up with some excuse for not being here," Anoushka said.

Winston started to deny this ridiculous accusation, but Maia cut him off. "Sit down, Winnie! We all have other things to do, you know. We don't want to spend the whole night talking about you."

He didn't particularly want to spend any of the night talking about him, but he sat down obediently.

"Okay," Maia said. "We all know that there have been a few extra problems in our lives since Winnie moved on our floor."

"Problems in blue jackets," someone commented.

Everyone but Winston started to giggle.

"It's true," Anoushka said. "It's been like the invasion of the Sigmas around here ever since Winnie got in with them. And it's driving most of us nuts."

"It's driving all of us nuts," Maia said. "You can barely walk into the dorm without tripping over one of Winston's frat brothers."

Candy put a hand on Winston's shoulder. "It's not that we have anything *against* the Sigmas . . ."

"Oh, I don't know about that," Debbie said. "I hold Jeff Cross against them."

"What about Bill, the man of a thousand hands?" Denise asked.

"What about Bruce Patman?"

"He's nothing compared to Peter the Great."

"Peter the Great Pain in the Butt."

"Let's not forget—"

"Ladies!" Maia was banging on the desk again. "Ladies, please. We don't have to go through all the ugly details. We know the ugly details. They're always asking us out. The only thing that concerns us tonight is the fact that the Sigmas think that just because Winnie lives with us, it gives them some special rights."

Anoushka nodded. "It's like they think because one of their friends lives on a certain piece of land, they're all allowed to hunt on it, never mind what the peaceful natives think."

Winston looked around at the roomful of intelligent, attractive, and angry faces. He wasn't so sure about them being peaceful natives. They looked more like an uprising to him.

"So what's the solution?" asked Tamara. "Is Winnie going to depledge the Sigmas?"

Winston started to choke. Candy pounded him on the back.

"Debbie and I thought of that," Anoushka said.

"But it would upset Winnie too much."

Winston threw her a grateful smile.

"So what are we going to do?" Tamara demanded.

Anoushka raised her right arm in the air, making a fist. "We're going to arm the natives."

"Steven, will you please get away from that window? You're acting like a jealous boyfriend."

Steven was standing with his back to the room, peering through the crack in the curtains at the street below. "I am not acting like a jealous boyfriend, Billie. I'm acting like a concerned older brother."

Billie sighed. He could picture the expression on her face. Her eyebrows were drawn together, and her mouth was somewhere between a pout and a sneer. He could picture this expression because he'd been seeing it a lot lately. Ever since the morning he found Jessica kissing Mike McAllery on the stoop.

"Steven . . . come on. I know you're concerned, but Jessica is a big girl now. You can give her advice, but she's going to have to make her own mistakes, just like everyone else."

Steven swung around. "I can't believe you, Billie. I really can't. Mike McAllery is not a *mistake*. Joining the wrong sorority or shaving your head and piercing your nose, *those* are mistakes. Next to them, Mike McAllery is World War III."

"And you are Bozo the Clown." She marched

over and shut the curtains. "This is ridiculous, Steven. You cannot spend the rest of your life waiting for Jessica to come back to Mike's. Dinner's ready and I'm hungry. Let's sit down and eat."

He parted the curtains again. "I'm not hungry."

"Steven!"

"I just have this feeling, Billie. I'm sure she's coming here tonight." He looked into the dark blue eyes that had given him so much sympathy and understanding since they'd met. She thought he was going insane. "Okay, so maybe you think it's crazy, but you have to remember how close my family is. And intuitive. Elizabeth and Jessica can practically read each other's minds."

"Nobody could read your mind," Billie said. "Everything in there is gobbledygook."

Steven threw his hands in the air. "What is it with you women? How can you be so intelligent and still be fooled so easily by a good-looking guy? Why can't you see how dangerous he is?"

Billie put her arms around him. "Steven, Michael McAllery is not Al Capone. I know he has a reputation for being a little wild, and I know there are a lot of women in and out of that apartment—"

"A lot of women! You'd think he was running a hair salon!"

"Steven, that does not make him a criminal."

"Have you seen that bike, Billie? Have you seen that car? Drug dealers drive cars like that. Over-sexed rock stars ride bikes like that."

127

Billie took her arms away. "Okay, Steven, if you want to spend the night standing at the window, then go right ahead. I'm going to eat."

He put his face to the glass again.

"Steven."

"What?"

"Can I ask you just one little question?"

"I thought you were hungry. Isn't there something burning on the stove?"

She ignored him. "I want to know why, if you're so concerned about Jessica, you don't just tell your parents. If it's anyone's responsibility, it's theirs, not yours."

He turned to her in amazement. "Tell my *parents*? Are you joking? You know what my parents are like. They could never handle something like this, Billie. They always blow things out of proportion."

Jessica's palms were sweating and her heart was pounding as though she'd run all the way from the dorm. Halfway there she'd started imagining what Isabella, Steven, and Elizabeth would say if they knew where she was going in her new silk sheath and matching underwear. Halfway to Mike's, Isabella's condoms in her bag, their arguments started making sense. He was too old and experienced. He was only using her. She knew nothing about him. She was letting her hormones rule her head.

She'd made herself so nervous that she'd almost turned around and gone back to the campus. But then she'd remembered what it felt like to have Mike's arms around her and his lips on hers.

Now that she was here, in his building, only feet away from him, the nervousness returned. *What if I've got the wrong night?* she asked herself as she stopped in front of his door. *What if he forgot? What if he had to go out for some emergency? What if he's with someone—* She closed her eyes. She wasn't even going to let herself think about that one. She counted to three, and then pressed the bell.

Mike answered on the second ring.

Her brother and her sister and her roommate were wrong. She was in the right place, with the right man. Jessica felt so happy at the sight of him that she thought her heart would explode.

"How's my baby tonight?"

His hair was hanging loose, and he was wearing black jeans and a long-sleeved T-shirt the same color as his eyes. If there had ever been another man as beautiful as this, it must have been a very long time ago. She didn't so much fall as float into his arms.

"She's fine now," Jessica whispered, all her fears and nervousness evaporating as she found his lips. "She's just fine."

Jessica wasn't sure how long they stood there kissing. It might have been a few minutes; it might have been a few days. Time didn't seem to have much meaning when she was with Mike. Not time or anything else.

Mike pulled away when he heard footsteps

coming down the stairs. "I'm not usually paranoid, but that might be your brother with a gun," he joked. "Maybe we'd better continue this inside."

"Inside sounds great to me." She laughed as he lifted her in his arms.

"I hope you're hungry," he said, setting her on her feet in the dining alcove and slipping off her jacket. "I've been slaving over a hot stove all day for you."

"Oh, Mike!"

Jessica looked around her. There were glowing candles and headily scented flowers all through the alcove and in the living room. Music played softly in the background—not the corny romantic music her parents liked, but raunchy, sensuous blues. The table was covered with a black cloth and set for two. On one of the plates was an orchid tinted the blue-green of the sea.

This can't be real, she told herself. *I must be in a movie or a fairy tale* . . . Mike came up behind her, cocooning her in his arms, his kisses like fireflies dancing on her skin. *Or in a dream* . . .

"I made salmon mousse to start," he whispered, the fireflies moving gently down her neck. "And chicken and mushrooms in wine and herbs for the entreé." The fireflies started a tango across her back. "And for dessert—"

She turned to let the fireflies warm the hollow of her neck. "Maybe we can skip dessert . . ." she whispered.

Once more Mike lifted her in his arms. "Maybe we can start with it," he said.

"My granny always said that it's patience that separates the saints from the sinners," Celine was saying as she studied her eyebrows in the mirror over the sink. She leaned forward and pulled a few imperfectly placed hairs from each eyebrow with her gold-tipped tweezers. "But to tell you the truth, I think I am beginning to run out of patience."

Celine turned to the girl at the sink on her right. "I've tried my best, but there are limits, aren't there? I mean, if the planet can run out of rain forests, a person can run out of patience, can't she?"

The girl, whose name was something like Jem, nodded sympathetically. "Of course there are limits," she said. "The idea of sharing a room with someone is that you *share*. Elizabeth must have missed that day of kindergarten."

"It's true," the girl on Celine's left said. "If one person's doing all the giving and the other's doing all the taking, then you've got a problem."

Celine looked sadly at her reflection. "I don't want to be unfair to Elizabeth. I'm sure she has her reasons—I mean, who knows what dreadful things she's suffered in her life . . ." Celine's reflection looked sadly back at her. "I've tried. The Lord knows I've tried, but maybe I haven't been understanding enough . . ."

The girl on Celine's left splashed water on her

face and looked over. "Don't start making excuses for her," she advised. "Admit it. You've got a problem. That's all there is to it."

Celine sighed. "I guess I do have to admit it," she said in a soft, reluctant, saintly voice. "I have got a problem. I am living with a person who thinks only of herself."

"Why don't you talk to her?" asked the girl whose name was maybe Em instead of Jem. "Maybe she just doesn't realize how much she's upsetting you. Sometimes just sitting down and talking really helps."

Celine gave her the smile of a martyr tied to the stake. "Oh, she knows." She shook her head. "I cannot tell you how many times I have tried to talk to her. I even told her I could live with the mess. I could live with her taking my things without asking. I could even get used to her playing her music when I'm trying to study." She smiled again. "But it's the running around all the time I can't handle . . . She's out till all hours, partying and carousing. Sometimes she even brings *boys* back to the room with her. I never know when she's going to burst in or what kind of mood she'll be in. . . ."

The girl on Celine's left finished drying her face. "Oh, I couldn't put up with that either," she said. "I can put up with snoring and weird eating habits, but I couldn't put up with that stuff."

Jem or Em shook her toothbrush in agreement. "Me neither. That's way over the top."

"I know," Celine said with another saintly sigh. "My granny would turn blue and swallow her dentures if she knew what I have to put up with."

"You mean your granny would turn blue and swallow her dentures if she knew how much you lie," said a voice that belonged to neither of the girls at the sinks.

Celine looked into the mirror. Nina Harper had just emerged from one of the shower cubicles and was standing directly behind her, wearing a striped terry-cloth robe and a disgusted expression.

Now, what's your problem? Celine wondered, hiding her frown. She'd been spreading so many rumors about Elizabeth since the beginning of term that she'd been certain she'd turned everyone on their floor against her. She'd convinced them that Elizabeth's shyness was snobbiness and that the reason she had so little to do with the other girls in the dorm wasn't because she thought they didn't like her, but because she didn't like them. Apparently, however, she'd been wrong. Nina Harper had slipped through her net.

"Why, Nina . . ." Celine turned slowly, her eyes wide with innocence and hurt. "I have no idea what you're talking about."

Both whatever her name was and the other girl had stopped their scrubbing and brushing and were staring at Celine.

"Don't you?" Nina threw her towel over her shoulder. "Well, I don't know what you're talking

133

about either," she said. "I happen to be a friend of Elizabeth's, and the person you're describing isn't like her at all."

Inwardly Celine was cursing herself. She'd known, of course, that Nina was a drip like Elizabeth, who was always in the library studying. One might be black on the outside and the other might be white, but inside they were obviously the same color: boring gray. Unfortunately, it had never occurred to Celine that the Dull Duo might actually have started talking to each other.

Outwardly Celine continued to look innocent and hurt. "I think I know Elizabeth a little better than you do," she said sweetly. "I am her roommate, after all."

"And I spend almost every night in the library study room with her," Nina said, just as sweetly.

The other two girls stopped staring at Celine and started staring at Nina.

"So where you get your stories about Elizabeth being out partying all the time is beyond me," Nina continued. "And how you'd know she was out is another question. Anybody who knows you knows that you're never in. I've never been to a party on this campus when you weren't there."

Feeling the eyes on her again, Celine opened her mouth to defend herself, her mind moving fast. Somehow she had to discredit Nina. Because she was always working and didn't really hang out with anyone, Nina wasn't much more popular than

Elizabeth in the dorm. It shouldn't be that hard to make her look like the liar.

"Why are you attacking me like this?" she asked, her voice quavering with emotion. "Is it because you blame my people for slavery? Is that it? Are you mad at me because I come from the South?"

For the first time the hard, disgusted expression left Nina's face. She started to laugh. Quietly at first, and then so loudly that everyone but Celine joined in.

"No, Celine," Nina gasped. "I'm not mad at you because you come from the South. I'm mad at you because you didn't stay there."

Celine was sitting with her feet up on Elizabeth's desk, idly searching through the drawers. The scene in the bathroom had thrown her, but it hadn't discouraged or defeated her. Celine's granny hadn't raised any giver-uppers. Her granny said that it wasn't the early bird who got the worm; it was the bird who hung around from the night before.

"Nothing," Celine murmured, slamming another drawer shut. "She doesn't even take extra bags of sugar from the snack bar."

She knew that Elizabeth hid her diary from her, but she still thought she'd find something just a teensy bit interesting lying around. Something that she could use against her.

Celine yawned. Even if she did find the diary itself, it probably wasn't going to yield any real dirt. Elizabeth had fewer secrets than a goldfish.

She yanked open the bottom drawer. Cigarette ash spilled over Elizabeth's things as Celine rummaged through them. Two unused notebooks. A spare pack of typewriter paper. Extra pens. A brand-new box of staples. Celine yawned again. What could be more boring than a girl who was afraid she might run out of staples in the middle of the night?

She was just about to shut the drawer when she noticed a piece of paper stuck at the back. Never one to overlook the smallest thing, Celine pulled it out.

The crumpled sheet had been torn from a blue-lined pad. There were a few incomprehensible notes scribbled on it in handwriting that was too loose and sloppy to be Elizabeth's. Most of the notes had been crossed out. Celine turned over the page. At the top, in Elizabeth's neat, precise writing, were the words *Illegal Recruitment of Athletes at SVU*. Underneath, also in Elizabeth's handwriting, was an outline for what was obviously an article of some kind.

"Now, what have we here? Don't tell me the Little Princess has a vindictive streak in her?" She laughed gleefully. "Don't tell me she's planning to get even with poor Todd for dumping her for someone else?"

A slow, self-satisfied smile spread across Celine's face like an oil slick on water. She folded the piece of paper and slipped it into her pocket. Maybe Mr. White wouldn't be quite so taken with Little Goody Two Shoes if he knew that she was really a mean and spiteful little witch.

Chapter Seven

Jessica woke up with sunlight pressing against the cloth blinds of the bedroom and Mike's arms around her. Hardly daring to move, she lay there listening to his rhythmic breathing and the steady beating of his heart. There were voices on the street outside and the sounds of traffic hurrying by. It was a normal day. A day just like any other day. Except for one thing. Except for the fact that last night, Jessica had made love for the first time.

Jessica pressed closer to Mike. *This is so weird,* she thought. *It doesn't seem like anything's changed.*

She'd expected to feel different. She was a woman now, a *real* woman, like Lila was. Jessica had always thought that when you became a woman, it was like joining a secret society. And it was true, in a way. She knew things this morning that she hadn't known yesterday morning; she'd experienced things last night that she had never experienced before.

Surely that was supposed to change you, make you and everything else in the world different. But it hadn't; everything felt exactly the same.

Careful not to disturb Mike, Jessica slid from the bed and crossed over to the mirror above the antique dresser. She stared at herself in the glass. She looked exactly the same too. If becoming a woman was like joining a secret society, it was a secret society with no special medallion or handshake, that was for sure.

She bent her head close to her body. Mike's faint aroma still lingered on her skin and in her hair. A little thrill ran through her. Jessica smiled at her reflection. There was no way anyone could look at her and know about the night she'd just spent. Because there was a change in her heart. She might have thought that she was in love with Mike before last night, but now she was sure.

In the mirror Jessica could see his hand searching for her as he slowly opened his eyes. "Baby," he said. "What are you doing way over there?"

Jessica turned and walked over to the bed. "I just wanted to see if I looked any different." She leaned down to kiss him. "You know, to see if I'd changed."

"You have changed," Mike said. He touched her cheek. "You look even more beautiful this morning than you did last night."

"I bet you say that to all the girls," she teased.

Mike made a thoughtful face. "No," he said,

shaking his head in mock seriousness. "Not to all of them."

On any other day, a remark like that would have sunk her into depression, but this morning she knew he was only teasing. She could see it in his deep, dark eyes.

"That's not what you're supposed to say!" Jessica made a movement to punch him, but he caught her arms and pulled her into another kiss.

"So how does my baby feel this morning?" he asked when they finally drew apart. "Or don't you feel like my baby anymore?" he asked with a smile.

"I'll tell you what I feel like," Jessica answered, yanking him off the bed with a laugh. "I feel like a cheese omelette and toast. I'm starving. For some reason, I didn't have any dinner last night."

As far as Isabella was concerned, there were some days that should be skipped altogether. Days when everything was going to go wrong. When you woke up and it was raining, and you'd forgotten to iron the blouse you were going to wear today, and you knew you would have cramps by lunchtime. Days when a girl should stay in bed, not answering the phone or answering the door, just waiting till it was dark and the good television shows came on.

The minute she opened her eyes that morning, Isabella had known that it was going to be one of those days.

"Oh, I don't believe this," she'd groaned out loud as her eyes fell on Jessica's untouched bed.

There wasn't a doubt in Isabella's mind that even after all the good advice and the strong warnings she'd given her roommate, Jessica had decided to sleep with Mike McAllery. And she also knew that Jessica might just as well have walked off a cliff with her eyes wide open and a smile on her face.

Isabella thumped into the bathroom. "Why are women such dopes sometimes?" she asked her reflection.

Her reflection gave her a wry smile. And Isabella forgot about Jessica for a moment as she remembered Tom Watts. Last night he'd been in her dream. She'd been walking across the quad and he'd been coming in the opposite direction. Unlike when she saw him in real life, in her dream he'd been glad to see her. He'd called her "Izzy" and stopped to talk. When he'd left, he'd smiled at her and kissed her on the cheek.

Isabella was still thinking about Tom when there was a knock on the door. She figured Jessica must have forgotten her key. "Just as long as she didn't forget the condoms . . ." Isabella muttered to herself as she hurried out of the bathroom.

But it wasn't Jessica. It was Alison Quinn, dressed all in white and looking as though she'd just come off a dry cleaner's rack. Even her hair looked as though it had been chemically cleaned.

Alison smiled, walking past Isabella and into the

suite as though she lived there. Alison was not a person to wait for invitations.

"I had to pass by here on my way to a Theta breakfast meeting," she said as she sailed into the living room. "You know, to discuss the pledges and that kind of thing." She stood in the center of the room, her eyes straying through the open door to the bedroom. "I thought I might have a word with Jessica about her sister," Alison said. "I'd like to be able to tell my sorority sisters that the matter is under control."

"I think I'll make some coffee," Isabella said brightly. "Would you like some?"

"Where is Jessica?" Alison asked. She glanced at her watch. "It's not even eight. Don't tell me she's gone to a class."

Isabella looked over the counter that separated the kitchenette from the living room. "Milk and sugar?"

But Alison was staring at Jessica's unslept-in bed. "Didn't she sleep here last night?" she asked.

Isabella didn't blink. She'd been at boarding schools and belonged to exclusive clubs and sororities most of her life. She was used to dealing with girls like Alison.

"I guess she stayed at her brother's," Isabella said. "You know Steven Wakefield, don't you? He lives over by Cayuga."

"Her brother?" Alison's eyes met Isabella's. Alison had been dealing with girls like Isabella all

141

her life too. She trusted no one. "Just so long as she is with her brother," she said menacingly. "I mean, I'd hate to think that she was spending the night with Mike McAllery. He isn't exactly our . . . type. I thought she understood that."

Isabella smiled. "You do take sugar, don't you, Alison?" she asked. *You could certainly use it.*

Celine hated the rain, and not just because it made her hair go limp. It was hard to carry on a conversation with someone when you were walking in the rain. Especially if that someone refused to get under your candy-striped umbrella but strode through the downpour so quickly that you practically had to run to keep up with him.

"You know what our girl reporter's up to now?" Celine asked, trying to sound casual despite the fact that she was jogging.

William White glanced over at her. Everyone else wore bright-colored ponchos and parkas in this weather, but not William. He wore a long black canvas coat and a black slouch hat. He looked like he'd just stepped out of a spaghetti Western. He was the cowboy you should never turn your back on. Celine hated him for looking so attractive as much as she hated the rain.

"Girl reporter?" William asked, slowing down just a little.

"Didn't I tell you that Elizabeth started working at the television station? Apparently she was

142

quite the journalist in high school, and now she's decided to go in for television reporting. It's supposed to be a big deal. She's getting special training or something."

William slowed down a little more. "With Tom?" he asked. "Tom Watts?"

There was something about the way he said the name that caught Celine's attention. It wasn't just dislike. William disliked almost everyone, anyway; there was nothing unusual in that. It was that she thought she'd heard the tiniest bit of . . . anxiety in his voice. Celine pushed the idea away. It was ridiculous, of course. William White wasn't afraid of anything. Not even her.

Celine shrugged and the umbrella bobbed. "I really don't know," she answered. "We haven't talked about it at any great length. I guess she's working with Tom. He's the big hotshot reporter there, isn't he?"

William nodded. "Yeah, he's the big hotshot reporter." He was walking beside her now, at her pace, his arm touching hers. "So what's the story Elizabeth's doing?" he asked. "I take it it's not about fall fashions or Homecoming."

"You can bet your last million that it's not about fashion." Celine smiled, sweetly and slyly.

He gave her elbow a squeeze. "So what is it about? You know I hate it when you play games with me, Celine."

Celine pulled away. As beautiful as William was,

he definitely had a lousy temper. "It's about the illegal recruitment of athletes on the SVU campus," she said slowly, pausing for the words to take effect.

"What? It's about what?"

"The illegal recruitment of athletes. You know," Celine explained, "when they give them special privileges and things so they'll come here instead of going somewhere else."

William nodded again. "Oh, is that all." He sounded relieved.

Celine looked at him sharply. *Is that all?* Had he missed the significance of this entirely?

"Well, I'm glad to see you're taking it so calmly," Celine continued. "Because I must say, I was a little shocked myself. I mean, I know Elizabeth and Todd Wilkins aren't together anymore, but I did think it was a little vindictive of her to try to get back at him like that."

William stopped. "Are you saying that Elizabeth's doing this story just to get her old boyfriend in trouble?" he asked.

She looked ' ack at him, innocent as a leaf. "I don't *know* for sure," Celine purred. "But it does seem a little tacky, doesn't it? I mean, to do a story that's going to cause a major scandal when you know your ex-boyfriend is one of the biggest new jocks on campus." She made a helpless, bewildered face. "What do you think? Don't you think it's a little strange?"

He wasn't revolted or outraged. He smiled. "I

think it must mean she doesn't love him anymore."

"This is incredible," Tom said, his voice openly admiring. "Absolutely incredible." He turned to Elizabeth, his eyes shining with excitement. "You've done an amazing job."

Elizabeth flushed at the praise. Coming from Tom, who everyone said gave praise sparingly, if ever, it really meant something. She looked into his eyes.

People always said that the eyes were the windows to the soul, but in Tom's case they were the shutters. His eyes were usually so guarded and wary that it was impossible to guess what was going on in his head, never mind his heart. But right now, his look was so open she almost thought that it wasn't just excitement that made his eyes shine, but pride as well.

"I'm just getting started," she said, forcing her gaze away from Tom's eyes. She pointed to the new outline she'd made for herself. "I still want to talk to alumni; you know, ex-players and team supporters. But also to people who were involved in athletics here before Coach Sanchez remade the department."

He looked up from her notes. "That's brilliant," he said. "If you can show just how systems, expectations, and attitudes have changed, you'll know exactly what you're looking for."

She nodded. "If I can make a comparison, I can

145

really show what's happened here. As it is, the change has been so gradual that nobody even questions what's been going on."

Tom laughed. It was a sound not often heard in the office of WSVU, but it was a sound that Elizabeth knew she could easily get used to.

They were sitting side by side at Tom's desk, so close that their arms were touching. If she'd leaned toward him just a little she would have felt his breath on her face.

Elizabeth had been with Todd for so long that she'd almost forgotten other men existed. She noticed if someone was attractive, but she didn't think whether or not he was attractive to *her*. That hadn't changed since her breakup with Todd, either. There was such a hole in her life where Todd used to be that she couldn't even begin to think of filling it with someone else.

And yet now she felt these surges of awkward, unexpected emotion she hadn't felt in so long. There was definitely something about Tom . . .

"Professor Sedder said you were exceptional," Tom said with a smile. "But he didn't say just how exceptional."

"He didn't say how exceptional you were, either." Elizabeth just sat there, looking into those wary, intelligent eyes, the color burning her cheeks. She hadn't meant to say that; she hadn't meant to say that at all. Confused, she turned back to her notes.

Tom turned back to her notes too. There was an uneasy silence between them.

"What about Todd Wilkins?" Tom asked suddenly.

Elizabeth dropped her pen. "What?" It was almost as though by thinking about Todd, she'd brought him into the room with them.

Tom leaned down and retrieved the pen for her. "Todd Wilkins," he repeated. "I know you two used to—" His eyes went back to the desktop. "I know you two used to go out." He took a deep breath, carefully choosing his words. "You realize that even from what you've got now, there is a chance Todd might be . . . implicated in all this. I wouldn't want you to—"

"It's not a problem," Elizabeth said quickly. For some reason, she didn't want Tom to think that she was doing this to get back at Todd because she was still so in love with him. "I know Todd really well, and whatever's going on, I'm sure he isn't part of it. He would never do anything that was even a little illegal."

"Right," Tom said, a little shortly. "I just thought—"

"He's one of the most honest people I know," Elizabeth added with a little more emotion than she'd intended. "There's no question about his role in this."

"All right," Tom said. His voice was calm and controlled, but the wary, guarded look was back in

147

his eyes. The mood of excitement and closeness that had passed between them was gone.

"I didn't mean to sound so . . . so bossy," she apologized.

"Don't mention it." He pushed back his chair. "I got the message. George Washington, Abe Lincoln, and Todd Wilkins—the three most honest men America has ever produced." He gave her a businesslike smile. "I wonder if this means Todd Wilkins is going to be the first basketball player in the White House."

Isabella was just about to leave for her first class when the door burst open and Jessica exploded into the suite.

"Guess what?" Jessica said as she threw her things on the couch and collapsed beside them. "Mike's going to take me to the Homecoming ball!" Jessica was almost glowing. "Isn't that wonderful? We're going to be the most fantastic couple there."

Isabella put her books down on the table. She'd promised herself that when Jessica got back from Mike's, she wasn't going to act like a mother hen. She'd vowed that she wasn't going to lose her temper and make a scene. After all, Isabella had been involved in serious relationships herself once or twice. It wasn't as though she couldn't sympathize with her friend.

"I can't wait to see Mike really dressed up,"

Jessica was babbling on. "He'll look so gorgeous, he should be illegal."

Isabella resisted the temptation to say that Mike McAllery probably already was illegal. She took a deep breath, and when she spoke, her voice was pleasant and normal. "Alison Quinn was looking for you," she said. "You missed her by ten or fifteen minutes."

Jessica broke off from wondering out loud whether or not Mike would wear a tux to the dance. "Alison Quinn," she said, looking puzzled. "What did she want? I already know I'm being pledged to the Thetas."

"She wanted to talk to you about Elizabeth. She wants you to tell Elizabeth what she has to do to prove her loyalty to the Thetas."

"I don't know what she has to do," Jessica said, stifling a yawn.

Isabella picked up a pale violet envelope with the silver sorority insignia on it. "You do now," she said, handing it to her.

Isabella watched Jessica reading the note, waiting for her reaction. She'd expected Jessica to be as outraged and horrified as she was, but she'd been wrong. The sea-green eyes looked a little dismayed; that was all.

Jessica tossed the violet notepaper aside as though it were no more than a shopping list. "I'll talk to Liz this afternoon. She's going to take some convincing—I mean, she isn't exactly Peter Wilbourne's biggest fan—but I'm sure she'll come around." She got up and stretched.

"Is that it?" asked Isabella.

"Is what it?"

"Is that all you have to say about it? After the way Peter Wilbourne treated you and Danny, and the way the Sigmas harassed you and Elizabeth, is that all you can say? 'She'll come around'?"

Jessica looked baffled. "What do you want me to say? That I won't join the Thetas because they want my sister to go out with Peter the Creep?"

"No," Isabella said, shaking her head. "I don't want you to drop the sorority, Jess; I just thought you'd be a little angry—you know, that you might stand up to Alison."

"Stand up to Alison—are you nuts, Isabella? The Thetas would drop me in a second if I did that."

"Not necessarily," Isabella argued. "You might convince them to give Elizabeth some other kind of test."

"*Might,*" Jessica said. "And they *might* not." She started toward the bathroom. "Well, it's not a chance I'm willing to take. Joining the Thetas is too important to me."

"Really?" Isabella said. "What about Mike, then? The Thetas don't approve of him either, you know."

Jessica swung around. "I knew it," she said. "I knew you'd get on me about Mike. That's what all this is about, isn't it? It has nothing to do with Elizabeth and the Thetas."

"Of course it has to do with Elizabeth and the Thetas—"

Jessica shook her head defiantly. "No, it doesn't. It's all because I slept with Mike." She made a face. "Well, you don't have to worry, Isabella. I took the condoms with me. I was very careful."

"It's not just your body I want you to be careful about!" Isabella shouted as the bathroom door slammed shut behind Jessica. "It's also your heart!"

Jessica was singing along to the love song playing on her Walkman as she entered Dickenson Hall, the dorm where her sister lived. Her argument with Isabella was already forgotten and her good mood restored. She had more important things to think about than Isabella Ricci or even Alison Quinn. She had Mike McAllery. No matter where she was or what she was supposed to be doing—eating, talking, walking across campus, listening to a lecture on some dead person with an unpronounceable name—it was Mike who filled her thoughts. She couldn't stay in a bad mood when she had him on her mind.

"It's not just for now, it's forever," Jessica sang as she climbed the stairs to Elizabeth's floor.

By now, Jessica had not only forgotten her argument with her roommate, she'd also convinced herself that the Thetas' request was really no big deal. So Elizabeth had to go out with Peter Wilbourne, so what? There wasn't a woman in the world who didn't go out with a complete creep now and then. It was the hazard of dating. You could never be sure that the guy who seemed okay when he asked you to the movies wouldn't turn out to be some loser who snored in the middle of the film or who spent the night talking about megabytes and binary-object files.

Jessica had had dozens of dates with guys just as bad as Peter Wilbourne III. She'd thought at the time the dates would never end, that she'd never survive, but when she looked back on them, they actually made her laugh. Elizabeth would go out with Peter for a few gruesome hours, and later she would laugh about it. "Remember the time I went out with that noxious waste, Peter Wilbourne?" she'd say. "Remember when I had to publicly apologize for telling the world what a septic tank he was? Wasn't that the funniest thing?"

Jessica didn't bother to knock.

Elizabeth was sitting at her desk, concentrating on something she was writing. She looked up as Jessica floated in, pulling off her headset and letting a fizzle of music into the room.

"I knew I'd find my beautiful twin here, working away like a slave on this beautiful autumn day," Jessica said.

Elizabeth looked from Jessica to the window

and back again. "It's raining, Jess," she said. "It may be beautiful out if you're a walrus, but for most of us humans a heavy downpour is less than ideal."

"Oh, come on, Liz." Jessica dropped her wet jacket on Elizabeth's bed and sat on the edge of her desk. "Didn't some poet say something about beauty depending on who's seeing it?" she asked.

Elizabeth smiled. "Something like that."

"Well?" Jessica raised her arms expansively. "When I look outside, I see a beautiful day!"

"I'm glad to hear that, Jess, but I wish you'd sit somewhere else." Elizabeth gave her a little shove. "You're wrinkling my notes."

"Oh, pardon me! I wouldn't want to be responsible for wrinkling your notes." Jessica slid to the floor, dragging several pages covered with Elizabeth's handwriting with her. She reached down to retrieve them. "Don't you ever get tired of doing work all the time?" she asked, not even bothering to glance at them as she put them back on the desk.

Elizabeth gave her an exasperated look. "It's an assignment for the station."

Jessica grinned. "Trying to get in good with the aloof but sexy Tom Watts?" she teased.

"Don't be ridiculous," Elizabeth said, turning away as she straightened out the papers on her desk. "I'm not interested in Tom Watts."

"I'm glad," Jessica said. "Isabella's got a thing

for Tom I'm-Not-Interested-in-Women Watts. I don't think I could stand having the two of you mooning over him."

Elizabeth dropped her pen on the floor. "Well, you don't have to worry about me," she said, her face to the carpet. "It just so happens that I'm not interested in men at the moment, and certainly not in Tom."

"Does that mean you don't have a date for the Homecoming game?" Jessica asked, leaning on the back of her sister's chair.

Elizabeth started writing again. "I'm not going to the game. I want to work on this as much as I can."

"I think you may be wrong about that," Jessica said, using her little-sister voice.

Elizabeth didn't look up. "Forget it, Jess. I don't care if you got yourself two dates for the game and you need me to take one of them—I'm not doing it. I'm staying here and working."

"But Liz . . ." Jessica crouched beside her sister's chair. "It's not that, it's much more important than that. My whole social life at SVU is on the line here."

Elizabeth stopped mid-word and looked at her. Jessica hated it when her sister stared at her like that, as if she could read her thoughts and didn't like what she saw. "This doesn't have something to do with the Thetas, does it?"

How did Elizabeth know things like that? Jes-

154

sica forced herself to smile. "They just want you to do one little thing to prove your loyalty."

"What little thing?" Elizabeth asked, not returning her smile.

"They just want you to go to the game with Peter Wilbourne," Jessica said in a rush. She was convinced that if she got it out fast enough, Elizabeth wouldn't object as much. "And apologize for reaming him out in public that time."

Elizabeth was looking at her as though she were sprouting fur and fangs.

"They what?"

"They want you—"

"Jessica Wakefield, have you lost your mind completely?" Elizabeth stood up so quickly that Jessica fell over. "Have you been inhaling too many car fumes from the back of Mike McAllery's bike or something? You can't seriously think that I'd go out with Peter Wilbourne!"

"Think of it this way, Liz," Jessica said reasonably, getting to her feet. "You haven't had one date since you've been here. Even though you don't like Peter Wilbourne, it can't hurt your reputation to be seen with the president of the Sigmas."

Elizabeth stared at her. "You are crazy," she said slowly. "You are out of your tiny mind."

"Oh, come on, Liz. It's only one date. A football game doesn't last that long, *and* it's all outdoors. All you have to do is sit there and watch the game and drink a soda and that's it. You don't even have to talk to him, except to apologize—which won't take a second. What could be simpler?"

Elizabeth shook her head. "Unbelievable. After the way that moron treated you and Danny . . . I just can't believe, I cannot believe you'd even suggest this."

"Liz, the Thetas will change their minds about pledging me if they change their minds about pledging you, and they'll definitely change their minds about you if you don't do this one little thing."

"I won't do it, Jessica."

Jessica started to wheedle. "Liz, be reasonable. This isn't the end of the world, you know. It's one lousy little date. You've been on bad dates before. You'll laugh about this later, Liz. I guarantee it. Years from now, all I'll have to say is 'Peter Wilbourne' and you'll go into hysterics."

But Elizabeth was way beyond wheedling.

"The only reason I've gone this far with the Thetas is because of you," she said calmly. "But this is where I stop. It's bad enough being on the same planet with scum like Peter Wilbourne; there is *no way* I'm going to date him. And there is absolutely no way in the universe that I would *apologize* to him."

So what'd you think? Tom was asking himself as he dribbled the ball past Danny. *Just because she looked at you like maybe you weren't just another reporter, like maybe you were a nice guy, did you think that meant she was interested? Did you think that because she was working so hard on the article, it meant that you'd been wrong about her still being in love with Wilkins? Did you really think she didn't care if he got in trouble? Are you an idiot, or what?* Tom raised his arms, aimed, jumped—and watched the ball bounce off the rim.

"Nice one, Tombo!" Danny shouted, scooping the ball in one deft motion and slipping around him. "You should've told me you were on my team!"

Tom raced after Danny.

I'm an idiot, that's what I am. A complete stooge. How could I have even thought that I might have a chance with Elizabeth? She probably wasn't even thinking about me when she was looking at me like that. She was probably thinking of him. *It's obvious she still worships the guy. She would have thrown that story back in my face if she'd thought for one second that he might get hurt by it.*

Danny raised the ball, he aimed, he jumped. Tom jumped too, trying to block the shot.

"Eleven–nothing!" Danny yelled as the ball dropped through the net. "Nothing, Tombo. As in none, zero, zilch, *nada*. Nothing to eleven. You want to quit while I'm ahead?"

And even if there was no Todd Wilkins, and even if her interest in you wasn't just professional, so then what? You're going to walk right into it, Tom? You're going to set yourself up to lose something else? If you don't have anything, you don't have anything to lose.

The ball bounced off Tom's head and fell to the ground.

"Hey, Spaceman Watts, I'm talking to you. You want keep going, or you want to quit?"

"I don't know," Tom said, still thinking about Elizabeth. "I just don't know."

Chapter Eight

"What do you mean, you have to go home?"

It took every bit of willpower Jessica possessed to disentangle herself from Mike's arms, but she managed to pull herself up to a sitting position.

"I just noticed the time," she said, pointing to the luminous numbers on the VCR. "I told you, I have to study tonight. I have to get back."

"Oh, baby . . ." He pulled her back down on the couch. "You don't really have to leave me. Stay here and I'll help you study."

"Oh, sure you will," Jessica said with a smile. "But this isn't biology, it's English."

"'Parting is such sweet sorrow . . .'" Mike whispered, his lips against her ear. "That's Shakespeare. You can't get any more English than that."

Jessica could feel her heart weakening. Maybe she didn't have to study *that* much. Tomorrow's exam wasn't the final or anything like that. It was just an exam. And they were allowed to refer to the text. How hard could it be when you had your book open in front of you?

But then a voice that wasn't Mike's started whispering in her ear. *You haven't finished one assignment, passed one test, or gone to more than two classes in a day since you started seeing Mike,* this voice was saying. *Never mind about what a sweet sorrow parting is. If you flunk out of college, your parents will have you back home before you and Mike have a chance to say good-bye.*

"No, Mike," Jessica said, once more struggling to a sitting position. "I really have to go. I've got to start paying more attention to my schoolwork or—"

Mike groaned. "I don't believe this. Isn't it bad enough I have to be jealous of every guy with eyes in Southern California—now I have to be jealous of some old textbook, too?"

She leaned into the hands that were caressing her. She could feel her body giving up the fight. Her body didn't want to go back to a dorm room and sit at a desk; her body wanted to stay here with these warm hands stroking it and that soft mouth on hers.

You have enough trouble with your brother, that unpleasant, whiny voice said. *If he finds out you're doing badly in school, he'll make sure you stop seeing Mike, don't think he won't.*

Jessica tore herself away from those hands. "Mike, please," she pleaded. "You know I'd rather stay here with you than go back to the dorm, but I have to get some work done or I'll get kicked out of school."

He ran his fingers tenderly down the side of her face. "Well, I've been thinking about this very thing, and I have the solution to the problem," he said softly. "I know how you can be with me *and* concentrate on school at the same time."

Jessica smiled. She had enough trouble concentrating on things like eating and sleeping when she was with Mike. "Oh, really? And what would that be?"

"Live here."

She couldn't have heard him right.

"What?"

"Live here." He looked as though this were the most normal, obvious proposal in the world. "Move in with me. Then you don't ever have to go home. You'll already be here." He touched his mouth to her hair. "Then I don't have to lie awake at night, thinking about you."

"But Michael—"

She didn't know what to say. She hadn't dared hope that he lay in bed at night thinking about her the way she lay awake thinking about him. She was afraid to ask him what his real feelings for her were.

"But what? It's the answer to everything. You move in, and then we can see each other all we want."

Her heart and her body wanted her to say yes. The idea of always being with him was almost too much happiness to bear. Every cell in her body seemed to be zinging with joy.

But that insistent little voice in her head had its doubts. *Move in with him?* it was shrieking. *You don't just move in with someone after a few weeks! Moving in with someone is a big step. A very big step. Do you have any idea what your parents would do if they found out? They'd kill you. And don't think they wouldn't find out. Steven lives upstairs, Jessica. Are you planning to buy a dark wig and wear sunglasses for the next four years?*

"Come on, baby, what's the problem? Just say yes."

Jessica could feel herself getting lost in those seductive golden eyes. "This is something I'm really going to have to think about, Mike," she said, forcing herself to her feet.

As much as she loved Mike, even Jessica knew that living with someone was different than being in love with them. It meant a real commitment. Commitment had never been one of her strong points.

"What's there to think about?" He stood up too, putting his arms around her. "Who would you rather live with? Me or Isabella?"

You! her heart screamed. *You!*

"It's not that I don't want to, Mike," she answered as the warmth of his lips touched her neck. "It's just that it's a big step. I really need some time to think it over."

"Okay," he whispered. "But don't take too long. You know I hate to be kept waiting."

*　　　*　　　*

"You know, Steven," Billie said, looking up from the paper she was reading. "I had a brilliant idea this morning for making a little extra money."

"Umph," Steven said. He was sitting on the sofa, staring into space.

"I was thinking we should get some of those outdoor wooden benches they sell at Hechingers, and paint them with flowers and all sorts of wild colors to sell at the flea market on Cantina Boulevard on Saturday for people's lawns."

"Umph," Steven said. He frowned in concentration, listening for something.

"It's the kind of thing people who shop at that flea market will love," Billie continued. "Don't you think?"

"Umph."

"How many do you think we could sell?"

"Umph."

Billie threw her paper onto the coffee table. "Steven Wakefield, have you heard one word I said?"

Steven didn't hear her. A motorcycle engine had started up outside and he was listening to that.

Billie sighed in frustration. "That's not Mike," she said as Steven jumped to his feet and went running to the window. "That's a BMW. He's got a Kawasaki engine."

Steven turned to look at her as the BMW pulled into the street. "How did you know that?"

"How did I know what?" Billie asked. "How

did I know Mike McAllery's bike has a Kawasaki engine? Or how did I know that was what you were listening for?"

He grinned sheepishly. "Both."

"I know what engine Mike's bike has because he explained it to me one day when I happened to run into him downstairs and asked him if he put the bike together himself." She gave Steven a look. "He did. I know you think he's probably a gun-runner for some guerrilla army, but he happens to be a first-class mechanic." She gave Steven another look. "And I knew that was what you were listening for because living with you is like living with a CIA agent. All you do lately is skulk around trying to catch Mike with Jessica."

The sheepish grin returned. "I know you think I'm crazy, Billie, but I can't help it. The thought of Jessica throwing herself away on a piece of trash like that—"

With another sigh, Billie went over and put her arms around him. "Steven," she said, "I love you. You know that, don't you? But you have got to get a grip on yourself. You know nothing about this man except that you don't like the way he looks—"

Steven stiffened. "That's not true, Billie. I know he's a womanizer. I know he runs around drinking and doing God knows what till all hours of the morning. I know he's always having an argument with someone."

"Steven, you're prelaw. You have also got to

164

know that all your evidence is circumstantial."

"It's not circumstantial, Billie, it's gut instinct."

She took her arms away. "And my gut instinct is making me rethink our whole relationship."

He looked at her in surprise. For the first time all evening he was thinking more about her than Mike McAllery. "What do you mean?"

"I mean that if we ever got married, I'm not so sure we should have children. If this is how you act when your *sister* starts having a serious relationship, how will you act when it's your own daughter?"

Steven laughed. "Oh, come on, Billie. That's ridiculous. That—"

He broke off as a sound from the street caught his attention. "Don't tell me *that's* not the motorcycle from hell," he said, sticking his head out the window. He made a fist. "It is!" he hissed. "He's taking her home."

Billie put a hand on his shoulder. "Well, that should make you happy. It isn't even nine o'clock and he's taking her home. She isn't spending the night."

"Why should that make me happy?" he asked, turning to face her. "He's probably just getting rid of Jess so he can have another date."

Lila Fowler—or the Contessa di Mondicci, as she was now known—appeared in Jessica's dream. She was wearing a tailored gray dress and matching coat and hat. She had a diamond as big as a Ping-

Pong ball on her left hand. The count was with her. He wore a dark business suit and had a distracted air. He talked on a cellular phone the whole time. The Contessa di Mondicci was bored.

"It's not that I don't love Tisiano to death," she told Jessica, "but he is *so* busy . . . and there are all these formal dinners and functions to go to." She shrugged, her wedding ring flashing like a strobe light. "Still, I can't complain. When I think of you, Jessica, living in a dorm with a bunch of *girls* . . . You can't really experience what it's like to be a woman until you live with a man."

Jessica was wearing a chartreuse cat suit and Mike's old motorcycle jacket. Her hair was blowing in the wind. She laughed. "Live in a dorm?" Jessica said. "But I don't live in a dorm."

"You don't?" Lila asked.

Jessica shook her head. "Of course not. And I know exactly what it's like to be a woman," she said as Mike pulled up behind her on his bike. "I live with *him*," she said, slipping into his arms and a passionate kiss. When finally they broke apart, Jessica turned back to the Contessa di Mondicci. "And believe me," she said, "I'm not bored . . ."

Jessica woke up, her lips still tingling with Mike's kiss. She'd been wrong to leave last night. And maybe she was wrong to hesitate about moving in with him too. All she could think of was seeing him again.

Frantic with love, Jessica looked at the clock. If she hurried, she could surprise him with his favorite breakfast, lemon croissants and blueberry jam, before her first class.

Jessica flung herself out of bed and started rummaging through the pile of clothes on her desk for something to wear.

Isabella rolled over, slowly opening her eyes. "Where are you going?" she asked sleepily. "The alarm hasn't even gone off yet."

"I'm hungry," Jessica said, her hand on the doorknob. "I'm going to get something to eat."

Jessica floated all the way to Mike's. *I've been a fool*, she told herself. *Of course I should move in with him. That's what you do when you love someone as much as I love him. You want to be with them as much as you can. You want to share everything with them, from breakfast to brushing your teeth at night.*

She hugged the warm croissants to her body as she raced along. How would Mike react when he opened his door and found her standing there; when she told him that she'd brought him the first of the thousands of breakfasts they were going to share? Would he be surprised? Would he pretend he'd known she'd give in? Or would he just be so overcome with joy that he'd take her into his arms without saying a word?

Jessica practically ran across the street to Mike's building and up the stairs. She was so excited, so nervous about actually telling him her decision, that she'd gone past his floor and was almost at her brother's landing before she realized her mistake.

Relax a little, she told herself. *Catch your breath. Walk, don't run. You're a woman now. Don't act like a teenager.*

Halfway back down the stairs to Mike's floor, she stopped suddenly.

"I want to thank you," a male voice was saying. A male voice that was imprinted on her soul. "That was terrific. It really was."

What was he doing up so early? What was he doing out in the hall? Maybe he'd had some emergency with the plumbing and he'd had to get the janitor out of bed to fix it. Sure, that was what had happened. He was talking to the janitor.

Jessica was just about to call out to him when another voice spoke. It was not the voice of the janitor. It was a female voice. A revoltingly sweet and cloying female voice.

"Don't mention it," it said. "You know you can call me anytime."

Jessica felt the stairs disappear out from under her. It was all she could do not to collapse. Horrified, she watched a very pretty redhead hurry down the stairs, smiling to herself. She heard Mike turn and go back to his apartment. She dropped the bag of croissants and followed the other girl down the stairs. Only Jessica wasn't smiling to herself. Jessica was sobbing.

"I'm not going to the Homecoming dance ei-

168

ther," Nina said as she and Elizabeth made their way through the breakfast line. "I have a big paper due for my history of science course." She put a glass of juice on her tray and gave Elizabeth a look. "What's your excuse?"

Elizabeth, counting calories in her head to determine whether she should have granola or oatmeal, frowned. "I don't need an excuse," she said. "No one's asked me."

Nina handed her a container of skim milk. "You know, I'm really, really sorry that I encouraged you to go see Todd that morning. I guess I should have warned you that I'm good when it comes to theoretical physics and advanced calculus, but not very good when it comes to men."

"Neither am I, anymore," Elizabeth said with a laugh. She picked up her tray and followed Nina into the dining hall. "And anyway, it's not your fault I got my signals crossed with Todd. I think I've finally come to terms with the fact that it really is over between us."

Nina led the way to a table in a corner. "It's really been hard for you, hasn't it?" she asked.

Elizabeth took a deep breath. "It's been easier losing the three quarters of a pound I've lost by living on air and water for the last few weeks than it has been getting used to the fact that Todd isn't part of my life anymore." She plunked down across from Nina and started to eat, her mind still on Todd. It was strange, but even though she knew in her heart that it wouldn't have worked between her and Todd, she still missed him.

"I guess it'll just take longer than I thought," she added with a bleak smile. "Doesn't everybody say that time heals all wounds?"

Nina laughed. "I always thought it was time wounds all heels," she said. "I find that very comforting."

Elizabeth laughed too. "You're right; I feel better already."

Nina nibbled thoughtfully on an English muffin. "You know what else they say, though, don't you?" she asked, eyeing her cautiously.

"Wait a minute, Nina," Elizabeth said, holding up her hands. "Remember what you just said. You're no good when it comes to men."

"But this isn't me," Nina protested. "This is tried and true. I'm sure I read it in one of those women's magazines that are always lying around the TV room."

Elizabeth sighed in mock resignation. "All right," she said, unable to keep herself from smiling. "What else does everybody say?"

The beads on Nina's braids clicked as she gleefully shook her head. "That the quickest way to get over one man is another man."

Elizabeth gazed back at her skeptically. "Really?"

"Uh huh. That's what they say." Nina crossed her heart. "It's tried and true. Handed down from one generation of women to another with

170

recipes for chocolate-chip cookies."

The skeptical look remained on Elizabeth's face. "I don't suppose you have any idea of who this other man might possibly be?" she teased.

Nina pretended to be thinking this over. "Well, there is the guy who always watches you in the library," she said at last.

Unbidden, Elizabeth's heart jumped half a beat. "You mean Tom? Tom Watts?"

Nina shook her head. "No, not Tom. The other one. The one you told me gave you the rose that Celine destroyed."

"William," Elizabeth said. "William White." She seemed to be considering William, but in reality she was thinking about the one who hadn't given her the rose.

"And don't forget, Elizabeth," Nina said, digging into her cereal. "You don't have to wait for him to ask you out. This is the nineties. You can ask him."

"Jessica. Jessica." Isabella sat down at the edge of Jessica's bed and put a tentative hand on her shoulder. "Jessica, why don't you come into the living room and I'll make some coffee and we can talk. You can tell me what happened."

Jessica pushed her hand away.

Isabella put it back. "Jessica, you can't lie here crying all afternoon—you're beginning to scare me." Which was true. Ever since she got back from her last class over half an hour ago, Isabella had been trying

171

unsuccessfully to get her roommate to talk to her.

Jessica raised her tearstained face from her pillow. Her skin was pale and blotchy and her eyes were swollen and red. "Yes, I can," she said in a hoarse, choked voice. "I'm going to lie here crying for the rest of my life."

"You can't," Isabella said. "The rate you're going, you'll be dried up by dinner."

"I don't care!" Jessica wailed, throwing herself back down on the bed. "I don't care what happens to me anymore. I don't care if I shrivel up and blow away."

Isabella gave her a shake. "Come on, Jess," she coaxed. "I'll make some coffee, and we'll sit on the couch and you can tell me exactly what happened. You'll feel better once you've talked about it."

"No, I won't," came the muffled reply. "I'll never feel better again."

The first time Elizabeth reached the door of the TV station, she kept right on walking.

"I can't do it," she mumbled to herself as she hurried by. "I just can't do it."

Ever since she and Tom had gone over her notes together, she hadn't been able to stop thinking about him. She couldn't figure him out. Sometimes she could sense a bond between them so strong that it almost frightened her, and other times he was so cold and distant that she was convinced he didn't like her at all.

It was crazy, but there had been a moment that afternoon when she almost felt as if he might kiss her. And then he'd brought up Todd, and an invisible wall had sprung up between them. She couldn't decide whether Tom thought she was helping him because she wanted to get back at Todd, or if he thought she would throw the story away if it did turn out that Todd was implicated in some way.

Elizabeth came to the end of the path. Maybe she should just keep going. She had an interview with Manny Clipper, the basketball coach, in half an hour. She might as well go a little early and use the time to see what she could pick up in the athletics office.

"That's what I'll do," Elizabeth announced to no one. "I'll go ahead to my interview."

Instead, she turned around and went back the way she'd just come.

Although she couldn't tell whether or not Tom liked her, Elizabeth was beginning to realize how she felt about him. She was terrified of starting a new relationship on the rebound from Todd, but in spite of this it was getting harder and harder to kid herself about Tom any longer. She felt enormously attracted to him. She had from the first moment she saw him. Not because of his unusual good looks, but because of his character and strength. Tom Watts wasn't fooled by appearances, and he didn't let anyone push him around.

Once more, Elizabeth found herself standing in

front of the door to the television station. She stared at the sign on the door as though she'd never seen it before. WSVU it said in bold black letters, and underneath in smaller print, *Studio and Office*.

It's not going to work, Elizabeth decided. *I just can't do it, and that's that.*

She spun on her heel and headed back in the other direction. Whether Tom liked her or didn't like her, whether she was interested in him because she was on the rebound from Todd or not, it didn't matter. She was never going to be able to ask him to the Homecoming ball, and that was all there was to it. Everyone knew that Tom Watts was a loner. He wasn't interested in women or having a relationship; he was interested only in the news.

I must be insane, Elizabeth told herself as she reached the end of the path once more, turned around, and marched back toward the station. *I must really be crazy. Of course he isn't interested in me. I'm just a reporter to him. That's all he cares about. That's all I'll ever be.*

She stopped in front of the door once again. She put her hand out toward the knob. She touched it. She pulled away and turned around so fast that she slammed into someone coming up behind her.

"Oh, I'm sorry!" Elizabeth gasped. "I'm really sorry."

She could feel herself blushing as she looked into his face, but his hands were on her shoulders, steadying her, and in that instant she knew she could do it. She could ask him to the dance. "Tom, I—"

He dropped his hands suddenly. "Wait a minute. What are you doing here?" Tom demanded. "You're supposed to be interviewing Coach Clipper this afternoon. You're going to be late."

"Me? I—"

"You're not changing your mind about this, are you? You aren't having second thoughts?"

He wasn't even looking at her. He was riffling around in his stupid notebook. "Because if you are—"

It was true. Why didn't she just face it? It was only about work. It would only ever be about work. "No!" Elizabeth said, resisting the urge to kick him in the shins. "I'm not changing my mind about *that*."

Jessica had been afraid that if she told Isabella about seeing the redhead coming out of Mike's apartment, Isabella would say the dreaded I-told-you-so. *What did you expect?* she'd imagined Isabella saying. *Didn't I try to warn you? Didn't I tell you what he's like?* She'd even been afraid that Isabella might know who the other girl was. *Tall and striking with legs to her earlobes? Oh, I know who she is. She and Mike go back a long way!*

But Isabella said none of those things. Instead, she made coffee, opened the chocolate macaroons she'd been saving for a special occasion, and listened silently while Jessica poured out her tale of woe.

"You poor thing," she said when Jessica was finished. There wasn't a trace of sarcasm in her voice or on her face. "How totally awful. No wonder you're so upset."

Jessica dried her eyes with one of the tissues from the box Isabella had put beside her.

"I just couldn't believe it, Isabella," Jessica said, her voice still thick with emotion. "After all that's happened between us . . ." *After making love to me, and calling me his baby, and begging me to live with him* . . . "It was like being knifed in the heart."

"I'm sure it was," Isabella said gently. "Believe me, Jess, I've been there once or twice myself, and I know exactly what you're going through." She sipped her coffee. "It's better you didn't confront him there and then," Isabella continued. "You know what men are like. He'd probably have a dozen excuses. She was his cousin, or his cleaning lady, or an old friend he owed money to." Isabella made a comical face. "You wouldn't believe the stories they come up with."

Feeling a little better just to have told someone, Jessica broke a cookie in half. Maybe she should have confronted Mike right then. She'd love to hear how he'd explain the redhead.

And then a thought occurred to Jessica that hadn't occurred to her before. What if he *could* explain her?

Isabella started telling her some of the excuses she'd heard men make, but Jessica wasn't really listening. She was thinking. Did it make any sense that a man would want you and need you one minute, and go off with someone else the next? Did it make any sense that a man would plead with you to live with him and then spend the night with somebody else? No, it didn't. It didn't make any sense at all. There had to be some other reason for the redhead. Obviously she wasn't his cleaning lady—cleaning ladies didn't wear Lycra shorts and tank tops. And she wasn't the janitor. The janitor in Steven's building was sixty and smoked cigars. On the other hand, the janitor might be sick and she might have been helping him out.

"So what are you going to do now?" Isabella asked. "You want me to drop off a Dear-Mike letter for you?"

Jessica looked up in surprise. "What?"

Isabella looked back at her with concern. "What are you going to *do*, Jess? If you don't want to talk to him, the best thing to do might be to write."

Jessica took another macaroon. "I don't know, Isabella. I don't want to be too rash."

"You what?"

She shrugged. "I mean, maybe it wasn't exactly the way it seemed. Maybe I overreacted a little."

"Overreacted?" Isabella repeated.

Jessica nodded. "And besides, I always fought for what was mine in the past. And now Mike

177

McAllery is mine. I can't give him up without a fight, can I?"

Isabella swallowed the rest of her coffee in one gulp. "If you say so."

"It's a good thing I don't have a gun," said Tom to his unopened container of juice. "I'd probably wind up shooting myself." He pushed his half-eaten sandwich away and put his head on his desk with a groan.

What was wrong with him, anyway? It was as if his emotions were a string and he was the yo-yo. One minute he wanted to take Elizabeth into his arms, and the next he was pushing her away.

Tom closed his eyes. He couldn't believe it when she fell into him this afternoon. He couldn't believe how small and fragile she felt in his hands. And she'd looked so lovely. Flushed, bright-eyed, and out of breath; he couldn't remember ever seeing her look more beautiful. She looked the way she had in his dream. Expectant, excited, happy to see him.

Had she been happy to see him? He didn't know anymore. He'd been so surprised to see her—as though she'd materialized out of his thoughts—and so rattled, that he couldn't get rid of her fast enough. Seeing her there when she should have been on her way to the athletics office, he'd been sure she was going to back out of the story. She'd looked so confused and so nervous that he knew she was going to tell him she couldn't go on. She'd been thinking it

178

over, and she couldn't risk hurting Todd. Not even when truth and fairness were at stake.

And that was why he'd yelled at her. He could still see the look on her face. She looked as though he'd slapped her.

"Tom?"

This is all I need, Tom thought. *Now I'm hearing her voice when I'm alone.*

"Tom?"

Not only was he hearing her voice, but her voice was upset and needed him.

"Tom, I'm really sorry to bother you, but . . ."

He raised his head and turned around.

She was standing in the doorway, strained and pale, her notebook clutched in her hand. It was hard to tell because half of the lights were off, but she looked as though she were close to tears.

"What is it, Elizabeth?" He got to his feet.

Slowly, as though this were a dream, she came toward him, holding out the book.

He took it from her. "Todd?" he asked.

She nodded. "You were right," she whispered. "He is implicated."

And he'd also been right that she was close to tears. "You want to forget about this?" he asked, chucking truth and justice out the window. "We can jack it, Elizabeth. Do something else."

But she was shaking her head. "All I want is to believe it isn't true."

Chapter Nine

Michael McAllery whistled an old rock song under his breath as he strode briskly through the night. He had his hands in his pockets and his collar up against the autumnal chill, and he walked with the air of a man who knew exactly where he was going and why. Halfway down the block he stopped to look in the window of the bookstore; at the corner he played with his keys while he waited for the light to change.

Yet all the while he was unaware that just a few yards behind, a dark figure followed his every step: speeding up when he sped up; stopping when he stopped; ducking into the shadows whenever he turned.

Jessica pulled the scarf more tightly around her face. *Maybe Isabella's right,* she thought as she warily rounded the corner after Mike. *Maybe I really am crazy. Maybe sex hormones have destroyed my brain.*

The idea of trailing Mike had come to her on the spur of the moment. Unable to eat, to concentrate on anything that wasn't him for more than three seconds, or even to cry anymore, Jessica had gone to his apartment to have it out. "Maybe you shouldn't surprise him again," Isabella had advised. "Maybe you should call first." But by then Jessica had convinced herself that he'd be sitting at home wondering why he hadn't heard from her, waiting for her to come by.

He was just leaving the building when she arrived. She'd been about to say something, but she stopped. Suddenly she knew that if she wanted to find out the truth, she needed to be with him when he didn't know she was there. He was probably just going around the corner to pick up some milk—but maybe he wasn't. Maybe he was going to pick up the redhead.

Mike slowed down. Jessica stopped in front of an appliance store, pretending to be mesmerized by the display of toasters and coffee makers while she watched him out of the corner of her eye. He came to a halt under a pink neon sign that said *Mojo's Bar and Grill*, pulled open the door, and disappeared inside.

Jessica's heart was stampeding and her whole body felt damp with sweat. *Stop it,* she told her heart. *Get a grip on yourself. Stop making so much noise.* She wiped her hands on her skirt, the one Mike had said was his favorite because it was the same color as her eyes. *Just give him some time to sit down and get a drink . . . then you can go in and see who he's with.*

Jessica stared at the gleaming appliances in their bright designer colors and shining chrome, but all she could see was fiery red hair.

She started slowly down the street toward the bar. It was impossible to see in. Lighted beer signs and a checkered café curtain filled the smoked-glass window, and even though it was a weeknight the place was packed. Jessica stepped into the doorway of the next place over as a group of men came out of Mojo's.

Mojo's wasn't a sophisticated club or café where a guy like Mike would bring a date. It was a neighborhood bar where a guy like Mike would go to have a drink and forget his troubles when he hadn't heard from his girlfriend all day.

Jessica closed her eyes. "Okay," she whispered out loud. "This is it. On the count of three. One . . . two . . . three . . ."

It took her a few minutes to find him. He was in the back room, playing pool with a lanky man with a long ponytail and a lopsided grin. Jessica got herself a soda from the bar and slid into a dark corner booth where she could watch Mike without his seeing her. Not that there was much chance of that. He was so intent on his game and the beer he was drinking that she probably could have come in wearing bells and flashing lights and he wouldn't have noticed her.

Safe in her corner, Jessica began to relax. She'd been right to follow him. Isabella was wrong. Mike wasn't the slimy two-timing creep she'd warned Jessica about. He wasn't sneaking around with other women. He was just a guy hanging out with his friends, shooting a little pool.

She smiled to herself as he systematically cleared the table while his friend watched in horror. The last ball vanished down the left-hand side pocket, and Mike looked up. His friend smiled and shook his hand. A few of the onlookers whooped and cheered. Jessica was so excited that she jumped to her feet. She was going to go over and congratulate him. She was going to throw her arms around him and give him a big, public kiss.

Jessica was only a few feet from the pool table when she realized that another woman had had the exact same idea. Only the other woman was quicker. She was already in Mike's arms.

Jessica shouted. It wasn't really words, it was just a wail of rage. Everyone in the back room turned to look at her, including Mike and the woman whose arms were around his neck.

"Who's the little tiger?" the woman asked, not moving her head from its position on his chest.

Mike smiled at Jessica. "Shelley's right, you do look like a tiger. What's the matter?"

Finally words came. "You two-timing creep! You lying jerk!"

"Looks like you've got yourself a real jealous one this time," Shelley said through her giggles.

Mike started laughing. "Oh, come on, Jess, you've got to be kidding."

But Jessica didn't answer him. She was already running from the bar.

Elizabeth sat at her study carrel, her eyes on the textbook in front of her, her notebook opened to a clean page and her pen in her hand ready to write, but her mind was a million miles away. Her mind was on Todd.

She'd been so sure that Todd couldn't be implicated in any scandal that she'd steamed ahead with the investigation without even thinking. Tom had only been trying to make her take a realistic look at what the outcome might be when he'd suggested that Todd could be involved, but she'd taken his remark as a personal insult. Elizabeth grimaced. How ironic that she, who had known Todd so well and for so long, should have been wrong, and Tom Watts, who probably had never even said hello to Todd, had been right.

Not that being right had made Tom generous or sympathetic. "I told you this might happen," he'd said. "I thought you understood that the truth can hurt." Elizabeth dropped her pen and laid her head on the desk. Maybe she wasn't cut out to be an investigative journalist after all. Maybe she should consider writing articles on food and fashion instead. How much trouble could she cause researching pasta recipes?

Elizabeth groaned inwardly. It was all Alexandra Rollins's fault. While Elizabeth was interviewing Coach Clipper, a few chance remarks Alex had made had come into her head. Something about Mark being lucky he didn't have to study much since his time wasn't taken up only with practice but with people wanting to give dinners for the players all the time. *The way athletes are treated on this campus, you'd think the place was designed for them,* Alex had said. She'd mentioned Mark's new Explorer and going to the spectacularly overpriced Da Vinci's for dinner. Sensing that she might really be on to something, Elizabeth had decided to drop her slightly probing, professional style with Coach Clipper and adopted an attitude of open admiration instead. Hiding behind her California good looks and the sweet, girlish smile that always worked so well for Jessica, Elizabeth had stopped asking for information and started wheedling it out of him.

Gently and innocently, Elizabeth had pumped Coach Clipper about the way the basketball team was treated. Coach Clipper had chatted unguardedly, thinking he was impressing her.

Hoping to open him up even more, Elizabeth had mentioned Todd. "My boyfriend, Todd Wilkins," she'd said, praying that Coach Clipper wouldn't know that she'd left out the tiny word *ex.*

He hadn't known. At the mention of Todd, the

185

coach became almost effusive. "One of the best players we've got," he'd boasted. "And believe me, it cost us the sun and moon to get him. But I'm sure I don't have to tell you how many top-notch universities were after him."

He hadn't had to tell her. Elizabeth had fought back a sour smile. She'd believed that Todd picked SVU and not one of the bigger schools because of her. Apparently she'd been wrong about that, too.

Elizabeth groaned out loud. She wished she'd never started this. She wished it were last week and Tom was showing her the stuff he'd uncovered, and instead of saying that she thought it looked like the biggest story she'd ever touched she'd said, "It's not one for me, Tom. Get somebody else."

"Elizabeth? I was hoping I'd find you here."

She didn't move. If she didn't move he might just go away. It wasn't all just Alexandra Rollins's fault, it was his fault too.

He came around the desk and knelt down beside her chair. "Elizabeth," he whispered. "I've gone over your notes again, and I've been giving this a lot of thought . . ."

She raised her head, brushing a few stray tears from her eyes. "And?"

"Here." Tom reached in his pocket and handed her a tissue. "And I've decided that we don't have to take this any further. I mean, what's the point? There's no question that the sports teams are really important to the school. Whatever's gone on that hasn't been completely aboveboard was to help SVU, not hurt it. It's not like these things have been done for any personal gain."

"What about truth and justice?" she whispered back, hardly able to speak. "What about fairness and honesty?"

Tom handed her another tissue. "Everybody has to compromise sometime, Elizabeth. Nothing's black and white. The trick is knowing when to compromise and when to push."

Elizabeth stared at Tom, torn between gratitude for the generosity of his gesture and disgust that her own weakness should have forced him to make such a sacrifice. Suddenly everything fell into place. The scandal and the shock and hurt it would cause when it broke wasn't Alexandra's fault, or Tom's fault, or even her fault. It was the fault of people who believed that the ends justified the means.

She took the tissue he was offering her and blew her nose. "In that case," she said, "I think this is the time to push."

"Is Elizabeth still working at the station with Tom Watts?" William asked.

Celine looked up from shaking ketchup on her fries. Ever since she'd told William that Tom was training Elizabeth, he didn't let a day go by without asking about it. She wouldn't have thought that someone like William would even be aware of

Tom's existence, but he was more than aware. He was disturbed.

"Working with him?" Celine smiled. "I'd say that those two might be doing a little bit more than working." She picked up a fry and bit off the end. "If you know what I mean."

William eyed her coldly over the rim of his coffee cup. "No, Celine, I don't know what you mean. Are you saying that Elizabeth's going out with Tom?"

"Oh, no, William. I didn't mean to imply that," Celine protested, even though that was exactly what she'd meant.

Ever since she'd discovered that William White was worried about Tom Watts, she'd been determined to give him something to worry about. It didn't matter to Celine if she had to stretch the truth now and then to do so. It didn't matter if she had to out-and-out lie. Tom Watts was a weak point in William, and she was going to make the most of it. How much Elizabeth actually saw Tom or how close they were wasn't important at all.

She finished her fry and delicately licked the oil from her fingertips. "All I meant was that Elizabeth seems to be spending quite a lot of time with Tom." Celine shrugged. "I guess it's this story they're working on. As far as I can tell, they're together every night."

William sipped his coffee without comment, but the glacier-blue eyes were deep in calculation.

"Frankly, I'm a little surprised," Celine went on. "I wouldn't have thought that Tom Watts was really the princess's type."

The pale eyelashes flickered, but he still didn't speak.

"I mean, he's not really a big man on campus, is he? Not anymore. I suppose some girls would find him attractive in a sort of renegade way, but he isn't what you'd call *classically* good looking, is he?" She bit into another fry. "Or blond," she added, wiping a dab of ketchup from the corner of her mouth.

The classically good-looking and blond William White continued to study her wordlessly.

Celine smiled. "Of course, you never can tell with these sweet, virginal types, can you?" she asked. "You think they're into poetry and moonlight walks and what they really want is some cowboy to pull them onto the back of his horse."

William put his cup into its saucer with a click. "There are times, Celine," he said softly, "when I'd really love some cowboy to pull *you* onto the back of a horse." His lips twitched. "Preferably one that bucks."

Why is my life like this? Winston wondered. *Why can't things be normal for me?*

Winston was sitting at a table in the center of the snack bar, surrounded by five of the most attractive girls on campus. He should have been

189

happy, he knew that. He could tell from the glances other guys gave him when they walked past that he should be happy. His ego should be in overdrive and he should be delirious with joy. But he wasn't. He felt like a piece of cheese waiting for the mouse, or, in this case, mice.

Anoushka's plan was simple. These five women of Oakley Hall, wing B, were going to show signs of giving in to the advances of the Sigmas. They were going to string them along for a few days and encourage them to ask them to the Homecoming ball. And then, at the very last minute, to a woman, they were going to say they already had dates. Total humiliation for the Sigmas and total triumph for the good women of Oakley Hall. Simple but fiendishly clever. Winston sighed. A plan like that could have come only from a female brain.

How did I ever get involved in this? he moaned silently.

"They're here," Anoushka said. "Bill just came through the door."

Winston stared at her. Anoushka and Debbie had their heads together and their faces buried in a math book.

"I don't know if I can go through with this," Debbie whispered. "What if I start laughing?"

"You better not," Denise said. She kicked Candy under the table. Winston knew she had because he was sitting next to Denise and her leg

190

brushed against his. Electric sparks went off in his kneecap.

Candy studied her nails. "They see us," she hissed. "They're nudging each other."

"They're headed this way," Maia said.

"I'm out of here," Winston announced. He started to get to his feet.

Denise grabbed his belt and yanked him back down. "Not so fast, Winnie. You can't go yet. If you leave, they won't come over."

Part of Winston didn't want Denise ever to let go of his belt, but another part felt the instinct of a fox who will gnaw off his own foot to get out of a trap.

"Sure they will—" he began.

A booming, boyish voice cut him off.

"Win, old man. How's it going?"

Winston looked up, but the girls continued to pretend that they were so involved in their books they hadn't noticed the gaggle of Sigmas looming over their table.

"Hey, Bill!" Winston could only hope that he looked surprised and not just scared out of his wits. "Jeff, Bruce, Tony, Miles . . ." He nodded to Bill's companions. "I think you've already met my dormmates . . ."

"Mind if we join you?" Bruce asked, already shoving a chair between Winston and Denise.

Jeff leaned over Debbie's shoulder. "What are you doing?" he asked.

191

If Winston had asked Debbie that question, she would have snapped back something like, "Picking my toenails, you idiot, what does it look like I'm doing?"

"I'm trying to understand how to construct a statistical graph," she said to Jeff, looking helpless and cute. Winston knew perfectly well she could draw up a statistical graph with her eyes closed and a parade coming through the room.

Jeff pulled up a chair. "Maybe I can help," he said, practically shoving Anoushka out of his way. "I'm pretty good at math."

Miles, meanwhile, was gazing at Candy like a sheep that had been locked out of the pasture for too long. "Can I . . . uh . . . give you a hand with something?" he said, looking around for another empty chair.

"I'm not doing anything," Candy said with a smile as sweet as her name.

"That's okay," Miles said agreeably. "I can help you with that."

Tom leaned back in his chair. After he'd walked Elizabeth to her dorm from the library, he'd returned to the station to do some more work on the sports-recruitment story, but for once working wasn't stopping him from thinking. It was the other way around.

Every time he looked down at his notebook he saw Elizabeth's face, her blue-green eyes rimmed

192

with tears. He was sure she'd made the right decision about going with the piece—and he was sure she was sure that she'd made the right decision too—but being right didn't always make you feel very good.

And as for being right, had he done the right thing, going after her like that? Tom wished he knew. His first attempts to comfort her had been so inadequate that he'd had to do something to try to make it up to her. *I thought you understood that the truth can hurt*. Tom groaned. What had made him say a cliché like that? *And I told you so*. He'd actually said *I told you so*. But his second attempts to comfort her hadn't been much better.

What he'd wanted to do was simply take her in his arms and whisper clichés into her ear till the library closed—till the universe closed, if it came to that. *Everything's going to be all right*, he longed to tell her. *You're not alone. I'll always be there for you. I'll always take care of you. Always . . .*

But, of course, he hadn't said any of those things. She frightened him so much; his feelings for her frightened him so much. . . .

Tom stared at the wall. This time it wasn't Elizabeth's face he was seeing; this time it was the faces of his family—his parents, his older sister, his little brother.

It was harder to picture them now. The time that had passed and the power of what he felt for them blurred the images. He still missed them so much it was like a physical ache.

It's me who's alone, he said to himself. It wasn't that Elizabeth needed him. It was he who needed her. And needing was something he didn't want to touch with the tip of his finger. It was even more terrifying than love.

What was it Danny had said to him the other day? "You can't start a fire, Tombo, without the risk of getting burned. But without a fire, you'll freeze to death."

Jessica parked the Jeep in the municipal lot and set off to meet Isabella for a mini-shopping spree. There was something about spending money that always cheered her up.

And I could definitely use a little cheering up today, she admitted as she turned onto the main street. *I made an absolute fool of myself last night.*

She could see that now. She'd be lucky if Mike ever spoke to her again after the way she behaved. Everyone in the bar must have laughed themselves silly after she stormed out like that.

Jessica shuddered at the thought. In the bright light of this beautiful afternoon it was easy to see that she had overreacted last night. Totally overreacted. After all, it wasn't as though Mike had gone to the bar with that woman. She was a waitress, that was all. Regulars in bars like that always hugged their favorite waitress. It didn't mean anything. It was like hugging your dog. Mike had probably known Shelley for years. He probably saw her two or three times a week. He probably bought little presents for her kids at Christmas.

Jessica stopped at the corner, waiting for the light to change.

On the other side of the street, a striking-looking couple was getting into a vintage convertible Karmann Ghia with a dented left fender and a lot of body rust. The woman was tall and dark, with the angular face and body of a high-fashion model.

The man was Mike.

This time Jessica was too numb to scream. Scream? If she'd had to jump out of the way of a runaway car, she would have been hit. *Three days, three different women!* her heart was shouting. *He probably has a different woman for every day of the week, like underwear!*

Even above the sounds of the street, she could hear the doors of the Karmann Ghia slam shut. She heard the engine start up. And she saw Mike see her as the high-fashion model pulled the car into traffic. But she couldn't see if he was smiling or not, because there were too many tears in her eyes.

"I don't know why you came here," Todd said as he nervously showed her into his room. "I thought we'd said just about everything there is to say."

Elizabeth stood in the center of the carpet, her arms folded in front of her. She wasn't quite sure why she'd come either, but after Tom left her at her dorm she'd decided she had to talk to Todd.

195

She had to tell him about the story, to warn him. But Todd wasn't making what was already hard any easier.

"Not quite everything, Todd. Something just happened that I really have to—"

"Here," he said, throwing a pile of books and sweaters from the armchair. "Why don't you sit down?" He smiled awkwardly. "Make yourself comfortable."

Comfortable? The only way she could feel comfortable right now was if somebody knocked her unconscious. Elizabeth shook her head. "I'd rather stand, if you don't mind. What I have to say won't take that long."

"How about coffee or a soda? There's a machine just down the hall."

Since when had he become the host of the year? Why wouldn't he just let her talk?

She shook her head again. "No, really, Todd. I just wanted to tell you—"

"Please, Liz," he interrupted. "I can't deal with this if you're going to stand there like that." He sat down on the edge of his bed. "Sit in the chair. Please?"

She sat in the chair. "Todd, I'm here because I wanted to—"

He cut her off again. "There's just no point in going over the same thing again and again," he said. "I still have feelings for you too, Liz, but you've got to get on with your life."

"Todd, this is not about *my* life. This is about *your* life. About—"

His voice rushed over hers. "My life includes Lauren now, Liz. You've got to understand that."

"Todd!" She shot out of the chair. "I don't care about Lauren! That's not why I'm here."

He stood up too. "Don't shout at me, Liz. I know you're upset about what's happened—"

"I have to shout or you won't listen!" she shouted. "Todd, I'm not here to talk about us. I'm here because there are going to be charges of illegal sports recruitment at this college. Charges in which you're implicated."

That shut him up. For one frozen second Todd just stood there looking at her.

"What?"

As succinctly as she could, Elizabeth told him about what she and Tom had uncovered. She explained that she'd agreed to do the story because she'd been so sure that he couldn't be involved. She told him what Coach Clipper had said.

"And you think that's true?" he asked when she was done. "You think that's why I came here? Because they offered me money and privileges?"

I thought you came here because of me. Because you loved me and couldn't stand to be apart. But she couldn't say that out loud, not anymore. Elizabeth stared back in silence, unable to speak.

Todd was shaking his head. "I can't believe you'd think that," he said. "I thought you knew

197

me a lot better than that."

"So did I," Elizabeth whispered.

"I'm sorry, Mike," Isabella said, "but as I've already told you three times, Jessica doesn't want to talk to you." Isabella didn't sound sorry at all.

Jessica kept her face in the cushion of the sofa, forcing herself not to jump up and grab the phone. Of course, *she* knew that Isabella had been right all along. *She* knew that Mike McAllery was nothing but a two-timing creep. *She* knew that the only thing she had to say to him was good-bye. But Jessica's stupid heart hadn't gotten the message yet. Jessica's heart still longed to hear his voice, to hear him call her baby.

"Mike, how can I put this so you'll understand?" Isabella said. "She doesn't want to speak to you."

Jessica sobbed into the couch. She was just going to have to be stronger than her heart. Especially in front of Isabella. Isabella had been comforting her for hours now. Jessica couldn't let her see that she felt anything for Mike except loathing.

Isabella's voice got louder and harder. "No, Mike. Even if you died and came back as someone else, she wouldn't want to speak to you."

Jessica looked up as Isabella slammed down the receiver. She wiped away another flood of tears. "I can't believe I was such a fool," she sniffled. "I just can't believe it . . ." She took another tissue from the box on the coffee table and blew her nose.

"Come on, Jess," Isabella said, setting down two steaming mugs. "Try some of Grandma Ricci's almond espresso. It'll make you feel better."

Fresh tears streamed down Jessica's cheeks. "I'll never feel better again as long as I live. I'll always feel like this. Like somebody's just run over my heart with a tractor."

Isabella sat down beside her on the couch. "No, you won't, Jess. In a little while you'll feel like your heart had a fender bender with a compact car, and then you'll feel like it walked into a wall, and then you'll be looking around for the next guy to mow it down."

"Not me," Jessica croaked. She would never love anyone the way she'd loved Mike. She wouldn't let herself. "I'm never going to be that stupid again. The next guy who asks me out is going to have to produce letters of reference and a ten-year guarantee."

Isabella handed her the coffee. "That's what you say now—"

"No, I mean it. I'm through with men." Jessica turned to Isabella with her old look of determination. "To think that I almost blew the Thetas for that creep. How could I? How could I have jeopardized my chances with them for *him*?"

"Drink the coffee," Isabella said. "Caffeine's wonderful for anger."

"That would have been too much!" Jessica

wailed. "To lose Mike *and* lose the Thetas. Then I'd really know my life was over."

Isabella looked at her uneasily. "This may not be the right time to mention it, Jess," she said hesitantly. "But you're not out of the woods yet."

Jessica looked at her sharply. "What are you—" Suddenly she drew in her breath. Elizabeth! She'd been so upset over Mike that she'd completely forgotten about Elizabeth! Elizabeth refused to go out with Peter Wilbourne. Elizabeth was going to sabotage Jessica's last chance at happiness.

"Oh, my God," Jessica groaned. "I forgot about Liz."

"Well, Alison Quinn hasn't forgotten about her. She was asking me today why Elizabeth hadn't gotten in touch with Peter the Terrible yet."

Jessica put her head in her hands. "What did you say?"

"I said I didn't know. I said I'd ask you." Isabella put a hand on her shoulder. "Maybe if I talk to Alison, Jess. You know, she and I go back a long way. Maybe if I try to explain—"

Jessica's head bobbed up. "Explain what?"

Isabella blinked. "Explain that Elizabeth refuses point-blank to go on the date."

"But she doesn't," Jessica said, a glint of excitement showing through the tears. "Liz is going out with Peter Wilbourne the Third. And she's going to have a great time."

Isabella stared back at her uncomprehendingly

for a few seconds, and then, slowly, understanding dawned. "You mean you're going to pretend to be your sister?"

For the first time since she saw Mike with Miss Karmann Ghia, Jessica allowed herself a small smile. "It's always worked before," she said. "There have been times when I've been Elizabeth better than she could have been herself."

Some guys got so nervous before a big game that they couldn't sleep or eat beforehand. If they did manage to get to sleep, they dreamed that they single-handedly lost the game, and woke up sweating. If they did manage to eat some breakfast, they'd throw it up in the locker room. All these guys had to do was imagine the bleachers filled with spectators and the coach watching from the sidelines, and they'd go to pieces.

But not Tom Watts. In the days when Tom was the biggest collegiate quarterback on the West Coast, he never got nervous before a game. He got excited and keyed up, sure, but not nervous. Not nervous like he was now.

In his jacket pocket was an envelope, and in the envelope was a poem he'd written to Elizabeth. He never could have explained his feelings out loud, but he had put them down in this poem. Not only had he told her exactly how he felt about her, but he'd also explained that there was something in his past that stopped him from taking any chances on love.

Although he'd already wiped his palms on his jeans at least six times since leaving the station, Tom wiped them again as Dickenson Hall came into view.

"I must be crazy," he muttered to himself as he came to a stop under a tree. "I must be at least ten cards short of a full deck."

It would have been crazy enough if he'd simply spent the evening writing an emotionally charged poem to Elizabeth. That in itself would have been grounds for having himself put away in some nice, quiet padded cell. But what was he doing actually *delivering* the poem? Didn't he have any sense left? Any self-respect? One tiny shred of self-preservation? Tom leaned his head against the tree. He couldn't decide if he was on automatic pilot or self-destruct.

This time Tom wiped his hands on the sleeve of his jacket. At least he wasn't so insane that he intended to hand it to her in person. He couldn't bear the thought of being there when she read it. What if she laughed? What if she was so horrified that he should have any feelings for her that she gave up her job at WSVU? No, he was going to slip it into her mailbox and be gone before anyone saw him.

Tom took a deep breath, his eyes on Dickenson Hall. That was, he was going to slip it into her mailbox if he could get himself across the street and through the doors of her dorm.

Just do it, he urged himself. *If you're going to do*

it, then do it. He took another deep breath. No, facing an opposing team of men built like Sherman tanks hadn't scared him at all. But being caught by Elizabeth with an envelope with her name on it terrified him into paralysis.

He removed the poem from his jacket pocket and held it in his hand. *So don't give it to her. If you're that upset about it, tear it up and throw it away,* said the sane, rational voice of his brain. *You wrote it, you got it out of your system, now chuck the stupid poem in the nearest garbage can.*

Tom stared down at the off-white envelope with Elizabeth Wakefield typed across the front. *You can't throw it away,* the insane, irrational voice of his heart said. *You just can't. Even if she laughs at you, even if she refuses to speak to you again, you have to try to make her understand. If you don't reach out for Elizabeth, you may never love anyone again.*

"So I guess I'm going to listen to my heart," Tom said as he started across the street. "I guess I'm on automatic *and* self-destruct."

Elizabeth looked up as the door burst open and Celine swooshed into the room. She'd been so sure that Celine wouldn't be back for hours that she couldn't hide a frown of disappointment.

"Don't get your pantyhose in a knot, princess," Celine said, noticing the frown. "I'm not staying." She dumped her books and several shopping bags on her bed. "I just want to change out of these grungy clothes. I've got a late date." She tossed an envelope onto the desk beside Elizabeth. "Here," Celine said, undoing her skirt and letting it drop to the floor.

Elizabeth looked down. "What's this?"

Celine tossed her blouse over a chair with a shrug. "How should I know? It was in our mailbox, and it has your name on it." She laughed sarcastically. "Maybe our perfect princess has a secret admirer. Stranger things have happened, haven't they?" She opened her closet.

"Yes," Elizabeth said sweetly. "*You* have admirers, after all."

"Oh, ha ha ha," Celine said. She pulled out something red and slinky and held it up to herself in front of the mirror. "Knowing you, it's probably just a note from the dorm monitor to thank you for always rinsing out the bathroom sink after you've used it."

Elizabeth scowled at Celine's back. The horrible truth was that Celine was probably right. It probably was a note from the dorm monitor, or someone like the dorm monitor. While Celine threw the red dress aside and pulled out something orange and made of Lycra, Elizabeth tore open the envelope.

It wasn't a note from the dorm monitor. Not at all. Elizabeth had to read the first stanza over several times before she understood what it was. It was a poem, a poem written for her.

Celine humphed and sighed and complained

about having nothing to wear as Elizabeth read the typed page in her hand with amazement. The poem was beautiful and poignant, and it moved her so much that she completely forgot she wasn't alone.

"What is that?" Celine's head appeared over her shoulder. "It looks like some kind of poem."

Elizabeth went to lay it facedown on the desk, but Celine was too fast. She snatched it out of her hand with a cry of delight. "It is!" she squealed. "Some poor deluded jerk is writing the princess poetry!"

"Give that back to me," Elizabeth ordered. "Or you really will have nothing to wear because I'll cut everything you own into tiny pieces."

"Be my guest." Celine opened her hand and let the poem float to the ground. "I'm certainly not interested in your pathetic love life." She slung her bag over her shoulder and banged out of the room.

As soon as she was sure Celine was gone, Elizabeth took the poem and sat on her bed to reread it. When she came to the end there was a catch in her voice as she read out loud, *"But I'm too afraid to try . . ."*

Elizabeth rested the page on her lap with a sigh. Who could have written such a beautiful piece of poetry? Who could have these feelings for her?

Tom. It was the first name that came into her head. The thought made her heart race. She picked up the poem again. Tom was an investigative reporter, not a poet, she reminded herself. He'd never shown any interest in poetry, not even when he'd seen the books she was reading.

She leaned back against her pillow. "Do you think it's Tom because it really might be Tom?" she wondered out loud. "Or is it because you want it to be him?"

Chapter
Ten

Steven came racing up the bleacher stairs with a cardboard tray filled with hot dogs, sodas, and popcorn. "This is the life!" he exclaimed as he sat down beside Billie. "A beautiful autumn day, a beautiful Homecoming game, and a beautiful woman to share them both with." He leaned over and kissed her. For today, at least, Steven had decided to put his concern for his sisters out of his mind and to have a good time.

"Never mind all that soppy stuff," Billie teased, kissing him back. "Unhand my frank."

Steven laughed, suddenly realizing that this was the most relaxed he'd felt in weeks. *Since the beginning of the term*, he told himself. *Since Elizabeth and Jessica arrived*. Steven sighed. The twins had been so cute and so much fun when they were little. He'd been the happiest big brother in the world. Now Elizabeth was lonely and miserable, and Jessica was spending far too much time with the cretin downstairs. It terrified him to think what either of them might do next.

Billie poked him with her elbow. "Stop it," she ordered.

"Stop what?" he asked innocently.

"Stop thinking about your sisters. You promised you wouldn't think about them all afternoon. You swore the only thing in your head would be football and me."

Steven grinned. "How did you know I was thinking about them?"

She gave him a wry smile. "Because you get the exact same look on your face my father used to get when I first started going out with boys."

"Well, Ms. Detective," Steven said. "It just might interest you to know that I wasn't really thinking about them. I was thinking how good it felt not to worry about them for a couple of hours."

"Well, stop thinking about it and just enjoy it. This is going to be a great game." She kissed his cheek.

"It's a great game already," Steven said, putting his arm around her. "And it hasn't even started yet."

He bit into his hot dog and gazed happily across the stands. It looked as though the entire school had turned out for it. He saw his sociology professor, three of his good friends from the prelaw program, Billie's friend Sandi and her boyfriend, and he saw Elizabeth and Peter Wilbourne.

The hot dog turned to sand in Steven's mouth. He gave Billie a shake. "Billie, look over there! Where those Thetas are sitting. Tell me what you see."

Billie followed the direction his hand was pointing. "I see Elizabeth and Peter Wilbourne."

Steven turned to her, disbelief on his face. "And that seems all right to you?"

Billie shrugged. "It seems a little strange. I thought Elizabeth didn't like Peter, but I guess she changed her mind."

"Billie," Steven said, fighting to remain calm. "Nobody with half a brain likes Peter. The guy's a power-happy bigot with an ego as big as Alaska."

She eyed him warily. "Oh, don't get started on him now, Steven. At least he doesn't drive a motorcycle and live in our building—that should make you happy."

"Well, it doesn't make me happy." He threw his hot dog back in the tray. "What is it with my sisters? Jessica's always been a little flaky, especially when it comes to boys, but Elizabeth was always rational. Elizabeth—"

"Steven!" Billie looked as if she was about to dump her soda over his head. "Stop it! When are you going to accept the fact that your sisters are adults now, and that they can go out whomever they want? They have to take responsibility for their own lives."

"I do accept that, Billie. It's just that—"

"The game's about to start, Steven. Let's just watch the game and have a good time, all right?"

"All right." He sat back. "Looks like they've got a good lineup this season, doesn't it?" he asked as the SVU Vanguards jogged onto the field.

Billie nodded. "It's amazing how Coach Sanchez has brought the team back after they lost Tom Watts, isn't it?" she asked.

"Yeah," Steven said. "He's really worked some miracles in the athletics department." But though his mouth was talking about football, he was still thinking about his sisters. *Jessica's with Mike McAllery, and Elizabeth is with Peter Wilbourne*, he thought miserably. *Maybe the twins are more identical than I thought. They both have really lousy taste in men.*

Tom shifted in his seat as the band came onto the field for half-time.

Danny looked over at him. "You ever miss it?" he asked.

Tom nodded. "Yeah. I don't regret giving it up, but I miss it all the time."

It wasn't the sport that he hadn't liked. He loved football. What he hadn't liked was the way being a superjock had made *him*—arrogant, thinking the world owed him a living. And what he hated was the fact that if he hadn't been so wound up in himself, his family would still be alive.

210

"Especially when we're getting massacred and I know I could've done something about it," Tom added with a small smile.

A raucous whoop went up from a group of Thetas and their dates a few rows below them.

"I wish someone could do something about them," Danny said, glancing down at them. "Football game, fraternity party, it's all the same to them."

Tom looked down the bleachers. "It's Wilbourne. You know he hates anything to take the attention away from him, even a Homecoming—" The word "game" died in Tom's throat as Peter Wilbourne and his date suddenly stood up in the center of their group.

"I don't believe it," Danny said. "It's Elizabeth Wakefield."

Tom couldn't take his eyes from the smiling couple. "You're sure that's Elizabeth?" he asked, laboring to keep his voice flat. "You went out with Jessica. Are you sure it's not her?"

Danny shook his head. "Look at the way she's dressed. Look at the way she moves. I'm sure that's not Jessica."

Tom's fingernails dug into the palms of his hands. What a jerk he was. What a fully paid-up member of the bozo club. He'd written her a poem! He'd poured his heart and soul out to her. He'd thought Elizabeth Wakefield was going to be the person to help him put his heart back together again. What a joke! She wasn't interested in him. She was interested in Peter Wilbourne III. What an ass she must think he was. She'd probably laughed herself silly when she read his poem.

Even as Tom watched in horror, Elizabeth and Peter kissed. Right there in the middle of the stadium, for the entire school to see.

Laughed? She'd probably read it to Peter Wilbourne and the two of them had laughed together.

"I don't mind admitting when I've been wrong," the girl who looked, acted, and sounded exactly like Elizabeth Wakefield was saying in a loud, clear voice. "And I was wrong about you, Peter. I was very wrong, and I'm sorry." She took Peter Wilbourne's hand. "I'm really and truly sorry."

Isabella smiled to herself. She had to hand it to Jessica—she was so convincing as her twin that even Isabella could believe she was Elizabeth.

"I accept your apology," Peter said solemnly. "And I forgive you." He pulled her to him. "Let's kiss and make up. You know it's what you've wanted all along."

Pass me a barf bag, Isabella thought. *I'm going to be sick.* She turned away as Peter moved in for his kiss. What a jerk he was. What a complete and total jerk.

The group of Thetas and Sigmas whistled and cheered.

Isabella glanced behind her, searching for

something to look at that wouldn't make her feel ill. And there he was, looking amazingly handsome in a hooded sweatshirt and a pair of old jeans, staring intently down at them. Isabella's heart banged against her ribs. Had she been wrong in thinking that Tom Watts didn't know or care that she was alive? Could it be that Tom was watching her?

Isabella put her hand over her eyes as though shielding them from the sun and pretended to scan the crowd, but in reality she was studying Tom's face. His expression was more than intent—it was pained. He almost looked as though he'd seen a ghost.

It's not me he's looking at at all, Isabella realized with a pang. *It's Jessica!* She turned back to the Thetas and the truth hit her like a runaway train. It wasn't Jessica that Tom was watching with such hurt and longing. It was Elizabeth.

There was so much emotion in that expression. She was certain of it. *So Tom Watts isn't the complete loner everyone says,* Isabella thought as she gazed vacantly down at the field. *He is capable of love*. It was just unfortunate that it wasn't Isabella he was in love with.

After that kiss, it wasn't easy for Jessica to convince Peter Wilbourne that she didn't want to spend the rest of the afternoon with him. Thank God, he already had a date for the Homecoming

213

dance or he would have expected her to go to that with him too. Jessica shuddered as she raced away after the game like Cinderella running out of the ball. She'd had about as much of Peter Wilbourne III as she could take for one lifetime. He had to be the most egotistical bore she'd ever met.

But all's well that ends well, Jessica told herself as she strode toward her dorm. *It was just like the dentist. You hate going, but when it's all over, you feel better.*

Alison had congratulated her as she was leaving on being pledged to the Thetas. "I can admit when I'm wrong too," Alison had said. "I think both you and Jessica will make terrific Thetas, and so does everyone else."

Jessica crossed the road to her hall. She didn't really smile, but the frown she'd been wearing since she discovered the truth about Mike faded a little. She'd probably never get over Mike, but at least she belonged to the best sorority in California. If she was going to have to learn to live with a broken heart, she'd rather do it as a Theta Alpha Theta than as a nobody.

Still thinking about Mike, Jessica entered her building. A group of girls she knew were in the lobby, making plans for the Homecoming dance that night. Jessica winced. She could have gotten another date for tonight if she'd really wanted to, but for the first time in her life she preferred just to stay home by herself. If she couldn't go with Mike,

214

then she didn't want to go at all. Dancing and laughing with someone else wouldn't make her happy, it would smash another hole in her heart.

The lift she'd gotten from fooling the Thetas into pledging both her and Elizabeth vanished completely as Jessica climbed the stairs to her floor.

I guess the good news is that this is the worst I'll feel for as long as I live, she thought as she reached her landing.

It was just at that moment that she heard it. So quietly at first . . . *Love me tender, love me true* . . . Jessica's hand was on the door, but she couldn't open it. Someone on her floor was playing an old crackling Elvis Presley record. And it wasn't just any song; it was the song Mike had played the night he made love to her. It was *their* song. *For my darling, I love you* . . . Tears welled up in Jessica's eyes and her breath caught in a sob. No, she couldn't imagine ever feeling worse than this. . . . *And I always will.*

Overwhelmed with the need to be in her room where she could be alone and cry what was left of her heart out, Jessica stumbled into the hallway. The song ended and then, to her horror, started again. The tears spilled over her cheeks as she hurried around the corner to her room.

Suddenly she pulled to a stop. Her body froze.

Mike McAllery was sitting on the floor outside her room, leaning against the door, a boom box beside him. *Love me tender, love me true* . . .

She studied his face, her heart hammering in her chest. He looked haggard and ravaged, as though he hadn't slept or eaten in days, as though . . .

And suddenly she was struck by an astonishing thought. A thought that gave her a weak feeling in the bottom of her stomach. Mike looked as though he might have a broken heart too.

. . . And I always will.

Mike didn't move, but stared straight into her eyes and held them. "I love you, Jessica," he said softly. "I really love you." Very slowly he got to his feet. "Maybe you've got a right to be mad at me, but if you'd give me a chance, I know I can explain." He opened his arms. "Let me explain, Jess. Please . . ."

Over the roar of her heart she could hear Isabella telling her not to listen to Mike's excuses. She could hear Steven and Elizabeth telling her to run for her life. But Jessica didn't care. It didn't matter what they thought. It didn't matter about those other women. Nothing mattered except the fact that Mike loved her. He loved her, and he was sorry for hurting her. He loved her, and he was begging her to take him back.

Without a second's hesitation, she threw herself into his waiting arms.

Celine had flounced off to the bathroom to finish putting on her makeup, with a "Do try to make my Homecoming date feel comfortable if he arrives before I'm back, won't you, princess?"

Elizabeth had to stop herself from saying, *You mean he won't be in a cage?* But she didn't want to fight with Celine tonight. She was feeling much too miserable. She hadn't even been cheered up by the fact that this afternoon when she weighed herself, Nina's scale had claimed that she'd lost three pounds. As though it wasn't bad enough that everyone else in the world but her was going to the dance tonight, but this afternoon the Pi Beta Phis had let her know that they weren't accepting her pledge. The Pis thought Elizabeth was more Theta material. And there was something slightly weird and hinty about the way they said it. It was so ironic that if she hadn't been so disappointed by the rejection, she might have laughed.

When the knock came announcing the arrival of Celine's date, Elizabeth put down the book she was reading with a sigh. The last thing she needed was to have to make pleasant conversation with one of Celine's Neanderthal boyfriends.

She got up from her desk and opened the door. The man standing there with a corsage in his hand and a polite smile on his face might have just left a poetry reading, but he definitely hadn't been let out of a cage.

"You!" Elizabeth was so surprised to find herself staring into the handsome, enigmatic face of William White that she blurted out the first thing that came to her mind. "What are you doing here?"

217

His eyes went up and down her, taking in the twist of golden hair pinned up on her head and the old jeans and plaid flannel shirt she was wearing. He looked even more surprised than she felt. "And why aren't you dressed for the dance?" he asked. "Or is that what the real style-setters are wearing this year?"

Feeling, for some reason, as though she'd just been complimented, Elizabeth finally returned his smile. "I know this outfit would make a real fashion statement," she said, "but the truth is I'm not going."

"Not going?" He looked almost happy. "A beautiful girl like you isn't going to the Homecoming ball?"

Now she knew she'd been complimented. She shook her head. "I decided to skip the dance this year." She shrugged and her smile brightened a little. "I'd actually rather stay here and read Whitman."

He followed her into the room. "Whitman's overrated," he said, stopping at her desk and picking up the volume of poems she'd left there. "He's got some good stuff, but I've always felt he was a little too earnest. If you'd actually spent an evening with him, he would probably have turned out to be an awful bore."

"It's just as well he didn't ask me to the dance, then, isn't it?" Elizabeth joked.

William White turned from the book to her. "Who did ask you?"

218

As surprised by the question as by the fact that the intelligent and elegant William White had a date with Celine, Elizabeth again told the truth. "No one." She felt herself flush. "I guess the men at this school were afraid to go to Homecoming with a woman dressed for hiking."

There was a sudden gleam in those cool blue eyes. "I wouldn't have been afraid." His voice sounded unusually warm and gentle.

Her cheeks turned a deeper pink. As impossible as it seemed, William White was flirting with her. Before she could recover herself enough to respond, Celine sailed into the room in a cloud of perfume and washed silk.

"William!" she purred. "I am so sorry to have kept you waiting. I hope Elizabeth made you feel at home."

He looked over at Celine, but when he spoke all warmth and gentleness were gone. "That's not the only thing you have to be sorry for," he said.

"We're sorry to barge in like this," Billie said as she sat down on Elizabeth's bed. "But you know what these big dances are like. Steven was afraid we wouldn't even have a chance to say hello to you if we didn't stop by on our way."

Steven shoved some of Celine's things to one side and positioned himself gingerly on the edge of her desk.

"Don't apologize," Elizabeth answered sin-

219

cerely. "It's really good to see you." Which was the truth. She was so rattled by her encounter with William White, she was glad for a dose of normalcy.

At least Billie was normal. She chatted happily about the evening ahead, asking Elizabeth what she thought about her hair and her dress and complaining that her shoes were too tight. Steven was not normal. Steven was looking at Elizabeth in a way that he usually reserved for Jessica: perplexed, frustrated, disappointed.

"Why aren't you dressed?" he asked when Billie's voice finally trailed off into silence. "Won't Peter Wilbourne be picking you up soon?"

Elizabeth's smile disappeared. "What?"

Steven was drumming his fingers on the desktop the way Mr. Wakefield did when he was upset about something. "You heard me," he said shortly. "You went to the game with Peter the Geek. Considering the way you were kissing him right there in broad daylight, I assumed you'd be going to the dance with him too."

Elizabeth could feel something going very wrong with her blood. It was turning to ice. "What?" she whispered.

Billie stood up. "Steven, you promised . . ."

Steven stood up too, refusing even to glance at Billie. "Come on, Liz. We saw you. Practically the whole school saw you." He shook his head. "After the way he treated you and Jess— I just can't *believe* you'd go out with a creep like that."

220

Billie's voice was sharp. "Steven—"

Elizabeth cut her off. "What are you talking about? I wouldn't go out with Peter Wilbourne if he was the last man on earth. I've been in this room the entire day."

Steven stared at her. Elizabeth stared back. The truth hit them both at exactly the same moment.

"Jessica!"

Billie let out her breath. "What a relief," she said, slipping her arm into Steven's. "Your brother's been driving me crazy because he thought you were going out with Peter."

Elizabeth wasn't relieved. She was furious. Of all the low-down, sneaky things her twin had done to her in the last eighteen years, this had to be the worst. Knowing how strongly Elizabeth felt about Peter, Jessica had gone ahead and impersonated her just so she could get into some obnoxious, stuck-up sorority.

"Elizabeth?" Steven said. Both he and Billie were looking at her with concern. "Are you okay? You look like you're about to explode."

Elizabeth's eyes were flashing and her jaw was set. "I am about to explode," she said. "I can't believe she did that to me. After I told her I wouldn't go out with him, not under any circumstances, no matter what the stupid Thetas wanted—" She broke off, too furious to go on.

Steven came over and put a hand on her shoulder. "I'll talk to her, Liz. Jessica's been getting

221

pretty carried away with herself lately. I want to try to reason with her if I can."

Suddenly Billie was standing beside him. "Why can't you let them work out their own problems?" she demanded. She picked up her bag from Elizabeth's desk. "Why do you have to interfere all the time?"

"Billie's right," Elizabeth said quickly. She didn't want Steven talking to Jessica. She wanted to wring Jessica's neck herself. "I'll handle Jess. Believe me, I know exactly what I want to say."

How could she have doubted Mike for even a few minutes? Jessica wondered as he opened the door to the Corvette and took her hand. He looked wonderful in his dark Italian suit. He *was* wonderful. After she'd given him a chance to explain, she'd realized that.

He hadn't been cheating on her with the woman in the Karmann Ghia. He'd been negotiating to buy the car for Jessica and fix it up.

Isabella was wrong. Mike wasn't into any shady dealings; Mike bought old cars and fixed them up. That's how he made money. That was what he'd done with his Corvette. That was what he was going to do with Whatever-her-name-was's Karmann Ghia.

"I love you," he whispered as she stepped out of the car and into his arms. "I've never said that to anybody before, Jess." He cupped her chin in his hands and gazed into her eyes. "I've never said it, because I never felt it."

Jessica felt more beautiful than she ever had before standing there with him on the sidewalk. Her golden hair was up in a twist, her neck and shoulders left bare by her long, strapless, fitted red dress.

"I love you, too," Jessica whispered back. "And I'm sorry I acted like such a jealous child. I—"

He put a finger to her lips. "Let's not talk about it anymore. Let's just forget it ever happened."

"Forget what happened?" she asked with a laugh.

Enid Rollins was so happy she couldn't stop smiling. She'd smiled all through the game this afternoon, sitting on the bleachers with Mark's arm around her, only half aware of what was happening on the field. She'd smiled all through the exquisite meal at Da Vinci's with Todd and Lauren. She'd smiled all the way back to campus in Mark's new Explorer, so happy that it didn't bother her even a little that the guys did nothing but talk about football the entire way. And she was smiling now as the four of them strolled through the warm night to the Homecoming ball.

"Someone may have to pinch me," she said with a laugh. "This day has been so unbelievably great I feel like I'm dreaming."

"Somebody better pinch me, too," Todd said from behind her. "I think the dream just turned into a nightmare."

Mark, Enid, and Lauren all saw what he was talking about at the same time, and they all stopped suddenly. Coming toward them in a direct line across their path was Elizabeth Wakefield. She had a sweater thrown over an old shirt and jeans, and she was moving fast. She looked upset.

"Elizabeth!" Enid said.

Elizabeth came to a halt. It was clear from the expression on her face that she hadn't seen them until this moment. Her eyes moved from Enid to Todd, and then to Lauren and Mark. They settled back on Enid as she forced something that was almost a smile onto her face.

For a second, Enid was afraid that none of them were going to be able to speak, that they were just going to stand there in an awkward silence for the rest of their lives. She tried desperately to think of something to say. But what? *We just had a wonderful dinner? Don't you think Todd looks handsome in his dinner jacket? My, but those jeans are very becoming on you, Liz?* Beside her, the guys cleared their throats, but no words came out.

It was Elizabeth who finally thought of something to say. "You look great, Alexandra," she said in a voice that was barely more than a whisper. "You look really great."

Enid smiled back. "Thanks," she said. "I— you—" She broke off, unable to continue.

Mark came to her rescue. "Why aren't you dressed up?" he said to Elizabeth. "Isn't Peter

Wilbourne taking you to the ball?"

Elizabeth looked as though he'd slapped her. Without any answer, she rushed away.

"Wow," Todd said as soon as Elizabeth was out of earshot. "That was unpleasant."

"Well, it's over now," Lauren said. "Let's just pretend that it didn't happen and go back to having a good time."

Enid pushed the memory of Elizabeth's stricken face from her mind. "Lauren's right," she said brightly. "This is a perfect day. Let's not let anything spoil it."

Winston tiptoed down the corridor, his arms filled with bags of chips and a two-liter bottle of soda, afraid to disturb the unearthly quiet of Oakley Hall.

"I feel like the last of the Mohicans," Winston mumbled to himself as he walked toward the common room.

"It's too bad I don't feel like studying," he continued. "It's the one night I could actually work without being disturbed by someone in a hair crisis or having a fight with her boyfriend."

But Winston didn't feel like studying. He felt like watching two or three really awful horror movies on the TV and eating himself into a coma on nachos and potato chips.

He shoved the common-room door open so hard that it banged against the wall.

225

"I can't believe it," Winston grumbled as he threw his things on the counter and fished through the stuff on the table for the TV guide. "My first college Homecoming ball and I'm not at it."

"Well, why aren't you?"

Winston caught his breath, not daring to turn around. There was no one else in the room. If there were, he would have seen them when he came in. *Good grief,* he thought, *this is what they've driven me to. I'm finally cracking up. I'm hearing voices.*

There was a ripple of laughter that sounded just like tiny silver bells.

Winston recognized that laugh. He turned around.

Denise was leaning over the back of the couch, grinning at him. "So why didn't you go?" she asked again. She smiled. "Don't tell me you were struck by the curse of the Sigmas and couldn't get a date."

He returned her grin. "It was more that I was afraid I'd be struck by the Sigmas themselves if I turned up with a date when they'd all been stood up," Winston confessed. Which was half the truth. The other half was vaulting over the couch, coming to see what food he had. He hadn't had the nerve to ask Denise, and she was the only girl he really wanted to go with.

"You're right," Denise said, stopping so close beside him that he could smell the shampoo she'd

226

just used to wash her hair. It was papaya. "They probably would have."

"What about you?" Winston asked. "Don't tell me you're not feeling well again?"

"Yum, salt-and-vinegar potato chips," Denise said. "My favorite." She tore herself away from the chips and gave him a smile. "No, I feel fine. I just didn't feel like going to the ball with Bill, and he's the only one who asked me."

Winston could hardly hide his surprise. "The only one?"

She shrugged. "Okay, one of the only ones. But I didn't want to go with any of the others, either. I thought I'd have more fun if I stayed here and washed my hair." She picked up the bag of her favorite potato chips. "And it looks like I was right."

Winston didn't trust himself to speak. The dorm was empty, the night was young, and he and Denise Waters were alone together with half-a-dozen bags of snack food and a two-liter bottle of soda. He must be cracking up. He wasn't only hearing voices, he was having hallucinations.

"So, Win," Denise said, shaking the television guide he was still holding in his hands. "What are we watching?"

Winston scooped up the chips and soda and followed her to the couch. "Well, there's a horror double-feature on that I was going to watch," he said hesitantly. "*Revenge of the Lost Corpse* and *Assassins from the Forbidden Planet*. But we could

227

watch something else, if you want."

Denise handed him the remote. "Are you kidding? *Assassins from the Forbidden Planet* is one of my all-time favorite movies. It's a classic."

He plopped down beside her, unable to believe the strange ways things happened. Five minutes ago he was facing one of the worst nights of his life. And now . . . *Assassins from the Forbidden Planet* and Denise Waters not two feet away from him.

"I'm so glad you didn't go to the dance, Win," Denise said. "I don't mind admitting that I was already feeling bored." She opened the bag of salt-and-vinegar potato chips. "But this is going to be really great. This is my idea of a perfect evening."

"Mine, too," Winston said, sinking into a state of bliss.

Elizabeth found herself walking almost blindly toward the TV station. She'd started out on a mission to find Jessica and have it out with her. And then, of course, she'd run into Alexandra and Todd. She felt the deep ache in her throat of tears about to come. She couldn't decide which was worse: seeing them all so dressed up and happy or discovering they thought she was dating Peter Wilbourne.

But Elizabeth was beyond caring. She didn't want to go back to the dorm, she didn't want to go anywhere there were bright lights and people. She wanted someplace she felt safe, where she could try to piece her heart back together again. And that place was Tom's office at WSVU. Tom wouldn't be there. He was probably at the ball with Isabella Ricci.

Which is better anyway, Elizabeth told herself as she slipped into the building. *I don't want him to be here. I just want to be alone. I don't want anything from anyone ever again.* She hurried down the corridor as a new wave of crying threatened to overtake her. *He won't be here, so it doesn't matter. But even if he were here, I wouldn't want him to be. Even if he did write that poem, I don't want him to be here. Even if . . .* her thoughts trailed off as she stepped into the office.

A light was on over the desk in the corner, and a figure was stooped over the desk.

Tom was there. Of course he was. And maybe she did want him to be there. Because she found herself fighting the most desperate urge to run to him. To throw herself in his arms and stay there forever.

Once again her mind turned back to the poem. The beautiful lines that made her eyes fill with tears. *Was it you, Tom?* She needed to know. She stepped silently toward him, unsure of what she was doing, carried by her heart.

Suddenly Tom turned around. His eyes locked on hers. She found herself frantically searching his face for the love and the tenderness she so desperately needed right now.

It wasn't there. She could see that immediately. The hardness in his eyes made her entire body freeze.

Tom turned his eyes from hers. "What are you doing here?" he asked coldly.

She'd been wrong. She wasn't safe here. And she'd been wrong about the poem. Tom hadn't written it. No one could have written those things and be looking at her now with such iciness, such detachment. Why had she let herself believe it could have been him? For the second time that night, Elizabeth turned and fled without a word.

She was halfway down the hall when she heard him running after her. "Elizabeth!" he shouted. "Elizabeth! Wait! I'm sorry—I—Elizabeth!"

Not as sorry as I am, Elizabeth thought.

She'd find no love here. It was time to accept that. The tears began to fall again as she reached the front doors and hurled herself into the black night. *Not as sorry as I am.*

Jessica felt as though she were floating on air as they entered the crowded hall, hand in hand. Hundreds of balloons in autumn colors shaded the lights and cascaded from the ceiling. The band stood on a stage lit by candles.

This is so perfect, so absolutely perfect, Jessica thought as she held Mike tight and looked around. *It's a perfect evening. I have the perfect boyfriend. I belong to the perfect sorority* . . . A feeling of joy bubbled through her. *My life is absolutely perfect.*

She could feel the eyes on them as they crossed the room. No one could deny that she and Mike were a stunning couple. Jessica smiled to herself. Peter Wilbourne III definitely looked stunned. Jessica flashed him her smuggest smile. Out of the corner of her eye she saw Isabella, standing to one side with Alison Quinn. Isabella looked pretty stunned too. Stunned and outraged. Jessica sighed to herself. At some point soon she was going to have to face Isabella and another lecture.

But not right now, she told herself as Mike took her in his arms and they began to dance. *Right now I just want to enjoy being the happiest girl in the world.*

"So tell me, Jess," Mike whispered as he pulled her close. "Will you move in with me?" He touched his lips to her hair. "If you live with me, you'll never have to be jealous again."

Jessica closed her eyes and leaned against his strong, hard chest. "Yes," she said, her heart soaring. "I'd love to."

And I'm going to be the happiest girl in the world for the rest of my life.